THE SWAN SYNDICATE

BOOK ONE

KIM ALLRED

STORM COAST PUBLISHING LLC

The Swan Syndicate
Book One
KIM ALLRED

Published by Storm Coast Publishing, LLC

Copyright © 2024 by Kim Allred
Cover Design by Dar Albert / Wicked Smart Designs
EPub edition August 2024 978-1-953832-32-0
Print Edition August 2024 978-1-953832-33-7
Large Print Edition August 2024 978-1-953832-34-4

CONTENTS

Life's roughest storms prove the strength of our anchors.

Author Unkown

1

Baywood, Oregon - Present Day

Stella Caldway sighed with pleasure as she pulled her red convertible, top currently up, into her driveway. Twinkling white lights wrapped around the small fir tree near the brick walkway leading to the front door. Another string ran along the roof line of her bungalow-style home.

She could have sworn she'd turned the Christmas lights off last night and must not have noticed when she raced out of the house that morning, already ten minutes late for her meeting with Alexis, another local Realtor.

Several months before, she'd returned to Baywood after a man from the past had kidnapped her and taken her through the fog to 1805 England. She'd known about time travel before it happened. Her best friend AJ had been taken to the past by her now husband, Finn Murphy, by way of ancient stones and a Celtic incantation.

Since then, she'd found little interest in her one-woman broker business. It was difficult for anything to hold her attention for long after being kidnapped twice and almost losing the love of her life in a power struggle for the stones. She decided to maintain a few long-time clients and slowly turned over the rest to Alexis.

She stared at the miniature lights until they blurred, wondering why she'd never considered decorating the outside of the house. Christmas was one of her favorite holidays, and she always went a little over the top on the interior decor. She smirked. After the trip to France during the previous year's holiday with AJ, Finn, and the entire family, the idea of outdoor lights had given her second thoughts.

Her gaze refocused, and she grinned as she tugged on a lock of her wavy auburn hair while viewing the yard. Beckworth, her significant other, lived with her. She wasn't really sure what to call him—boyfriend didn't quite fit. Lover?

He didn't have electricity where he'd come from, and he'd been like a kid in a candy shop when they went shopping for decorations. The sparkling lights weren't the only items that caught his interest. He fell hard and fast for the whole spirit of the holidays. He'd firmly secured three reindeer and a fat Santa on the lawn. She'd also caught him whispering to Finn, who was an inspiring furniture maker, about building a sled.

Oh, Teddy. What am I going to do with you?

Viscount Theodore Beckworth of Waverly Manor, aka Teddy to only a handful, was a man out of time. A man from two hundred years ago, who had left his hard-fought title and manor in England to be with her. He'd had a mercurial background, once considered an enemy when he'd kidnapped AJ and taken her and the stones to France. But, after helping AJ find Finn when he'd been near death, he slowly earned their trust.

It wasn't like he was the only one. Finn was also from the past but had lived in Baywood for some time and was well-acclimated to the present day. Three others from Napoleon's era had traveled forward to spend the rest of their lives in present-day Oregon.

Time travel between the past and present had somehow become common place for their small clutch of family and friends. Though most had agreed that the stones they'd brought with them for safekeeping should remain locked away.

She was still smiling as she entered the house and took a whiff of blue spruce seeping out from the family room. They would have to take the tree down soon, but it was fun to cuddle on the couch and watch old movies with the Christmas tree providing the only light.

After dropping her purse on a side table, she wandered through the house, expecting Beckworth to be in the living room, kitchen, or bedroom. There was an office, but he rarely spent time there, preferring to create his own private study that he'd set up in the guest room. He wasn't there either.

As a last resort, she glanced through the sliding glass door that led to the back patio. The skies were winter gray, but the air was dry if cool. The enclosed intimate yard was a gardener's paradise. She'd spent countless hours outside with AJ, gossiping and laughing over a bottle of wine. Even though it wasn't just the two of them anymore, they still found a way to squeeze in girl time.

"What are you doing out here?" Stella stepped onto the patio and studied the man. He was on his knees, bending over a grouping of hostas. Her gaze landed on his blue jean-covered backside and didn't think she'd seen anything so sexy.

"I'm cutting off the spent flowers and noticed something had been burrowing, so I thought I'd cover up the hole." Beckworth leaned back to rest on his heels. He waved to the other side of the garden. "Mrs. Simpson brought over a small cutting of heather. I think she overheard me talking to Mr. Chopra about the wild heather in England. There was an open spot in the far corner. I think it will do well there."

When she didn't respond, he turned his cornflower-blue eyes up at her. "What is it?"

She must have been wearing a silly grin because the confusion on his face was priceless. If she only had her phone to snap a picture. God knew he'd taken hundreds of her in the last seven months. Who would have thought this man, who'd mingled with aristocrats in London and had been a dangerous spy for the Crown, would end up tending her garden? "I'm imagining you in that same pose in the gardens at Waverly."

He pushed his ash-blond hair back before giving her a smile that made her heart skip a beat. "Don't tell anyone, but during fall cleanup, when most of the manor believed I'd gone to Eleanor's, I dressed in the gardener's livery and tilled the soil in the far side of the garden. Sometimes, on the way back from Eleanor's, when the flowers were in bloom, I'd been known to cut a dead flower here and there."

She clapped her hands together. "As Dame Ellingsworth would say, how marvelous." It was crazy to think about what they were about to do. "I'd like to see that when we go back."

His smile faded. "Are you sure you want to go? I'd understand if it's too much to ask. It's just that I feel a responsibility to check in."

She marched over and held out her hands. He took them, and when he stood, she pulled him in for a long, slow kiss. He wrapped an arm around her lower back and tugged her closer. It was a couple of minutes before he let her go.

She wiped a touch of lipstick off his lip. "I can't deny I'm nervous, but I trust Maire. She's the best at deciphering and rewording the incantations. And I don't want you going anywhere that I can't go, too. Well, not unless it's like a guy's weekend or something like that. Then it would be okay. Unless you were going to Vegas. Or one of those resorts for singles. I suppose that would obviously upset me. What?"

His grin matched the humor in his gaze. In fact, it was likely he was ready to burst with hysterical laughter.

She grinned. "Sorry. I got sidetracked."

"I believe that means you have the normal jitters of anyone who's purposely traveling back two hundred years for a short holiday."

Her throaty laugher escaped. "Exactly."

His tone became serious. "How is AJ dealing with this?"

She stepped away and picked up the garden tools, rinsing them off at her garden workstation. She set them down to dry, then wiped her hands on a towel.

"Stella. You've told her—right?"

She kept her back to him. "I've been so busy, I haven't found the right time."

"We leave in three days. Don't you think you should say something before Maire or Sebastian let it slip?"

She shrugged then fussed with cleaning off the workstation. His grip on her shoulders forced her to stop, and she blinked away tears that came out of nowhere. Good grief.

He didn't turn her around to make her face him, instead he massaged her shoulders. "What's this all about?"

When she didn't answer, he gave her shoulders a quick squeeze then kissed her cheek.

"Do you know what I'm in the mood for?"

She rubbed at her eyes. "What's that?"

"One of Donna's pies. The sisters made their own pies when I lived with them. Then AJ had to bring home one of those pies from Donna's. Now, I can't think of a better pie. I like the Dutch apple the best. I'm going to change and then we'll go get one. How's that?"

He was up to something, but it was impossible to tell what it was. The sisters were Louise and Edith, widowed for several years, and they lived together in a quaint coastal neighborhood a couple miles south of town. A year or so ago, when Beckworth had been pulled from the past to the future, he'd fallen into their driveway—dazed and confused from an injury and the effects of traveling through the fog to a different time. They pampered him to the point of irritation, yet Beckworth had forged a strange friendship with them that remained strong even now.

He met her in the kitchen in jeans and a dazzling blue shirt that matched the color of his cornflower-blue eyes. His dark brown blazer and a scarf finished his look. Even in this modern time, Beckworth retained his fashion sense.

"I'll drive." He grabbed his keys from a blown-glass dish on the counter and patted her backside.

He was definitely up to something, but she couldn't see any reason to complain or argue, so she inwardly sighed and grabbed her purse on the way out. He chattered about every-thing and nothing on their way, and, once they were at Donna's, which she had to agree, had arguably the best pies she'd ever tasted, and she'd tested quite a few in her life, they both got lost in staring at the numerous selections.

They bought a Dutch apple, a strawberry, and a Marion-berry because they lived in Oregon, and everyone had to have the best blackberry pie. He put the pies in the car then took her for coffee.

"I know Mary and Hensley will be able to join us at Waverly for a hunting weekend, but I'm not sure about Elizabeth. She tends to make plans several weeks out."

Stella loved Dame Elizabeth Ellingsworth. She scared the bejesus out of AJ, but Stella found her to be a woman out of time. Basically, not one to mess with. She knew all the ways of manipulation and machinations to get things just her way.

Stella snickered to herself. A skill all young women should learn.

"I'd miss her if she weren't able to attend, but a weekend with Eleanor and Mary will be just as fun. Eleanor will come, right?"

"In the past, it's always depended on her mood and whether she felt like company. But if we're there, she'll want to catch up."

"Does the hunting take up the whole day?"

He laughed. "No. Just a few hours, and sometimes we come home with nothing to show for our efforts."

"So, it's kind of a guy thing to get away from the women?"

"Not at all. Women join the hunt as well. Mary and Eleanor wouldn't be interested, but you could join us."

She shuddered at the thought of racing around the countryside on a horse. Though, surprisingly, her skills on horseback had improved since the first time when she had to share one with Beckworth during their escape from Gemini.

"Let's wait and see how that goes."

He chuckled and gave her a swift kiss before picking up her empty cup and tossing it in the trash. "Let's get these pies home."

When he missed the turn for home, she didn't question him. He liked to take the long way, still getting familiar with the streets. It was instinctual for him to want to know where he lived. He grew up a street urchin in London, working for the gangs, which required knowledge of the city and quick escape routes. Not something he needed now, but when he'd been in Baywood previously, he'd been the enemy. It was a habit he couldn't shake.

He didn't make any other turns, and the city began to give way to the coast. Her knee began to bounce.

"Where are you going?"

"You didn't think we were going to eat all those pies with the few days we have left."

"You tricked me." Her fingers played at the edge of her sweater, and when Beckworth glanced over, he smirked. "What?"

"I should have brought some paper for you."

"You think making a few swans will make up for this?" She glanced out the window as he made a turn into the driveway of the Westcliffe Inn, the non-functioning bread and breakfast hotel that AJ and Finn called home. She suppressed a smile, reminding herself she should be angry with him. Her penchant for making origami swans was widely known among her friends both in this time period and in 1805. She made them when she was nervous, bored, or working through problems. So, pretty much all the time.

She didn't just create swans. She could fold a single sheet of paper into a crane or a fish, but she preferred swans and could make them with her eyes closed. Charlotte, AJ's niece, had become adept at making origami figures, pushing Stella to learn more shapes to satisfy the youngster, who'd begun to idolize her "auntie."

"I simply thought it would be an easier discussion with family." Beckworth didn't seem fazed by her grumpy attitude.

She understood how important it was for him to see Waverly. For a kid raised in the harsh streets of London, he'd worked hard and, admittedly, had performed some unscrupulous tasks while working for the Duke of Dunsmore. It paid off with the acquisition of Waverly Manor and the title of Viscount.

Most might consider the manor to have been bought from tainted money, but how else was someone from the streets able to rise above their station? Besides, Beckworth, the bastard son of the duke, had tried to make a connection with his father, only to have it all thrown back in his face. If Finn hadn't killed the man, she would have done it—just on principle.

When he gently squeezed her hand, she had to admit this was the best way. She expected AJ and Finn to push back on their crazy idea to call the fog. It wasn't like time travel was a science. The mysterious stones and secret incantations, discovered in an ancient text written by paranoid Druids before the time of Julius Caesar, would be considered outlandish, if not a downright immediate path to a sanitarium, which should make most people question their actions.

But AJ and Finn had traversed the mysterious fog several times—not completely by choice—and lived to tell the tale.

"This will all work out. You'll see."

Stella had expected Beckworth to call in the entire army, but the only other car besides AJ's and Finn's was the large black SUV Ethan drove. The small group was, as expected, sitting around the dinner table in the kitchen. The French doors that led to the wrap-around deck overlooking the Oregon coast were closed against the chilled air.

Though everyone appeared to be drinking coffee, except for Sebastian, the elderly monk from France who preferred tea, there was a new bottle of Jameson whiskey in the center of the table with seven short glasses circling it.

Something told Stella, AJ and Finn might have an inkling of what was going on. She should have known Maire wouldn't be able to keep a secret from AJ, and while she should be mad, she was grateful someone else had dropped the bombshell. Now, all Stella had to do was pick her way through the remaining shards of AJ's anger.

It wasn't that she'd been scared to tell her. It was that AJ would harp every day until they left about how dangerous it could be, that they wouldn't know what they would be walking into, and all the worrisome things AJ had dealt with when everyone was chasing the stones. Those days were over. Most of the stones were in this century now as was *The Book of Stones.* But still, best friends shouldn't keep these types of secrets.

All eyes turned to her as she walked through the entry to the kitchen. She took a step back, but Beckworth was right behind her, blocking a quick exit.

"The beans have been spilled," AJ growled. "You might as well sit your ass down and explain what the hell the two of you are thinking."

2

____

Stella didn't move, thrown off by AJ's tone more than her words. Beckworth pushed past her with the pies and placed the Marionberry in front of AJ and the strawberry by Maire. Stella's gaze snapped to Finn. He held his practiced poker face, which was no help in sensing the mood of the room. Maire's focus was on the pie—strawberries were her favorite—but she couldn't stop a small grin. Stella wasn't sure if the smile was for the pie or a reaction to AJ's outburst. Ethan's expression was as stoic as Finn's.

So, she glanced at Sebastian. He was a monk who normally had very little to say but wore his thoughts on his face or, more accurately, in his eyes. And they were currently shining with mirth, which eased her shoulders that had risen toward her ears.

AJ was bound to be irritated, and it wouldn't be the first time it had been directed at Stella. She would have her misgivings about their plan to go back, but it was obvious AJ was more hurt by the fact everyone else appeared to know before she did. Her best friend should have been the first one Stella told.

"You think pie is a fair apology." AJ eyed the pie as she said it, her gaze shifting toward the fork in the place settings that had been laid out for dinner. She might be pissed off, but she had a thing for Donna's pies, and Marionberry was her favorite.

Stella would have words with Beckworth later, but it was obvious he'd planned ahead to butter up AJ with support from Maire. One thing about him, he was as good at strategizing as Finn and Ethan were and knew how to mold a situation to his advantage. In other words, a manipulator when it suited him. And now was an excellent time to play off his thoughtfulness. He did all of this for her, after all.

"Some news is better when heard among friends." Stella made her way to the coffee pot, poured the last remaining dregs into a cup, then started a new pot. She swallowed the remnants then turned to the table where all eyes were still on her.

"Oh, for god's sake, let's just get to it. Yes, Teddy asked if I was interested in going back to Waverly for a New Year's celebration. We should make it in time to invite Hensley and Mary so they can stop on their way to London for the season. What's wrong with that?"

"You make it sound like you're just taking a drive down the coast to see friends." AJ pushed the pie aside, though it was still within easy reach.

"Except for the trip through the fog," Maire chimed in, "and the gut-wrenching pain, it's really nothing more than that."

AJ gave Maire a look that clearly stated she didn't need that kind of help. "You're betting everything on the fact you won't have a problem with the stones. What if... I don't know." She searched around the room as if chasing her thoughts. "What if you lost both rings? You'd be stuck there forever."

Everyone chuckled, and AJ had to smile at the absurdity.

"I'm not sure if it's a good idea to use the stones as a constant doorway to the past." Finn ran a finger over the table, following a wood grain. "But I think we've proven that the travel has become more reliable. And yes, there's always a chance the two stones could be lost, but if they don't come back within a reasonable allotted time, Ethan has a stone, and we have the Heart Stone, which gives us what we need to go find them."

Stella hadn't been prepared for Finn's support, but perhaps he liked the idea of being able to go back in time to see old friends. She sat at the table, pulled over a stack of napkins, and began creating an origami swan. She'd learned the art several years before during a self-improvement phase. Of the dozen courses she'd taken, none of them stuck except for origami.

It had become a joke between her and Beckworth. Whether it had been while they were on the run from Gemini's man or when the game changed to pursue Gemini and her gang, he always made sure she had paper to make her swans.

AJ turned to Sebastian, who'd been following along even as he turned pages in whatever ancient text he'd found at an estate sale. Being a man of the nineteenth century, he had been fascinated by the idea of estate sales. AJ was an antiques broker and liked to hit the sales early on the first day before all the good stuff was gone. She always took Sebastian with her. Sometimes Maire went along, but she wasn't as fond of the outings. Stella thought it was more that she preferred to wait and see what Sebastian brought home for her.

"Sebastian," AJ started with an even tone. "I know you gave the two stones to Stella and Beckworth in the hopes they'd find each other in one of their time periods, but you can't be in favor of them going back just for a holiday gathering."

He set his book aside and glanced at the group, taking a moment to study each person before moving to the next. His odd behavior used to make Stella fidget until she remembered he was a monk. He didn't read expressions; he looked deep inside and read a person's soul. That was creepy as hell, but at the same time, it was peaceful.

"I haven't been in this time period for very long, but there seems to be risks just crossing one of your city streets." Sebastian chuckled. "Though I must say, having been in London several times in my life, the risk is greater getting hit by a wagon or carriage in the narrow streets of the city by drivers with little regard to another's life. I suppose that's not the best analogy for sending someone back in time, but Maire and I have had many discussions about the stones and the latest set of incantations. If Stella and Beckworth use the correct incantations, I don't see a problem." His fingers played at the edges of an envelope he'd been using as a bookmark. "I must admit, I'm curious to know what's happening back home and hoped they'd take a letter back with them. Hensley said he'd stay in touch with the monastery."

"And before you ask," Ethan piped in as the only one who hadn't provided his opinion. "I do side with AJ on it being an unnecessary risk. At the same time, I haven't left anything behind except good friends, which was difficult enough. If the earl were still alive, I would want to go back. Beckworth has left more behind than Finn, Maire, or I." He took Maire's hand. "We're making a fine life here. But I understand Beckworth's need to spend time at Waverly. I doubt this will be their only trip. Once he finds his calling here, he won't have as much need to return to Waverly." He glanced at Beckworth. "Just my opinion, mate."

Beckworth shrugged. "We could debate all evening as to my motives for returning to Waverly. But that isn't the point of the conversation. Stella and I discussed it thoroughly, and we're in agreement." He smiled at Stella. "Unless she's changed her mind."

Stella focused on the swan, doing her best to ignore the entire discussion. She knew the conversation would devolve into the whys and why-nots. It was her own fault. She should have told AJ days ago, but the discomfort she sensed in the room lessened. Beckworth's solution was working. And she was such a chicken shit.

"I haven't changed my mind." Stella set down the swan. "We did agree. And we've spoken with Sebastian and Maire several times regarding the risks. They're minimal. Safer than air travel."

Finn barked out a laugh, and AJ snickered.

"Fine." AJ pulled the pie back. "I should know better than argue the merits of time travel with Maire or Sebastian. If you want to jump back, feel like your guts are being ripped out, and then toss your cookies, by all means, have a wonderful time." She turned her attention to Finn. "Get the plates. I need pie."

<hr>

AJ strolled around Stella's bedroom, picking up a knickknack, dusting it off, and then setting it back down. She folded a scarf that had been tossed over the back of a small armchair and placed it in a drawer.

"Why didn't you tell me you were going back?"

AJ's question was said loud enough for Stella to hear from the closet, where she was reviewing last-minute options. Stella's shoulders tensed as she considered the question. After that dinner a couple of days before, everything seemed back to normal between her and her best friend.

They'd gone shopping twice, searching for the best pants and shirt for her to wear through the fog. She still had the set she'd worn when traveling home from Waverly, but AJ thought something that fit Stella's curves would be more comfortable. After realizing she'd lost the battle on Stella going back, AJ seemed eager to ensure she was well-equipped.

Not once during the thrift stores, lunches, and coffee breaks had AJ's question come up. Not once was there any weird vibe coming from her that she was unsettled by Stella's unwillingness to share her plans with her. Now that they were a day away from travel, she popped the question.

After one last review of her closet, she ran her fingers over the moss robe she'd brought with her from Waverly. She refused to take it with her—it was Beckworth's favorite. She smiled at all the times he'd taken it off her. With a last sigh and not seeing anything else to pack, she straightened her shoulders and strode into the bedroom. Her first stop was the table by the armchair, where an almost empty bottle of wine and two glasses sat. She refilled the glasses and handed one to AJ.

She sat cross-legged on the bed without spilling a drop and patted the bed. "Come sit."

AJ smirked and joined her, preferring to lean against the headboard as she rested the glass on her belly.

"Back when I'd been kidnapped and dragged through the fog, you'd been terrified for my safety." Stella stared into her wine, searching for the best words. "Your worry grew as you and Finn searched for me, even when you knew Beckworth was protecting me. I get it. I worried about you every time you stepped through the fog.

"The thing is, we each had a right to be worried. But it had nothing to do with the time travel. It had everything to do with the bad guys who wanted control of the stones and the chronicles. The bad guys have been vanquished. The stones are safe. *The Book of Stones* is safe. We're safe."

"All true." AJ sipped wine. "That doesn't explain why you didn't tell me you wanted to go back to Waverly."

"In a way, it does. When I followed you and Finn home to this century and left Beckworth behind, you were worried I'd go back. Hell, I even had the powers of attorney set up for that very possibility. I wanted to be with Beckworth, but that's not the same thing as wanting to be at Waverly."

Stella sighed and scooted back, leaning against the headboard so she was next to AJ. She took her friend's hand. "We're only going to visit. Beckworth still has a strong attachment to what he built and the people he left behind. But he's committed to this future. He likes it here now that he's had time to see it from the perspective of friends. We're coming back. Think of it as a trip to see family."

AJ snorted. "It's not exactly a flight to the East Coast."

Stella laughed. "Exactly. Sure, the first couple minutes are uncomfortable, but it's not like I'll have some kid behind me, kicking my seat all the way there and back."

"Well, that's one way to look at it." AJ took another sip. "I wish there was a way to stay in contact while you're in a different century. And god, doesn't that sound strange." She sighed while she picked at her chipped nail polish. "I don't understand why you didn't just blurt it out days ago. I would have been upset, but I would have preferred hearing it from you. I guess it's my turn to sit home and wait. Once I spoke with Sebastian and Maire, I was partially appeased. When Beckworth found out I knew, I have to admit, I was surprised by his solution."

"He knew you knew?" Stella sprang up, wine jostling but not breaching the rim.

AJ laughed and couldn't seem to stop. Stella took her glass before she sloshed wine over the bedspread. She couldn't believe Beckworth hadn't told her. He'd been more manipulative that she'd guessed. She set the glasses on the nightstand and leaned against the headboard while AJ controlled her giggles.

Could she blame him? He'd asked several times if she'd talked to AJ. Had suggested Stella take her to lunch, drive down the coast to their favorite tourist trap, or discuss it over a fancy dinner with AJ and Finn. When she ignored all his suggestions, then discovered AJ already knew about the trip, most likely through Finn, he'd come up with his own solution—break the news in a large group with the support of friends. The anger that had been building at being duped melted away.

"Promise me you'll stay out of trouble." AJ gripped Stella's hand.

"It's a weekend hunting party. I'll be eating cake and strolling through Waverly gardens helping Mary plan her spring garden parties and gossiping over which balls she'll attend in London. What trouble could I get in?"

"Just a weekend?"

"Probably more like a week or two, but you know that's only a day or two in this timeline. We never spoke about how long we'd be gone, but let's say, from your perspective, no more than a week."

"You know that's like two or three months in the past."

Stella squeezed AJ's hand and stood. "I know he only mentioned Waverly, but I'm wondering if he might also want to see his friends in London. It's possible—" she held up a hand at the protest AJ was beginning to raise. "I'm just saying, he might consider continuing to London with Hensley and Mary for a few days and then returning to Waverly for a few more before coming home."

AJ considered it. "I have to admit, the London parties were fun, though I didn't get to experience many. If you made the jump, it makes sense to get the most out of it before coming home. And you're right, with the trouble with the stones behind us, there shouldn't be anything to worry about." She jumped off the bed. "So, let's get you packed before Beckworth comes home. I think Finn wanted to go out to dinner for your send-off."

"And then some god-forsaken early morning jump. I don't know what he was thinking."

"I think the key is that it's before breakfast. You'll thank him once the fog spits you out."

They were both laughing as they continued packing.

"Do you have the first aid kit?" AJ asked.

"You've asked me that twice already."

"Yet, still no answer."

Stella sighed and walked into the bathroom and came out waving the kit, which she dropped in the duffel. "Satisfied?"

AJ searched through the duffel, moving the first aid kit in between a pair of pants and a jacket. "I am now." She continued to shuffle through the bag, not surprised to find a couple bags of coffee beans, lock picks that made her snort, then held up a pair of red boots with four-inch heels. Her brow lifted.

Stella blushed. "Don't ask and stop snooping."

AJ snorted. "Says the snoop queen."

Stella grinned. "Ironic much." She pulled out the periwinkle dress Beckworth had made for her on her first day in London. She ran her hands over it and sniffed the material. Then she put it back.

"You're not taking it? It's beautiful."

Stella rubbed the opal hanging around her neck, her thoughts flickering back to that weekend. The first time she'd made love with Beckworth. Teddy. She shook her head before AJ got nosier. "Teddy asked me to leave the clothes I brought back with me. He had two day dresses made for me to take back."

AJ's brow lifted again.

Stella raised her hands in a give-up gesture. "Don't ask. He won't say why. In fact, his exact words were 'I won't stop you from taking them with you, I'm just asking you not to.'"

"Oh, man. He didn't."

"Yep. Guilted me right into doing as he asked."

AJ giggled. "Man. He's got it bad."

Stella grinned. "I know."

"Hey, what about seasick medicine?

She turned a bit green at the thought. "Why would I need that?"

"One thing I've learned about time travel, even without worrying about the stones, it's best to be prepared for anything."

3

Beckworth, a duffel slung over his shoulder, strode down the path that led from the inn to a lone dock in a private bay. Finn and Ethan matched his pace. The quiet bay was deep enough to have once moored the *Daphne Marie*, an eighteenth-century tall ship that Finn brought through the fog when first arriving in this century.

There was a second path on the other side of the inn that ended at a tidal pool. When the tide was out, it offered a narrow beach from which to search the pools. AJ had once told him that her father had brought her there often when she was a child, and the inn seemed an appropriate home for Finn, who'd left his ship behind when he decided to live in her timeline.

Beckworth glanced over his shoulder at the women who walked with Sebastian. "Is AJ alright with this?"

"She's had time to get past her fear for you and Stella. It's difficult to remember the past without thinking about the stones and keeping one eye over your shoulder."

"I'm somewhat aware of that feeling." They'd all been impacted by the stones, but they'd landed on their feet—luck or fate on their side. "To be fair, Stella was a bit on the fence about it, but the more we talked about it, the more she remembered the good times we had. She's excited about seeing Waverly's gardens."

"I think Maire is a bit jealous she's not going." Ethan walked with his hands in his pockets. When Beckworth first met him, Ethan had been uptight and rigid. Over the last couple of weeks, it was easy to see the change in him. He was almost as relaxed as Finn, and Beckworth imagined Maire played a large part in his transformation.

"Maybe next time we could all go for a short trip. I've found it more difficult than I thought to leave so many friends behind." But he'd do it all over again to be with Stella. If this trip went well, perhaps they could have the best of both worlds.

"There's one thing we wanted to share with you before you jumped." Finn's tone turned serious, and Beckworth wasn't sure he wanted to hear what was coming. "It could be different than our experience since the troubles with the stones are behind us, but you might discover yourself overly protective of Stella."

"If I remember correctly, I spent most of the time keeping Gemini away from her. To the point of turning myself over in exchange for her."

Ethan nodded. "True. But you've spent, what, about nine months in this time period now. Between this time and the women's proven ability to handle themselves in difficult situations, we still need to be the protectors—more so in the past than in this timeline."

Beckworth understood what they were attempting to say, though he didn't believe there was any difference. Besides, the trip was a holiday, not running for their lives.

Finn patted him on the back. "I see your doubts. All we can do is share our experience. It's up to you on how you handle it. Because trust me, whether in peacetime or war, you'll need to be prepared."

Both men chuckled as they left him on the dock. He was still mulling over their words, believing them to be joking, when Sebastian joined him.

The monk pulled a stack of letters from his pocket and handed them to Beckworth. "I was wondering if you could give these to Hensley. The top one provides directions on where to send the letters. There are five in all."

Beckworth noted the parchment on which the letters were written. "Did you bring this paper with you from the past or did Maire?"

"They're from my journal." He scratched his head and peered back at the others, who were saying their goodbyes to Stella. "I was wondering, if you have the time and remember, could you bring me more paper and a new journal?"

Beckworth eyed the old monk. "You know there's better paper and writing instruments in this time period."

"Oh, yes, and I use them almost exclusively." He held out his hands. "Some of the ink stains from the quill are beginning to fade. Oh, that reminds me. I could use a few more quills and ink pots. Maire has located some, but the quality isn't the same."

Beckworth studied Sebastian, whose eyes sparkled with mischief. "You old dog. You knew if I came to the future, I'd end up going back."

Sebastian only smiled. "Hensley might have a message or two for me. If you don't mind bringing those back, I would appreciate it."

"You expect me to play messenger between the two of you?"

The monk shrugged. "I'd go myself, but at my age, I find the travel too difficult."

"You're a crafty old man. When you gave Stella and me each a stone, you had this all laid out."

He smiled and patted Beckworth's hand. "I prefer to think of myself as a careful planner. Safe travels." With that being said, he turned and shuffled back to the group as Stella made her way onto the dock.

The two stopped long enough for a hug and a few words before parting, then Stella stepped next to Beckworth.

"I take it you got his letters." She winked at him.

"You knew what he was up to?"

"Not until last night. Who knew monks could be so devious?"

"It seems to be a trait we all share."

She chuckled and pulled out the incantation before glancing at her ring. After releasing a long sigh, she asked, "You ready for this?"

"Have you been practicing your Celtic?"

She nodded. "I ran through it a few times last night with Sebastian and Maire. They say I've got it."

"Okay." He took her hand and turned them to face their friends.

Stella read the incantation, and he glanced over his shoulder. The fog was rolling in. Stella yelled, "Don't forget the swans and fish I left for Charlotte." Charlotte was AJ's young niece, who was becoming an expert origami practitioner at the tender age of five.

AJ's response was lost as the fog overtook them. Then, nothing but a light so bright, even with his eyes closed, they burned.

Stella's grip tightened as the fog tore them away from this time period. At one point, he was certain his insides were being ripped out. The next, it seemed his organs were being squeezed in an attempt to make them implode. When he didn't think he could take anymore, the light receded as he slammed into the ground—hard.

Perhaps he would need to rethink the time traveling.

After dry heaving into the grass, he glanced up to see Stella pushing the duffel off her before rolling over into a fetal position.

When he regained his focus, he stared up into the smiling face of Fitz, the first mate of the *Daphne Marie*.

The young man nodded his head with apparent glee. "Looks like I won the bet."

***

Waverly Manor, England - 1806

"When did you grow a beard?" Stella had rolled over at the sound of Fitz's voice and stared up at him. His face was upside down, but that was definitely a beard.

Fitz ran a hand over it and rocked back and forth on his heels. "Oh, I guess it was during the sail to Chepstow when we traveled to Hereford for Ethan and Maire's wedding." He stepped next to her and held out a hand. When he pulled her up, he added, "The ladies seem to like it."

Stella gave him a long perusal and matched his smile. "I can see why."

Beckworth snorted. "Good lord, woman, he doesn't need to hear that."

They all laughed as Beckworth picked up his duffel and Fitz retrieved Stella's.

"How did you know to be waiting for us?" Beckworth asked. "I told Barrington the date we'd attempt, but I didn't think he'd post men to watch for us."

"He didn't. I just happened to be on my way back from Eleanor's when I saw the fog. That's a sight you never forget."

"And that's what the bet was about?" Stella asked. Fitz would bet the sun wouldn't rise in the morning if the odds were worth it. What she really wanted to know was why he was at Eleanor's, but she'd find out soon enough.

He gave her a wolfish grin. "You know what they say about the luck of the Irish."

Stella followed the men as they chattered about changes to the manor's security now that the matter of the stones was over. And there was a new foal from one of Beckworth's prize stallions. It wasn't difficult to see he wanted to go straight to the stables, but he stayed the course as Fitz walked them through the kitchen.

Fitz stopped at the staff's long dining table where a meat pie, a biscuit, and a mug she assumed was ale waited for him. He gave the cook a kiss on her cheek, which made her blush, then he sat down. "They'll be in your west study. Last I heard, there was some disagreement on who to invite to the hunting party."

Beckworth stopped before turning for the stairs. "They haven't sent the invitations yet?"

Fitz finished chewing his first bite of meat pie. "You'll have to talk to Hensley about it. The hunt has been postponed for a fortnight."

Stella glanced at Beckworth. His brows scrunched, forming those cute lines between his eyes. He didn't respond and quickened his pace as he hurried up the stairs, leaving her to race behind him.

"Can you slow down? Where's the fire?" she huffed, grateful she'd worn a used pair of old hiking boots she'd found at a thrift store. They were durable, comfortable, and plain enough to get by without much notice.

He paused when he reached the main floor and hooked his arm through hers. "I apologize. I suppose I was expecting a different homecoming."

"Perhaps a more quiet one."

He smiled and kissed the tip of her nose. "Exactly."

"And you thought the life of a viscount would be boring."

"In retrospect, that was silly of me." He stopped at the main staircase where Libby waited.

"It's a pleasure to see the lord of the manor home safe and sound." She curtsied.

Beckworth shook his head. "Good to see the staff still has a sense of humor." From Stella's understanding, he ran a very loose household compared to other aristocrats when he didn't have guests. Libby always tested the boundaries.

Libby glanced past him to Stella. "Does Lady Stella want to go to her room to rest or join the men in the study?"

"I'm not ready to rest yet." She held a hand over her belly. "I'm still waiting for my stomach to settle. What time is it, anyway? How soon before the next meal?"

"Lunch is still a couple of hours away. I'll have cook send something to the study." She winked at Beckworth. "It is good to have you home, sir."

Beckworth touched her shoulder. "And it's good to be home. Thank you, Libby."

Fitz hadn't mentioned who would be in the study, but apparently, Hensley had commandeered it. If Fitz was at the manor, then either Jamie, the captain of the *Daphne Marie*, or Lando, his second mate, could be there. She was hoping they all were.

But why postpone the hunting party? Hensley must be planning a mission. She glanced at Beckworth. There was a faraway look in his gaze along with a furrowed brow—he was processing.

"Are you sure you'd rather not go up and unpack?" he asked.

She passed him a look he knew all too well. "Not a chance in hell. I want to know what Hensley is up to as much as you do."

"I'm sure the delay in the hunt is nothing more than finding a time when everyone will be available."

"Uh-huh."

He didn't respond because they both knew he'd gloss over what they were both thinking. Hensley didn't get involved in weekend party arrangements. That would be Mary's task. While Beckworth led them deeper into the manor, stopping to say hello to any staff they ran into, she glanced in the rooms, wondering exactly where Hensley's wife was.

Beckworth stopped in front of his study door, which was closed. He chuckled. "I'm not sure whether to knock. Being gone for almost nine months, and with Hensley here, it feels odd."

She rubbed his arm. "It's like we walked onto the set of the *Twilight Zone*." He preferred the old black-and-white episodes to the newer versions. "You should probably knock, wait a heartbeat, and then walk in. This is still your manor, but the knock is polite."

He stared into her eyes. Maybe they should both go upstairs and unpack. Whatever waited for them behind the study door would still be there after they tested out the bed. His gaze warmed, and she knew he was thinking the same thing. His kiss was thorough, heated with passion, and ended far too soon.

"I can't tell you how much it meant that you came home with me."

She pushed a strand of loose hair back into his queue. How most of it stayed intact through the fog was anyone's guess. Her hair had to be a mess. She ignored his comment about coming home. This would always be his home. To her, it was more like a vacation home. But a little kernel settled in the back of her brain, refusing to budge. What would happen after the hunting party was over and it was time to go back to Baywood?

Before she could give it another thought, Beckworth gave a sharp rap on the door with his knuckles, waited a beat, then opened the door.

Five faces turned in their direction. It was obvious they

hadn't expected them, or at least not at that moment. They looked like the cat who ate the proverbial canary, and it seemed to catch Beckworth off guard.

So, Stella did what she always did and took the first step in breaking the ice.

"Hello, boys. Did you miss me?"

4

"We've been expecting you but weren't sure how well the incantations worked. And, of course, you've been greatly missed." Barrington, the Waverly butler, was a long-time friend of Beckworth's from their early days running with a London crew—Beckworth's term for a gang.

Stella was overcome with emotion when the aloof butler bent and kissed her cheek. She was saved from displaying what his affection meant to her when Jamie and Lando gave her welcomed bear hugs.

"We weren't sure if Beckworth could remember how to use the stones." Jamie gave Beckworth a good-natured punch on his shoulder before shaking hands. "It's good to see you home."

Hensley, the steadfast leader of a network of spies working for the Crown, wasn't willing to let go of his English stuffiness, but she managed to give him a kiss on each cheek, forcing a blush. He waited patiently for Beckworth to make his way to the desk and then held out his hand.

"When I asked Barrington to invite you and Mary to the hunting party, it was meant as a restful weekend without any business." Beckworth held the handshake a bit longer than normal, and Stella caught the meaningful look that passed between them.

There was definitely a mission being planned.

Her curiosity only grew deeper when she noted Thomas—she never caught his last name—lounging in a far corner chair. She hadn't spent much time around him when he'd helped with the mission to take down Gemini. So, it was surprising when he smiled and nodded at her. It was more than she expected.

Thomas had worked as Sergeant of Arms for the Earl of Hereford. A job previously held by Ethan. After the earl succumbed to age-related maladies, Stella assumed Thomas would hold the same position for the earl's nephew, the new lord of Brun Manor. Maybe the mission involved the nephew.

She glanced at the men, settling her gaze on Hensley. Would he update Beckworth on the conversation they'd interrupted while she was in the room? This wasn't the twenty-first century, and while she'd previously been included in the mission meetings, it was only because she'd been a victim with insight into Gemini. AJ and Maire always had a role to play, but they were typically included for the skills they brought to the team.

Beckworth's eyes gleamed as he chatted with his friends. Would this still be the holiday they'd planned? She glanced around for an available seat. The west study was similar to the one at Hensley's manor and larger than Beckworth's personal study in the east wing. A massive desk took a prominent stage surrounded by stuffed bookcases, a floor globe, and a cart containing a stocked bar.

Beckworth's fascination with books extended to the east study and a stunning library filled with chairs and sofas for reading and dozens of bookcases. Beckworth's favorite hobbies besides gardening were chess and collecting books. In Baywood, he'd managed to stuff books into any open space he could find. He joked about adding an extension to the house for a library, though she wasn't positive he was kidding.

A small seating area with a sofa and two stuffed chairs surrounded the hearth, where low flames licked at the remaining embers. She took a seat on the sofa and turned to face the desk, making herself at home rather than waiting to see if she'd be invited.

They might want her to leave, but they'd have to kick her out.

While the men chatted about the new foal, Hensley returned to his seat behind the desk. And though it was obvious he was listening to what they said, since he had his own collection of stallions, his eyes kept darting to her.

What made her take note of it wasn't glares or looks meant to remind her she was in the men's study. He didn't do either of those things. No. If she had to put a name to it, his gaze was one of curiosity.

Hensley was older than the others. Perhaps in his fifties. Age wasn't easy to discern in this time period with a lack of proper diets and occasions to drink enough alcohol that made her look like a teetotaler. He was an aristocrat, though she never heard him called by a title other than lord, which was the proper way to address most men with titles. But he'd been in Parliament and hobnobbed in the King's court.

Yet, for all his propriety, he worked well with people in all social classes, which made him excellent in his role as spymaster. He was impossible to beat at chess, though she'd come close a couple of times. Somewhere along the way, the two of them had developed a bond that gave her a certain latitude, but she'd be an idiot to ever cross a line with him.

She tucked her musings away as Hensley cleared his throat.

"Now that we have the lord of the manor back, it's time to return to our discussion. He can share his new life in the future during dinner when Mary returns."

"Where is Mary?" Beckworth took a seat in a chair next to the sofa. "I would have expected her to be running Mrs. Walker ragged with supervising the housekeeping duties."

"She's spending a couple of days with Eleanor." Hensley dabbed at his forehead before shuffling paper around.

"Something about needing time away from all the men in the manor." Jamie grinned.

Lando, who always preferred standing, as if itching to have someplace to go, leaned against one of the bookcases and nodded with a huge grin.

Hensley's cheeks reddened, and Stella held back a smile.

"And you sent Fitz to check on them?" Beckworth asked.

"Is that where he went?" Jamie asked. "I thought he was checking on the foal."

"He probably got a craving for Eleanor's meat pies," Lando responded.

"Well, it must have been a difficult walk from Eleanor's. We left him in the kitchen with another meat pie." Stella grinned and fingered her opal.

"He's never been one to sit long." Lando moved to a straight-backed chair that Stella was positive would be considered an antique even in this era.

She had to give AJ, a burgeoning antiques broker, credit for not bringing home items to sell. Stella made it a personal mission if she had the opportunity, to buy something for her. AJ might not have the best memories of her time in this century, but she'd made friends that she'd left behind. It wouldn't hurt to have a memento or two to remember the good times. Maybe a hair ornament like the one Beckworth had bought her.

"So, Hensley, why is it my carefully made plans for a hunting party have been delayed for a fortnight?" Beckworth leaned back and appeared comfortable with a leg crossing over a knee.

She suspected his casual appearance wasn't the full story. He wasn't angry, or she'd see it reflected in a tightened jaw. It was more a combination of the curiosity she'd seen earlier on Hensley and concern over what was so important it forced his guests to rearrange schedules. If nothing else, Beckworth was a consummate host. His first thoughts would be of his guests— more specifically, Dame Elizabeth Ellingsworth.

"Not to worry, Beckworth." Hensley reviewed a letter, set it aside, and picked up another one. "I caught Barrington before the invitations went out and replaced them with an apology on behalf of the Crown for the delay."

Mention of the Crown made Beckworth and Stella sit a bit taller. If Hensley was tossing around the Crown as the reason for the postponement, this had to be important. England was at war with Napoleon. When Stella was last at Waverly and had considered asking Beckworth to go home with her, she'd backed off when she'd overheard a conversation between him, Hensley, and Jamie. She racked her brain. It had been months since that day, but it came back easily enough. There had been word of a possible spy in the war council. Big stuff. Was this the same concern?

"What's so important to the Crown that you'd need a ship?" Beckworth jogged loose a question she hadn't considered. Which was strange considering the men in the room. "And I must ask, as good as it is to see Thomas, does this also touch the new master of Brun Manor? Or is he an earl already?"

Thomas answered first. "He's not an earl and has quite a lot to learn before that day ever comes. When I first met him, he seemed like a man I could work for. But when he moved in, he brought his own men to form an elite guard. I was invited to stay on in a minor security position." He clenched a hand into a fist. "If the earl were alive to see the caliber of men the new lord brought with him, he'd run them off his land. Not a single man has seen battle, nor do they have the experience to train fighting men. I took the last of my pay and headed south."

"And it was fortunate that his first stop was in Bristol." Hensley's smile was sincere. "The loss of the earl was quite a blow, but death comes for us all." He paused a moment, then turned to Beckworth. "Thomas has been working with the network for the last couple of weeks, mostly working with our contacts to meet the players. The reason we're here and why I need a ship has to do with something Jamie and Fitz uncovered while the rest of you searched for the missing Mórdha Stone Chronicles."

"I only heard parts of that story." Beckworth scratched his head. "Something to do with smugglers?"

Jamie nodded and took up the tale. "We'd just dropped Maire and Ethan off in Newport for their run to Bransford. Before we turned for London, we sailed to Dublin to pick up cargo."

"You mean Irish whiskey," Beckworth corrected.

"It's a popular cargo during wartime or peace."

Beckworth chuckled. "No doubt. I'm remembering now. Something about someone who should have hung at Newgate."

The door opened at the right time as Fitz strolled in. He must have heard the conversation before entering because he finished Beckworth's statement with, "Thaddeus MacDuff." He shut the door and found a spot on the floor, drawing up his legs. "He'd been sailing along the southern coast of Ireland, stopping at ports and riling up the locals with talk of France being our salvation to rid ourselves of the English."

"More like finding the best ports to run his smuggling operation." Jamie stood and walked to a map on the wall that showed the British Isles and the northern coast of Europe. "From what we've been able to pickup through our contacts and ship captains, MacDuff has been seen along both coasts—Ireland and England. His travels take him from just north of Dublin to the southern tip of Ireland and along the western coast of England."

"Could be typical smuggling operations," Lando said.

"Or a way to bring French spies to England while finding isolated ports to moor French ships." Fitz pulled out a pipe and stuck it in his mouth but didn't light it.

Stella didn't remember Fitz smoking a pipe, and she considered the first mate. He was a decent-looking man. Not as roguish as Finn or Jamie, but he carried a carefree attitude that seemed to lure women to his bed. Or so Beckworth had told her. And while not her type, she sensed the magnetism. At first, she'd considered him a roughneck sailor and nothing more. But she'd been on a few missions with him. He was competent and somewhat of a chameleon, easily adapting his persona to fit a situation, similar to Beckworth's ability. Perfect spy material for Hensley.

"Though frowned upon, the Crown isn't overly concerned about smuggling at this time." Hensley stood and replenished his glass with an amber liquid. Some of that Irish whiskey, if Stella was to guess. Once he returned to his seat, he continued. "England doesn't have the resources, not while battling Napoleon."

"But the rumors about possible French spies must have the War Council concerned." Beckworth tapped his fingers on the armrest, his brows knitted.

"Yes, but with the Royal Navy focused on France, we simply don't have the ships to waste chasing MacDuff between ports, especially when we don't currently have a location for him. We could use British patrols, but they don't have the skills to deal with someone like MacDuff. And the last thing we need is him going to ground if he smells a patrol."

"Now it makes sense," Beckworth added, and Stella had a good idea where this was going.

Hensley nodded. "I need the *Daphne* and her crew to find MacDuff."

5

After Hensley dropped the bomb about the pending mission, the group broke up so Beckworth and Stella could get settled in. It was a reasonable expectation, but she also knew they didn't want to discuss any more of the mission while she was in the room. There was a moment of irritation that she squelched, reminding herself they were in a different century, and she needed to pick her battles.

She was headstrong. Stella knew that. In her opinion, it was one of her best attributes and the reason she was the best-selling broker in the county. But that was in Baywood. Here, she was an unmarried woman with no father or brother to see to her needs. Beckworth didn't see it in the same light, and for that, she was grateful. He'd grown up with a single mom and understood some of it, even if it was colored with the social etiquettes and trappings of the early nineteenth century.

After the meeting in the study, Beckworth went to the stables to see the foal while Stella went upstairs to unpack. She shouldn't have bothered. She hadn't packed much, but Libby had hung the dresses, placed the rest in a dresser, and stuffed the empty duffel in the dressing room.

Libby, her personal lady's maid while she was in residence, was also one of Beckworth's best spies. She wasn't sure Mrs. Walker approved the decision, especially when the female guests would begin arriving for the hunting party. Lady Agatha Osborne always asked for Libby, as did others. Beckworth had assured Stella that it was common practice that the lady of the manor didn't share her maid, and Lady Agatha would have to deal with it.

Whether by design or his nature to surround himself with trustworthy friends, he employed several people he'd known in London, quietly building his own crew at Waverly. Libby was one of those, but she knew how to follow proper decorum— when it was expected. She was a wild one—rebellious and outspoken. Stella considered her a perfect match as her lady's maid.

Beckworth hadn't been born into the aristocracy, even though his father was a duke. He grew up poor on the streets of London, a bastard son. When he rose out of the East End through various means—some questionable—he had a clear understanding of the haves and have-nots. So, when there weren't any visitors at Waverly, he allowed the staff more freedoms. They knew the requisite etiquette and applied it when required. It wasn't easy for many of them to relax, having come from generations of the service class, but they knew a good thing when they had it.

With the unpacking done and nothing else to do, she stepped onto the balcony and scanned the gardens in their drab winter color. Bits of green and small clumps of winter flowers played hide-and-seek through the dead leaves. Evergreens of various shapes and sizes added to the ethereal January landscape. Beyond it all were the deciduous trees, bare of leaves, and where they'd arrived through the fog.

She found a shawl and wrapped it around her, selecting a

patio chair in the hazy sunlight. Less than two hours since arriving, and they faced a dilemma. Beckworth's interest in the mission might be nothing more than pure curiosity. He would want to be involved in developing a strategy for finding MacDuff, but he was fine waiting with her at Waverly while they prepared for the hunting party. Jamie and his crew would take the *Daphne* and track down the smuggler. They'd be back in time to join the hunt and regale them at dinner with their tales. Of course, Fitz would embellish everything and leave everyone in stitches.

The other possibility was that Beckworth would be unable to resist the challenge. He'd want to go with Jamie, promising to be back in time, and trusting her and Barrington to have everything prepared for their guests. That was not how she'd planned on spending her holiday.

There was a third option. But the odds were fifty to one against her—a long shot indeed.

The outer door burst open, and voices filled the bedroom. Libby was ordering someone to place a trunk in the room. Curious, Stella wandered in to see what her lady's maid was up to.

Libby dropped two large boxes on the bed and startled when she turned around. "Lady Stella. I thought you were still downstairs."

Two footmen nodded at them before leaving the room.

Libby tapped the two boxes. "I'll get these ready in time for dinner." She opened the trunk. "I'll need to air the rest of these out so they'll be ready for tomorrow."

"What's all this?" Stella opened one of the boxes to find an emerald-green evening gown. She lifted it out and admired the hand-stitched beadwork.

"Your royal-blue gown is in the trunk as well other the other items you left behind. Beckworth had them all stored in a trunk." She clucked her tongue. "He must have known you'd come back." She draped a couple dresses over the open lid, stepped next to Stella, and removed the top from the second box. "These are your underthings for this evening and your shoes."

"Do you know when Mary will be returning? And will Eleanor be coming with her?"

"They'll be here this afternoon. Mary will want a nap before dinner, and Eleanor will see if Mrs. Walker needs help." She hung the dress and emptied the boxes. "Oh, I forgot. Barrington asked to see you. He's in the east study."

Perfect timing, as she wanted to see him. Besides Libby, Barrington was the only other person, except for Eleanor, who would honestly tell her what's been happening since they'd been gone. With any luck, she might maneuver him into telling her what he knew of Hensley's mission.

Libby helped her change out of her pants and shirt and into one of the day dresses she brought with her.

Before Stella left to meet with Barrington, she nodded toward the clothes she'd traveled in. "Do me a favor. Can you have those freshened and then pack them in my duffel along with my boots? There was another set in the trunk. Could you add those and two sets of the undergarments I brought with me as well?"

Libby nodded, and though her brows had lifted at the request, she didn't say anything until Stella was walking out the door. There was humor in her tone. "You need to tell me about those red boots before the party."

Stella grinned as she strolled down the hall, nodding at the same two footmen who now followed Nigel, Beckworth's valet, with another trunk.

Barrington was behind Beckworth's desk in the secluded east-wing study. Beckworth used the larger west-wing office for manor business and meeting with his guests. This room was his personal study, and only a handful of people were allowed inside—Barrington being one.

The butler was reading documents and making notes on a separate page, most likely identifying major points for Beckworth so he wouldn't have to read the entire document if he didn't want to. There was a long-standing trust between the two that Stella had only glimpsed. She'd eventually pull away the layers of what she expected was a complex story.

"You wanted to see me?" She leaned against the doorframe, her arms crossed in front of her chest, a grin on her face.

He glanced up and, with a straight face, motioned for her to take a seat. "Close the door if you don't mind."

She strolled in, taking time to read the titles in the bookcases before plopping into one of two chairs in front of the desk. There was a paisley-print sofa against one wall and another straight-backed chair, which gave the room an air of openness, but anything more and it would make the room appear as small as it truly was in comparison to the west study.

She leaned back and gave Barrington her undivided attention even though he was still making notes. The silence grew, and instead of the ticking of a clock one might expect, there was only the scratching of quill on paper.

"Beckworth thought you might like to have your own office while you're here. And though he might make use of this room at times, he thought this one might fit your needs."

She was stunned. "What do I need an office for?"

When Barrington lifted his head, he held a tight grin, but his gaze was full of merriment. "Traditionally, the lady of the manor would have her own desk and stationary to carry out her duties. Some keep an office next to their bedroom, some use a salon, and others have a desk in the library. He felt you would prefer something more private."

"Why?"

His lips twitched. "I've supplied you with two stacks of paper." He nodded toward the two piles to his left that she hadn't paid any attention. "It was apparent from the note you left Beckworth when you returned home that you could use some practice with the quill."

She snickered but said nothing. He ignored her.

"While several of the servants in the manor know about time travel, most don't. And it would be unseemly that someone of your station doesn't know how to write. There are several invitations that need to be sent for the hunting party, and while Beckworth will attend to most of them, he thought it best for you to send a couple."

She held back a snort. "And who would I be sending invitations to? Eleanor and Bart?" Bart was another friend of Beckworth's who lived several miles away. He was a surgeon who once practiced in London before he left it all behind for a cabin in the woods. Even though it had been years since he'd lived in London, he still held clout at the College of Surgeons. He'd also been instrumental in healing AJ, Finn, Beckworth, and others during their troubles with the stones.

"I believe he was thinking more of Dame Ellingsworth and Lord and Lady Osborne."

She eyed the two stacks. Writing with quill and ink wasn't as easy as it looked, and she'd left splotches of ink all over her first attempts. Of course, writing a goodbye letter to Beckworth hadn't helped since her eyes kept blurring as she wrote. She'd finally written a clean version, though a couple ink spots had still dotted the page.

There was a lot of paper in those two piles, and she was a bit annoyed that Barrington thought she'd need an entire ream of paper to write a couple of invitations.

"Do you think you brought enough paper for me to practice in the solitude of my office?" Beckworth wasn't wrong that she'd prefer to perform this task behind closed doors. Sebastian had helped her with the single letter she'd finally left for Beckworth.

He finished his last note and set the quill aside, closing the inkpot. "The first stack is for practicing. I understand Fitz has started a pool on how many pages will be required before you can complete a clean invitation."

Try as she might, she couldn't hold back the snort. "Good to see everyone finds my lack of skills entertaining. I'd like to get in on the bet." It had to be difficult for Barrington to remain impassive because there was no doubt he found this more than humorous. "So what's the second stack for?"

He stared at her as if she were daft. "For your swans, of course."

She blinked away the stabbing pain in the back of her eyes that threatened waterworks was close at hand. "Of course," she managed to spurt out. She twisted her hands together, realized what she was doing, then pressed the palm of her hands on her dress, slowly pressing out non-existent wrinkles. She caught Barrington's grin as she lifted her gaze seconds before it disappeared.

"The second reason I needed to speak with you was to go over the current guest list for the hunting weekend." When she simply stared, unsure how to respond, he continued, "It's a common duty for the lady of the manor to care for the guest list, the meal menus, the entertainment between hunts, and so forth." He grinned as the blood left her face. "You're fortunate that Mary happens to be here early."

Her eyes narrowed. "You're having fun with this."

He chuckled. "A bit."

They spent thirty minutes going over the list while Barrington explained who everyone was, providing titles and why they were important to Beckworth. She'd assumed Beckworth had met most of them while working for the duke, and she was mostly correct. The interesting part was that most of them despised the duke yet seemed to hold a fondness for Beckworth. The man was a charmer.

Once she was comfortable with the list, he gave her tips on how to work the quill and gave her the seat behind the desk.

Before he left, he gave a last glance back.

"What?"

"Beckworth is going to need time to acclimate."

"I know."

He studied her for a long moment, his thumb playing at the silver ring on his finger she hadn't noticed him wearing the last time she'd been at Waverly. She'd have to ask Beckworth about it. When he seemed satisfied with whatever he saw, he gave her a brief nod and closed the door behind him.

She stood and stretched, glancing around the room. She'd only spent a few days at Waverly before leaving for Baywood, but she felt like she knew the manor. Though the only room she knew intimately was Beckworth's bedroom.

She smiled.

She'd already spoken with Libby about the evening she'd planned for their first night back. Candles, wine, and a roaring fire that would burn to embers before they finished making love. Her eyes closed as the image played through her mind. Then they snapped open.

After tomorrow, once her plan was underway, there would be no telling the next time they'd make love. She snorted. Sometimes, her conniving ways were worth the risk.

She turned to the desk and selected a page from each stack. They were the same, and she laid one on the desk and returned the other to what would be her swan stack.

When she'd returned to Baywood, brokenhearted at leaving Beckworth, she'd stopped making the swans. After he miraculously traveled to the future to find her and decided to stay, she picked up the habit again. She didn't make them as often as she used to, but she appreciated having the paper available.

Unable to think of any other reason to procrastinate, she cleared a spot on the desk, grabbed several pages and set them to her left. She opened the inkpot and set the blotting sand behind it. Barrington said the quill was a goose feather and it felt familiar in her hand. The first time she'd attempted to write she'd used too much pressure and stopped writing before the quill ran out of ink, creating splotches.

She rolled up her sleeves and ran the quill over the paper without ink, getting a feel for the rhythm and flow. Then she dipped the quill in the inkpot, gently tapped the side to expel excess ink and wrote her first words.

The quick brown fox jumped over the lazy dog.

She laughed out loud, surprised at the unexpected memory. When she was a little girl, her mother borrowed a library book and a friend's typewriter to learn how to type. She kept it in the washroom, covered with an old towel when she wasn't practicing. The only time her mom would practice was when her father was at work. The quick brown fox passage was the standard as it used all twenty-six letters of the alphabet.

She frowned and wiped an eye. One day, her father had come home early from work. He'd injured his hand in an accident. Mother hadn't expected him, and he'd walked in while she was hunched over the typewriter, completely immersed in her typing.

Father saw Stella in the kitchen and made her go to Mrs. Brewster's to see if they had any eggs. She didn't understand at the time because they had their own chickens and plenty of eggs, but after one glance at her mother's face, she raced out of the house.

When she came home, Mother was in the kitchen making dinner and refused to look at her. Father was in the living room watching TV and drinking a beer. There was no sign of the typewriter, and Stella had never seen it again.

She wadded up the paper, forcing the memory away, and tossed it across the room. This wasn't difficult. It doesn't have to be perfect the first time out. She placed a new sheet in front of her, dipped the quill, and, using a light touch, began again.

This is the journal of Stella, the Swan, Caldway.

She grinned. That was better. She lost herself in the writing, not realizing she was journaling. It was scattered—her kidnapping, meeting Beckworth, and then Sebastian, her first trip across the Channel to France, and the ensuing storm. Tears welled when she recounted the hunt for the chronicles and Beckworth trading himself for her, then her riding to the East End in London, calling upon Beckworth's friends to help find him. And they did.

Once she completed recording her time in the past, she turned to memories of Baywood. She'd barely started when the door burst open, making her jump. Fortunately, the quill had run dry, or her new dress would have been covered in ink spots.

"I didn't mean to startle you. Barrington said you'd be here." Beckworth leaned against the doorframe. He was dressed in his viscount attire—tan breeches, a dark blue waistcoat and cravat, and a white shirt. His hair had been pulled back, and his cheeks were red.

"How's the foal?" she asked.

"He's the spitting image of his father. Would you like to see him?"

"Yes, but I think it needs to wait until tomorrow." She laid down the quill and stretched. The stack of written pages had grown. "I didn't realize how long I've been here. Have you been with the foal all this time?"

"No. I went with Fitz to retrieve Mary and Eleanor. Mary is resting upstairs. Eleanor wants to see you, but she wanted to check in with Mrs. Walker first." He picked up the half-filled page and nodded. "I think you've mastered the quill."

He laid the paper down and pulled her up from the chair. His kiss was passionate and lasted longer than she expected since the study door was open. She tugged him closer.

When he finally pulled back, she quirked a smile. "I thought Eleanor was looking for me."

He grinned. "She is. And that wasn't a prelude for something more. I'm afraid we'll have to continue this after dinner. But first, I want to take you on a tour of Waverly. You can work on the invitations tomorrow." He took her hand and led her to the door.

"I've seen Waverly."

His gaze filled with mischief. "Not all of it. Eleanor can catch up."

6

———

Exhaustion plagued Stella with each step she climbed. It seemed someone added more steps to reach the second floor. Would this day ever end?

When she finally made it to the bedroom, she sighed with relief to see Libby laying out her nightgown and robe. She had left her moss-colored robe behind, but the lavender-colored one waiting for her was just as silky. Her thoughts immediately imagined Beckworth taking it off her inch-by-inch.

"Do you want me to help you with your hair?" Libby asked as she lit another lamp.

"The dress first, then just get the hairpins out. I could drop dead asleep standing here."

"It was a busy first day." Libby laughed as she loosened the ties. "Did Beckworth really drag you through all the secret passages?"

"I couldn't believe there were that many. He said several aren't used very often, but they look cleaner than I expected."

"They aren't, but Barrington has someone clean them every week."

"I suppose I should thank him. I knew about the one that

ends at that old cabin. We used that to get in when Gemini had overtaken Waverly, but I didn't realize there would be a dozen more."

"The maids use a couple of them, but most aren't necessary."

"I can't imagine living in a time where they were needed because of what religion you followed."

"Well, they came in handy when Dugan and Reginald were here." Libby took the dress as soon as Stella stepped out of it and laid it on a chair.

Stella put on the nightgown and sat at the dressing table. Libby removed the hairpins but put a hand on Stella's shoulder to prevent her from standing while she reached for the brush. Stella inwardly sighed, preferring to brush her own hair, but Libby seemed to enjoy the task. She grinned as Libby caught her up with the current gossip. Something told her this would be a common theme while at the manor. And why not? Libby could keep her updated without Stella having to get involved with the daily dramas.

Libby laid down the brush and picked up the dress Stella had been wearing. "I'll take care of the dress in the morning, and I've moved your special evening to tomorrow night."

"Perfect. I'd hate to waste all the candles. We'll be sleeping in, but if the footman can bring up coffee at whatever time Beckworth normally wakes up, that would be great. I'm afraid I wasn't here long enough to figure that out."

She winked at her. "Not a problem. Have a good evening."

"You too."

Libby had barely left the room before Beckworth sauntered in, looking almost as haggard as she felt. When his valet followed him in, she shooed him away. She had two choices. Either ask about the mission or leave it for tomorrow and enjoy their first night back at Waverly without an argument.

He turned once she'd removed his jacket and pulled her to him. She wrapped her arms around his waist and laid her cheek on his chest. Although she'd spent a couple of hours with him during the tour, managing to sneak in several long kisses, she missed him. In Baywood, they spent most of their days together. Not every day, but most. She'd deal with how they'd spend their days on holiday tomorrow.

He nestled his nose in her hair and breathed deeply. "I love the smell of you."

She snorted. "It's a good thing I washed it before we left this morning. God, I can't believe I just said that. Like it's a normal day to wake in the twenty-first century and go to sleep in the nineteenth."

"Fortunately, it's not an everyday occurrence." He pulled back to give her a tender kiss. "Help me with my boots."

She wasted no time getting him naked, and she tossed her robe before whipping the nightgown over her head. They were soon nestled within the sheets, holding each other.

"I think I miss our bed at home already." She could already feel a lump but couldn't keep her eyes open to care.

"I can't argue with that, but I doubt we'll notice. It's been a long day for both of us." He kissed her forehead. "I'm so glad we're here together."

That was the last thing she heard, and it made her smile.

Stella turned a slow circle in front of the standing mirror, pleased with the robin-egg-blue day dress Beckworth had made in Baywood. He never mentioned the name of the tailor, nor did she go to any fittings, yet it was a perfect fit. He'd already commissioned more day and evening dresses since their visit would be longer than they'd originally planned.

When she'd asked for a riding habit, he'd laughed so hard she thought he'd pass out from loss of oxygen. She managed to hold a straight face, but it had been difficult.

Her history with horses wasn't the best, but she'd gone from gripping the saddle until her fingers ached to riding a horse on her own. She wasn't as comfortable as she should be, and the horse never moved faster than a trot, but she hadn't completely given up on improving her skills. At dinner the evening before, she'd met everyone's laughter with her own when Hensley mentioned he'd brought Smudge from London and was now in Waverly's stables.

Smudge was an ugly, mottled-colored gelding she'd ridden from London to Ipswich and back on that fateful mission when Beckworth had traded himself to Gemini in exchange for Stella. To everyone's dismay at the time, she'd also ridden the horse alone through London's East End to meet with Beckworth's crew to plan his rescue.

Though she hadn't given the horse much praise at dinner, she'd been touched that Hensley had brought him to Waverly. And it was that horse that would be her excuse to visit the stables.

After a slow morning of sweet lovemaking and coffee in bed, Beckworth had gone for a morning ride with Thomas and Fitz. Jamie had stayed behind to discuss other business with Hensley, but she'd heard from Eleanor that Jamie had just left the manor to check on the new foal.

This was her moment.

She passed through the kitchen on her way to the stables, stopping to greet the staff and cook, who handed her a mug that was typically used for ale but was filled with coffee. God bless that woman. When she stepped outside, she pulled her cloak tighter against the morning chill and tilted her head to the hazy sun. It provided little warmth, but it uplifted her spirits just the same.

A young stable boy smiled when she approached. "You here to see the foal?"

"I actually came to see Smudge, but I would love to see the new baby. And what's your name? I don't think we've ever been introduced."

The lad's cheeks turned a bright red. "It's Jax. Baby is a funny name for a horse."

"I suppose I should have said baby horse."

"Is that mottled gelding that arrived a few days ago your horse?" He led her into the stables. "He's not very handsome."

She laughed. "I agree he's not pretty, but he's always been good to me."

"That's more important than looks."

"You're a wise young man."

It was hard to see in the dark stable, but she would bet money his cheeks burned with another blush.

He stopped at Smudge's stall. The horse's head was down and seemed to be asleep.

"Hello, Smudge." Stella pulled out a carrot she'd pilfered from a bin in the kitchen. Smudge turned his head toward her and gave a light chuff before lumbering over. He nodded a couple of times, his lips extending in search of the treat.

She laughed with delight as she fed him the carrot, then scratched his cheek. "Don't worry. I'll get you out for a ride. You're probably being horribly ignored."

Jax leaned over and whispered, "We don't talk about it, but one of us usually takes him for a ride every other day. He might be uglier than a one-eyed, three-legged ewe, but you're right that he has a good heart."

She squeezed the boy's shoulder. "Thank you for taking

such good care of him." She gave the horse a last scratch and looked around the barn. "Now, where's that foal?"

Her first concern was that she'd dawdled too long and missed Jamie. How long did one spend with a foal? But her concerns were dashed when she found not only Jamie but Hensley with the foal.

She hadn't expected Hensley. Her strategy might not work with him there. It wouldn't be the first time she'd had to adapt to a situation. Chester's words came back to her. He was a crew leader in London and a long-time friend to Beckworth and Barrington, all three having worked in the same gang when they were lads. Chester had once told her the reason he included her in his missions was her ability to adapt.

She had every intention of putting that to work.

The men were inside a larger stall that allowed mama and baby to move around. The mare was dark brown with a tiny white blaze and white socks that ran up to her knees. The foal, who was currently hiding behind its mom, appeared to be jet black, but she couldn't see its head.

"Is the baby alright?" she asked.

Hensley and Jamie both turned. While Hensley's eyes widened for just an instant, Jamie gave her a smile that made her think he'd been expecting her. She weighed whether that was a good thing as she returned a grin.

"I came down to see Smudge, but I've never seen a baby horse up close." She leaned over the stable door and gulped her coffee. "A boy or girl. Fitz never said."

Jamie opened the door. "Come in and see for yourself."

Stella set the mug down on a nearby barrel and tiptoed in, not wanting to scare the mare, who seemed calm with the men.

"He's a fine-looking colt." Hensley walked toward the mom, forcing her to move aside, which gave Stella a clear look at the young horse.

He was jet black from tail to nose with one exception—a long white star on his forehead. She gave a low whistle, and the mare's ears perked, then she chuffed. The foal took a step toward her but wasn't brave enough to leave his mama's side.

"He likes you." Jamie picked up a bucket of grain and hung it on a hook. The mare instantly forgot them as she began to eat. Then he squatted and waited. The young foal took a few tentative steps toward Jamie until he was close enough for Jamie to touch, but he didn't. "It's good to have them feel comfortable with you when they're young. I find it easier to train them once they're older."

"I wouldn't think you'd have time for horses as a ship's captain." Stella stayed a few steps behind Jamie, not wanting to scare the foal.

"Not as much anymore, to be sure, but it was a full-time job when I was young."

"Beckworth and I are of the same opinion as Jamie." Hensley positioned himself near the mare's head and stroked her neck. "Though Beckworth's a bit more hands-on than I am. There's no question he made an excellent breeding decision with this boy. He'll make a fine stallion."

"Is the sire here?" she asked.

"Beckworth took him out this morning." Jamie motioned her closer.

"Aah. I know the horse." Stella picked up her skirts and squatted so she was eye level with the tiny creature that stumbled on his long legs. He slowly approached, and she waited, allowing him to take a gentle sniff before he made a funny leap and raced back to his mama's side. She laughed, and Jamie helped her up. "This is one horse I wouldn't mind being around."

"If memory serves, you didn't seem to have any issue with a

horse when you road to East End." Hensley sounded amused, though he hadn't been when he'd first heard about it.

"They seem to be growing on me. Tell me, Hensley, is this mission of yours just a reconnaissance mission?"

The men glanced at each other before Hensley answered. "It is. Why do you ask?"

"The timing seems interesting. That something so important would come up the same time Beckworth was scheduled to travel back to Waverly."

"A truly amazing coincidence." Hensley patted the mare, then strode through the stable door, turning as he relatched it. He gave her one of his unreadable expressions though his lips twitched. "I have some time this afternoon if you're interested in a game of chess."

"I'll meet you in the library." She watched him stroll down the aisle, stopping to glance into stalls, taking a moment to admire a horse. Once he was far enough away, she turned to Jamie. "Have you already asked him to go with you?"

"He just returned home after several months. There's much to catch up on before the hunting party."

"From what he told me, he'd left detailed instructions with Barrington, his property manager, and Mrs. Walker before leaving for Baywood. He spoke with all of them for an hour last night and, being a rather intelligent man, is probably all caught up. So, let's cut to the chase, shall we?"

Jamie gave a last look at the foal then motioned Stella out of the stall. She picked up her coffee, and though it had grown cold, still tasted good. He seemed to be collecting his thoughts, so she remained silent as they walked back to the manor. But instead of leading her inside, he took her for a stroll through the garden.

A thin haze still covered the sun, and a light film of clouds had moved in. The air was damp, like any Oregon winter day, and it felt good on her skin as they walked among the long-dead flowers. She took note of the few winter flowers that poked through the weathered garden remains.

"Has Beckworth mentioned the mission?" Jamie asked.

"He doesn't have to."

Jamie chuckled. "The two of you seem to know each other quite well. You're alike in many ways."

"Nosy and interfering?"

Jamie's laugh echoed through the garden and could probably be heard in the manor. "I was going to say curious and resolute."

She grinned. "Finn said you were becoming a fine diplomat."

"One has to be as a ship's captain. It's not easy keeping dozens of men happy on a sea voyage."

"I never considered that. I just assumed you'd keep them busy with tasks."

"I should add wise to your list of attributes."

"Wise enough to know when you're skirting the issue."

He huffed out a breath. "I can't speak for Hensley, and he hasn't said much about it. When he first asked me to meet him at Waverly and mentioned his problem, he did let something slip. I suppose more of an off-handed comment that it was too bad Beckworth wasn't part of his network anymore. There's no question this job suits his talents. And Beckworth confirmed last night that, to his knowledge, had never seen MacDuff. But I won't lie. Hensley's timing for bringing us together at Waverly under the guise of a mere postponement of the hunting party hasn't fooled any of us."

She let silence walk with them before switching the topic. "I'm still learning about this time period, but some things aren't that different in mine. Men tend to ignore women, except for those they want to bed."

Jamie barked a laugh. "We need to spend more time together. You are a bold one."

She grinned. "I would have thought AJ had prepared you for the modern woman."

"I think you raise the stakes a bit higher."

"You're not wrong there."

They had reached the back of the manor. He stopped at the door to the solarium and turned to her. "Most of our time will be spent at sea. I hear you don't do well on ships."

"It was better on my second voyage, but I brought medicine for it this time."

His brow lifted. "For a weekend hunting party."

She gave him a sly smile. "I believe in being prepared. Now, I must go. It seems the lady of the manor's work is more trying than I could imagine. Mrs. Walker has questions about the hunting party, Barrington tells me Mary has arranged for afternoon tea with Eleanor, assuming we can stop her from following the housemaids around, and now I have to fit in a game or two of chess with Hensley. Thank you for the walk through the garden." She leaned in and gave him a kiss on the cheek that he clearly hadn't expected.

She grinned. It wasn't the most subtle seed she'd ever planted, but Jamie was a quick study. It was the best she could do for now.

7

Mary, Hensley's wife and expert party planner, leaned back while the footman placed platters of sandwiches and tiny cakes on the table and refilled teacups. She repositioned her napkin and glanced around the solarium. "I never paid much attention to this particular room. It seems to have a feminine touch I wouldn't expect from Teddy."

Stella surveyed the room as if seeing it for the first time and considered the rest of the manor. "The decor might be left over from the previous viscountess. From what Beckworth tells me, he's been slowly replacing items with pieces more suited to his own taste." She chuckled. "I'm not sure what in this place actually reflects Beckworth."

Eleanor chortled. "He keeps it that way on purpose and has used that excuse for too long. Though, to be fair, he hasn't spent much time at Waverly these last couple of years." She took a sip of tea and took two sandwiches from the platter. "But if I had to pick one room, I'd say the library. It's where he spends most of his time when he doesn't have guests."

Stella wanted to see that side of him. She'd learned his behavior patterns when they were in Baywood. He preferred tea in the evening after his brandy. On most days, he was an early riser, but on rainy mornings, he brought a coffee urn and two mugs to the bedroom and snuggled next to her. Sometimes, they wouldn't leave the bedroom until mid-afternoon after long discussions and a round of lovemaking. And surprisingly, or perhaps not that much, he was learning computer skills faster than she would have expected. He finally admitted that Edith and Louise, the two older sisters who'd taken him in during his first unhappy trip to the future, back when he was considered the enemy, had trained him how to search the internet. With that knowledge and his consulting work at Ethan's security business, he was almost as savvy as her with software apps.

With all that, it was his habits here in the manor that she wanted—no, *needed* to know. Did he prefer to sit by the fire in the library or his study? Did he always go for a ride first thing in the morning? What business did he really do running an estate?

"Stella, dear, did you hear Mary?" Eleanor asked.

"Hmm. Oh. Sorry. Wow, my mind had definitely left the building." She smiled at their expressions and made a mental note to tone down the twenty-first-century language. "I was just trying to picture Beckworth spending a leisurely day at Waverly."

Mary smiled with a twinkle in her eye. "I can't tell you how thrilled I am that Teddy found you. But I hate that you're living in a different time." She held her hand in front of her mouth. "I can't believe I just said that." They laughed, then she continued, "I don't suppose there's any word of posting banns."

Stella had just taken a sip of tea and choked but managed to swallow it before spitting it across the table.

Eleanor didn't bother with etiquette. "I'm sure Beckworth is waiting for the right moment. He won't do anything until he feels secure enough to support you."

The statement made Stella pause. She hadn't considered

that would be an issue. He had his own money but not a job. Not something that gave him purpose. It was one of the reasons she'd left this century and him behind. She pushed the concern aside. He just needed time, and she wasn't in a hurry to get married. Not yet. There was more to learn about each other. Loving someone and marriage didn't always go hand in hand.

She gave Mary and Eleanor the best response she could. "We met under very traumatic circumstances, and the last few months have been focused on getting him reacquainted with my time period. We're finally at the stage where we can spend time getting to know each other better."

"In this day and age," Mary countered, "we get to know each other during the first couple years of marriage. But I understand it could be confusing trying to blend two different time periods. But AJ and Finn made it work, and their adventure wasn't any less fraught with danger."

Stella licked cream frosting off what she would call a little-bitty cupcake. "You're right. That's something to consider. But don't worry. When it's time to run the banns, you'll be the first to know."

She didn't think it would be anytime soon. She'd seen the light in Beckworth's gaze when Hensley mentioned that the *Daphne* would be tracking down the smuggler. Their pending argument was right around the corner.

Beckworth approached the bedroom but stopped before entering. He'd been avoiding discussing the mission with Stella. It would be easy to blame the long days when they had no opportunity to discuss private matters. He snorted. On their first night home, neither could stay awake long enough to do anything but hold each other.

He reached for the doorknob then stopped. Why hadn't Stella asked? He took a step back. She seemed fine at dinner. Even gave him a kiss on the cheek before he followed the men into the study. Had she been waiting for him to come to bed to ask him? If she were any other woman, he'd assume she wouldn't understand how important Hensley's mission was. Wouldn't understand how it would intrigue him.

Stella wasn't any other woman. So, what was she up to? He thought back to the moment they found the men in his study. He hadn't witnessed any suspicious behavior. Had he missed something?

His thoughts were interrupted when a housemaid walked by, a dress hanging over her arm.

"Good evening, sir. Do you need anything?"

He gave the young girl a smile. "No. I'm fine, Abigail. Have a good night."

She nodded and hurried on.

Good god. He was scared to walk into his own bedroom. The last thing he needed was another person seeing him standing outside his room. He could already hear them gossiping in the kitchen. Without another thought, he pushed open the door.

The room was ablaze with dozens of candles. Shadows fluttered among the light cast by the flames dancing in the hearth. All his previous concerns disappeared as he searched for Stella. Like a wood nymph rising from the floor, she propped herself up on her elbow. The fire glowed around her, and though it cast her in shadows, there was no doubt she was naked. Waiting for him.

He wanted to rip his clothes off, but he tempered his burning desire to race to her. His movements slowed as he pulled off his jacket. After the boots, the waistcoat and cravat went next. He stepped closer until the contours of her body were visible, beckoning him forward. Memories of the first time they'd made love rushed back. How could he want her even more now than he had then? He untied his shirt and pulled it over his head, dropping it at his feet.

He heard her soft intake of breath, and he smiled. She pushed her hair back, exposing her long neck. He wanted to run his lips over the sensitive skin. He pushed his pants down and stepped out of them. Her eyes followed his movements, and she did the unthinkable. She licked her lips—and he came undone. Nothing else mattered but this woman.

She'd upended his world until she'd chipped away the wall he'd built around his heart and claimed it for her own.

How had he existed before her?

He knelt in front of her and pulled her up to him, running a hand over her cheek then down the length of her neck. She leaned her head back, giving him access to kiss the soft hollow at the base of her neck. He sighed at how well reality matched the vision.

She ran her fingertips up his arms and over his shoulders until she caressed the back of his neck.

He pushed her down to the blankets, his mouth moving to a breast. His moans of pleasure increased when she ran her hand through his hair, urging him on. He took his time until she cried out in frustration, and he couldn't help smiling with satisfaction. It was her sign that she couldn't take another moment before he took her, and if he didn't, she'd take matters into her own hands. And there were many times when he let her. But not this night. Tonight was his.

When they joined, her passion ignited as she wrapped her legs around him. He kissed her, her body thrumming to match his own. Then, without warning, their legs tangled, and with a swift push, she rolled him until she was on top.

She stretched back, her hands on the floor as she rocked, and his breath caught. His auburn beauty. His wildest desire. He stroked her breasts until she shuddered with release. Then he rolled her onto her back and thrust until she screamed for more. And when his own pleasure peaked, she opened her eyes, sensing it.

He knew that look. He belonged to her, and she'd never let him go.

They napped for a short period before her fingers ran down his chest, then moved up until she pinched his chin. "Did you want wine?"

Beckworth lifted his head. "There's wine?"

Her throaty chuckle stirred him. "Of course." She crawled toward the sofa, where a tray sat on the floor. What a marvelous view of her backside. She returned with an opened bottle and two glasses. He sat up and took the proffered glass.

He sniffed it, tasted it, and grinned. "Barrington must have retrieved this from the cellar."

"Libby might have had a hand in it."

He pulled over a blanket and spread it across their laps. "You thought of everything."

She grinned. "That also might have been Libby."

"I'm deciding whether it had been a mistake to have Libby assigned to you or a moment of sheer genius."

"We're a perfect match—either way you look at it."

"Did you have tea with Mary and Eleanor?"

She laughed. "Eleanor really hates that stuff."

He grimaced. "She doesn't seem to live in either world—not the aristocrats or the serving class. She wasn't happy as a house-maid. I gave her a higher position to take some of the load off, but that wasn't the problem."

"She wasn't used to service."

He sipped the wine and shifted to lean against a chair, then waited for Stella to move beside him. "None of her family was. You know, she's not too different than you."

"Wanting her independence?"

He nodded. "I found a small cabin with a bit of property just down the road. Turned out she already had her eye on a place. She said it was both close and just far enough away." He shook his head.

"You bought the property?"

"She insisted on a loan."

Stella turned and rubbed his arm. Her touch sent a shot of warmth up his spine. "She still owes you money?"

"You know how stubborn she is." He pushed a hand through his hair as he considered his friend. "But no, not anymore."

She leaned back, staring into the fire. "Good."

He watched her, gauging what her reaction would be. "It was paid off with a portion of the coins from Gemini's trunk." Gemini had kept a small trunk filled with all types of coins. After her death, Stella had asked Barrington to hide it from the magistrate, preferring Beckworth find a good use of them.

"How had she been paying you back?" Stella liked Eleanor from the first time they'd met. They'd been on the run, but when they showed up on Eleanor's doorstep, Stella had rolled up her sleeves and helped with dinner.

"She's one of the best seamstresses this side of London. You know how well she sews. She makes enough to only work when she needs to."

Stella considered his answer. "I suppose knowing it was Gemini's coins, she didn't argue."

He put an arm around her, and she leaned her head on his shoulder, the wineglass resting against her thigh. "Her only concern was whether there would be enough coins to help others."

She stared up at him, her green eyes lit with amusement. "But you didn't keep any of the coins."

"No. I used a small amount toward repairs to the manor, but

only because you requested it. The staff received extremely nice bonuses, and I gave the rest to Barrington. He traveled to London after I left for Baywood and gave it to Chester to share with the crews."

She stabbed his chest with her finger. "I thought you'd give some of it to a charity like an orphanage or something."

He grinned. "The Viscount of Waverly already donates money to several needy organizations both in Corsham and London. Philanthropy is alive in the aristocracy."

"You're a good man, Teddy." She took his glass and set both out of the way before grabbing the blanket and crawling toward the hearth.

He crawled after her then grabbed her around the waist and rolled her to the floor. She giggled as he hugged her close. She'd be safe with Barrington and Hensley to watch over her. He was the luckiest man in the world. His only concern was in keeping her safe. They'd still have plenty of time together before the hunting party.

He ran his fingers over a lock of her hair and pushed it behind her ear. Then he let his hand wander down to her bare hip. "Do you have any idea what I'm going to do to you tonight?"

"You don't scare me, Lord Beckworth." Her hand touched his thigh, and an involuntary shiver coursed through him.

His chuckle was deep as he bent to lick a nipple. He took his time, enjoying and relishing every part of her. A body he already knew so well. It would be days before he'd see her again, and he wanted this night to be something she kept close until he returned.

For a brief moment, he wanted to ask her to come with him. What a fool. She needed to stay where she would be safe. Barrington would keep her occupied, teaching her the role of lady of the manor.

But her scent drove him mad, and when Stella pulled him to

her, there was nothing but her. Why was he planning on leaving her? The missions weren't his concern anymore. Jamie and the crew of the *Daphne* were enough for surveillance.

"I love you, Stella."

"I'm all yours, Teddy."

He kissed her, then turned her over, running his hand up her back. "Then prepare yourself, Lady Caldway. Lord Beckworth is far from finished with you this evening."

Her throaty chuckle was followed by moans of pleasure that lasted through the night.

8

Beckworth whistled as he strode through the manor. He'd just come from the stables, pleased with how well the foal and mare were doing. It was good to be home. He took a deep breath, enjoying the herbal scent that flowed through the house. Something Mrs. Walker insisted on, and his guests never complained, so he let her be.

Over the last few years, most of his time at Waverly had been spent under the yoke of his bastard father. Then he got caught up in the mystery of the Mórdha stones that took his time and almost his life. Once that business was done, Hensley lured him into his network of spies working on behalf of the Crown, primarily in London.

He rubbed his hands together against the chill in the air. They hadn't been back a day, and Hensley laid a mission at his door. He hadn't considered Beckworth for the task, or so he said. It was a mission for Jamie, which only made sense. To catch a smuggler, one would need a ship, and the *Daphne Marie* was a sleek schooner with a seasoned and well-captained crew. A crew that was also masterful in the art of subterfuge and misdirection.

The thought of going with Jamie had lit a spark in him he hadn't felt for some time. And with that thought, he made a quick turn into a rarely used drawing room, shutting the door behind him. He found a chair in the far corner where he would be almost invisible if someone were to enter.

He rubbed his face then pushed his hands over his head, pulling strands from his queue. What had he been thinking?

He wasn't a single man anymore. It had been easy enough to remember that while living in Stella's house, surrounded by her things and the new life they were building. He'd even added a few touches of his own in the house and garden. It was a good life but held little in the way of challenge.

He'd been working as a consultant in Ethan's security business, and he kept busy learning about technology, but there wasn't any mystery in it for him. The thrill of pursuit. Stella had confided a few weeks after he'd traveled to the future that she was concerned he wouldn't find fulfillment. It had been one of his concerns as well.

On the other hand, his time period would be equally difficult for her over time. If she were a more submissive or demure woman, she could cope with the behavior expected of a woman. And if she had been that woman when he met her, he wouldn't have given her a second thought other than to help because she was AJ's friend.

But he loved Stella and chose her time period.

He never thought he'd find such deep and sustaining love. Hadn't believed it truly existed. In this time—his time— marriages were nothing more than business arrangements or ones of convenience. He'd bedded his share of women, flirted, courted in a fashion, but love? The first time he'd caught a glimpse of it had been with AJ and Finn, but he'd assumed that to be a special case.

Then he came face to face with the ginger-haired beauty

with a fiery will to match his own. Someone he could see living the rest of his life with. Perhaps building a family with.

Now, he'd been lured into one of Hensley's missions. He didn't have to join the team. It would be as simple as wishing them well then spending two glorious weeks with Stella, preparing for his guests. Maybe take her for a ride or two.

He grinned. She'd asked for a riding habit. The woman surprised him at every turn. She couldn't be happy with the thought of him leaving, yet she must know he'd go. It was only surveillance. A few days roaming the ports along the English coast. Perhaps a quick run down the southern coast of Ireland. They'd be back before the guests arrived, and then he'd convince her to stay a few more days. By the time they returned to Baywood, only a couple of days would have passed.

He stared at the horrific portrait on the wall across from him. The painting was a leftover from the previous viscount. He'd spent years trading out the art and furniture left behind in favor of new purchases, but it was a slow process. It was time to make some changes in this room. A perfect job for Stella.

He ran his hand over his hair one more time, poking loose strands back into place, then stood, ready to face Stella with his decision.

Down one hallway and then another, he peeked into rooms but couldn't find anyone who could tell him where Stella might be. He was debating whether to visit the kitchen or run up to the second floor when Douglas, one of his footmen and part-time spy, entered the foyer, heading for the sitting room.

"Where is everyone?" Beckworth asked.

"Barrington is in your east study, Mrs. Walker is downstairs doing inventory, and Lady Stella is upstairs in your room. Oh, and Captain Jamie wants to leave in an hour to catch the tide."

"Thank you, Douglas. I'll need two footmen to gather my trunk. Give me a half hour to finish packing."

He stopped by his office to give Barrington last-minute directions. He was still wondering over his butler's strange smile when he opened the door to his bedroom.

"There you are."

Stella turned and smiled. "Have you been looking for me?"

"Only for the last half hour. I never realized how large the manor is when needing to find someone. I barely found Douglas to tell me where everyone was."

"Mrs. Walker has everyone doing inventory. I've given several dinner parties, and I'm used to just running into town to grab last-minute items. Not something you can do here. Mary and Eleanor took a stroll in the garden, and I assumed Hensley and Jamie were in the stables with you.

He laughed. "Planning for a long weekend party can take a toll on the staff. By the way, Barrington showed me the invitations. They're perfect. It seems you've mastered the quill."

She shook her hands in what he assumed was a reflexive action. "Not without wasting dozens of sheets of paper and giving me carpal tunnel."

He strode toward the dressing room, surprised Stella hadn't said anything about the open trunk. When he glanced down to see what his valet had packed, he stopped short.

Next to his clothes were the pants and long-sleeved shirt Stella had worn through the fog on their arrival, similar to those while on the run from Gemini. He reached in and looked under them. Another set, and then a day dress under that.

He shook his head. "No."

Stella didn't turn from whatever she was doing at the dressing table. "I'm sorry. What did you say?"

"I said no." Beckworth almost growled the sentiment.

"I must not have heard you correctly."

"You're not going with us."

Stella chuckled. "Says who?"

"Says me. We talked about this."

She spun around, hands on hips, and his jaw clenched. He was not going to listen to one of her lists. "Exactly when did we discuss it? After Hensley mentioned the mission within the first hour after our jump here? Or maybe it was during the tour of the manor. Nope. Maybe after we crawled into bed that evening or during our breakfast coffee the next morning? No. Not then, either. The first indication of your decision was the open trunk the footmen left after you strolled out of the bedroom this morning."

She had given him a list, but it wasn't one he'd been prepared for. "You could have asked." As soon as it was out of his mouth, he knew it was a mistake. It had been his responsibility to discuss it with her, but he hadn't because of this very issue—her wanting to go with him. He hadn't wanted their first days back to be in an argument. Up until now, she'd been sweet and patient and, damn it, had been the perfect lady of the manor. And all the time, she knew what his intentions had been. He blurted out the only thing he could think of. "Besides, it's too dangerous."

"Says you."

"Yes." He all but roared. He had played this all wrong. She stood there, completely uncaring about his concerns, somehow thinking she'd won. How would Finn handle this? He took a deep breath in an attempt to dispel his temper, but it wasn't working. He managed somewhat of a defense. "I've been on countless missions. I have experience in these matters."

She simply shrugged. "Hensley gave me a role in the mission. I can be of use." Then she turned back to what she'd been doing.

He stepped to the side to get a better view. She was going through the first aid kit AJ had given her. She was serious about this. Well, so was he.

"We'll see about this." He stormed out of the room, not bothering to shut the door behind him.

What had the spymaster been thinking? Of all the preposterous notions.

He marched through the manor, sorry for making two housemaids and a footman back away as he passed by. It took several strides before he stopped and glanced back. He thought he'd scared them, but on reflection, had they been smiling? He didn't see anything funny about the situation.

He burst into his west-wing study where Hensley was writing a letter. He didn't seem surprised to see him.

"What's this about giving Stella a role in the mission?"

Hensley held back a grin, but it appeared to require every ounce of his unflappable countenance to do it. He dipped the quill and continued to write. "That wasn't quite what I said."

Beckworth calmed. "What exactly did you say?"

"I said a woman might provide alternatives to the mission, but she'd have to abide by Jamie's decision on who has a role."

"I should have expected her to shape the words to her benefit." He paced in front of the windows that looked out to the garden.

"Yes, you should have." Hensley set down the quill and sprinkled pounce over it.

"Well, I still say she can't go."

Hensley chortled. "But that's up to her and Jamie, isn't it?"

"Not if I say otherwise."

Hensley's brows lifted. "Did the two of you get married that I wasn't aware of?"

"No. It hasn't been the right time to consider it."

"Fair enough. But that leaves it with her to decide."

"But she's under my care while we're here."

"She might be under your protection, but not your decisions. You're not her husband, father, uncle, or brother. Therefore, all you can do is guide her. You know that."

Beckworth sat, then stood, and strode to his liquor cart where he poured a finger of whiskey that he swallowed whole. He lifted the bottle toward Hensley, who nodded, and he poured two fingers for him and replenished his own glass.

"This has become more difficult than I thought. Now Finn's words before we jumped make sense."

"And what were those?"

"He said traveling back to this time after living in the future has a way of changing one's perspective. That I might become overly protective or some nonsense."

"Finn has the experience in this area."

"Bloody hell, the woman gets seasick. Why would she want to travel onboard a ship to track down a smuggler? It would be simpler to wait here."

"Did you consider this might have something to do with you leaving her behind?"

He finished the whiskey. "And when did you become so wise?"

"After many years of marriage." Hensley folded the letter, then picked up the quill, dipping it in ink to scratch out a name. When he reached for the wax, he offered another suggestion.

"You can try bargaining with Jamie. He's having the carriage hitched up."

He shook his head, but it was worth a try.

After leaving Hensley, he strode to the stables, though the farther he walked, the less his heart was in it. Once Stella got an idea in her head it was almost impossible to change it. On occasion, he'd been able to adjust her notions to their mutual satisfaction with a well-laid-out countermove. He was hard-pressed to think of one for this situation. Her issues with seasickness had been his only play. Why the devil had she thought to bring medicine to counteract it?

The carriage was hitched and ready, but it didn't take long to find Jamie, who was with the foal. The colt was becoming comfortable with people, and he pranced around Jamie, still wobbly on his legs.

"If you've come about Stella, the decision has already been made." Jamie reached out a hand, and the foal sniffed it before running for the mare. The young captain had a way with horses.

"Why?" There was no point in explaining what he was asking; Jamie understood.

"She came to me and raised a good point." Jamie pet the mare's neck, then left the stall to meet Beckworth in the aisle. "And before you get any angrier, let me just say this. I once asked Finn why he allowed AJ to learn the proper use of the dagger and bow and then gave her roles in our missions." He steered Beckworth outside, then lifted his face to the sun. "His answer was that AJ was a woman from the future—independent and strong-willed. He said women were equal to men, for the most part.

"Stella doesn't see you going off on this mission as the lord of the manor or one of Hensley's spies...I'm not saying this right. She understands your desire to go. When she came to me, it wasn't to talk you out of going. She thinks of herself as your partner. Where you go, she goes. And quite frankly, she had a point. Women in this century go mostly unseen. She can be eyes and ears for us. And before you say anything, yes, Fitz is excellent at collecting information. But, honestly, we'll be looking for a needle in a haystack. We could use all the help we can get. And if she gets seasick, we can drop her off at a port with one of my men, who will see her back to Waverly."

Well, damn. It would be a waste of a man if Jamie had to do that. But he wouldn't have a problem finding a sailor willing to escort her, giving them time for the pubs in Bristol while waiting for the *Daphne's* return.

"She's thought it all through." Beckworth stared at the manor. She no doubt finished her packing and had the trunk delivered to the foyer while he was down here on a fool's mission.

"Did you expect anything less?" Jamie patted his back. "She's proven herself. And if I thought she'd be at risk, I wouldn't have agreed. But this is a simple find mission. Nothing more. If we can learn where MacDuff has been and the direction he's traveling, it will make Hensley's next move easier." Then he gave Beckworth a side glance and a wicked smile. "But it's up to you to keep her out of the way while she's onboard."

Then he strolled off, whistling some Irish ditty. And to think, not an hour ago, Beckworth had been whistling as well, not prepared for the storm Stella had kicked up.

Resigned that he'd done everything he could, he decided on one last effort and headed for the manor. Stella was no longer in the bedroom, the solarium, or the library. Barrington found Beckworth heading for the kitchen.

"She went out to feed the ducks in the pond." Barrington continued on his way but called over his shoulder, "And she'll be fine."

"You're only saying that because you won't have to deal with her stomping around the halls while I'm gone."

The butler's chortle made him shake his head. Did no one agree with him?

She was sitting on a bench with her gray cape wrapped around her. A raft of ducks swarmed in a constantly moving circle as she tossed breadcrumbs into the water.

He sat next to her, and she dumped the rest of the treats in before turning to him.

"You're still mad."

He ran a hand over his face. "It's not that I'm mad. I'm worried. This isn't the same as before. We were on the run from Gemini and her men. You'd been dragged into a dangerous situation and had no choice." He had to make her see the difference.

"You didn't have a problem letting me go to Ipswich. You said it was my choice."

"And look where that got us," he muttered.

She leaned back. "I'll never forget my mistake and where that got us."

He grabbed her hands and squeezed hard. "Don't ever say you made a mistake. What happened in Ipswich wasn't your fault. I only mentioned it to point out how badly a mission can go. And because you frustrate me."

"The team trusted me to go on the mission to rescue you on the *Phoenix*." She gently removed her hands from his grip. "You trusted me to go with Chester in search of the illegal real estate transactions."

"That was different." He hated that his voice sounded petulant. "Besides, you get seasick. Most of our time will be onboard the *Daphne*."

"I brought seasick medicine from home, and Eleanor gave me fresh herbs. You know, like the ones you bought me before."

Bloody hell. She'd even turned his closest friends against him. She squeezed his knee and trailed a finger up his leg before stopping just below his manhood, which couldn't help but twitch.

"It's up to you on whether we share a cabin or we each get our own." She kissed his cheek, then stood and walked back to the manor, leaving a floral scent trailing behind her.

Love. It was going to be the death of him.

9

The carriage arrived in Bristol and stopped on the pier alongside the *Daphne Marie*. Beckworth immediately jumped out, said something about returning the horses but most likely wanted to put some distance between himself and Stella. Jamie had ridden inside with them while Fitz rode on the bench with the coachman. Lando had ridden ahead to ensure the ship was prepared for sail.

Jamie grinned as he watched Beckworth stride off before helping Stella out of the carriage. He'd engaged Stella in conversation the entire way, ignoring the frosty air between her and Beckworth during the several-hour-long ride from Waverly.

Once her feet were on the ground, she took a deep whiff of sea air and ignored the more unpleasant smells coming from the busy port. She reached for the opal necklace Beckworth had given her the first time she'd been in London, but her neck was bare. Concerned about losing it, she'd left it at Waverly, carefully tucked away with the Mórdha stone rings in one of Beckworth's hidden compartments.

It had been two days since they'd jumped. If anyone had told her she'd be boarding the *Daphne Marie* in search of smugglers, she would have considered them mad. What would AJ think?

She barely heard the carriage drive off after Beckworth's trunk had been removed. Her eyes were locked on the ship, her focus on her whirling emotions.

"If you want to change your mind, there's still time." Jamie waited patiently by her side. "The carriage is close by, waiting on Beckworth's orders."

She shook her head. "To be honest, I'm not sure how I feel. Mixed emotions, I suppose. The first time Beckworth told me we had to cross the Channel to escape Gemini, I freaked out. It wasn't that I feared the sea, although I had second thoughts when the storm almost tossed me overboard." She rubbed her stomach, thankful she remembered to take her seasickness pill. "I've always had a sensitive stomach, whether it was road trips in a car or on a boat."

"And now?"

"The second trip across the Channel wasn't as bad, and I'd been locked in a cage in the hold for the entire trip. The herbs Beckworth bought me and eating smaller meals seemed to be the solution. I guess we'll find out if that holds true."

They stood side by side as they gazed at the ship.

"She's a beautiful ship. I haven't seen her since that day on the dock at the Westcliffe Inn in Baywood. Finn had taken AJ for a sailing lesson on a smaller sailboat. We'd only just met him and when I hadn't heard back from AJ within our agreed time-frame, I drove to the dock to wait."

"Was there trouble?"

She laughed. "They simply forgot about the time. Although she returned with damp hair and clothes while Finn was dry from head to toe. At the time, Finn passed it off as ocean spray, but she confided later that she almost fell out of the boat."

"You said you had mixed emotions."

"I'm not as scared as my first trip now that I know what to expect. My worry is about getting in the way." Her gaze scanned the other ships and the sailors running back and forth either loading or unloading cargo. The crew of the *Daphne* were working the sails. Stella rocked back and forth between her heels and toes then glanced up at Jamie and grinned. "But this will be quite the adventure."

He laughed. "That's the spirit. We'll find you something to keep you occupied while onboard. And our first port isn't that far."

She touched his arm. "I appreciate you trusting me."

"You know his only concern is for your welfare."

"I know all about worry. It was with me each time AJ went through the fog, but she had Finn. When they returned and I heard about their journey, while at the time never wanting to experience it, I was sorry I didn't have a true sense of what she'd been through. I got a closer glimpse when we traveled to France to visit the monastery. Then I was kidnapped and forced back to this time. It wasn't as bad as I expected."

"Weren't you scared being kidnapped?"

She considered the question before snapping out a response. "Terribly, but at the same time, I was so angry. But I didn't freeze up. I wanted to, but I guess my survival instincts are stronger than I expected."

"And then Beckworth came along."

She laughed. "He didn't have an easy time with me."

Jamie could only shake his head. "And I don't think he would have appreciated it any other way."

"I suppose."

"So, one cabin or two?"

She took his arm as he led her to the gangplank. "Let's assume he'll get over his anger and go with one. But we could use extra blankets in case he ends up sleeping on the floor."

Jamie was still laughing when Lando greeted them on the deck of the *Daphne*.

Lando bowed his head and gave her an apologetic grin. "It's good to have you onboard, Lady Stella..."

"Just Stella."

He nodded and glanced out to sea before continuing. "Stella. I hate to ask, but Fitz mentioned you'd offered to help while onboard. After I show you to your cabin, we could use your help in the galley. The stores came in late, and if we're going to make tide I could use as many of the men as I can get."

She rubbed her hands together. "I can find the cabin later. Take me to the galley."

Lando lifted a brow and looked at Jamie.

Jamie shrugged. "Don't look at me. I have my own tasks." With a broad smile, he strode off toward a group of sailors, his head turning left and right as he watched the men at work.

Lando led Stella down the stairs to the galley and introduced her to Michelson, who assumed various roles as part-time sailor, part-time doctor, and part-time cook. He was a thin man with a receding hairline emphasized by his ponytail and was somewhere in his thirties if Stella had to guess. He had gentle eyes and a soft voice.

"This is Stella. She's here as part of our mission but willing to help out. I thought you could use a hand stowing the supplies. I'll be taking your two helpers."

Michelson stood with hands on his hips as he scanned the galley that was filled with crates and sacks of staples. He scratched his head. "I'll use whatever help I can get." He glanced at Stella. "Let me show you the pantry. Everything has its place so it can be found quickly. Then we can start moving the stores."

"Show me the way."

Stella trailed behind Michelson and took stock of the pantry and, after five minutes, nodded as she understood their system. Not how she would have done it, but easy enough to follow.

"Let's start with this stack." Michelson strode to the first group of items, which was a combination of sacks and small kegs. "Just starting packing everything into the pantry."

"I know this is my first time onboard, but can I make a suggestion?"

He straightened from the crate he was opening. "Go ahead."

"Well, the alleyway is kind of narrow. If we end up filling up the front before the back, it will take us longer. If we can find the items that get stored at the back and work forward, we can both haul items at the same time without running into each other."

He grinned. "I should have thought of that. I'm not the one who normally handles the cargo."

Stella walked around the stacks. "Here we go. Let's start with these." She picked up a sack, straining under what had to be thirty pounds of dried beans. "What do you normally do when it's time to set sail, if those are the correct words."

"Close enough, and I'm usually on deck."

"Well, we should be able to move through this pretty quickly once we set a pace." She disappeared into the pantry and dropped the sack in its spot, making sure to level it out so several more could be stacked on top.

She wasn't sure how long they'd been working when she rolled a keg into place and lifted it to its flat side.

"I've always said no one organizes better than a woman."

She turned to find Beckworth dropping a sack onto a growing stack of corn flour. "At least you're talking to me again."

He ran a hand through his hair then pulled at his cuffs. "I still believe this mission to be too dangerous, but we are where we are." He glanced away. "And I'm not sleeping on the floor."

She grinned. "Jamie told you?"

His lips twitched. "He didn't have to. I saw the pile of blankets with a pillow on top."

"Jamie's kind. I hadn't mentioned a pillow." She held her smile, and his shoulders relaxed. "Have you been at the stables all this time?" She glanced at the growing stack of inventory. "It seems like I've been down here awhile."

"I had to make a quick run to the mercantile then looked for you in the cabin."

Stella moved past him, slowing as she brushed against him in the narrow aisle. "Follow me if you want to talk. We need to get this put away. I felt the ship shift."

"They're raising the sails, so I sent Michelson up top. I'll help you finish this."

They worked for another two hours, and Stella shuffled behind Beckworth as he led them to their cabin, which, fortunately, wasn't too far from the galley. She fell face-first onto the bed.

"I think I found the cure for seasickness."

Beckworth chuckled. "We've barely left port, and it will be some time before we leave the river for the sea."

"Not sure it matters."

Strong fingers ran over her shoulders, massaging her sore muscles. She moaned as he worked his way down her back. He untied her dress, and his warm hands made her skin tingle. When his lips followed the path of his hands, she snuggled into the covers. She tried to turn over when he reached her lower back, but her arms refused to work. One too many sacks of flour. She grunted when he rolled her over and continued his kisses over her belly—her ticklish spot. Her throaty laugh only spurred him on.

He moved off the bed, and she managed to lift her head in time to see him toss his jacket away. She tugged a pillow under her head and continued to watch as he unbuttoned his waist-coat. His gaze was molten.

She glanced behind him. "Did you lock the door?"

"The men will be busy for another couple of hours." He pulled the shirt over his head and untied his breeches.

She considered her clothing, and though she could muster the energy, decided to let him take the lead. He needed this, and once the mission was underway, they'd have little alone time. Once he was naked, she lifted her arms, and he pulled her up. He kissed her neck before removing her dress.

She ran a hand over his face before pushing her fingers through his hair, pulling strands from his ponytail. "I know I can be difficult, but I love you."

He kissed her. Nothing quick. It started slow and tender, then it grew bolder as his hand moved between her legs. When he lifted his head, his gaze sparked with humor. "I'm beginning to see the advantages of bringing you along."

Her sultry laugh turned his merriment back to lust, and he moved down her body inch by erotic inch.

She closed her eyes and gave in to the sensations he drew from her. This was going to be an amazing voyage...then she shrieked when he nipped her.

An hour later, they spooned under the covers. She relished the strength of his arms around her, his chest warm against her back.

He kissed her neck. "It feels like we've left the river. The men will be looking for food soon. I heard someone in the galley."

"I'm not sure I have any muscles left to move." She had no desire to leave their cocoon.

"I know something that might help."

The bed shifted as he moved away, and she quietly groaned at the loss of his warmth. She wanted more cuddle time.

The trunk opened and closed. Then he was back, but he hadn't returned empty-handed.

She turned over and found him sitting up, the covers over his lap. His muscled chest gave her other thoughts.

When he noticed her ogling, he grinned. "None of that. Look what I bought at the mercantile."

She glanced down. A stack of paper. Her heart swelled. She'd forgotten to pack the papers from her new office at the manor.

She ran her hand over the pages. "For my swans."

"Of course." He kissed her nose. "And I dropped off an extra sack of coffee beans in the pantry. I can't have you drinking all the crew's coffee."

She laughed. "Maybe just half of it." She ran a hand down his chest. "I'm sorry I'm such a bother."

"I knew what I was getting into. And as I've told you many times, I'd have it no other way." He softly pinched her chin, and his tone turned serious. "But now that the mission has begun, you need to listen to Jamie. He's in charge, not me."

"All business. I understand."

His head tilted to one side, and his eyes moved to the ceiling. "They're still working the sails." He picked up the paper and dropped it on the floor. "We should take the opportunity—"

He never had a chance to finish his words when she tugged him back to bed.

10

———————

Stella stood at the railing and watched the *Daphne* moor in a small port just north of Bristol. Beckworth didn't expect to learn much from their stop, but he'd agreed it was worth investigating when he'd spoken about their route with Jamie at lunch.

She'd helped with the dishes and had just finished stowing the last pot when Beckworth pulled her away to review the mission plan prior to docking. Though there wasn't much to the port, several ships dotted the bay. One of their tasks, besides listening for rumors of MacDuff, was to learn the name of his ship.

It was one thing Jamie and Fitz had never determined while trailing MacDuff along Ireland's southern coast several months before. He'd been seen often enough through the seaside villages, stirring up insurrection, but no one could name a ship and had assumed he'd grabbed passage wherever he could find it.

Before they'd left Waverly, Hensley had agreed with Jamie and Beckworth that if MacDuff was making a more significant play with France, luring Ireland ports to their side, then he might be paying a merchant vessel. With word that MacDuff's smuggling operation had grown since his run down the Irish coast, it only made sense he'd have his own ship now.

Stella noted a number of ships moored in the bay rather than dockside. Luck was with the *Daphne* after two ships had departed, leaving an opening alongside the pier.

"Why are there so many ships in such a small village?" Stella leaned over to catch a glimpse of a small boat moving between a ship and a small pier that seemed built for that purpose. Lando had called them jolly boats.

"It's one of the reasons Jamie wanted to stop here." Beckworth stood close enough for their arms to brush. "Unless they have a reason to stop in Bristol, most captains would rather not take the time to sail upriver. So, ships will stop in Portishead at the mouth of the river or travel north to here."

He took her hand as the *Daphne* was secured to the dock. "Are you comfortable with your role?"

Her response died on her lips as she watched two young lads shimmy down a rope from one of the ships. They landed on their feet and raced toward town as a burly man yelled at them from the ship's railing.

She laughed. "Were those two stowaways?"

Beckworth turned to see the two boys running away. "Most likely. They either hid when they moved from port to port, or they might have been caught and forced to work then decided sailing wasn't for them. It's not uncommon."

"A rough life, even in the small towns."

He shrugged. "They could be orphans or simply thought life would be easier at sea. I think we both understand that life at home isn't always the best, regardless of the century."

Not wanting to go down that dark hole, Stella steered the question back to Beckworth's question. "Our task seems simple enough. We're a married couple traveling north to visit family. We have a meal and drink then watch and listen."

"Do you have your dagger?"

She patted her pocket. "Right here."

"Good. Fitz will visit the pubs and inns first and determine which ones are the type MacDuff would want to visit. They'll most likely be the rougher ones where the only women tend to be the servers. We'll most likely be assigned to the inns, but that doesn't mean it won't be dangerous."

"If I can be kidnapped out of an inn, then I should expect anything."

Beckworth tensed when she mentioned the time she'd been kidnapped from bed with him at her side.

She squeezed his arm. "Let it go. Your guilt for that night in Saint-Malo is as bad as mine about Ipswich."

"What a pair we make, Lady Caldway."

"Indeed, Lord Beckworth.'"

They grinned, bumping shoulders, then turned when Jamie called for them. She took his arm as they strolled to the gangplank.

"Fitz says neither inn has any vacancy." Jamie pulled out a timepiece not too dissimilar to Beckworth's. "Lando and Michelson will take the inn on the north side and you two will take the other."

"Wouldn't it be more likely we'll catch them in the evening?" Stella asked.

"Maybe," Jamie answered. "But when we chased him in Ireland, it seemed he wasn't particular to the time of day to hawk his rebellion. He might have seen it differently when he was riling up the townspeople with the advantages of siding with the French. If his focus is now solely on smuggling, he'll be more careful about being seen. So, we'll monitor now and stay overnight. This type of work requires patience and diligence."

Stella understood. "Like any stakeout."

"What's this about a stakeout?" Lando asked.

She turned as Lando and Michelson strode up. "In my time, cops—what you refer to as guards—sometimes perform what they call stakeouts. They find an inconspicuous place to watch a home or place of business, waiting for their mark to see what type of criminal activity they might be up to."

The men nodded, and Jamie said, "Then we're all aware of how long and unfulfilling most of our days will be."

With that uplifting thought, they made their way down to the dock.

"Where will you be?" Beckworth asked.

Jamie took a left as soon as they reached the pier. "I'm going to visit the ship captains. Just one smuggler to another." Then he strode off, humming a sea shanty.

Stella hadn't considered other captains as a source of information. She figured they'd be tight-lipped about such matters. The talk would probably be about the weather and the best ports to hide in or maybe where the British patrols were. But something might come of it.

Arm in arm, she followed Beckworth toward their assigned inn, giving Lando and Michelson one last glance over her shoulder.

The inn was crowded with men and a handful of women. It was loud and overly warm. Beckworth found one of the few empty tables across the room near the hearth. They waited some time for the overworked server to bring their ales and a single platter of food that Stella picked at.

"If we're going to spend our time at inns, no more eating on the ship. I think I'm going to bust." She watched Beckworth finish the plate.

"That's a good idea. How did you fare with the ship?"

"A bit queasy after breakfast, but it's more likely my stomach is getting used to the food again."

They spoke little after that, each of them listening to other conversations. And while it felt awkward not to be talking, no one would think it odd. She remembered seeing other couples at inns eating in silence. It was common in her own time. It just wasn't typical for her. She squelched several thoughts she wanted to share, especially when Beckworth tilted his head ever so slightly as if he was having difficulty hearing a discussion.

After an hour, the empty plate had been removed, and beads of sweat that had been building since they'd first sat down were leaving rings of sweat under her armpits. She had to get some air, but if she left the inn, Beckworth would follow, and he seemed interested in whatever the men at the table behind them were saying.

Their mugs were low, so she picked them up. "I'll be right back."

It broke his concentration, and he frowned. "The server will take care of it."

"I need some air and won't go any farther than the bar." It wasn't really a bar. More like a plank of wood over a few barrels, but several men stood next to it, chatting amongst themselves or the innkeeper.

She set the mugs down in between two old-timers who looked ready to pass out and three men who kept glancing at the door. If she was correct, the men would ignore her for several minutes. The air, while still stuffy and smelling of tobacco, alcohol, cooking meat, and unwashed bodies strong enough to bring on tears, was cooler than where she'd been sitting. She rubbed her stomach, which had finally settled.

For the first few minutes, she focused on the two old drunks. It would be far from the first time that someone spilled something they shouldn't under the influence of alcohol. But she soon determined their argument over the best type of bait would last for some time. She grinned. Some things never changed. Even in two hundred years.

Her focus shifted to the men to her right. They sounded like locals, one of them complaining about too many ships in town while another muttered something about smugglers, which caught her interest. Though to be honest, she was filling in the gaps through their garbled English. Beckworth mentioned the *Daphne* would be running along the coast of Wales. It was possible some of the speech she didn't understand could be Welsh. She focused on individual words, specifically listening for the name MacDuff, but it never came up. It didn't take long to realize that the words she was able to grasp weren't worth storing away.

She'd always been known for her excellent memory and recall, which was another reason Jamie had agreed to her role. Now, if she could only understand what she was hearing. The innkeeper noticed her after about ten minutes and took the mugs to refill them.

She only had a few more minutes before she'd have to go back to the table when the men bent their heads lower, and she silently cursed. No doubt they were talking about something juicy, which could easily be about a woman rather than a smuggler. When the words Cheval and the horseman floated to her, they seemed out of context, and she took note.

As soon as the name was out of the man's mouth, another hushed him then ducked his head lower. By then, the innkeeper had given her two fresh mugs, and she had no reason to stay. She thanked him, got an odd stare—which she assumed had to do with her accent—and picked up the mugs.

She set them on the table before she dropped into her seat. The men Beckworth had been listening to were gone, replaced by an older man and younger woman.

"Did you hear anything of value?" she asked.

He shrugged. "It was a group of sailors from one of the fishing boats. There's been an increase in the number of smugglers in the area, but they think it has to do with the increase in British patrols south of Bristol, forcing them farther north."

He took a swig of ale then pushed it away. "Too many of these and I'll sleep the rest of the afternoon."

She winked. "That wouldn't be such a bad idea."

He smiled. "Don't encourage me." He glanced at the bar then leaned close. "Did you hear anything? Those men look like locals."

"That was my thought, but they hardly spoke any English."

"Welsh. That can be a bit of a problem along this part of the coast."

She took a sip of ale, then stood. "I need to go. The heat is getting to me."

Beckworth was at her side in a heartbeat, giving her a searching look. "You look flushed." He put an arm around her shoulder as two men looking for a table approached. Beckworth nodded toward their mugs. "We've only taken a sip or two, they're yours if you like."

After getting a hearty slap on his shoulder for the offer, Beckworth steered them out of the inn. When they'd walked several yards, he turned her to him. "Are you alright? Or was that a ruse to leave?"

"I got overheated. It was too hot in the room to be sitting that close to a fire. I think I'd have preferred standing at the bar."

"Duly noted." He walked them along the stores, and she motioned toward the mercantile.

"I need a different dress. Something plainer. I don't think anyone noticed, but I'd blend more with the crowd."

He chuckled. "I counted at least eight men who noticed you standing at the bar, pretending not to be eavesdropping on the men next to you."

She stopped. "Was I that obvious?"

He laughed and tugged her along. "Only to me. But I agree on something more simple."

She waited by the door of the mercantile while Beckworth paid for a couple dresses and a warm shawl. There was a notice posted on the door about stocking materials for ship repairs. She snapped her fingers, suddenly remembering something she'd overheard at the inn. "My god, I must have had a heat stroke."

"What are you talking about?" Beckworth stepped next to her and peered outside. "Did you see someone? Stella?"

"Huh." She looked at him. "Oh. I didn't hear you."

He stood straighter and squinted. "Are you alright?"

"I could use a drink."

"You just had two ales and another good swallow of a third."

"I think the heat sweated the alcohol out of me."

"Do you need to sit down?" He took her elbow and glanced around for a place to sit.

She tugged her arm away. "I'm fine. That's not it. I forgot to tell you that I heard those three men mention something. I can't believe I didn't remember sooner."

"No harm done." Then one of his maddening smiles slipped out. "Though, is it normal for you to forget things when you're overheated? Do they have a name for that?"

"Are you laughing at me?"

"I was just curious if it's something to be added to the list."

She swatted his arm. "I'm sure it was a combination of the alcohol and the heat." Her cheeks warmed, and she held her grin when Beckworth's lips twitched. When they'd first met and had been running from Gemini, he'd discovered a few things about her that he kept on an imaginary list. They were common fears—claustrophobia, heights, and horses to name a few. There was also the seasickness, and though it wasn't a fear, it still went on the list.

"So, what did you hear?" He stopped when they reached the ship and nonchalantly scanned the area.

It was probably nothing. And what she'd heard had been taken out of context since it was just a couple of words in a sentence. Though, to her, one had sounded French. She was sure of it, which seemed odd with the rest of the conversation spoken in Welsh.

"It sounded like Cheval. I'm not good with languages, but does it sound like French to you?"

"Cheval? Are you sure?"

Her eyes narrowed. "Yes, I'm positive. They also said horseman. Does that mean something to you?"

He glanced around again. This time with purpose as if searching for someone. "I'm afraid it does. And if what you heard is true, we have a problem."

11

Beckworth paced a short path in their cabin. There was enough space for a comfortable-sized bed for two, a table with two chairs, a small bookcase, and a washstand with a mirror. It was a duplicate of the cabin next door. The two rooms hadn't existed when Finn owned the ship, but with the war, Jamie discovered additional income sources by transporting the occasional passengers from England to France or vice versa. So, he'd given up a cargo hold and made the two cabins. The only problem with the cabin's size was not having enough room to pace.

Stella sat on the bed, making her swans. He could only shake his head at the mercurial woman he'd fallen in love with. Most women would want jewelry or more evening gowns. Stella was satisfied with a good bottle of wine, bold coffee, and a stack of paper. A modern-day woman indeed. The thought almost removed the concern squeezing his chest from what she'd learned at the inn.

It was most likely a mistake. She didn't understand Welsh. The words could have easily been misunderstood. But even so, she had a sharp intellect and an excellent memory. He grinned. A memory that sometimes worked to his disadvantage.

Jamie had returned to the ship shortly after they arrived but went straight to his cabin without a word.

"Stop pacing and come sit with me." Stella stood to move the paper aside and lined up her birds on the bookcase. She plopped back on the bed and patted the spot next to her. When he stopped but didn't make a move toward her, she clucked her tongue. "Five minutes, and then you can continue stomping around."

"I'm pacing, not stomping."

"That depends on one's viewpoint."

He sighed. It was easier to submit than to argue a point he'd end up losing. He had to pick his battles with Stella, and honestly, he could use the distraction.

He sat next to her, and she moved to squeeze between his back and the wall. She massaged his muscles and neck with soft circular motions, gently teasing the stress out of him.

"Jamie will call us together any moment now. It's almost dinner time, anyway."

"How do you know that?"

"I can smell the stew and fresh rolls."

That released a chuckle. "I meant about Jamie. I'm not so completely absorbed that I can't smell fresh bread baking."

"He's learned a great deal from Finn, and I've had a long time to study Finn's behavior. He's a strategist. He thinks things over, sometimes for what seems forever, before coming to his own conclusions and decisions."

"And you learned all this during the year or so that you've known him. That is, from your timeline."

She whispered in his ear. "I admit, AJ's told me a lot, but I also watched him and Ethan work out ways to catch you your first time in Baywood."

A shiver ran through him at the memory. "Fair enough." He

didn't like talking about those times. That was when he was still the duke's man, not the man he was now.

She rubbed his shoulders. "Shake it off. Everyone knows who the true Beckworth is."

"Everyone?"

"Those who matter. And maybe Jamie has other things on his mind. We're at port. It's time for everyone to rest and have time for themselves."

He had nothing to counter with because she was right. Even the captain needed space from the men.

"Are you really worried about what I overheard?"

Before he had a chance to answer, a knock at the door made him jump from the bed. He took a couple of steps and yanked the door open.

"Hello, little man." Lando gave him a huge grin, knowing how much Beckworth hated the moniker Lando had given him back when they still questioned his loyalties. "Jamie wants to meet before dinner. Half an hour in the galley." He glanced past him to Stella. "And you're looking well, Miss Stella. Cook wanted to know if you could spare some time after the meeting to help in the galley. He has friends in port he wanted to visit."

"Of course. I'll work out a schedule with him if it's easier. You know—while we're at sea versus when we're at port. Although, if we're in a storm, I'll probably be worthless."

Lando nodded and gave her a wide grin. "I think Cook is already in love with you. If Beckworth isn't careful, you'll have a marriage proposal before the mission is over." Then the burly man scurried away faster than Beckworth thought possible.

Stella's throaty laugh made him lock the door. He pulled his shirt over his head and dropped it to the floor as he stalked to the bed. Her laughter soon turned into moans of pleasure, and his worries about Cheval disappeared for a time.

When they arrived in the galley for Jamie's meeting, Beckworth's earlier concerns were still forefront in his mind, but the anxiety it brought had been reduced with his time in Stella's arms. It wasn't the act of lovemaking, though it was a small part. It was that she understood what drove him, what made him irritable, and what made him smile. Sometimes she knew what he needed before he did. It more than made up for her stubborn streaks and making questionable decisions without him. Those were behaviors he wouldn't be able to change, and based on Finn's advice and observations of him with AJ, he had to discover a happy middle ground. Some days were easier than others.

Stella took a seat between him and Fitz, who was already munching on a hunk of cheese and a leftover roll from breakfast. The first mate ate constantly yet never gained an ounce. But the man barely rested, usually working double shifts while at sea and then running various tasks while in port. Fitz was also an excellent spy. He could modify his appearance and voice when needed to the point people rarely noticed him, and those who did were left with a memory of a man who wasn't real. His usual physical changes were an added limp, a drunken posture, or a twitchy eye. His ability to physically adapt to a situation was similar to Beckworth's own skills after years working with the London gangs—or crews, as he referred to them.

Lando and Michelson sat across from them along with two other sailors Beckworth had seen before but had never been introduced to. They had been working the pubs with Fitz. The was a pitcher of ale, and Stella filled mugs.

Jamie sauntered in five minutes later, looking like he'd just woken up. That explained his earlier disappearance. He wasn't much of a talker when he was tired. Like someone had extinguished his inner light.

He'd barely sat when Cook set a mug of coffee in front of him. He took a sip and wiped his face before staring at the assembled group. "Sorry for being late. Never visit more than one or two captains while in port. I think it might be a while before I can look at another glass of whiskey."

The men's forlorn expressions matched Jamie's, as if mourning the loss of a good friend. It wasn't wise to step between an Irishman and his whiskey, so Beckworth nodded with his own condolences and tried not to grin at Stella's roll of her eyes.

She'd brought a few pages of paper and had begun making a swan. Her movements were slower than usual, most likely trying to keep the inventory low. She typically gave the swans away to children or acquaintances she knew who had kids. No one onboard the *Daphne* would want one, but perhaps a merchant in port would be interested. He wouldn't be surprised if she unfolded and refolded the same swan several times over. She'd done it before, but that was when she'd only had a single sheet of paper to work with for days.

Jamie cleared his throat, bringing Beckworth back to the present. Now that he had the opportunity to share Stella's observations, had paced the cabin with the need to share, he wasn't ready to discuss it. So, he let Jamie gather the other reports first.

"Lando. You mentioned earlier that you didn't hear anything about MacDuff."

"The inn was crowded with sailors, so we thought we'd hear something about smuggling." Lando stopped to take a drink then wiped his mouth with his sleeve. "Michelson thought he'd heard something, but it turned out the captains are concerned about British patrols boarding ships without cause."

Michelson nodded his agreement. "No mention of specific smugglers or ships."

"It's only our first run at it, and as Stella mentioned earlier, we might have better luck in the evening." Jamie turned to Fitz. "What did you, Lane, and Carmichael come up with?"

"Same as Lando and Michelson." Fitz chewed a piece of cheese while considering whether his quick response was true. "Lane mentioned a strange group." He lifted a chin toward Lane to continue.

Lane matched Lando in size, though not as beefy or thick around the chest, and his arms were well-muscled from working the sails. His bushy brown beard matched the color of his shaggy hair, and his nose was crooked either from a fight or a painful run-in with a yardarm.

"It wasn't anything they said," Lane said. "They barely spoke at all." His voice was soft, and Beckworth leaned forward. "I'd been in the pub for about an hour when these three men strode in. They ordered ales then studied the crowd. They didn't appear to be searching for anyone in particular, but they might have been."

"Or looking for a guard," Fitz suggested.

"Maybe." Lane scratched his neck. "They stayed about fifteen minutes. When they did speak, they spoke quietly, like they were sharing a secret. It seemed odd enough to mention."

"Were they sailors?" Beckworth asked.

Lane considered it. "Could have been, but if I had to take a quick guess, I'd say no. They looked like trouble."

"Anything else?" Jamie waited for each of the three men to glance at each other before they all shook their heads.

"I'm afraid what Lane reported might explain something Stella heard at the inn." Beckworth almost grinned at Stella's surprised glance. Had she forgotten what she'd overheard? She wouldn't have if she knew what it meant. "Does the name Cheval or a ship called *The Horseman* sound familiar to anyone?"

The men erupted into conversation as everyone talked over the other. As the voices increased in volume, Stella's hands moved faster as she made each precise fold, which involved little thought after the number of swans she'd made over the years.

She jumped when Jamie slammed a fist on the table, even though she expected someone to do it. She'd been thinking of doing it herself to quiet the men, but her mind was racing. When she'd first heard the words Cheval and horseman, she thought it might be something the team needed to hear, but without the full context of the sentence, nothing proved the two words were connected.

When Beckworth became anxious after hearing her report, she knew she'd hit pay dirt. The fact he didn't want to talk about it meant it was going to be bad.

While the men fussed over Stella's unexpected discovery, she tuned them out, turned her attention to the swan, and let her mind wander. She'd always been one who preferred to live in the moment. Her childhood hadn't been a happy one, and she'd left home as soon as she was old enough, traveling to the end of the road in northern Oregon. It was sheer luck she ended up working at a brokerage firm owned by a strong-willed woman who took pity on her and taught her the ropes.

When she found she'd inherited most of the woman's estate after her death, she traveled south and set up her own real estate office. She'd become a successful businesswoman with a healthy bank account, her future financially set. It was a career she was passionate about—until she met Beckworth.

She worked part-time now, taking on one or two clients a month, preferring to spend her time acclimating Beckworth to his new time period. Her sabbatical from work wouldn't last forever, but the two of them required time to learn more about the other. Their romance had been rushed and fraught with traumatic events.

She had to know if there was more to their relationship. That their confessed love hadn't been created by their forced proximity while racing away from danger or running toward it. Would they still feel the same when faced with a normal everyday life? Would their lust-filled attraction die?

She never spoke of her uncertainty but suspected he had the same questions. For now, they were enjoying their life and their time together. And she had to admit, as AJ had discovered, that the touch of adventure and danger had sparked something inside her that had yet to be quenched.

Now, as she glanced at the men around the table, she realized their mission had somehow changed. It had become precarious, which would explain Beckworth's unease. It wasn't for himself. It was for her. They might have been able to set it aside when they'd been alone in their cabin, but now that the team was involved, whatever was coming would be another test in their relationship.

She also realized that the table had quieted, and everyone was staring at her. They were waiting for her report. She took a cue from Maire, who never rushed when she had important news to impart, and completed the swan she'd been working on before setting it in the center of the table.

"We'd finished our meal, and the heat from the crowd and the fire was too much. Which probably explains why the tables hadn't been occupied. Beckworth was listening to the conversation at a nearby table and wouldn't want me going outside on my own, so I went to the bar to refill our mugs. I had to get away from the fire."

She ran a hand over her neckline as if wiping away sweat from that moment. "There were three men at the end of the bar, and I moved in between them and two old drunks who were debating the advantages of different fish bait. I couldn't determine if the three men were locals or not and most of their words sounded garbled, but they didn't appear drunk."

"Speaking Welsh," Fitz said.

"That's what Beckworth said. I picked up a word or two, but nothing of interest, or at least nothing I could put together. I was getting ready to leave when a couple of words caught my attention. But I didn't understand the whole sentence so wasn't sure if they were important." She glanced around the table. Even though Beckworth had said the words, it was apparent they wanted to hear it from her. At first, she thought she might have misunderstood, but the more she replayed the event the more she was certain of the words. The tightening of Beckworth's jaw and the slight crease in his forehead shouted for her to get on with it.

She straightened in her seat and looked Jamie in the eye. "I heard the words Cheval and horseman. I wasn't positive at first, but once we were outside and I had time to consider it, I had no doubts. I still don't."

"Dammit to hell." Lando pounded a fist on the table and stood, almost knocking the chair over.

"Do we send a letter to Hensley?" Fitz asked.

"We need confirmation." Jamie nodded at Fitz, who took the last bite of cheese and grabbed the remaining roll before he strode from the galley and raced up the stairs.

"Where's he going?" Stella asked.

"He'll check the inns and pubs to see if he hears the same from anyone else. Then he'll check the ships for *The Horseman*," Beckworth replied.

"It never occurred to me the way they said the horseman that it could be a ship." Stella fiddled with the edge of a new piece of paper, preparing for the first fold.

"Cheval is the captain of *The Horseman*." Jamie finished his coffee and poured ale in the mug. He took a long swig before leaning his elbows on the table. "He's actually an Englishman and a smuggler, though he pretends to be a merchant. He's traded with the French over the years and picked up the name Cheval along the way. And to complete the picture for you, the name Cheval means horse in old French."

"So does he work for the English or the French?" she asked.

"He works for whoever can pay him the most," Lando snarled from where he leaned against the wall.

"He's more a man without a true country." Beckworth refilled mugs. "And like MacDuff, has escaped the hangman's knot on more than one occasion. He'll smuggle anything from goods to people, but his favorite cargo are flintlocks, cannonballs, and gunpowder."

"Hensley has tried to catch him several times without success," Jamie added.

"Not from lack of trying," Lando growled. "We've lost good men to him."

Stella pressed down the first fold in the paper. Cheval sounded like a scary man, and when she glanced at Beckworth, he was watching her. He wanted to send her back to Waverly. He didn't have to say it, and she sure as hell wasn't going to mention it.

"Do you think Hensley will want you to change your mission?" she asked, turning her attention back to Jamie.

"We have standing orders for Cheval," Lando answered. "The question comes down to who Hensley wants worse—him or MacDuff."

"Right now, we don't have enough information on either man." Jamie finished his ale in a long swallow. "All we have is Cheval's name and his ship, but we have no idea what the conversation was about. They could have been sharing a tall tale for all we know. And we've only begun the mission Hensley gave us. Let's see what Fitz comes up with. Until then, we'll share a meal then return to the pubs and inns later this evening. We need to gather more information. Unless we hear something more substantial, we'll continue our route north tomorrow."

Stella stood and collected her paper and the single finished swan. "I'll just take this back to the cabin then help Cook." She gave Beckworth a quick glance. His eyes were on her, but his focus was distant. He was working through something. Regardless of what the team discovered that evening, if he intended to remove her from the ship, he was going to have a fight on his hands.

12

———

When Stella returned to the galley, Beckworth was gone and Lando had taken his seat. Curious where he might have gone but unwilling to sound like a harpy who had to know his every move, she focused on helping Cook.

His name was Stiller, but everyone called him Cook. While he was in charge of the meals, he was also an accomplished sailor and often spoke about his days at sea. He was a few inches shorter than her but claimed his height made it easier to climb the ratlines and help with the sails. He kept his hair short, and it was always messy as if he constantly ran his hands through it, though she'd never seen him do it. The pinky on his left hand was missing, and the scar looked old. He didn't offer how it happened, and she didn't ask. She hadn't known what to expect working with the crew, but she spent most of her time in the galley laughing at his tales.

Cook advised to finish the stew and serve it with fresh bread and cheese. A skeleton crew was kept active, and the men came down in shifts to eat. Once she was satisfied the crew was moving through the buffet line she'd set up, she dropped into a chair where Jamie and Lando were looking over a map, their empty plates and bowls pushed to the side.

"Are you working out the next leg of our journey?" Stella asked.

Lando looked up from the map. "The next two stops, actually. Unless something changes along the way."

"You mean if we hear any more about MacDuff or Cheval."

He nodded and pointed to a spot on the map. "This is where we are currently."

Stella leaned closer. It was impossible to tell how far it was between points. "This is Bristol here?" She tapped a spot near the mouth of a river just south of where Lando had pointed.

"Exactly. And this is our next stop. Baglan on the River Neath just short of Swansea, which is too populated for our purposes. Baglan is a bit larger than this port and is favored by some of the smugglers in these ports for restocking their ships."

"This sounds more promising."

"Possibly, but we'll have to be more careful." Jamie sat back and gave her a long look. "Thank you for helping Cook. He's been waiting for a chance to visit his family."

She shrugged. "I know my way around a kitchen, though I'm not much of a cook."

"One of those modern-day women things?" he asked.

She laughed. "I suppose that's part of it. Both men and women enjoy cooking, I'm just not one of them. Being a broker —or what you call an Estate Agent—tends to make for long evenings. If I need to show a house, a lot of times it's after the client gets off work or on the weekends." She winked at Jamie. "And there's as much paperwork in my job as there is for a ship's captain."

Jamie grinned but he seemed to consider her again. For what, she didn't know. "Which is why you recognized the estate contracts Gemini had hidden away."

She laughed at the memory, which wasn't so funny at the time. "I'd just been kidnapped by Gemini's henchman, Gaines, and walked for miles in shoes that weren't meant for walking, let alone over dirt and mud paths, only to be surrounded by crazy, scary men once we'd reached our destination.

"I knew AJ and Finn would come for me, but I had no idea how long that would take, and Beckworth hadn't shown up yet. I'd been going through the trunks, somewhat interested in the fashions." She chuckled, and the men laughed with her. "But when I found the stack of papers, it was the first thing that reminded me of home."

"You were quite brave from what Beckworth shared." Lando crossed his arms and his brows knit together. "And stubborn."

She barked out a laugh. "I have my moments."

"I'd say several," Jamie looked in his mug before taking a drink. "Beckworth gave me an earful about letting you come with us on this mission."

She shrugged, then played at the edges of her sleeves, almost laughing at the thought she might have picked up Beckworth's habit of pulling at his cuffs. "He's not talking about sending me back to Waverly, is he?"

"Not yet, but depending on what we hear about Cheval, that might change."

She felt her temper rise but took a deep breath instead. She considered using AJ's technique of counting to ten, but it had never worked for her. "I'm not going to be sent home like some errant child."

Jamie raised his hands in surrender. "I'm only stating what Beckworth might ask. I agree with Hensley that your role on this mission is between you and me. But it would be unwise not to listen to his advice and opinion. Though he'll be looking at it from a different perspective."

"I know he wants to protect me. And though this trip back in time was supposed to be a holiday for us, I wouldn't think of stopping him from following his heart. But neither will I step aside and let him go on his own. Besides, if trouble starts, the ship should be a safe enough haven."

Jamie smiled. "Then we don't have a problem."

She gave them her best broker smile. "Excellent. Then I'll finish up in the galley and take a rest before our evening at the inn." She picked up their plates and mugs and spent the next hour cleaning the galley. When she returned to the cabin, Beckworth hadn't returned. She managed to untie her dress and crawl into bed. She didn't have time to wonder what he might be up to before sleep took her.

———

Beckworth leaned against a stack of crates and watched the schooner make last-minute preparations for sail. There was nothing special about the ship, no different than the four others floating dockside. It wasn't *The Horseman* or MacDuff's ship, but he'd overheard two men at the pub talk about their next destination and the apparent secrecy of their cargo, so he followed them back to their ship.

If this were any other mission, his gut instinct would be to follow the lead. But the only way to follow was by ship, and that was too much of a risk for the slim information he'd overheard. For now, he wanted to ensure he'd recognize the ship if they came across it again. He took note of her name, and his patience finally won out when a man strolled to the railing, looked up to the sails, and yelled an order.

Though daylight was fading, he was able to make out the man's features, and whether he was captain or first mate; it was enough for now. Once the man moved away from the railing,

Beckworth backed up several steps then turned and headed for the *Daphne*.

His thoughts turned to Stella. Would she be mad that he took off without telling her? He didn't think so. In Baywood, they always told each other where they were going when leaving the house. It made sense in that timeline. But this wasn't Baywood or Waverly. They were on a mission. One that might have grown more dangerous than anticipated.

His natural instinct was to send her back to Waverly. He chuckled to himself as he strolled along the docks, keeping an eye open for anyone who looked familiar. She would fight him at this point of their travels, and he doubted he'd have any support from Jamie. Not yet. Rumors weren't enough. The problem was, the more trouble they found, the less likely she'd agree to return to Waverly.

The damn woman was as protective of him as he was of her. And the sentiment made him smile. Not that long ago, he once believed he'd find a woman who followed normal conventions. A wife like Hensley's Mary, who managed the manor, went to dinner parties, and planned ones for Waverly. A woman excited about the London season and would spend months there visiting friends, going to balls, and attending luncheons. There would be friendship and tenderness between them, and perhaps eventually some form of love. Then Stella dropped into his life and ripped away all his future plans.

At first, he'd thought it nothing more than a passionate love affair, knowing she'd go home to her place in the future. He'd had no desire to leave Waverly. Yet, once she'd returned home, his manor held nothing for him but memories of her.

Fortunately, Sebastian—the monk who'd been the one to get them involved in the Mórdha stones in the first place—had provided him the answer. He'd given Beckworth one of the stones and a new incantation that would allow him to live in both worlds with little risk. But to be honest with himself, even without the new incantation, he would have walked away from Waverly for her.

The question was whether their infatuation with each other would survive everyday life. Their first meeting and eventual romance had occurred under dire circumstances. Yet, when they'd found safety in London, she wanted to meet his friends from the old days when he was running with the crews.

He snorted. That had been part of his problem. He'd lived in two worlds his entire life, and chances were, with any other noblewoman, he would have to hide his past from her. But not Stella. She saw him for who he was and seemed to love him all the more for it. And while she continued to chip away at the hard shell he'd placed over his heart, she also made him crazy with her willingness to jump into the fray, risking her own life for him.

That had been unexpected, unnecessary, and downright irritating. She knew the risk—to a point. But he'd seen loved ones die for nothing. Ones he wasn't able to save. And he didn't like how his chest tightened with the thought he could lose her just as quickly.

The *Daphne* was quiet when he boarded her with dusk fading to darkness. A few sailors were top deck working on repairs that were difficult to care for while at sea. Soon they would be in their bunks or at the pubs. He nodded at the men as he made his way toward the stairs, passing through the galley on the way to their cabin. He knocked softly before entering and smiled.

Stella was face down in the bed, wearing nothing but her undergarments, her head turned to one side. Her dress had been thrown over a chair. She was a heavy sleeper when she felt safe and didn't stir as he removed his jacket and boots. They would leave soon for their evening mission, but there was enough time to join her for a nap.

Once he'd stripped down to his own underwear, he crawled onto the bed and lay next to her. Though she never woke, she seemed to sense him and leaned into his embrace, her head close to his. The sounds of her slow, steady breaths lulled him to sleep.

Something flicked his nose, and he turned his head away. In his drowsy sleep, he swatted at the next light touch, thinking it an irritating fly. When it happened a third time, his eyes popped open, somewhat disoriented.

"Wake up, sleepy head."

The sultry voice cleared his sleep-befuddled brain, and he turned as she brushed one of her swans over his nose.

He grinned and pulled her down for a kiss. When he tried to tug her into bed, she stepped away from him.

Her gaze suggested she wanted to jump in with him, but instead, she tossed him his pants and shirt. "Lando, Lane, and Michelson have already left. Jamie says Fitz never returned, so he wanted us to find him before going to the inn."

He sighed. She was already in mission mode. "The last I saw of him was at the pub on the far side of the docks. He was just heading in. It's a bit of a rough crowd but it should be safe enough for a quick drink before the inn."

She wore one of the new dresses he'd bought earlier. It was plain and better fitting for this port and their task. But unless they did something with that auburn hair and her face, men would easily pick her out of a crowd.

"It's a shame Eleanor couldn't have come with us. Her knowledge of theater makeup would come in handy."

She gave him a questioning look. "Why would I need that?" She handed him his jacket, and he dropped it on the bed and pulled her to him, giving her a long, promising look.

"To keep the men from staring at you each time you walk into a room."

His words produced a lovely blush, which was what he was aiming for.

"You always know the right thing to say. And I expect you to follow up on that kiss when we return." She stepped away and flipped through her clothing until she found a warm shawl.

The weather wasn't too dissimilar to a winter day in Baywood, but with a bit more of a bite, especially along the coast. They'd been fortunate to avoid the rain.

He straightened his jacket and opened the cabin door. "Was Jamie staying on the ship?"

"He claims to have paperwork to catch up on, and after making the rounds with the ships earlier today, he wants to avoid being seen too often."

"He never said if he'd learned anything from his visits. Did he say anything at dinner?"

She tilted her head. "Nothing that I remember, so his afternoon was a bust too."

"Not necessarily. He might be waiting for one of our reports to validate something he might have heard."

"And they say women are better at secrets." She sauntered out of the cabin and stopped to ask the three sailors in the galley if they needed anything more to eat before they left.

They were surprised by her question but smiled and nodded their appreciation. Most of them knew AJ Murphy from earlier missions and no longer seemed to question the wisdom of having women on board. He nodded at the men as he followed Stella to the stairs.

The docks were more crowded than earlier with sailors, merchants, and other locals milling around the pubs and inns. The locals would soon be on their way home, but the pubs would remain busy long into the night.

Stella walked behind him as he entered the pub where he'd last seen Fitz. He strode toward an open table when a drunk heading for the door ran into him.

"Watch where you're going, mate."

The Irish accent was thick, and Beckworth growled a response as his gaze flashed around the room. Fitz was in full disguise, and his bumping into him was a warning as he exited the pub. Beckworth turned toward a table while he scanned the room, his gaze landing on three men at the bar who appeared to be watching Fitz.

One of the men, tall and thick with a heavy beard, moved toward the door. He could be leaving for any number of reasons that had nothing to do with Fitz. If he didn't have Stella with him, he'd do something to slow the man down. But he wouldn't risk her safety. Fitz would easily slip into the crowd of sailors. He knew what he was doing.

The man grew close, but his focus was clearly on the door. Beckworth held his ground as the man passed by. A low grunt, the scraping of wooden legs on the floor, and several sharp remarks made him turn around.

Stella was on the ground and the burly man was pushing up from a chair he'd fallen into. Beckworth assumed he must have collided with her. He held out his hand, and she grabbed it. Once she was standing, she shook out her dress and patted her hair.

"Oh, my. He came out of nowhere," Stella explained to Beckworth.

"You stepped into me." The burly man had gained his footing and stood over her, a good foot taller.

She didn't back down, and when Beckworth placed a hand on her arm, she knocked it away. "I'm not asking for an apology. So, no harm done."

The man stepped closer, his eyes narrowing to slits. "I know you."

She stepped back, and Beckworth put his arm through hers. "I've never seen you before you plowed into me."

He snapped his fingers. "Earlier today. You were at the inn."

She didn't hesitate in responding. "Yes. I ate lunch there." She gave him a stern look. "Are you following me?" She turned to Beckworth. "I think he's following me."

For the first time, the man looked at Beckworth. Then he noticed the attention they were getting from the crowd. He glanced over his shoulder to his buddies and scowled. "Like you said. No harm done."

He pushed past them and quickened his pace until the door shut behind him.

Beckworth looked at the two remaining men who'd stood when their friend ran into Stella but held their ground during the altercation. They glanced at each other and then at Beckworth before taking their seats.

He squeezed Stella's arm and turned her toward the door.

"Why are we leaving?"

Her words weren't loud, but the few men who heard her chuckled. That was good. Most of the men saw the entire incident as a good-natured accident and probably liked Stella's spunk at standing up to a man a good foot taller than her. The question was whether the men at the table bought her ploy.

13

———

Stella folded a swan while she listened to Beckworth repeat their short evening at the pub for a second time.

When they'd left the pub, Beckworth dragged her down the dock, mumbling "What were you thinking?" over and over. At first, she wasn't sure whether he was asking the question of himself or if he was speaking to her. She decided both answers were probably correct and it would be best not to interrupt. It appeared they were returning to the ship, and she'd hear an earful there.

She'd sighed in relief when they met Fitz in the galley, feet on the table as he nursed a whiskey, but her brow rose at seeing Lando sitting next to him.

"I'd just left Lane and Michelson at the inn and was going back to a pub I'd been at earlier," he explained. "It wasn't difficult to pick out Fitz ducking in and out of the crowd in his rush to the ship. I've seen that limp a dozen times and knew something was wrong. I updated Lane and Michelson and then hurried back here. They'll be along shortly."

Beckworth had been halfway through the first telling of their evening when the two sailors arrived, and he began from

117

the beginning. Once the story was finished, Lando went to find Jamie.

The young captain must have been asleep because he yawned before he dropped into the closest chair. Since Cook was visiting his family, Michelson brought him a tin of coffee. Jamie looked quite irresistible with his bedhead look. She'd have to pay more attention to what type of woman interested him, for Mary and Elizabeth, of course. They loved to play matchmaker. She grinned as she made the next fold. At his age, he probably didn't have a type yet and was most likely not fussy. Ah, to be young again.

Beckworth must have finished the second telling because Jamie sat straighter and his eyes regained a focused brightness. He poured a shot's worth of whiskey into his coffee. If he was going to comment, he never had a chance as Beckworth turned toward her and unleashed his pent-up frustration.

"I can't believe you stood up to him. We're supposed to be unobtrusive." He stood with hands on hips, and she bit a lip so she wouldn't grin. If he weren't so mad, she'd point out that he was using her angry pose now that the tables were turned.

Rather than throw gas on the flames, she tried for a middle-of-the-road approach. "He looked like he was following Fitz. I thought I'd give him a head start."

"Fitz is a professional. He knows what he's doing."

"Actually," Fitz cut in. "The delay got me to the ship before anyone could follow."

Beckworth turned on Fitz. "You're not helping."

"You have to admit, he caved quickly once he realized we'd drawn a crowd." Stella finished her last fold and set the swan on the table, lightly tapping a wing before giving him her full attention.

"Except now he knows you. He remembered you from earlier today, and he won't forget the next time."

"We're leaving tomorrow." Her reasoning seemed sound. "There won't be a next time."

"Alright, the lot of you. I've heard enough," Jamie barked.

"Well, that might not be exactly true." Fitz had removed his boots from the table when Jamie had joined them, and he now leaned his elbows on it instead, knowing he'd gotten their attention.

When it didn't appear he was going to continue, Beckworth sighed and asked, "What isn't true?"

He shrugged and pulled out his pipe but didn't light it. "You've all been so interested in Stella's daring that you've overlooked the important part." He gave them each a long look. "The reason why I was hurrying out of there in the first place."

Everyone glanced at each other and realized at the same time he was right. The laughter eased the tension, and when Stella glanced at Fitz, happy he redirected the conversation, he gave her a wink as he polished a spot on his pipe. Once the laughter stopped, the men leaned in to hear what the first mate had to say.

"I'd been to two other pubs before this one and just happened to find a spot toward the end of the bar between a couple blokes more interested in their mugs than conversation. I was hunched over, listening to a nearby table while keeping my face hidden. So, when these three men strode by, I was able to get a decent look at them, but as far as I could tell, they never looked at me.

"They stopped at the end of the bar on the other side of the man to my right. Since my mate was the quiet type, I was able to listen to them while still paying attention to the discussion at a nearby table." He tapped his ears. "I've trained them to do that."

Stella understood. She'd developed a similar skill after listening to husbands and wives who spoke over each other when voicing their likes and dislikes as they toured a house for sale. She gave him a nod in understanding, and he grinned as he moved on with his tale.

"This new group was speaking Welsh, which made me think about what Stella reported earlier. I was able to pick up a few words—shipments, a cove just north of here, and then a ship. *The Horseman*." He shook his head. "And that was right about the time some drunken sod ran into me, which caught the attention of the three men. One of them had been giving me a glance every few minutes, but I didn't think he found me of any interest. But the drunk wouldn't stop apologizing, and that's when I decided a swift exit was the best. I knew when I was halfway to the door that one of them was following me. Not a better time for Beckworth and Stella to enter."

He sat back. His eyes were hard, and his lips thinned as he gripped the pipe. "I know we have our mission, but can we really forget what we're hearing? You know what must be in those shipments."

Stella glanced around the table as they all nodded, expressions solemn. "Well, I don't."

"Flintlocks. Possibly direct from France," Beckworth answered her question.

"More than that if I know Cheval." Jamie stood and went to the galley, returning with a pitcher of ale. He filled his mug and then the others.

"Didn't you say this MacDuff person you're trying to find was somehow connected with the French?" Stella folded a second swan, allowing the men to determine if her question made sense.

"The two captains working together." Beckworth considered it as he rubbed his jaw. "An interesting thought, but so far, all we have are rumors that MacDuff is active again, men dropping Cheval's name in pubs, and a group of men talking of secret shipments and *The Horsemen*."

"Were the men at the pub the same ones at the inn earlier today?" Jamie asked Beckworth.

"Their backs were to me at the inn. Stella, did you get a look at the men at the pub?"

She nodded. "I didn't recognize the man who ran into me." She grinned and so did the men, knowing quite well she'd been the one to run into him. "But one of the men at the inn kept his back to me. His size was the same, and since the bruiser who knocked me to the ground recognized me, then I'd say they're one and the same."

Jamie's face relaxed except for the wrinkled forehead. It was the same look Finn got when he was ready to make a decision. "So, we have men in town ready to make a run. It's possible they're meeting up with Cheval. Or maybe they want to avoid him."

"A competitor?" Lando asked.

Jamie shrugged. "Something we need to consider. Beckworth, did you happen to bring those spyglasses AJ always used?"

"I did."

"Lando, let's take note of the ships that leave port tonight and with the next tide. We'll stay in port until mid-day tomorrow."

"We're going to check out the cove?" Beckworth asked.

"Our route takes us that way. Seems a waste not to."

***

Beckworth packed a canvas bag while Stella paced the room. It didn't hold much—binoculars, a second pistol, and gunpowder cartridges. He carried his Queen Ann's pistol in his jacket and his dagger on his hip.

Stella had dressed in pants and a shirt when she woke that morning since she'd stay onboard until the next port.

"You know you can't go." He glanced at her as she made a turn.

"I know."

"Then why the pacing?"

"Can't I be worried for you?"

He sighed as he closed the bag and set it next to the door. When she made another pass, he grabbed her. His kiss was swift before he stepped back to give her a long perusal. "How's your stomach?"

She considered the question. "To be honest, all I've thought about is this new mission. I haven't had time to worry about being seasick. The trip here was calm enough, and I've only been using the herbs. After the first day, I decided to keep the seasickness medicine for stormy seas."

"Good thinking. What are your plans while we're gone?"

She hugged him. "I'll help Cook with breakfast and then clean up. It will keep me busy." She held on tight, and he rubbed her back. "I should have brought my own binoculars so I could watch you."

"We'll be out of sight once we get past the cliff."

The *Daphne* had remained in port until the middle of the previous day as Jamie had ordered. The teams returned to the pubs and inns that morning, but there was no sign of the men from the previous night nor word of MacDuff.

Two ships had left a couple of hours before dawn, both of them known to Lando and Fitz. Ships the *Daphne* stayed clear of when possible. Jamie had sailed the coast of England dozens of times as captain and many times more as second mate. Most captains knew Jamie, and he knew them, so he'd learned quickly who to avoid. He didn't want his name or face known too widely, especially when he was spying for Hensley. So, when

Lando and Fitz reported on which ships had left, it wasn't surprising they were known to be well-known smugglers. Chances were good the mission had confirmed its first solid lead.

The *Daphne* had reached the cove close to midnight and sailed past, running dark. The lookout in the crow's nest had seen a light he assumed to be from a ship. Jamie concurred it was worth checking out. He ordered the ship to make a wide turn in order to anchor just south of the cove. Then they waited.

"We won't be long. It's a simple fact-finding trip." He picked up his bag and gave her a last heated kiss before leaving the cabin.

She trailed behind him to the railing where Jamie, Lando, and Fitz waited.

"I don't want the *Daphne* to be seen if it can be helped. Get the names of the ships and whether anyone is going on shore. Simple surveillance."

"Understood." Fitz gave a nod to Lando, who slipped over the railing onto the rope ladder before dropping into the jolly boat.

Beckworth went next, with Fitz giving a final nod to Jamie before following in the predawn light. Beckworth glanced up to find Stella peering down at him. She dropped something and it floated in the air. He had to reach out over the water to grab it.

A swan.

He tucked it in his pocket and gave her a wave as Lando and Fitz picked up oars and moved them away from the ship. Beckworth found a seat and helped with rowing. The tide helped carry them to a thin strip of beach where they pulled the boat ashore. From there, Lando and Fitz grabbed ropes, and after a brief discussion, they decided on the best spot to start their climb.

The hardest part was the first fifty feet, which proved to be a moderate climb. From there, after dropping the rope, they jogged up the gently sloping landscape. When they reached the top, they fell to the ground, breathing hard as they peered over the ridge. Two ships were in the cove, and Fitz nodded to Lando, who took the lead as they worked their way closer.

After a hundred yards, Lando dropped to his belly.

"Can't we get closer?" Beckworth asked.

"There's someone in the crow's nest," Lando answered. "Give me those glasses."

Beckworth had them handy and passed them over.

Fitz had his spyglass out and nodded. "He's keeping his eyes on the bay and the shore, but seems more interested in that jolly boat approaching on the starboard side."

Beckworth squinted. There was indeed movement in the crow's nest. The boat had been hidden by the other ship until just before coming alongside. Lines were already thrown over the side of the ship.

"They're bringing cargo onboard." Lando adjusted the glasses. "There must be a cave where they've been storing their goods."

"Can you tell what the cargo might be?" Beckworth asked.

"Based on the way they're rigging the lines, it's not kegs. I'd say long crates."

A couple of minutes later, the lines were pulled taut, and with arm gestures from the sailors on the jolly boat, the cargo began to lift. From Beckworth's vantage point, it was easy to see they were indeed long crates. "The perfect size for flintlocks."

"Could be anything, but I agree." Lando continued to watch. "I don't see any markings on them."

"We need to go." Fitz put his spyglass away. "Now."

"What's wrong?" Beckworth asked, grabbing the glasses Lando passed back to him as they slowly backed away from the ridge.

"The other ship is preparing to raise sails."

No one needed any more encouragement. Once they were far enough away not to be seen, they raced back to where they'd left the ropes, which they anchored and tossed over the cliff. They moved quickly as they began their descent.

Beckworth focused on the sound of oars slicing through the water as he considered what they'd seen, curious as to what was in the crates. Then he thought about Stella and what she might be up to other than worrying about him. Then he thought about their evening together, and that occupied some time. He wanted to think of anything other than what would happen if they didn't make it to the *Daphne* before either ship left the cove.

14

─────────

Stella watched the jolly boat as it made its way to the beach. She was so focused trying to make out Beckworth she jumped when Jamie stepped next to her.

"Why don't you get breakfast while you can? Cook could use the help."

She nodded as she watched the men start climbing. "I could use a bite. Have you eaten?"

"Aye. But if there are any of Cook's sweet rolls left..." He shrugged, and she pictured him as a little boy begging his mother for a treat.

She snorted. "I'll see what I can do."

The tables in the galley were full, but it appeared most were finishing up. Cook was busy preparing another pot of porridge.

"Hasn't everyone eaten already?" she asked.

"No. The captain wants the crew on watch to wait until after we've set sail."

That made sense. Jamie had told Fitz he didn't want the ship seen, so the *Daphne* had to be ready to sail as soon as the team returned. "What can I do to help?"

"Have you eaten, girl?"

She shook her head.

"Well, grab a bowl and eat something. Then go topside and wait for your man. I won't need you until after everyone's eaten."

"Are you sure?"

He nodded, then he jutted his chin toward a towel-covered plate. "I saved a sweet roll for the captain. If you'd be so kind to take it to him."

She grinned. "He was hoping you saved him one."

Cook chuckled. "He says that every time, though he knows I always save him an extra."

"Will he want coffee with it?"

That got a bark of laughter. "Oh, to have a woman onboard. He would, but since he refuses to keep a cabin boy, there's no one to cater to his needs."

"Well, he has someone now. At least for this mission." She grabbed a bowl of porridge and a mug of coffee and looked around for a seat. She thought she saw an open seat when Michelson waved her over.

"Are you worried about Beckworth?" Michelson asked.

She swallowed her first bite of porridge. "No. At least not with his current task."

He laughed. "Fair enough. How are you holding up? You know, with your stomach."

She grimaced. "Does everyone know about my seasickness?"

"Oh, I'd say only about half the crew."

She shook her head and sipped her coffee. "I've been a bit queasy a couple of times, but nothing like I've experienced before. The herbs really help."

They spoke of the fair skies that followed them, and then Michelson shared tales of when AJ and Finn had been onboard.

"I hear AJ spent a lot of time in the crow's nest." Stella scraped the last of the porridge from her bowl.

"She seemed to enjoy her time up there." Michelson got a gleam in his eye. "I don't suppose you want to give it a try."

She snorted. "Not a chance in hell. I don't do heights."

He chuckled. "Well, Cook can always use an extra hand."

"And I don't mind, but for now, he doesn't need me until after the next shift gets their breakfast. I guess I'm on my own."

Michelson nodded as he finished his second bowl. He crossed his arms on the table and leaned close. "What do you know about rigging?"

"Not a thing."

"Would you like to learn?"

She turned on her broker smile. "If it means fresh air, then I'm game."

When Michelson stood to collect his bowl and mug, Stella grabbed them along with hers. "Give me a minute."

She collected the sweet roll and a mug of coffee, then whispered to Cook, "Make sure there's a pot of coffee for me."

He gave her a wink, and, still smiling, she met Michelson at the stairs.

Jamie sighed when she handed him the sweet roll and mug of coffee. "I'm not sure we're going to be willing to let you go when the mission is done."

"As long as you only plan on sailing the English coast I might give it some thought."

He grinned. "I'm afraid that would be a problem."

"Well, I suppose it wasn't meant to be."

"You are a bold one, Lady Stella."

She followed Michelson as he strode to where a massive number of taut lines from sails and masts wrapped around a row of wooden pegs.

She leaned against the railing, grateful they were port side, otherwise she'd spend all her time focused on the cliffs, waiting for Beckworth to appear. Michelson had to be aware of that and was simply trying to keep her busy.

The tangle of lines wasn't as complicated as they appeared, but the terminology wasn't something easily grasped. She pointed to a set of lines. "So you use these lines to keep the sails taut so they can catch more wind to make the ship go faster?"

"If speed is what the captain wants then yes. But we can manipulate the sails to catch less wind if we need to slow, heave to, or prepare for a turn."

"Heave to?"

"Stop."

"Ah. I see. What if something happened and one of the lines broke?"

"That depends on which line and whether it was one or several. Typically, one or two wouldn't be a problem, but too many could be disastrous.

"How so?"

"If the ship caught a good wind and we lost a set of sails, the ship would turn without us expecting it. We could lose someone overboard or hit something if we were riding close to shore or another ship. If it happened during a storm, and the ship caught a rogue wave at the same time, we could capsize."

Stella paled. "I see."

Michelson must have noticed because he tried to backtrack. "I shouldn't have said any of that. It would be a rare occasion to be sure and could never happen on the *Daphne*."

She tilted her head. The poor guy thought he'd upset her. He did, but it hadn't been his fault. She hadn't needed the finer details, but she had asked. "So tell me why it wouldn't happen on the *Daphne*?"

He took a breath and focused on her question. "Because caring for the rigging and the lines is one of Captain Jamie's primary tasks for the crew. I mean, he has several, but everyone knows to look at the lines for signs of chafe whenever we work them. And they're always part of regular maintenance."

She chuckled, feeling better, but wondered what would happen if a cannonball hit the rigging. With her stellar memory, parts of Michelson's words would probably carry over into her dreams. Then she remembered something AJ had told her when she'd first met Finn. Every time she visited the ship, he was always carrying a bucket around, working on the ship.

"I'm guessing Jamie learned that from Finn."

Michelson nodded and smiled. "Captain Murphy was the finest captain. Captain Jamie is certainly following in his shoes. Of course, he has Lando and Fitz to help mold him."

She touched his arm. "He has the whole crew to help him. Loyalty is important."

Before Michelson could respond, a shout came from the other side of the ship.

"Prepare for sail."

They must be on their way back. She raced across the deck a step behind Michelson. Before they reached the railing, Michelson swung to his right and began climbing the shroud— one term she'd learned from Beckworth on their first Channel crossing. He must be going to his duty station, or whatever they called it.

She kept her trajectory for the railing with the best vantage point. Jamie strode down the deck, yelling orders. She leaned over the railing, assuming the jolly boat was alongside. It wasn't. She looked toward the beach, holding a hand over her eyes to shield them from the reflective glare of the morning sun on the water.

They were still quite a ways out. Even over the shouts of the crew, she heard the command to weigh anchor.

She didn't understand. Why wasn't he waiting for the boat?

It was torture watching the boat's slow progress as the three men rowed quickly against the tide. She glanced behind her and then up. The sails were slowly lifting.

The ship began to move, but instead of moving toward sea, it moved toward shore. She glanced over the railing, her focus going beyond the water in an attempt to gauge its depth. She couldn't see anything past its dark surface. That was probably for the best.

Then the ship stopped. Heaved to as Michelson had called it. Jamie had moved the ship closer so the men wouldn't have to row as far. And it had made a difference.

She could see Beckworth's face. His expression was focused. He didn't look back, and only occasionally glanced up. When she looked at Fitz and Lando, they were equally grim at their task. Suddenly, Jamie was next to her.

"I need you to stand farther forward. We need the men here to help with the lines."

"Of course." It took her a moment as she considered which way was forward, then took several steps toward the front of the ship until Jamie nodded for her to stop. She immediately returned her sight to the jolly boat that was coming alongside. Lando and Beckworth used the oars to keep the boat in place as Fitz stood. With the grace of a dancer, he caught the lines and anchored the jolly boat to the ship. One of the crew threw a rope ladder over the side.

Within minutes, all three men were onboard, and they turned to help the men lift the jolly boat onto the deck. Once the boat was tied down, Fitz turned to Jamie.

"The ship was preparing for sail, but they were still loading crates."

Jamie nodded and turned to Stella. "Get these men breakfast and tell Cook to get up here." Then he was off shouting orders again.

Stella grabbed Fitz's shirt when he started to follow Jamie. "You heard the order. Breakfast, then you can help."

She'd expected Lando to argue, but he took Fitz by the shoulder and turned him around. Fitz growled, but it seemed good-natured as he marched toward the door leading to the lower decks.

Stella put an arm around Beckworth's waist and gave him a swift kiss. His heart was still racing. "Fitz mentioned crates."

He nodded. "We'll give a full report once we're far enough away from the other ship. We can't be sure what's in them, but they appear the right size for flintlocks."

<hr>

Once the men were fed and rushed back up to help Jamie, Stella turned her focus to the galley. Cook didn't want to leave her with everything, but an order was an order. She was okay with that.

The more she stayed busy, the less she thought about the ship or being seasick. The herbs helped, but she was running low. She'd been taking more than necessary, but better safe than sorry was a motto she could agree with. And she didn't want to waste the motion sickness pills if she didn't have to. With any luck, there would be an apothecary at the next port.

She'd take half a pill later and conserve what herbs were left. Her concerns resolved for the moment, she rolled up her sleeves and got to work. She was comfortable in the galley, and it didn't take long to have dishes and pots cleaned and stowed.

She cleaned off the tables, swept the floor, and then scanned the area, searching for anything out of place or forgotten. Satisfied with a job well done, she considered putting coffee on for Jamie's meeting. Before she had a chance, Cook raced down the steps and pulled up short. He glanced around the room.

"You put me to shame," he said. "I don't think the galley has ever looked so clean."

She grinned. "I think you've been around the Irish too long with that silver tongue."

"I was just coming down to start the coffee and prepare something for the meeting. Jamie says he'll be ready in an hour. Then I'll need to start preparing something more substantial for lunch."

"I was just thinking about coffee."

He donned an apron that could use a good cleaning around his waist. "You should get some rest. You've been on your feet since you woke."

She was going to argue, but he was right, and it had little to do with how much she worked. The bed was calling her name. She wasn't used to getting up before dawn. "I'll agree as long as you don't argue when it's time to help with lunch."

He just waved her away, but she caught his grin. The closer she got to the cabin, the heavier her legs grew. With the earlier excitement and then the cleaning, the last bits of her adrenaline were fading.

When she opened the cabin door, she was surprised to find Beckworth on the bed. He was fully clothed, lying on his back with a pillow stuffed under his head and a book resting on his chest. He'd fallen asleep while reading.

She loved these moments when she could just look at him. He was such a handsome man, and sometimes she wanted to pinch herself whenever she was reminded how much he loved her and how much she loved him. She removed her shirt and pants but left on her undergarments.

She carefully removed the book and checked the title—*Tales of an Uneventful Voyage*—before laying it on the side table. No wonder he fell asleep. She crept onto the bed and lay next to him, her head resting on his shoulder. His steady breathing never changed, and for the first time since they'd left the cove, she noted the movements of the ship. The gentle rocking in combination with Beckworth's rhythmic heartbeat lulled her toward sleep.

"I love you, Teddy," slipped out as the world morphed into a dream.

Warm hands stroked her body. They started along her thighs and worked their way over her hips and belly, lightly squeezing a nipple before sliding back down again. A hard chest nestled along her back, and tender kisses touched her shoulder before sliding to her neck, creating heat in her lower belly as the hand roamed lower.

An eye popped open.

Small circles played on her hip, and she smiled.

Not dreaming after all.

She gave a soft moan, encouraging the man pressed against her. He nuzzled deeper into her neck.

"I love you, too." The soft circles on her hip turned into a light massage. "Even when you drive me mad with your antics."

Her laugh was a throaty chuckle as she rolled over, her breasts meeting his chest. His kiss was slow and tender. Like the mornings when they spent hours in bed—talking, making love, and planning the rest of their day.

Through the haze of growing passion, the slight lurch of the ship reminded her of where they were.

"Isn't Jamie calling for a meeting soon?"

"There's time." He rolled over, wrapping a leg around hers. His ministrations intensified until she melted under the touches and continuing strokes. "There's always time for us."

She ran her hands over his shoulders before scraping her nails down his back. This man put up with her stubbornness. Had sacrificed so much for her. At times was filled with such frustration she wondered why he stayed.

There were so many good times. Laughter and wonder. Each day full of discoveries—how he thought, what he found funny, his attempts at cooking, his favorite movies. Did he find her just as interesting?

His kiss wasn't as tender this time, and she hugged him tight, terrified to let go. He had to see how much she wanted to be his partner. Not someone he left behind. She made a personal commitment to show him how well they worked together.

Then he pushed his knee between her legs, and she arched her back, wrapping her legs around his waist. She stopped thinking and worrying. It was impossible with the thrumming of her body as it shut down her mind as emotions and sensations took control. They were one, and she held back her scream as her release came. Then his lips covered hers to smother her moans.

She held on, nipping at his chin, then his ear until his own pleasure ripped out of him. It took a moment before he moved, but he didn't go far. His arm lay over her, claiming her.

This was the best holiday getaway ever.

15

———————

Stella decided on the other plain day dress Beckworth had bought for her as he dressed beside her. They would have finished sooner but kept stopping to smooch, smiling and laughing as they leaned into each other when Beckworth lost his balance putting on his pants.

They would have still been in bed if Lando hadn't pounded on their cabin door announcing the meeting in fifteen minutes. She gave Beckworth a long perusal, then brushed back his hair, preferring his tangled locks, but it might give the men the wrong idea. Well, not wrong, but she didn't want the men passing him winks. Satisfied he looked presentable, even with his goofy grin, she turned for the door.

He pulled her back and gave her a long kiss, his hands running through her own tangles. She held on tight before he stepped back, leaving her with a matching grin. He tugged on her hair with a quizzical stare. She raced to the washstand and grabbed the brush. After a few strokes, she turned around.

"Better?"

"I preferred you before the brushing, but that's for my eyes only."

Her cheeks heated. The man could still make her blush. She strolled out when he opened the door but not before slapping his backside.

He chuckled, patting hers as she made her way to the galley.

The men were in various conversations around a table filled with a pitcher of ale, mugs, and a platter of cheese, meats, and bread.

Her stomach growled at the sight. She found an open seat next to Lando, and Beckworth sat between Fitz and Jamie. Michelson and Lane were also present, belaboring the benefits of mead over ale. Jamie listened patiently, a twitch to his lips as they continued their personal assertions. They were so involved in defending their positions that neither appeared to notice Stella and Beckworth arrive and jumped when Jamie landed a fist on the table.

"Now that everyone is here, Lando, tell us about your trip to shore."

"There were two ships in the cove, *The Horseman* and the *Tidewater*. We believe the men from the inn and pub were from this second ship, but it's only a guess. We arrived in time to spot a jolly boat as it came alongside *The Horseman*, but all we could see were long crates being hauled onboard. From our view, there didn't appear to be any markings on the crates. When Fitz spotted the other ship preparing for sale, we made a swift retreat."

Michelson laughed. "It's been a while since I've seen men paddle so quickly."

"I thought me arms were going to fall off." Fitz shook his head as he grabbed a hunk of cheese, two slices of meat, and bread, but he was grinning.

The men had a chuckle until the seriousness of the situation returned.

"Why two ships?" Stella asked. "Had they already taken cargo to the first ship?"

Jamie shook his head after setting down his mug. "The first one is more likely a decoy. When you're in a private cove, it can be dangerous sailing out without knowing what might be waiting for you. It's not typically done, but with the war and the increase in British patrols, it's more common."

She nodded. "So, they board the first one, don't find anything, and sail away. The second ship is safe."

"It doesn't always work," Beckworth added. "The patrols are becoming wise to that, but they also can't sit in front of the cove for days. If the first smuggler ship doesn't go far and waits for the second one to leave, they could outflank the patrol, which puts them at great risk."

Stella frowned. "A risky game indeed."

"So, where does that leave us?" Lane asked.

"We continue on with our mission," Jamie replied. "I'll send a message to Hensley at the next port with our speculations." When Fitz and Lando growled, he added, "We don't know enough to change the mission we've been given. As far as we know, they could be smuggling fine silks, laces, and china. We know our route. With any luck, Hensley's response will reach us at one of our next ports."

The men nodded, knowing Jamie's decision made sense, but Stella guessed they all wanted to pursue Cheval—even Beckworth. Jamie once told her he didn't work for Hensley, but since he agreed to the paid mission, he had to follow the plan regardless of his own feelings. If they weren't on an assignment, she had no doubt the discussion would have gone differently.

"We should make port by evening." Jamie stood. "That should give us time to run through the pubs. This is a larger port, so we'll probably need one more two-man team to ensure we cover them all."

"We should rotate the teams through the pubs every hour," Fitz suggested. "It will be less suspicious."

"Agreed." Jamie turned to Beckworth. "I believe Michelson explained the rigging to Stella this morning. Why don't you give her a full tour of the ship?" He smiled at Stella. "With Cheval out there, it's best you know the workings of the ship. I don't expect trouble, but I would feel better if you can find your way around if you need to help Michelson with injured sailors."

Beckworth started the tour of the ship by walking Stella around the top deck, explaining how the sails worked, when they used the anchor, and the lines used to moor the ship when docking. He'd been surprised when he stopped to explain the rigging, and she interrupted with what Michelson had taught her.

"So, you've already had a tour." Beckworth leaned against the railing, squinting at the coastline in the far distance, but it was too far away to distinguish anything without the glasses.

"No tour." She turned her head to see what he was looking at. She had a beautiful profile. A shapely nose, not small nor large, and a graceful neckline. "When you went off to check the cove, Michelson kept me occupied by explaining the lines and rigging. There are two types of rigging, right?" She turned to find him watching her. "What?"

He pulled her close but refrained from kissing her with the men around them. "Nothing. I just like looking at you." When she blushed, he grinned. He liked that he could still make her blush, considering how bold of a woman she was, her demure side was a rarity. "When would Jamie use a standing rigging?"

"Always. They're used to support the masts."

He nodded. "And the running rigging?"

"That's what Michelson showed me. They're used to control the sails."

"And, of course, you know about the crow's nest—AJ's favorite job."

She laughed. "It really is. It's the climbing and being up high where she can be alone with the wind and the sky. She learned to rock climb after her father died."

"His heart I believe."

She nodded, then shielded her eyes as she glanced up to the nest. "The climbing focused her. He'd been a mentor and a good friend in addition to being her father. It was a hard loss for her. But, as is her nature, she became obsessed with learning everything she could and now climbs several times a week." Her gaze fell on Beckworth with an impish grin. "From the way Finn tells it, she'd gotten a sparkle in her eye the first time she glanced up and saw the ladder. That's what you call it right? The ropes they use to climb up?"

"I think you have the basics." He tapped the tip of her nose. "You're getting too much sun. Let's explore the lower decks."

He kept a hand at her waist as he steered her below. Although she was familiar with the galley, he pointed out where the first aid station was located next to the pantry. "When you have time, you should probably review everything in here. From what I've been told, it usually holds sutures, bandages, and the like. But when Maire spent time onboard, she added a fresh selection of various herbs and tinctures. There should also be a few bottles of medicine that Bart supplies, mostly for pain and infections."

"I miss that old man. Does Jamie send someone out to his cabin in the woods and hope not to get shot?" There was humor in her question.

"Bart puts a package together every few months, and Lincoln delivers them to Hensley. Jamie picks them up whenever he's in Bristol." He led her to the navigation table where Jamie kept his maps neatly stowed except for two that were currently spread across the surface. Four small brass figurines of what looked like mermaids held down the corners. A compass, pencils, an hourglass, and a journal lay on the topmost map.

He explained how the charts worked, and Stella followed along for a while, but he could tell when her interest waned. It wasn't obvious. To most people, you'd assume she was still listening, but her fingers played at the edge of the map.

"I think that's enough of that." He clasped her fingers. "If I don't stop, Jamie will discover his charts have turned into giant swans."

"Sorry. I get the gist of it. This was another area AJ loved. It's interesting, but I'm afraid I'll never understand all the squiggles on the maps."

They were alone at the table, so he took the opportunity for a sweet kiss—gentle but with lots of promise. Her hand ran along his thigh, and he stepped back. A wicked smile crossed her face, but she moved past him and turned right down a hall.

He cleared his throat. "That's the way to the captain's cabin." He turned her left, past their cabin and the one next to it.

The lower deck contained cargo holds, extra stores for the galley, and the crew's quarters that included a network of hammocks. When they worked their way up to the top deck, he walked her past the line of guns.

She pulled away from him, set her fists on her hips, and narrowed her eyes. "We're not going to just walk through here without you explaining how the cannons work."

He sighed. She'd probably been waiting through the entire tour for this moment. He'd understood when two days after they met she'd demanded to learn about flintlocks. They'd been running for their lives, and she required a way to defend herself, especially if something happened to him. But guns were a different matter entirely.

He quirked a patient smile. "Is this just general curiosity, or do you imagine Jamie asking you to run down here in the middle of a sea battle to help the master gunner?"

She smirked. "General curiosity. AJ says it's pretty loud when they're fired."

It hadn't taken him long to learn that it was easier to satisfy her curiosity or else she'd nag him to death. Or, as he'd discovered on other occasions, rather than bargain or fight with him, she'd find someone else to answer her questions. That didn't always work in his favor.

"First, they're called guns, not cannons." He stepped next to the first one in the line of four port-side guns. "These appear to be what they call twelve-pound guns, which is the weight of the shot—or balls. The process is the same as loading a rifle—load the gunpowder, add the ball, tamp it down, add wadding, then add serpentine powder to the gunlock on top, which is nothing more than another term for a flintlock. Once they fire the gun, it will recoil backward—and if anyone is behind it, serious injuries can occur. They use the rope to run the gun forward when it's time to fire again."

"What's serpentine powder?"

"A finer grade of gunpowder. It ignites quickly." He nodded to a flask hanging on a nail in a post.

She nodded. "I understand. So, this is all like loading my flintlock times a hundred."

"Exactly." He took her arm and guided her out of the room and back toward the galley. "Shall we see if they left us anything for lunch?"

"Perhaps a picnic in our cabin?"

"Do you need to help in the galley?"

She shook her head. "I arranged to take care of dinner and clean up."

"Then a picnic it is." He stopped her in the hallway. "Whatever shall we do with the rest of our afternoon?"

She leaned in for a kiss then ran a hand up his thigh and squeezed his ass. "I have a thought or two."

<hr>

The next morning, Stella rolled over and ran a hand along Beckworth's chest. "Morning, Teddy."

He groaned but managed to grab her hand before it reached his lower extremities. "It can't be."

She raised up to an elbow and stared down at him. His eyes were closed, and she marveled at the length of his lashes. Something she'd never paid that much attention to. When his eyes were open, his sultry blue gaze always took her breath away.

It wasn't often she woke before him. He'd always been an early riser, even in Baywood.

"I told you not to drink any more whiskey. You shouldn't let Fitz encourage you."

He threw an arm across his forehead. "I think I have—what do you call it? A drunk over?"

She chuckled. "A hangover. And fortunately for you, I have something that might help." She shoved the covers off her, and without bothering to grab her robe, dug through her duffel and pulled out the first aid kit. "I blame it on Jamie and Lando for starting the game of hazards in the first place."

"It was a way to burn off our frustration. Four hours of pubs and inns and not a single sighting or mention of either MacDuff or Cheval." He pushed himself up and grabbed his head.

She pulled out a single tablet and poured a glass of water

from the pitcher. She handed him both before climbing back into bed.

"This should relieve your headache."

He stared at the pill.

She sighed. "It's just an aspirin."

"Bart usually crushed up his pills and put them in water."

"I'm afraid I left my pestle and mortar back in Baywood. Just put the pill on your tongue and swallow it down with water. All the grown men from my time do it."

He growled but did as he was told, and she shook her head. Men acting like children when they didn't feel well must have begun at the beginning of time.

She took the glass of water and set it on the table. "Now, what can Stella do to make it all better?" She climbed into bed and stroked his body until it went limp as his headache receded. "Just lay back and let the medicine work."

She massaged his arms and legs, but when her hands slid to his chest, he rolled her over against her protests. His gaze was heated, with no sign of his earlier pain. She didn't think it had anything to do with the medicine. She'd wanted to be the seducer, and she tried to push him off so she could get on top, but he pinned her down.

"Hush, woman. I've discovered a better cure for hangovers."

Her laughter was throaty, which only encouraged him. He was always a generous lover, and this time was no different. And when his thrusts increased, he smothered her screams with a heated kiss.

There was no question about it. This was turning out to be a fantastic holiday after all.

16

———

Stella stood back and scanned the galley as she wiped her hands on a towel. The breakfast dishes were done, the pantry restocked, and she'd left the makings for lunch and dinner on the counter for when Cook was ready.

Beckworth was supposed to take her shopping while in port. Instead, he'd gone off with Fitz for morning sleuthing while most of the sailors on other ships were sleeping off their night in the pubs or caring for ship tasks.

"If you continue to keep the galley spotless, I'm going to think of ways to permanently keep you aboard."

Stella turned and smiled at Jamie. "I believe we've had this discussion before. You know I'm only good if you stay close to shore."

He frowned. "Have you been getting seasick?"

"No. But I'm not sure I want to chance a trip to Ireland. I understand the sea between here and there can get stormy."

"Aye. It has its moments."

"Beckworth was going to take me shopping so I could get more herbs. Do you know how long he'll be gone?"

"If he was on his own, maybe a couple of hours, but with

Fitz along? It depends on what piques their interest. It could be a good portion of the day."

"You mentioned at breakfast that this was a safe port. Safe enough for me to take a stroll?"

"Yes, but I'm not willing to face Beckworth's wrath if he knew I let you go alone. Lando has spare time, and there are few items he could pick up for the ship."

She sighed. As much as she enjoyed her time in this century, her inability to go anywhere without someone trailing behind her grated. She had her dagger and her pistol, but apparently, they weren't enough, even in broad daylight.

She put on her best smile. "That would be lovely."

Jamie had watched her wrestle with his offer, and though his lips might have twitched, he nodded. "Lando's finishing up a repair. I'll let him know you'll be up when you're ready." He turned, but before he reached the stairs, she called out.

"Thank you, Jamie."

He looked back, and this time he did smile. "Try to stay out of trouble."

She winked, and he climbed the stairs, his chuckle floating back down to her.

She took her time, finally settling on one of the day dresses she'd brought from Waverly. Not too fancy, but a step or two up from the dresses she'd worn for the evening pub crawls. It should prevent most of the sailors from pestering her.

Eleanor had created larger pockets for the dress so she could carry her dagger in one and her pistol in the other. The pistol was heavy, and she considered leaving it behind since Lando would be with her, but she needed to get used to carrying it.

While she brushed out her hair and worked on pinning it up, she considered changing into her pants and shirt. Then she could carry her pistol in a holster under her jacket. Would she be safer dressed like that in port?

She decided to stay with the dress and would ask Lando once they were in town. He had a different way of looking at things, and he never sugar-coated his answers. Not that Beckworth or Jamie would lie, but they sometimes modified their answers in such a way that made the other person believe they were getting the answer they wanted to hear. She wasn't fooled, and she grinned as she turned, trying to get a better look in the small mirror. The men usually thought they won a verbal discussion with a woman, but they rarely did. It was fun to watch them try, though.

Lando waited at the gangplank, leaning against the railing and watching the people mill about the docks. He had a good view of a few pubs and two inns.

"Notice anyone suspicious?" She stepped next to him and took in the scene. They had arrived after dark the night before and this was the first time she'd seen the port during the day. This town was larger than the last one.

"Everyone."

She laughed. "That makes finding our targets more difficult."

"That's why it's better to listen rather than look."

"Wise words."

He leaned over. "Say that again when Fitz is around. He has a hard time remembering I'm smarter than him."

She chuckled again. "Have I kept you waiting long after pulling you away from your tasks?"

"No. The men know what they're doing and don't need me looking over their shoulders for minor repairs. Besides, there's no better way to view a port than aboard a ship." He stepped back and studied her. "I think for this walk around town, I'll act as your bodyguard. I'll stick close until you feel safe, then I'll stay a few steps behind."

She took his arm. "I would love a stroll with you by my side. I'll let you know when I need my space."

He snorted. "Beckworth must have his hands full with you."

"Be careful what you say. Before you know it, you'll have your own hands busy with a lovely lass."

Lando was true to his word, and they walked along the dockside merchants then strolled several blocks with more shops and fewer pubs. After an hour of viewing the various stores, he stopped in front of the apothecary.

"I need to see the blacksmith. I shouldn't be long. If you finish before me, you can walk around the mercantile next door."

After watching him cross the street, she glanced around and not seeing anything suspicious, stepped inside the store. She restocked her seasickness herbs, added something for headaches, then handed the list of first aid supplies Michelson had given her to the clerk. While she waited, she added a bag of dried lavender for their cabin.

Lando wasn't waiting for her outside, nor did she see him at the blacksmith. He must have gone inside. So, she turned for the mercantile. She didn't have anything else to buy, but it wouldn't hurt to take a walk-through. Maybe she could find something special for Beckworth.

Without thinking she turned right instead of left, shook her head at her mistake, then stopped when she looked through the shop window. It was a tobacco and cigar shop, but sitting on a side table was the most beautiful travel-sized chess set. She clutched her coin purse. Michelson had given her money for the first aid supplies, and Beckworth had left her money for the herbs but had given her extra in case she saw anything else she might want. And, of course, being the independent woman she was, had also brought her own coins.

For a reason he wouldn't explain, Barrington had saved a

small portion of the coins from Gemini's treasure chest. When Gemini had been killed during her hostile takeover of Waverly, Stella had made Barrington hide the miniature trunk so the magistrate wouldn't get his hands on it. The money was to be used to repair damages to the estate that had occurred during the swift battle to wrestle back the manor, provide bonuses to the staff, and then give the rest to charities.

Why Barrington had thought to save coins for her was a mystery. Yet, he must have expected her to return one day, and the thought still made her tear up.

She entered the shop and, after a short negotiation, took possession of the wrapped chess set with a huge smile. She'd taken a few steps out the door when she stopped. Maybe she should have bought Fitz some pipe tobacco.

She glanced across the street for Lando while turning to go back inside when she heard an "oomph" and felt a foot beneath hers. Her hand flew to her mouth, unsure whether to apologize or laugh. Then her gaze locked with warm amber eyes.

"Oh, god, I'm so sorry." She blinked, and when she noticed the man's hand on her elbow, she stepped back until he released her. He was a good-looking man in a roguish way, similar to Finn.

He gave her a long perusal, his grin wicked. "I seriously doubt God had anything to do with it." He had an accent similar to Finn and Jamie's, but not exactly.

For some reason, she thought Scot but had no idea why and shook it off.

She returned his grin. "I suppose not, but it was worth blaming it on someone else."

He laughed out loud, his head thrown back as if he hadn't heard anything so funny in days. She knew she had a humorous side but rarely said anything that funny. But this was a different era.

"You are a bold one."

Oh, boy. She had to remember to be more demure around strangers. She shrugged. "My mother always thought I was a bit odd."

He studied her. "You're not English."

"Neither are you."

He chuckled again. "True enough."

Suddenly, Lando was at her side. "Lady Swan, is everything alright here?"

Stella, more surprised by Lando's greeting than his popping out of thin air, juggled her packages while the man studied Lando. She thought she'd caught the errant packages, but when she felt the chess set slipping, she dropped the bag of herbs rather than take a chance on breaking the chessboard or any of its pieces.

Lando, quicker than the other man, bent over to pick up the package. Before he stood, a paper swan dropped to the ground. Stella caught the drop but couldn't remember giving Lando a swan. The man's eyes snapped to the swan but didn't say anything while Lando hurriedly stuffed it in his pocket.

She placed a hand on Lando's arm when he attempted to move her along. "It's alright. I'm afraid it was all my fault. I got turned around and ran into this nice gentleman." She turned to her new friend. "I'm sorry. My bodyguard tends to be rather overprotective."

"As he should be for such a beautiful woman." The man bowed his head to Lando. "These ports aren't safe for a woman on her own."

"We must go, my lady. The ship will be leaving soon." Lando extended an arm, which Stella took.

"You're traveling?" the man asked as he walked on the other side of her as Lando led them toward the docks.

She wasn't sure how to play this or why Lando was acting

like he was until she caught Fitz walking by. His back was to them, but she caught the quick side glance he'd given the trio before passing them. She looked at the man next to her, who didn't seem to notice Fitz since his gaze never seemed to have left her. Thank heavens Beckworth wasn't there. Would he be as congenial as Lando was being?

If Fitz was monitoring the situation, she shouldn't mention smuggling. She held back a snort. That would be like walking up to some shady-looking man in Baywood and asking them if they were a drug lord. But this man must be someone important. Why else would Lando have dropped the swan? Maybe he's Cheval or his first mate. There hadn't been any recognition in the man's eyes when Lando showed up. She gave the man a more studious appraisal, now curious what she might have stumbled into, and took a leap of faith. Maybe the man would find it puzzling why she'd taken so long to answer him.

"We're actually on a cargo run up the coast." The words were barely out of her mouth when Lando gave her elbow a light squeeze. Did that mean she said something wrong or something right? Or had he meant for the man to see it as if Lando had wanted to keep their cargo a secret? They really should have given her a playbook on what all the silent gestures meant.

"You have a ship?" MacDuff made it sound like he didn't care one way or another.

She laughed, using one of her more sultry ones, and knew she hit a cord when his gaze darkened with interest. "I believe that's the easiest way to transport cargo along the coast."

He laughed with her. "You are a delight."

When they reached the dock, she stopped Lando and gave the man her hand as she'd seen Dame Ellingsworth and Mary do at London parties.

"It was a pleasure speaking with you, but this is where we must part company." She fluttered her lashes. "I think you heard my name mentioned, but I never got yours. May I be so bold as to ask?"

"Aye, my lady. The name is Thaddeus MacDuff, at your service." He gave her a bow suitable for any London party while she took the moment to clamp down her accelerated heart rate.

"Perhaps we'll meet again, Mister MacDuff."

"As I have my own ship and also run cargo, we'll let fate steer our course." He kissed her hand, gave Lando a solemn nod, then strode away, whistling a song she didn't know but assumed was some sea shanty.

Lando led her toward the *Daphne*, taking his time so they didn't appear rushed. "That was perfect."

Her heart was still racing, and her legs were shaky. "A little warning would have been nice." Stella wanted to look back to see if MacDuff was watching them but didn't dare.

"Sorry about that, lass. Jamie and Fitz had seen MacDuff come out of the inn down the street. When you ran into him, it was a bit of a last-minute decision."

She tsked. "Not too last minute if you just happened to have one of my swans fall out of your pocket." They were setting her up for something.

"It was Jamie's idea."

"Why was he even off the ship?"

"He couldn't remember if he asked me to stop by the blacksmith."

Jamie and Fitz waited for them at the gangplank.

"I think we've just found our way in." Jamie's grin filled his face, and Fitz actually rubbed his hands together.

Stella was pretty sure he was already calculating his odds in a betting pool. What they would be betting on, she'd prefer not to know. She gave all three men a steadied gaze then shook her head.

"I'm not saying it's not a great idea. But have you spoken to Beckworth about it?"

"Are you all mad?" Beckworth paced as he blew off steam after Jamie explained what happened with MacDuff. "You will not put Stella in the middle of this reckless plan. What even possessed you to do such a thing?"

Stella placed a hand on his arm as he passed by her, but the act that usually calmed him had no effect. Instead, he gave her a hard glare and continued his pacing. How could she think he'd approve of such a plan, but then he caught the pointed look she gave Jamie. Maybe this had been his idea all along.

"None of this was planned." Jamie leaned back in his chair, and though his demeanor appeared calm, Beckworth wasn't convinced. "As I clearly stated when I went through it the first time. Instead of making more of it than it is, take a seat so we can discuss our options."

Beckworth stopped his pacing and leaned against a table. Jamie's tone might be calm, but he'd be a fool not to sense the heat that clearly simmered beneath the words. He didn't feel like sitting, but he stopped pacing and crossed his arms over his chest. "Go through it again."

Fitz took over, always happy to spin a tale. "I was coming back from the pub where we split up after searching for ships moored in the bay when I ran into Jamie. He'd been headed for the blacksmith, but on his way, he noticed MacDuff leave the inn and stroll by the shops without a care in the world. We decided to follow, you know, at a discreet distance, and see what he was up to. He was dressed like the gentry."

He took a swallow of ale and, after wiping his mouth,

nodded toward Lando. "We ran into the big man, who stopped by the blacksmith while Stella was shopping."

"And why was she alone in the first place?" Beckworth interrupted.

Stella rolled her eyes but let Lando explain.

"She agreed to stay at the apothecary or the mercantile next door." Lando stated it with no apology in his tone.

"And you expected her to do that?" Beckworth asked.

"Hey!" Stella gave him a sour look, and he instantly regretted his words. "This isn't my fault. I went to the tobacco shop next door and was just leaving it when I ran into a man. I had no idea who he was."

Beckworth ran a hand over his face. He stood, ready to resume pacing but dropped into a chair instead. "Apologies. Go on."

"The three of us were discussing options when I remembered the swan I've been carrying around." Jamie fished in his pocket and pulled out another one. He grinned at Beckworth. "I got the idea from you, mate."

"I can hardly wait to hear this," Beckworth grumbled.

"Weren't you the first one to leave a swan for Gemini's men to find in the cargo hold of the *Phoenix*? Then you left another one with the dead man who'd been snooping around Eleanor's."

Beckworth began to say something but thought better of it and grabbed a mug, filling it with ale. After a long drink, he slammed the mug down, sloshing some onto the table. He gave Jamie a side glance. "Go on."

"We have no intention of putting Stella in the middle of anything. But have a think on this. What would MacDuff do if there was another smuggler out there? Someone with a ship and perhaps no loyalty to England."

Beckworth considered Jamie's reasoning. It was a decent question, but then another thought spoiled the moment. He stared Jamie down. "You thought of this possibility the first time Stella began sweet-talking you into a role in this mission."

Jamie shrugged with no remorse. "How many women do you have working in your crew?"

"That's different." Beckworth wasn't ready to back down, though he felt the noose tightening.

"Because you have a personal relationship with her?" Jamie remained calm and didn't once look at Stella.

"Because she doesn't have the training or experience of someone like Libby, if that's where you're going with this."

"Fair enough. But you have to admit, she handled herself quite well during her ordeal with Gemini. She's quick of wit, remains calm under tense situations, and has skills that set her apart from the rest of us."

When Beckworth lifted an eye, Jamie laughed. "She knows how to manipulate a man."

"Hey!" Stella sat up. "I'm sitting right here, you know."

Jamie lifted a hand. "Only when required."

She rolled her eyes and crossed her arms over her chest as she leaned back. Beckworth almost laughed. She wasn't satisfied with Jamie's response, but she couldn't refute the statement.

"Enough of this. What's done is done, and—" Stella gave Beckworth an irritated scowl. "Nothing happened and nothing more needs to be done if that's what we decide—as a team." She turned to Fitz. "You said you were looking for ships moored in the bay. Did you find any?"

She glanced at Beckworth, and though he was still upset, there wasn't anything he could do at the moment. Their mission was to find MacDuff and advise Hensley of his direction, not chase him or trade with him. But he was grateful for the change in topic. He'd have words with Stella later.

Fitz, who'd been watching the exchange with amusement, straightened. "We thought we might find *The Horseman* out there since this has been a safe haven for smugglers—though we know how quickly that can change. Anyway, the ship is here, moored down by the spit."

"There's a second ship anchored near it, but we weren't able to get close enough to see the name," Beckworth offered. "But we'll recognize her the next time we see her."

"Do you think Cheval is working with MacDuff?" Jamie asked.

Fitz shrugged. "Hard to tell. It's not the *Tidewater* that played decoy in the cove. In fact, we haven't seen her at all. Not at the port and not moored in the bay."

"Interesting," Lando said.

"Did the blacksmith have anything to report?" Jamie asked.

Beckworth lifted a brow. Jamie had a spy in port. He must have several along the coast. Smart man.

"He hadn't spotted MacDuff but confirmed smuggling activities had increased in the last few months," Lando reported.

"If he hadn't seen MacDuff, then he must have just arrived." Stella sat up, her fingers fidgeting between gripping her mug and playing with the sleeves of her dress. She hadn't thought to bring her paper.

Jamie nodded. "Chances are he'll spend at least one night at port. We'll use the same routine as the last port. Let's see if we can find out more about MacDuff—name of his ship, his next port, if possible, and any other tidbits that might be helpful."

"Maybe we'll see him with Cheval," Stella suggested.

"With any luck."

"I'm still not happy about this." Beckworth frowned as he studied his mug. "But at this point, I'm not sure it's in our best interest for Stella to be seen with me. At least, not yet."

"Aye." Jamie rubbed his chin. "The fewer people he sees from the *Daphne*, the better. Let's mix up the teams. Since he's already seen Lando, it's best he go with Stella to an inn. There won't be a question of her seeking dinner off the ship. Lane can go with Fitz, and Michelson with Beckworth. I'll remain on the ship."

He glanced at Beckworth. "Is that safe enough for you?"

Beckworth glanced at Stella. He'd prefer she stayed on board until they left port, but he could already imagine the list she'd give him of why she should participate. And other than being terrified by how far she could be dragged into this, going to the inn wasn't an unreasonable request. His gaze shifted to Lando, who smiled.

"Don't worry, little man. I'll watch over her."

17

———

Stella added finishing touches to her hair with Beckworth's reluctant help.

"How is it you always seem to be in the wrong place at the wrong time?" He used the last hairpin then pulled out a lock so it curled about her face. He kissed her temple.

"Some might say it's the right place at the right time." She gave his cheek a pinch and smiled. He had dressed in his travel pants and jacket, which looked a bit worn for wear. They needed a decent cleaning, but he preferred to keep one set of clothes appearing unkempt for his surveillance. The easier to blend with the masses.

"You're way too daring for my comfort." He retrieved two of the growing flock of swans she'd set on the side table and stuffed them in his jacket pocket.

"Why are you taking swans if you don't like Jamie's plan?"

He checked his pistol and counted the gunpowder cartridges. "I didn't say I didn't like his plan. Jamie was correct that I started this business with the swans. I just didn't think they'd go any farther than Gemini."

She stepped up behind him and ran her hands over his

shoulders then down his arms before wrapping hers around his middle, resting her head against his back. "This is just surveillance. Assuming MacDuff even shows up at the inn, Lando will get to see who he's hanging out with. He already had lunch there. It's more likely he'll go to the pubs if he leaves his ship at all."

He turned around and held her against him, letting his chin rest on top of her head. "If all else fails, Lord Swan will come to your rescue."

She chuckled. "It is somewhat exciting. Like going undercover with an alias. What would AJ think?"

"She'd either think you mad or, much to Finn's dismay, want to go with you."

She stepped back and patted her hair. She appreciated Beckworth's help but missed Libby's assistance—especially with her hair. There were enough pins in it now; a storm at sea wouldn't be enough to disturb it. "You're not wrong." She snapped her fingers. "I forgot to ask. Did Hensley send a return message?"

He shook his head. "If he did, it will be waiting at the next port. Jamie will send another one before we leave."

"And when will that be?"

"It was supposed to be tomorrow, but it will depend on whether we can determine which ship MacDuff is on. We'll follow a few hours after he departs."

"How will we know where he goes?"

"We won't. Not for certain. Jamie will still go to the next port to check for Hensley's message. It's better to trail MacDuff than for him to fall behind us."

"That makes sense. Lando and I are to stay at the inn as long as we can without appearing suspicious. Are you and the other men making the same one-hour rounds?"

"Yes. Unless we spot either MacDuff or Cheval. Then one of

us will follow them at a safe distance. If they go into another pub, we'll regroup. At this point, we're just hoping MacDuff is still in port and can lead us back to his ship."

"He might have been picking up last-minute supplies before leaving."

"Possible. And if he's gone, there might be men more willing to talk about him or his ship."

Stella glanced around for her coin purse and tucked it into the same pocket as her dagger. With her pistol in the other pocket, her skirt weighed heavily on her left side, but she was unwilling to leave without it. She might be with Lando, but Beckworth preferred her armed while in port, and she saw no reason to disagree.

"Do you have your pistol?" Beckworth asked.

"Yes." They'd been working on her dagger skills at least once a day since boarding the *Daphne* in Bristol. The flintlock pistol wasn't a problem, but her dagger skills had become rusty while in Baywood. "The dagger feels more natural than it had leaving Bristol, but I'd like to increase my training. Would it be possible to include one of the other men going forward?"

He opened the cabin door and waited for her to exit. "Now that you're more involved in the operation, I agree. There's a nice spot near the forecastle that should keep us out of the way while we're under sail. We might have an opportunity for a session before we leave port. I'll discuss it with Jamie."

She waited for him to close the door behind them, then turned into him for a kiss. "For luck."

Beckworth and Michelson found a table at the back of the pub. It was one of the better pubs in town. The food tastier, the ale fresher, and the whiskey more palatable. The crowd was mostly sailors, but he spotted several locals in the group, easily standing out from the others.

He sat with his back partially facing the door. He wouldn't be able to spot MacDuff since he'd never seen him. They both listened to the conversations around them, but Michelson was also monitoring faces while Beckworth focused on the more subtle nuances in the crowd. The loners and those who spoke in hushed groups, their eyes constantly scanning the room.

When their hour to observe before moving to another pub was almost up, he refocused on a group that had arrived twenty minutes earlier. Three men huddled at a table too far away to hear their discussion. They drank ale with little talking, but being sailors, it wasn't an uncommon sight. If they were from the same ship, they might just want the company without the chatter. No harm in that. But he kept an eye on them as he and Michelson listened to closer conversations that told them nothing.

A woman with gray running through her hair dropped two fresh ales on their table and removed their plates. She'd barely rushed off when a man walked through the crowd and joined the table Beckworth had been watching. Cheval. He glanced at Michelson, who gave a slight nod before sampling the new mug.

Beckworth wanted to get closer, but there wasn't a way to do that without appearing suspicious. They had to remain unnoticed by the men at the table, so they kept their heads down and focused on their ale. With an occasional side glance, the talk at the table had notably increased as they drank, ate, and laughed.

Earlier that day, when he'd been with Fitz searching for any ship that might be MacDuff's, they'd only found one suspicious ship moored close to the mouth of the bay. Though the ship was anchored and their sails lowered, Fitz said the ship appeared ready to leave as soon as word was given. Beckworth couldn't see any major repairs being done, and the men remained at their stations performing small tasks like checking the lines and cleaning the deck. Even he could tell they weren't in port for long.

While he was considering options on how to get closer to that ship, Michelson nudged his boot. He took another drink of ale as he turned around. A man dressed in finer clothes than anyone in the pub—and possibly the entire village—strode directly to Cheval's table.

Beckworth lowered his head when he set the mug down and bent over it. Michelson had been keeping his head down, only lifting it—as a scattering of others did—when someone new entered.

The man shook hands with Cheval, and that's when he noticed a second man. A bodyguard? Two of the men who'd been at the table earlier stood and shoved two men from a nearby table out of their chairs, giving them to the two men who'd just arrived. One look at the growing group of men and the two who'd lost their seats grabbed their mugs and hustled to the bar.

"That's MacDuff." Michelson kept his voice low, and Beckworth strained to hear him over the crowd.

He'd expected that as soon as the man had walked through the door. His suspicion only grew when he'd shaken hands with Cheval.

Interesting.

"Finish your ale," Beckworth said. "Then find a place outside where you can watch the door and the docks. I'll follow along in a few minutes to find Fitz."

Michelson took his time with the ale, then quietly left the table at the same time as two other men. The only man at MacDuff's table who took notice was the man who'd followed MacDuff. His muscle. Beckworth waited until the gray-haired woman stopped at Cheval's table with a new pitcher of ale and more mugs before using the distraction to leave. He kept his head down and added a slight limp to his walk.

He never looked back as he exited the pub. The inn where Stella and Lando were keeping watch was to his left. Fitz was going to take the pub on the far side of the inn, but it had been an hour and if no one of interest had showed up, the first mate would have moved to another pub.

Then he spotted Michelson leaning against a post off to his left, a mug in his hand. He lifted his head long enough to shake his head. That confirmed his earlier thoughts. Michelson had already checked, and Fitz wasn't in the pub anymore.

Beckworth, keeping his limp, turned right and staggered toward the two pubs at the end of the pier. He'd taken several steps across an alley when he was pulled aside. Before he could struggle, he heard the first mate's whisper.

"Jamie has an assignment for us. Keep your stagger and limp and follow me."

Beckworth watched Fitz as he moved out into the street with a slow walk, occasionally listing to one side. He shook his head and followed. He had a good guess what the assignment would be.

Stella sat back, rubbing her stomach. "The fish isn't sitting well." She pulled out a hard-sided coin purse she'd brought from Baywood, which was different than the coin pouches used in this century. Instead of coins, she used it as a mini first aid kit.

She carried motion sickness pills, a small amount of ginger, and several tablets of an antacid. After glancing around and not seeing anyone paying attention to her, she slipped an antacid under her tongue.

"I told you to stick with the chicken." Lando filled their mugs with ale and shoved one toward her. "This will settle your stomach faster than whatever you just took."

"It never hurts to double down on this type of thing." She glanced around again. "I hope the others are having better luck than us. Most of these people don't look like sailors to me." Her belly gurgled, but with the current noise level, she doubted Lando heard it. If he did, he was gentleman enough not to mention it.

"If MacDuff is still in port, even if he isn't meeting anyone, he's likely to come for dinner. Most get tired of the same fare available onboard. Some will even eat the fish."

"Funny." But she gave him a wink. She took another sip of ale, not expecting the burp that came afterward. The combination of ale and antacid worked well. Good to know.

They went silent, each in their own thoughts, though Lando never stopped scanning the room. Based on other couples she'd seen her first time in this century, a man and a woman eating at an inn rarely spoke. She quietly snorted. Sometimes not all that different in her time period.

"How much longer should we stay?" Stella asked. "We're going to start looking strange if we just sit here."

"Give it another fifteen minutes. Time to finish our ale."

"Can we try one of the pubs?"

He shook his head. "You know better than to ask."

She sighed. Next time she'd dress in pants and shirt and wear a hat. Not that she had one, but she'd seen a few at the mercantile. Before she had time to think on it further, Michelson entered the inn. He glanced around as if looking for someone and walked their way, then dropped something on the floor by their table.

He bent down until he was eye level with them. "Jamie wants everyone back to the ship. No delay." He picked up whatever he dropped, then surveyed the room and with a light shrug left the inn.

If Lando was surprised by the order, he didn't show it.

"What do you think that means?" Stella whispered.

"Don't know. Finish your ale and let's find out."

When they reached the galley, everyone from their evening surveillance was there except Beckworth and Fitz. Her stomach gurgled, but she didn't think it was from the fish.

She sat and didn't bother waiting for Jamie to start the meeting. "Where's Beckworth?"

Jamie appeared to be writing a letter. He dipped the quill but paused to look at her. "That's why I called everyone back. Give me a moment and we'll begin." He wrote for another ten long minutes. When he was finished, he sprinkled blotting sand over it then set it aside. He leaned back and took a sip of whiskey. "I wanted to finish this letter to Hensley. I'll be sending a rider in the morning."

"It must be important if you're sending someone rather than using our normal system." Lando didn't appear concerned, but she didn't understand how their typical communication route worked. But if they were changing it up, something important must have happened.

"Beckworth and Fitz might not return for a while, so I'll tell you what I know, which isn't much." Jamie must know enough to send a message to Hensley with a rider, but Stella kept her mouth shut and waited for him to continue.

"Cheval showed up at the pub Beckworth and Michelson were monitoring."

"They were too far away for us to hear anything," Michelson added. "At first, it appeared to be nothing more than a night of drinking, eating, and telling stories, based on their laughter. We were considering leaving when someone else joined their table." He waited until everyone focused on him, and Stella laid a hand over her stomach.

"MacDuff and a bodyguard."

No one spoke. They simply stared around the table at each other as if trying to make sense out of it. Clearly, they hadn't expected MacDuff to join the party. But to her, it only meant one thing, and being new to this, decided to just ask.

"You mean they're working together?"

"That's what we need to find out." Jamie finished off his whiskey and pushed the glass away.

Boots running down the stairs made them all turn. Fitz strutted in, and Stella held her breath until Beckworth trailed in a minute later. He looked tired, and when his gaze landed on hers, she knew they had trouble.

"Where were you?" she asked Fitz, but her focus was on Beckworth as he joined them at the table.

Fitz poured a whiskey for himself and one for Beckworth. "Lane and I worked our way through three pubs, but it wasn't until we left to double back and start over that I caught sight of two men leaving a jolly boat. A third man remained behind with the boat. We managed to step into an alley and watch them. Once they got close to the pubs, it didn't take long to recognize MacDuff."

Lane, who rarely spoke, couldn't seem to hold back. "When

we noticed the pub they entered was where Beckworth and Michelson were, we thought it best to notify Jamie."

Fitz nodded. "So, I sent Lane back to report while I waited in case Beckworth and Michelson moved to another pub. Lane made it back to tell me Jamie was lowering a boat. That's when Michelson came out alone. I waited, expecting Beckworth to come find me."

"I almost stabbed you with a dagger when you pulled me into the alley." Beckworth swallowed the whiskey and grimaced as it went down.

"What made you stop?" Fitz asked.

Beckworth grinned. "That sweet scent from your pipe. It could have been anybody, but I decided it best to confirm."

Fitz chuckled and rubbed his belly. "I appreciate your caution." He glanced around. "Did Cook leave anything to eat?"

Stella immediately stood. "There should be some cheese and bread handy." She didn't want to miss the conversation but needed time to pull her rollercoaster emotions together. Excitement, fear, and worry for Beckworth made her stomach upset again. Maybe some bread would settle it. She didn't have to go far to find something. Cook kept a spot in the front of the pantry where he kept cheese, rolls, dried meat, and fruit—when they had it—in case someone needed a quick meal. She was surprised to find a handful of meat pies left over so she grabbed those too.

With no one else in the galley, it was easy to listen as the men continued their discussion.

"We rowed the jolly boat out to the ship moored at the mouth of the bay," Beckworth started.

Then Fitz took over. "We needed the name, but it wasn't easy. We counted three watchmen, but no one sounded an alarm."

"They probably assumed if anyone was interested they'd

come directly from the docks." Beckworth rolled his shoulder. "I can't remember a time I rowed so much in two days."

"We decided to approach straight out of the bay from the *Daphne*, then turn to come in from behind the ship." Fitz chuckled. "Any closer to the sea and we might have gotten sucked out with the tide."

Stella shivered at the thought as she set a platter on the table. "Does anyone want coffee?"

They all shook their heads, so she returned to her seat and smiled. The scene reminded her of being in Baywood with everyone sitting around the kitchen table at the inn, working out their troubles over the Mórdha stones. Before she'd been kidnapped, she never had anything to add to the topic, though she listened and asked the occasional question. For some reason, perhaps because she had nothing to contribute, she needed something to keep her busy, especially hearing the precarious situations AJ found herself in. So, she became the hostess in their home. It appeared she was picking up her old habits aboard the *Daphne*.

"We took down names of other ships moored in the bay, but none were familiar to us," Beckworth continued since Fitz was eating. "We rowed back toward the *Daphne* and waited to see if MacDuff's boat would return to one of the ships. We didn't wait long. As we suspected, a boat with three men rowed out to the ship."

"So, we have the name of the ship?" Jamie pulled the letter he'd written closer and opened the inkpot.

"The *Grey Ghost*."

"Apropos," Lando grunted.

Jamie scratched out a few words. "What was your impression? Was the meeting of the two men coincidental or planned?"

Beckworth glanced at Michelson. "No question in my mind

it was planned. MacDuff walked in and barely scanned the room before walking straight to Cheval."

"I agree." Michelson picked at a biscuit. "If it was by chance, I don't think he would have done anything more than nod or perhaps stop to give their regards before going to their own table. The men at the table seemed to have expected them."

Beckworth nodded when Jamie looked at him.

"This complicates our mission." Lando frowned and stood but didn't go far, deciding to sit on the edge of a table.

Jamie sat back, nursing his whiskey. He flicked a finger at the letter he'd written. "I have Simmons riding to Waverly in the morning. But even if Barrington sends the manor's fastest horse, it will be several days before we get a response. We can consider our options, but until we hear back from Hensley, we stick with our mission. We'll stay in port long enough to see which direction MacDuff goes, then we'll head for Gowerton."

"Even if MacDuff turns south? Or what if he sails for Ireland?" Stella asked.

"Ireland is always an option, but I think he'll stick to the English coast unless British patrols come up this way. Gowerton is where we expect Hensley's first response, and it's where we'll wait for the next one. As long as we know which direction MacDuff sailed, we'll find him."

***

Stella rolled over as the first scent of coffee tickled her nose. She opened an eye, blinked to refocus, then smiled at the scene. Beckworth sat at the table studying a chart. A pot of coffee was on the table along with a plate of biscuits and jam. He dipped a quill and made notes on a sheet of paper, pausing to sip coffee before returning his attention to the map.

Curiosity poked at her, but she pushed it away, preferring to watch him. After Jamie's decision to continue on to Gowerton, she'd returned to the cabin with Beckworth where they'd fallen into bed exhausted from the day's events. He'd kissed her and spooned her, and she'd felt the tension roll off him. It might have been that he was tired. It might have been the rapidly changing mission he had no control over. But at the heart of it, he was most likely irritated that she'd come along. Maybe irritated wasn't the best word, though she'd understand if it was part of it.

This was supposed to be surveillance, but it was becoming increasingly something more.

He was worried about her. It was why he hadn't wanted her to come in the first place, and just as AJ had predicted, Beckworth was becoming the viscount. His need to protect her was mounting.

And she had no idea how to deal with that.

If Eleanor or Dame Ellingsworth were there, she'd have someone to talk to about it. They'd both known him for years. Understood how he thought and would have advice. Mary would tell her to behave more like this century's woman and stay out of the men's business, preferring her gentle manipulations.

She snorted. There was no way she was going to remove herself from the mission. Not at this point. Everyone knew she wasn't one for subtlety, but she'd admit there were times when it was necessary. This moment didn't call so much for nuance as it did for distraction. It wouldn't last for long, but she'd take what she could get.

She watched him for several more minutes—how he held the quill, his brow furrowed as he traced a finger over the map, and the three taps of the quill on the inkpot before writing. Not two taps and not four. Always three. She'd have to try that.

Was he searching the map for something or trying to determine the smugglers' next move? When the need for coffee outweighed her desire to watch him, she moaned and stretched, giving him time to come out of his work.

What mood would he be in?

Beckworth turned with a smile on his face. That was promising. "Morning. The coffee is still warm, but I can get it refreshed." He closed the inkpot. "You looked too peaceful to wake."

She sat up, her breasts peeking over the covers as she pushed her hair back and rubbed her eyes. His eyes warmed. "Did I hear you leave earlier this morning?"

He nodded. "I couldn't sleep and heard the crew busy on deck. I thought Jamie might be leaving port, and I wanted to send a message to Barrington before Simmons rode for Waverly."

Stella tilted her head. The ship wasn't rolling like it usually did at sea. "We're still docked."

"Yes. But we'll be leaving in the next couple of hours."

"MacDuff left?"

"About an hour ago, but not before receiving a shipment from Cheval."

She crawled out of bed, and as much as she'd love to parade around nude to entice him, it was too damn cold. She pulled on her undergarments and her pants and shirt as she asked, "How do you know? Did Jamie see the handoff?"

"Fitz and Lando rowed to a point on our side of the bay before dawn."

"Were they supposed to sit there all day?"

He chuckled as he poured her coffee. "You know how Fitz gets, what do you call it, a sixth sense about these things. I have to admit, the thought had occurred to me as well. The two men could have met for any number of reasons, assuming their meeting last night wasn't by accident."

"Or they could have been meeting to transfer cargo. But why take the chance in port and not do it someplace less noticeable?"

He shrugged and gave her a kiss before handing her the mug. "There's no British patrol. And the cargo could be nothing more than restocking their stores, satisfying a previous agreement to trade supplies, or one of them lost a bet in a game of hazards."

"So how do we know what's in the crates?"

"We won't know without opening them, but according to Fitz and Lando, the crates are the same size and shape as what Cheval pulled out of the cave."

"Enough to be suspicious." She stared at the chart. "What have you been doing?" She pulled the sheet of paper closer. Names of ports?

"Jamie has an idea of where MacDuff might go next. He wanted me to have a look."

The names meant nothing to her. "Are these towns along the coast?"

"A few. Some are names given to coves or points. Any place where smugglers can store goods."

She spread jam on a biscuit and nibbled it as she reviewed the chart. Jamie had told her the charts and lines reflected shorelines, longitude and latitude, and ocean features to help sailors plot their routes. She could follow a road atlas but, like most people, depended on her GPS. So, she ignored the lines and focused on the symbols that reflected ports along the coast.

She'd been so focused matching the names on the sheet of paper with points on the map that she hadn't heard Beckworth moving about the cabin. She jumped when he placed a wrapped package on the table.

"Did you get this in town?"

She swallowed the last bite of biscuit too quickly and washed it down with coffee before she choked. "Oh my god. I forgot all about this with all the MacDuff excitement." She patted the chair next to her. "Sit and open it."

He gave the package a suspicious look but after a moment, he sat and gave her a side glance before searching for the best place to start unwrapping. He settled on ripping the paper from a corner. Once the paper was torn off, he tossed it to the floor.

He stared at the chess set. Without saying a word, he opened it and ran a finger over the pieces. He picked up the carved ebony queen and rubbed it between his fingers—his face a perfect mask. It wasn't the first time she'd seen the expression and knew it was his way of hiding his emotions. And he was excellent at not providing any indication of what was running through his head.

"What's this?"

She snorted. She couldn't help it. He was so serious. Especially when the object was self-explanatory. But that wasn't his question. He wanted to know why. Silly man.

"There's only so much reading, walking the deck, or cleaning the galley that can be done when sailing between ports. I thought this would be a nice change."

"This is for us?"

"Who else?"

"I thought perhaps a gift."

"It is. For you."

She stood and took the queen he was still holding, placing it back inside the chessboard. She tugged on him until he stood, and she began removing his jacket.

"I need to get my letter to Simmons."

She sighed and let go of his jacket but not before rubbing up against him.

His kiss was swift and possessive. He didn't want to go, but his task was important, so she stepped back.

He picked up his letter, glanced at the chess set, then gave a last look at her before opening the door.

She grinned at him. "Don't be long." She tilted her head. "Have you ever heard of strip chess?"

18

―――――

Stella, dressed in pants and shirt, her hair rustling with the soft coastal breeze, sat on a barrel on the starboard side of the ship, watching the portion of the dock visible to her. Her fingers worked rapidly on creating another swan. Six of them had been tucked into a partially enclosed gap in the railing, but they still fluttered with the breeze as if wanting to take flight.

The sail to Gowerton had been uneventful, and she was proud that she'd discovered the best formula of herbs to balance her equilibrium, keeping her motion sickness at bay. Her time was spent helping Cook in the galley, walking the deck as she watched the men at their work, sometimes asking a question if they were chatty, and alone time with Beckworth, playing chess in bed.

They'd bought a beautiful chess set in Baywood and kept it near the window in the living room, giving them time to enjoy the neighborhood while waiting for the other person to make a move. She would need to buy a smaller set for the bedroom and their lazy Sunday mornings.

They'd been in port for two days, waiting on word from Hensley. She'd spent the first day taking walks around town, adjusting to being on land again. The port wasn't as large as the last port, which meant fewer shops and activities to occupy her time. Beckworth and Lando spent most of their days running surveillance at the pubs and inns while also monitoring the ships that came and went.

Jamie, making sure she remained occupied, asked her to help with the inventory records until he discovered a minor problem.

"You can't write?"

"I can, but I'm not used to working with a quill. I managed to complete the invitations for the hunting party." She glanced at the floor and bit her lower lip. She sighed as she admitted, "It required several attempts and wasted several pieces of paper. Barrington hid the wasted attempts from the staff."

He laughed. "Is it so different in your time?"

"First, we don't use inkpots anymore." She picked up the quill lying on his desk. "Though I do find the idea of using a feather as a writing instrument quite inspirational."

He pushed a piece of paper over. "Sit and write." He waved a hand. "It doesn't have to make sense, but the only way you'll improve is with consistent writing."

"You sound like Barrington."

"A wise man."

She sat and pulled the paper to her, then glanced up. "I probably should have asked first. Would you prefer I take this to the galley?"

"No, stay here." He stood and put on his jacket. "It's time to go up and see what the men are up to." Before he left, he said, "You know he worries for you."

She laid down the quill and turned to face him. His brows had scrunched with his own worry, maybe for her, but thought it was more for Beckworth. The two had developed a lasting friendship after some difficult times when Beckworth worked for the duke. Her first instinct was to make light of the concern, but their simple surveillance mission was turning into something more. How much more they wouldn't know until Hensley's message arrived. Perhaps his request would be to simply watch and monitor. Yet, her gut said it wouldn't be that easy.

"I know he struggles at times with how to deal with me." She picked up the quill again. "But it's a two-way street." When Jamie's brow rose, she chuckled. "A modern-day term, meaning I grapple with the same thing. In this day and age, women worry for their men when they leave for war or—" she smiled, "—to sail the seas. But they've been taught their place is to care for their home and children. All they can do is hope for the occasional letter, but they don't stop worrying until their husband walks through the door.

"I suppose in some ways it's still the same in my time. Men leave for work or military duty. The difference is that in my time, women also leave for work or join the military, and the men are left behind to worry." She shrugged, noted the quill in her hand, and ran her fingers over the sturdy feathers. "I guess all of that is to say the two of us need to find a balance. Neither of us will stop worrying about the other. So, we have to find the strength to let the other do what's important to them and then do the best we can to support their endeavors, either through action or with patience." She laughed. "And that's as much philosophy as I can spare for one day."

Jamie considered her words. "You're a complex woman, Lady Caldway."

She turned back to her task. "You don't know the half of it, but I'll take that as a compliment."

She'd written two pages of nonsense, discovering she'd remembered everything from composing the invitations. Beckworth's three taps of the quill had been a perfect discovery. Why hadn't Barrington mentioned it? Before she knew it, she was copying the inventory Jamie had identified from his ledger to a separate piece of paper. She assumed it was some form of checklist. When she added the last item to the page, she closed the inkpot, dried off the tip of the quill, then left the page to dry on its own.

It was at that moment that she realized she knew next to nothing about how the cargo business operated. Or smuggling for that matter. If they were dealing with smugglers, she had to understand how everything worked.

On a mission to learn, she went topside, but Jamie and Fitz were busy and Beckworth and Lando hadn't returned. She considered Michelson or Lane but decided she could wait. The day was warm for winter and the sun had made an unexpected appearance.

With nothing else to do, she'd returned to the cabin to grab a few sheets of paper and ended up where she currently sat, making another swan as she watched the docks and a nearby ship as the crew prepared it for sail.

A whistle made her glance up. One of the sailors waved at Fitz, who was working with two others to mend a sail. Fitz laid his portion of the sail down and called for another to resume the repair. He met a man running up the gangplank who handed him a letter.

It had to be the message they were waiting for. When they'd first arrived in port, the first response from Hensley had been waiting with only two words—keep monitoring. From what Beckworth told her, it wasn't surprising since the only thing they'd been able to tell Hensley was that they'd run across Cheval.

Since Jamie's last letter to Hensley had explained that the two smugglers seemed to be in partnership and they'd witnessed the movement of unknown cargo between them, this letter was sure to say more. She was sure of it. The question was whether the order would be to continue monitoring or get more involved.

Excitement tingled through her as she folded the last couple sheets of paper in half, gathered her swans, and stuffed everything in her pocket before making a beeline for the gangplank where several men had gathered. They were waiting for Jamie, who slowly made his way toward them, stopping to check the repair of the sail before arriving to shoo the men away.

"Let's get back to work, gentlemen." Jamie took the letter from Fitz. "Everyone will know if our mission has changed once I've had time to consider Hensley's answer." He glanced at Stella. "I know how curious some of you are."

Stella felt the blush creep up, but she was too giddy to care. She turned to scan the docks, searching for any sign of Beckworth or Lando. There wasn't any, and when she turned around, Jamie had walked off. Disappointed he didn't open the letter but understanding why he hadn't, she huffed a sigh and leaned against the railing. If he was anything like Finn or Hensley, he'd shut himself up in his cabin while he considered the response.

She stared up at the masts and the blue sky beyond. The waiting would test every last ounce of patience.

"We'll know soon enough, lass." Fitz had stepped next to her as they watched Jamie disappear through the door.

"It doesn't make the waiting any easier." She studied Fitz. His gaze was full of mischief, and she chuckled. "You already have a betting pool going, don't you?"

"You want in?" He rocked back and forth on his heels.

"You know I'm not the best with how the money works, but how about a crown that says Hensley wants to break up MacDuff's and Cheval's little party."

He rubbed his hands together. "That's something I can work with."

"You think otherwise?"

He glanced around the deck, then leaned over and lowered his voice. "I think when the men hear a crown's been added to the pool, they'll wager the opposite just for the chance of winning."

"Which way are you betting?"

He gave her a grin. "There's not a chance in hell Hensley will risk those two smugglers joining forces. It's a sure bet."

Then he strode away, whistling as he went, tapping a sailor on his shoulder and taking the man's place to finish work on the sail.

Pleased she'd bet on the winning side, she suddenly frowned. Was this how Beckworth felt when a new assignment came along? A mix of excitement with a touch of dread. And what did it mean for her participation? Would he ask, or demand, that Jamie remove her from the ship and send her to Waverly?

She rolled up her sleeves. They could give it their best shot. Regardless of what the letter said, she wasn't getting off this boat. Feeling a mood coming on, she stormed across the deck, raced down the stairs, and made her way to the galley.

She pulled out pots and pans, a stack of ingredients, coffee beans, and the coffee pot and went to work. If the sailors hadn't already completed the task, she would have scrubbed the deck. Busy work was what she needed, and since it was close to lunchtime, she didn't wait for Cook as she started cutting turnips for the stew.

While she sliced and diced, she mentally created a list of all the reasons it made sense for her to remain aboard the ship. She grinned. Beckworth just loved her lists.

L ando crawled to the boulder Beckworth was hiding behind. He wiped his brow and, staying low, turned his back on the three men loading kegs and crates into the back of a wagon.

Beckworth continued his watch, and when the men returned to the old barn, he stayed low as he worked his way back to their horses. Lando didn't make a sound, but he knew the big man was behind him.

Once they reached the horses, Beckworth rubbed his forehead. "Do you think they're part of Cheval's crew or MacDuff's?"

Lando shrugged. "Could be either or someone else."

"Your merchant friend seemed to think it was Cheval."

He nodded. "And most of the time he's right. But he's been wrong a time or two."

"He wasn't wrong about the barn or the firearms."

"We're not sure about the weapons."

"Those weren't kegs of whiskey or ale."

Lando grinned. "Maybe they were filled with mead."

Beckworth laughed. "You're right. They could have been filled with anything, but a smuggler is still a smuggler. And even Cheval knows the value of carrying more than fine lace or Irish whiskey."

Lando ran a hand over his short-cropped hair. "That doesn't help us. Do we follow?"

"We haven't been out here long. Even if Jamie gets a response from Hensley today, I doubt he'll want to leave before morning."

Lando nodded. "What are you thinking?"

"They don't have many options with a wagon. I doubt they're taking their cargo back to the docks, but it's possible."

"You think they have a ship nearby?"

"How well do you know the area?"

Lando scratched his chin then turned in a half circle. He pointed to his left, which led to the road they'd traveled to get to where they currently stood. "Let's get the horses well off the road. They should come this way. There's a narrow path that veers to the right about a mile before town, just wide enough for a wagon. It leads down to a small cove."

"It's worth checking out."

They walked their horses deeper into the woods. With it being winter, the trees were bare, and it required a longer walk than he preferred, but it wouldn't take long to catch up to a wagon once it passed. They settled the horses by a patch of winter grass to keep them quiet and found a spot to wait.

"Did any of those men look familiar to you?" Beckworth hadn't recognized them.

"Maybe. But not anyone I would have considered following."

"Probably a quick pick of sailors happening to be standing by the captain when he gave the order."

A half-hour passed before they heard the wagon. Once it passed and the sound of the hooves and a squeaky wheel faded, Lando took off on foot. He was back in five minutes.

"They took the road to the cove."

"Let's give them another fifteen or twenty minutes."

Once enough time had passed, they mounted and followed the trail. The path curved around a scattering of trees before sloping down to the cove. They tied the horses in the trees and slowly worked their way toward the edge of the road where it began its curving path around boulders to the shoreline. There was a wide section of dirt where a wagon could turn around.

The men were already loading the cargo onto two jolly boats. Beckworth and Lando were close enough to easily make out the ship, but Beckworth pulled out his binoculars to get a closer look at the men onboard.

"Cheval?" Lando asked.

Beckworth nodded. "And I recognize one of the men from the pub. He might be the first mate." He passed the binoculars to Lando.

"I've seen the one next to the first mate. He was on the boat at the cove where they loaded the crates they traded to MacDuff."

"Looks like they're getting ready for another trade."

"Stay put. I'll be right back." Lando handed him the binoculars and crawled away.

Beckworth resumed his watch with the glasses, taking in the men on the beach and those watching from the ship. Was this the last of their cargo, or did they have more stops to make? If they were working their way north, then chances were likely the meeting spot would be north, but not a guarantee.

He watched for another five minutes before he heard the snap of a branch and froze. It might be Lando, but it was rare for the big man to make a sound while on surveillance. When he heard another rustling of feet stirring up forest debris, he put the glasses away.

The sound of a flintlock being primed made him turn. A man, not more than twenty feet away, pointed a pistol at him. He should have moved when he heard the twig break.

"Who are you?" the man asked.

"Just someone out for a ride." Beckworth stood and shifted his weight to his left foot, rubbed his hands together, and shrugged. "I must admit, I'm a bit of a curious sort and saw a wagon head down this path. I thought there might be another dock I wasn't aware of."

"Unfortunately, your curiosity has gotten you into some trouble."

Now that Beckworth had time to get a look at the man, he was one of the men at the pub. Not good. And he appeared to be smarter than the average sailor. Probably the second mate or perhaps Cheval's muscle. Neither he nor Lando had considered there might be a fourth man. He might have been returning from town on another errand and it was just their bad luck.

Beckworth spread his arms wide. "If you just let me on my way, we'll just call this a misunderstanding."

"I wish I could do that, but you don't appear to be the trustworthy type."

That hurt. He'd shared his best smile. "I assure you, I'm known to be quite trustworthy."

The man seemed to consider it for a moment, but Beckworth knew it was a ruse. The man was going to shoot him. No doubt about it. So, without hesitation, when Lando swung his rifle, slamming it against the man's head, Beckworth dove to his left.

The man pulled the trigger as he fell, but the shot went wide in the opposite direction of Beckworth, who rolled and came up in a crouch.

He glanced up at Lando. "How did you know?"

The big man shrugged. "Just had a feeling."

They looked down at the man.

"Someone will be coming," Lando said.

Beckworth checked the man's jacket and pulled out a piece of paper from an inside pocket. "Look at this." He passed the paper to Lando, who took a few seconds to look it over before handing it back. Beckworth folded it as he'd found it and tucked it back in the pocket then tugged the jacket in place.

"Shall we leave him alive?" Lando asked.

Beckworth nodded. "Let's go."

The two ran for their horses. They didn't mount but walked the horses north of their position, taking the long way around before mounting at the main road. They raced the horses toward town, though the wagon would never be able to catch them.

They slowed as they approached the first buildings.

"He's seen your face." Lando turned down a street that led to the stables.

"And he knows there were two of us, but we could have been anyone," Beckworth said.

"Was he at the pub?"

"Yes, and he's likely to remember when he has time to think it over. Worse case, they change their plans. If they assume we ran before checking pockets, they might consider themselves lucky, though they'll be more cautious."

"Let's see what Jamie makes of the map."

19

———

Stella stared at the ceiling from the bed in their cabin. After preparing everything Cook needed for lunch and resorting the pantry, which had gotten out of order, she'd collapsed on the bed and fallen asleep. When she woke, the ship creaked but was otherwise quiet.

When the knock came, she jumped up and, with two long strides, pulled the door open. She startled Fitz, whose fist was raised to knock again.

He gave her a grin. "Catch you asleep?"

She patted her hair and frowned. "Guilty. Is it time?"

"Aye. Jamie doesn't want to wait on Beckworth and Lando."

"So, they haven't returned." If they had, she would have expected Beckworth to seek her out, but he might have gone straight to Jamie if they'd found anything.

"Nothing to worry about. Gathering information is a slow process."

She pulled on her jacket, grabbed a piece of paper, and followed Fitz, expecting to find the group at a table in the galley but instead found the men in Jamie's office. Michelson and Lane sat on stools, and, after closing the door, Fitz offered Stella a chair while he took the other one.

Jamie wore his typical smile, but he seemed to be studying her again. Small lines creased his forehead as he watched her take a seat. Was he considering whether she should still be on board? She pushed the thought away and straightened her shoulders. When his grin widened and his face relaxed, she understood he'd come to a decision, but was it in her favor?

"I'd hoped Beckworth and Lando would be back by now, but I've stewed over Hensley's message long enough, and we have plans to make." Jamie lifted what looked like the letter that had arrived earlier. "Hensley's first message advised to keep monitoring. Now, after hearing Cheval and MacDuff seem to have a business arrangement, of which we're only assuming at this point, Hensley has asked us to dig deeper."

The men eyed each other, and Stella was ready to ask what that meant when the sound of heavy boots made its way toward the cabin. After a swift knock, the door opened and Lando stuck his head in, then pushed it wider when he noted the others in the room. Beckworth followed him in, gave Stella a stern look, and found a seat.

She wasn't sure what his look was about but had an idea. They'd learned something new, and he didn't like the direction the mission was taking. And his misgivings had nothing to do with smugglers and everything to do with her.

"Good timing, gentlemen." Jamie raised a hand when Beckworth opened his mouth. "We've just started, so let me restate Hensley's second message that arrived a couple of hours ago. He's concerned by the meeting between MacDuff and Cheval. He wants to know what they're up to. This has now moved from mere surveillance to something more. We need to find out if they're working together to increase their smuggling operation or if it goes deeper. Specifically, are they working with France and stirring up a rebellion?

"Now, based on Hensley's request..." Jamie looked at Lando. "What can you tell us of your scouting mission. It appears you've discovered something."

Stella was surprised when he asked Lando rather than Beckworth, but he must have had a reason. Perhaps calmer heads, since Beckworth fidgeted in his seat. Maybe he was thinking this would be a good time for both of them to leave and go back to the safety of Waverly and hunting parties. To be honest, she'd be good with that as well—but only if they went together.

"We received information that Cheval might be picking up more cargo and was directed to an old barn north of town. There were three men removing crates and kegs from the barn and loading them into a wagon." He continued to tell them of the trail that led to a small cove and when they followed it, they found the cargo being loaded onto *The Horseman*."

Lando nodded to Beckworth, who seemed to have calmed during the telling.

"Lando left me, and, at the time, I assumed he went to search for a better vantage point or to check on the horses. While he was gone, another man showed up, pistol in hand with every intention of shooting me whether I answered his questions or not." He slid a side glance to Stella but continued. "Fortunately, Lando arrived in time to help, but not before the man got a shot off."

Stella kept her gaze on Beckworth, though he didn't look at her again. He could have been killed, and he was acting like it was no big deal. It *was* a big deal. What would she have done if he hadn't returned? She blinked away the burning sensation at the back of her eyes. How could she return to Waverly knowing the game had changed? Was she supposed to help Mary plan a hunting party while constantly wondering if Beckworth was in trouble or worse? Not a chance in hell.

"We decided not to kill him," Lando jumped in, shaking Stella out of her growing irritation. "But Beckworth had the foresight to check the man's pockets. Which was a good thing."

Beckworth nodded, still avoiding eye contact with her. "He was carrying a map, roughly drawn, but it reflected three points along the coast near ports north of here."

"Do you have the map?" Jamie asked.

Both men shook their heads, but Lando answered. "We didn't want to give Cheval any reason to change their plans." He rubbed his head. "Though he might anyway."

"Doubtful," was Beckworth's only response.

Fitz stood and grabbed a bottle of whiskey from a sideboard and poured several glasses, which he then handed out. Stella took a long swallow and held in the choking burn.

Jamie stared into his glass for several long seconds then only took a sip. "This puts Cheval in a difficult position. There wasn't just one unknown man watching them but at least two, and possibly more. But he has an advantage that his man has seen Beckworth's face. Did you recognize the man?"

"He was one of the men at the pub."

"So, someone highly trusted. Did he recognize you?"

Beckworth shook his head. "No. There was no sign of it, but I suspect he'll eventually remember."

"That gives them nothing," Fitz said. "Too many variables. For all Cheval knows, he could have competition following them. If those kegs were gunpowder and the crates filled with weapons or cannonballs, they'd be valuable to any smuggler."

The men nodded.

"How easily could they change their plans?" Stella asked. The men glanced at her, probably having forgotten she was in the room—except for Beckworth. Her presence must have weighed heavy based on his stubborn avoidance to glance her way. She ignored him. "I mean, any remaining cargo Cheval wants to retrieve is wherever he hid it. It's not like they can just beam it up to the ship." When they gave her a strange look, a grin slipped out, and she caught Beckworth trying to hold one in. "Sorry, that's a bit futuristic even for my time. But if they're worried someone's on to them, they still have to get their cargo or leave it behind for another time. And how would they get a message to MacDuff? God knows, we've been sitting here for days waiting for a communique. They're not on land where messages, as slow as they are, can get to them quickly. They have to dock somewhere."

The men glanced at each other, most of them turning their focus to their whiskey, holding back their own grins.

Jamie was the first one to laugh out loud. At first, she thought she'd said something stupid until he said, "You certainly know how to get to the heart of the matter. You're absolutely correct."

She straightened in her seat but held her tongue.

"Which only makes his problem worse." Beckworth hadn't taken a drink. He'd crossed a leg over a knee and balanced the glass on his leg, slowly turning it as he considered the situation. "He won't change his plans, at least not until his next meeting with MacDuff. But he will tighten his security."

"Aye, which makes it tougher to get close." Fitz emptied his glass and leaned against the sideboard.

"The best answer would be to get a sailor onboard one of the ships." Lando's frown and scrunched brows suggested other-wise. "If we had more time that might work, but not now. Any new sailor brought on will be constantly watched."

"We know his next three ports." Jamie tapped his fingers on the desk, then fingered Hensley's note again. "But spending time in pubs and inns won't get us close enough."

The men went silent, each seeming to consider their options.

"So, why not play into Cheval's fear?" Stella asked.

The men turned to her, and Beckworth was the first to nod. "It's not unheard of for a smuggler to take over someone else's operations."

Jamie glanced at Stella, who was folding a new swan but watched him out of the corner of her eye. He smiled. "Aye. But not take over Cheval's operation. We need to convince MacDuff to work with us rather than him."

———

Jamie ended the meeting with a request to meet again after dinner. Beckworth remained sitting as Stella rose and stepped toward him on her way out. He took her hand and kissed it.

"I'll meet you in the cabin in a few minutes." He held her gaze, though hers flickered to Jamie for an instant before she smiled.

"Of course." She squeezed his hand and then turned it over to deposit the swan in his palm.

Then she strode out of the room ahead of the other men. Fitz was the last one out, and he turned back for a moment then shut the door behind him.

"Did you have something else to report?" Jamie asked, though his grin was back.

"You know that's not why I'm still here."

Jamie's grin faded, though Beckworth doubted it had gone far. The man thought this was a joke. No. That wasn't right. He, of all people, understood the dangers. But he had a mission. And while the crew of the *Daphne*, mostly Irishmen, had no particular love of England, they had no desire to live under

Napoleon's yoke. At the end of the day, they desired coin that could be sent home to family. If MacDuff and Cheval were making plans with France and using their smuggling operation as a ruse, it had to be uncovered.

Jamie, similar to what Hensley had once told him of Finn, never took a job that would hurt Ireland or its people. Break up a smuggling operation? Locate spies who weren't good for Ireland? They were there—happy to oblige—for a decent payday.

And like his predecessor on the *Daphne*, Jamie's crew wasn't above a bit of smuggling themselves. They had even colluded with Sebastian, the French monk, who ran his own smuggling syndicate once their team had rid the monastery of the duke.

At the heart of it all, Jamie was above reproach when it came to a mission. And he would do whatever it took to keep his crew safe as well as his team. That included himself and Stella. But still.

"We have no other way in with MacDuff." Jamie laid it out for him.

"She only had one run-in with the man. I doubt he'd even remember her."

Jamie barked out a laugh. "A blind man would remember her."

Beckworth growled. He had to put this in perspective. If it were Libby or any of the other women who worked with the London crews, he wouldn't hesitate. The best decision would be to put her off the ship first thing in the morning. He should go with her. But this was an important mission.

God's blood, why had he fallen in love?

"What would she have to do?"

"We need to plan another accidental meeting. From what Lando told me, MacDuff found Stella intriguing. I have no doubt he'd invite her to dinner if they crossed paths. She mentioned she was running cargo up the coast. He's bound to ask what type of cargo. She just needs to drop a few hints. Perhaps mention some important names."

Beckworth nodded. "I can think of a few. And I suppose the *Daphne* is her ship."

"Naturally. With any luck, she can entice him into a trade." Jamie pointed to the swan Beckworth was holding. "Lando called her Lady Swan. I think we need a stash of those. They'll be her calling card."

"This is a bad idea."

"You started it, mate." Jamie's grin was back.

"And I'm regretting that decision every day." Beckworth had started it. He'd used the swans when they'd been running from Gemini. Then Barrington had used them again when the team searched for him. It had seemed such a good idea at the time.

He stood and dropped the swan, now with a bit of a bent wing, on the desk.

Before he left, Jamie said, "We'll protect her."

He nodded and closed the door behind him. His first inclination was to find where Fitz had stashed Jamie's case of whiskey, but his feet took him back to their cabin. Jamie's words echoed in his ears. They'll protect her. He had to give Jamie credit for giving it a go, considering his own attempts, Beckworth had never seemed capable of doing it himself.

Beckworth gave a light tap on the cabin door and held his breath before entering. Would she be defiant? Curious? Demanding to know every detail? He wasn't expecting what he found instead.

He closed the door behind him. She took his breath away as she'd never done before.

She sat in the middle of the bed, her arms locked around her knees. At that moment, she appeared so tiny until his gaze locked on her face surrounded by untamed auburn locks. Her green eyes were huge, which would give most men a false idea that she was wounded.

Fragile.

He almost snorted. He knew this face. Stubborn. And though he caught a spark of fear, she was ready for a fight.

She didn't speak as he removed his jacket and then his boots. He let the gentle sway of the ship keep the peace between them as he crawled onto the bed and sat next to her. They didn't touch, but he was close.

His first thought was to immediately tell her what he and Jamie had spoken about. To explain what they needed from her in the next phase of the mission. Hell, he wanted to tell her how worried he was for her, but that he'd be there to protect her.

Instead, he said nothing. Something was troubling her, and he wanted to know what it was. While they'd been in Baywood, it seemed there wasn't any thought they didn't share. He wasn't sure if that was normal or because their relationship was still young. Yet, the minute they traveled to this time, walls went up.

Would that have happened if they had arrived and hadn't found Hensley waiting with a mission? He could assume or rationalize, but the truth was, he didn't know. All of this was so new. He'd never had anyone care so much when he left for a mission. Not the way she did.

He continued to wait.

After another minute of silence, she rested her head on his shoulder.

"Are you sending me back to Waverly?"

God's blood. It never occurred to him that she'd think that. But why not? He'd thought it dozens of times.

He took her hand and gently rubbed it with his thumb. It

was a small hand. Delicate. He turned it over and ran a finger across the fine lines of her palm. There were thin callouses from her gardening shears and perhaps from helping with the lines as Michelson showed her how to trim the sails.

"It crossed my mind." He waited while her body tensed then slowly relaxed. "But I'd have a fight on my hands, wouldn't I?"

With her head still resting on his shoulder, she said, "Damn straight."

He chuckled and slowly moved her so he could wrap an arm around her. He kissed the top of her head. "You know I worry for you."

"I worry for you, too."

"What a pair we make, Lady Caldway."

"Indeed, Lord Beckworth."

He held her for some time. Her simple presence, the feel of her in his arms, soothed him. Settled him. And he wanted the moment to last as long as possible before he told her. She'd be excited, which would only increase his worry. He suddenly wished they were at Waverly, dealing with the madness of preparing the manor for a weekend of friends.

He released a slow breath. They had a mission. She would do her part and play her role, but asking her to do this would be the most difficult thing he'd ever done. Even more than when he'd stood in the woods at Waverly and watched her disappear into the fog with AJ and Finn.

The day his heart broke. He couldn't lose her again.

He gave her a long hug then released her.

"Jamie has an assignment for you."

She popped up, her face as bright as if the sun was shining on it. "Really?"

He grimaced at her excitement. "We need you to continue your persona as Lady Swan."

Lines appeared across her forehead as she considered the

statement. Then she slowly nodded. "You need me to get close to MacDuff."

"We need him to believe you're another smuggler with cargo that would be of interest to him."

"Why? Oh, you need me to find out when and where he's meeting with Cheval to trade cargo."

"It's a bit more delicate than that."

She gave it more thought, and he gave her the time. She liked to figure things out for herself and typically did so with exceptional speed.

She moved, rising to kneel, then sitting back on her heels. No question as to whether she would accept the assignment. Her answer was written all over her shining eyes and breathtaking smile. "You want me to find out what his end game is."

He grimaced again. She was going to get herself killed.

He rose to face her. "You need to move slowly. This is a very dangerous game."

Her face relaxed, her expression instantly changing to one of concern. She placed her palm on his cheek, and he couldn't help but lean into it.

"I understand the stakes. I'll take this seriously and do exactly what the team tells me. I won't do anything to risk myself or the crew."

He nodded, thankful she understood the risk. Then she destroyed his calm.

She wrapped her arms around him and almost shrieked her words. "I'm just so damn excited."

20

The sail to Burry Port was uneventful though a bit stormy. Not willing to take chances, Stella had taken one of her motion sickness tablets in addition to her daily dose of herbs. At the last port, Fitz and Lando had been able to garner enough eggs for the crew to enjoy poached eggs, sausage, and biscuits for breakfast.

After helping clean the galley, she'd spent the rest of the morning in the cabin while the men met with Jamie to discuss plans for the day. Their first task would be to search for the *Grey Ghost* and *The Horseman*. If they didn't find the ships in port, they would most likely still run surveillance around town and the pubs in case they heard news of either MacDuff or Cheval.

All she'd been told was that Lando would take her for a walk around town after lunch. She'd been too nervous to eat so she read until she fell asleep, only waking when Cook sent a tray of cheese and bread to the cabin with two mugs of ale. If nothing else, the ale calmed her nerves.

Now fully rested and fed, she tugged at the bodice of her nicest day dress. If this was going to require more than one meeting with MacDuff, she'd need more dresses. She turned around.

"How do I look?"

Beckworth gave her a long perusal. "I prefer the dowdy dresses I bought you at the first port."

She grinned and tapped his shoulder with the tip of her dagger's sheath before it disappeared into her oversized pocket. "You're only saying that because I'm dressing for another man."

He pulled her close, his arm snug around her waist. "Don't forget who your only man is."

She stared into his heated gaze then stood on tiptoes for a long passionate kiss that, if this had been a movie, would have made her toes curl.

When they stepped back they both rearranged their clothes, and Stella ran a hand over her hair, ensuring all the hairpins were still in place.

"I won't be far away." Beckworth's brows furrowed, his lips thinned, and his eyes got that hazy look that said he was rethinking a decision. Maybe he was thinking of tying her to the bed until they left port.

"Where's your hat?" She glanced around the cabin but didn't see it.

"Lane is lending me a knitted cap."

She stood back. He was once again dressed in his dusty pants and shirt, and she wasn't sure who would look more like a vagabond, him or Fitz. She gave him an approving nod.

"Are we sure MacDuff will show up?"

"No. But it's best not to second guess what Cheval has planned. And, as you stated before, unless Cheval has some way of contacting MacDuff when not in port, this is Cheval's next stop. Whether MacDuff was to meet him here is the only thing we don't know for sure." He took her elbow and steered her out the door and up the stairs to the gangplank where Lando waited.

"Who's going to be my messenger?" she asked.

"Billy." Lando looked around, searching for him.

A small lad poked him from behind. "I'm here, sir."

Lando spun around and made a grab for the boy, but Billy had been expecting it, and he jumped back, his laughter causing the sailors around them to join in.

"Keep it up, lad, and you'll wake up tied upside down in the lines for your trouble." Lando grinned as he swatted at the boy. "Now, what's your assignment?"

"Stay close but out of sight until you give the signal." Billy tugged at his ear, which Stella assumed was their sign. "Then I come to meet Lady Stella, I mean Lady Swan, who'll hand me a paper swan. Then I'll run off and get lost in the crowd so no one can see where I went. I'll hide for a bit then sneak back to the ship."

"Good lad." Lando held out an arm for Stella and led her to the dock.

She glanced over her shoulder. Beckworth fussed with the knit cap, but his gaze followed her. In addition to him, Fitz, Lane, and Mickelson would take various positions around the village while keeping her and Lando within sight as they watched for any sign of MacDuff.

Beckworth had shown the team hand signals he used with the London crews that would allow them to stay in communication should anyone spot MacDuff or any other trouble. Stella understood the signs but would rely on Lando to watch for them then steer her in the right direction that might cross the smuggler's path.

They spent an hour walking around town before they stopped at a pub to rest. They ate a simple meal and were finishing their ale when Lane worked his way through the crowd. He bumped Stella's chair and his hat fell off.

When Lane stooped to pick it up, he said, "MacDuff's ship just arrived but is still mooring. You should return to the ship." Then he disappeared, pushing his way past newly arriving sailors.

"Why are we returning?" Stella asked.

"It will take time to moor the ship. We'll come back this evening."

"Then I'd like to stop at the mercantile and the apothecary on our way back."

"Do you need more herbs already?" Lando asked. It was a reasonable question since she'd just bought some a few days ago and they'd spent more time at port than at sea.

"No." She stood and arranged her dress, reassured that she had two swans in one pocket and her dagger in the other. "Let's go."

Without another word and not waiting for Lando, she strode from the pub. Whether it was the fact she was a woman or was followed by a large imposing man, the crowd parted for her like the Red Sea. She flashed the men her broker smile as she passed, pleased by the returned grins.

A girl had to have some fun.

Once outside, she glanced up at the parting clouds and paused for a moment as the cool air from the sea washed the scent of the crowded pub away while the sun warmed her cheeks. Lando, staying in character, waited next to her.

She caught sight of Michelson near a stack of crates by the side of a building but no one else. They were out there—she sensed them. Confidence with a dash of independence emboldened her, knowing she was aggravating Beckworth, if not the others, by ignoring the order to return to the ship. She turned toward the pier where she remembered spotting the mercantile and apothecary.

"We've been given an order." Lando had to lean down to whisper as she briskly worked her way through milling sailors and locals.

"This won't take long. If we don't expect anyone until later, what can it hurt? Besides, I've been locked onboard that ship for too long. As long as we stay in character, no one will be the wiser."

The harumph sound only made her smile as she ducked into the apothecary. She purchased ginger though she still had a good supply. Better safe than sorry her mother as well as millions of others had advised their children. It was one of the few words of wisdom her mother had imparted that she found to be of any value. She also procured two different remedies for headaches.

When they exited the shop, she noticed Beckworth and Fitz at the blacksmith across a narrow alley from the mercantile. Fitz was speaking with the smithy, his arms held out as if explaining the size of something. Whether he was planning to buy something or not, the blacksmith was fully engaged.

Beckworth on the other hand, was hunched next to a post, his body facing toward Fitz, but his head had turned to watch her. He was too far away to catch the nuances in his expression, but he would be irritated by her refusal to follow Jamie's command. One more stop and they could all go back to the ship.

The mercantile was cool inside, and a handful of customers wandered about the place. The clerk was busy with a customer, and another man helped a woman pick through a bin of root vegetables.

Stella strode to the back of the store where she spotted a bookcase. After glancing through the titles, she picked one up to review. She hadn't heard of the author or the title, but what had she expected? An entire stack of classics? She'd read a couple of books Jamie had lent them to pass the time, but one could only read so many sailing adventures. She suspected he kept the good stuff in his cabin, maybe not wanting to show off how smart he was.

Halfway through the bookshelf, she glanced back. Lando had moved off to the right, staying close to the door, either doing some shopping of his own or remaining in character. She would have to tell Jamie she refused to follow his order. The last thing she wanted was to get Lando in trouble.

She returned to scanning the books, hoping to find something to buy. One of the books on the bottom shelf was *The Odyssey*. Who would have guessed this wayward village on the coast would have such an old classic? Spurred on by her find, she glanced at the last few books and grabbed the last one —*Robinson Crusoe*.

What a find. She could read them, Beckworth probably already had, and then take them home to AJ. True classics from this era would be an antique broker's dream in her time, though she doubted AJ would think of selling them. They would be a perfect addition to the inn's library.

"You have an interesting selection of books there."

The familiar male voice sent a tingle through her. It couldn't be.

She glanced up into the smiling face of MacDuff. How did he get here so fast if his ship was still mooring? They must have dropped a jolly boat beforehand.

She kept her facial expression fixed as her gaze took in his features. He was smiling and humor danced in his eyes. He was a handsome man and confident in his bearing.

"Do you read, sir?"

He held a hand to his chest. "You wound me. I thought you

might remember me." He didn't look hurt as his smile widened. This man was an outrageous flirt. Evenly matched was her first thought.

She tilted her head then released a slow smile. "You ran into me in Baglan."

He laughed. "I think it was the other way around."

"I believe that depends on who's telling the story."

"So it does." He took both books from her and gave them a quick scan. "You read?"

"Of course." Not many women in this time period did, but Mary and Elizabeth did, as did Eleanor, so it wasn't completely unheard of.

His brow lifted. "Very different books. Do you like adventure, Lady Swan?"

He remembered her name. They were off to a good start. "Who doesn't love a grand adventure?"

He chuckled, and his smile warmed. "Not many women do."

She shrugged and took the books back. "Perhaps, but I'm not any woman."

"Clearly."

She squared her shoulders. "You're not following me, are you, Mister—" She let the rest of her statement trail off as if she couldn't remember.

"MacDuff. Again, you wound me."

"It must be all the men I meet at these ports. Business and all. I'm surprised you remember me for such a quick, accidental meeting."

His smile never wavered. "A woman in a literal sea of men, you shine like the sun."

She gave him one of her sultry laughs. "I think I saw a book of poetry you might be interested in."

He threw his head back and laughed with her. "You are a

charming woman." He glanced around the store then at her. "It appears your guard is returning. Are you in port for long?"

"I'm afraid we leave in the morning."

"Then you must allow me to treat you to dinner this evening. The inn has a wonderful way with fish."

She glanced at Lando, who'd positioned himself several paces to her right, as she considered MacDuff's invitation.

"Your man can tag along, but I prefer he sits a couple tables away."

She gave it another few seconds, not wanting to appear too eager. Then she gave him a slow nod. "I think that would be acceptable. How could I pass up such an enticing meal?"

"Excellent. Which ship are you traveling on?"

"Why don't I meet you at the inn?"

He considered her answer, but rather than frown at her illusiveness, he appeared intrigued. Perfect.

"Shall we say eight o'clock? My ship is currently mooring, and I have much to do before then."

"Then don't let me take any more of your valuable time. I have my own business to see to." Before she could walk away, he took her hand. Her first instinct was to pull away, but she pushed the impulse aside as he placed a warm kiss on it.

"Until this evening, my lady."

She was ready to turn away when Billy raced over.

"I'm sorry, Lady Swan. I thought I'd find you at the apothecary."

Good grief. She'd forgotten all about Billy and their plans as soon as they'd called off the surveillance. She rearranged the books in her hands.

"I'm sorry, young master." It was a phrase she'd heard Beckworth use with the youngsters in the London crews, making them feel special. "I'd almost forgotten." She pulled out one of her paper swans and handed it to him. "Make sure he gets it before his ship leaves, or my trip will be wasted."

Billy nodded. "No worries, mistress." Then he scampered out the door.

MacDuff appeared interested in the exchange but had the good manners not to ask. His brow had definitely lifted when he saw the swan and no doubt remembered the one Lando dropped at their first meeting.

"Until later, Mr. MacDuff."

"Thaddeus, if you please."

She gave him her best broker smile. "Thaddeus."

She strode to the clerk on shaky legs, where Lando met her and took the books from her. Neither spoke as he paid for them, tucked the wrapped package under his arm, and followed her out the door.

She squared her shoulders and lifted her head, walking at a sedate pace through the crowd, hoping to blend in. MacDuff could still be watching, trying to discern which ship she was on.

Lando steered her gently by the elbow until Fitz wandered by, head down, and said, "All clear to return to the ship."

Then he glanced at her. "And a fine job, Lady Swan." He gave her one of his charming grins before hurrying away.

His words—a fine job—made her smile all the way to the *Daphne.*

21

Stella tossed the day dress on the bed and turned her back to Beckworth. "I need new dresses. Nothing fancy, but I can't possibly be expected to play a proper role without the right accessories."

She thought that might get a chuckle out of him but all she got was a tug on the ties as he loosened them. He slid the dress off her and held her hand as she stepped out of it. He pulled her to him and gave her a kiss that sent shivers through her body.

He wrapped his arms around her, and she laid her head on his shoulder and closed her eyes. He hadn't said a word when they'd returned to the ship. Lando had told her to go to the cabin while he followed Beckworth to where Jamie stood on the far side of the deck.

Her first instinct was to follow, but Beckworth was already on edge, and she'd disobeyed Jamie's orders. Things had turned out better than expected, but there was always that slim possibility that something could have just as easily gone wrong. She could talk her way out of Jamie's rebuke, but she didn't want to have to do it in front of Beckworth.

Fitz came to the cabin thirty minutes later. Beckworth had

been sent on another assignment, but he'd return before her dinner with MacDuff. Then he winked at her.

"I don't care what the others say, nice job. None of us expected MacDuff to be around while the ship was being moored. Lando was impressed by how you handled yourself. Just do the same thing at dinner. Conversation and a little flirting, then find a way to slip in the smuggling."

She'd laughed. It all sounded so simple. Just drop a hint about smuggling. Maybe right after dinner was served. It was more likely she'd mention it before racing out of the inn for the safety of the ship.

When Beckworth returned, he'd been sullen, but his earlier kiss had told her everything she needed to know. She pulled away from his arms and placed a chase kiss on his lips.

"Dinner, a little conversation, and then back to the ship." How would that work? "He's going to want to walk me back to the ship."

Beckworth nodded, and his game face appeared. "We discussed that. Michelson will already be inside the inn to keep an eye on things. Lando will remain outside the inn while you have dinner. It will show some trust in MacDuff. Once dinner is finished, he might want to take you for an evening stroll. If so, Lando will stick with you. We prefer that MacDuff doesn't discover what ship you're on. Not yet. Though chances are he'll have his own people watching you."

This time her shiver was cold and not the heated one that Beckworth always produced. "That's a rather unsettling thought."

"Lando will step in as necessary. Just find out what port he's going to next if you can."

"Alright. Help me into this dress."

Once she was properly attired, Beckworth tugged at one of her locks.

"Do you need help with your hair?"

"I thought I'd leave it loose and pull back the sides with a couple of hairpins." Once she completed the task she turned to him. When his gaze immediately heated, she grinned, then glanced around. "Where's my dagger?"

He picked up the dress she'd worn earlier and searched the pockets. "These pockets are big enough to hide a small child."

"Funny. All the dresses I brought from Waverly have them. I guess AJ started the trend based on the hidden spaces Maire kept in her trunk. They come in handy."

"Finn and Ethan were right."

"How so?"

"Women are devious."

She took the dagger from him and stuffed it in a pocket. "Always a good thing to keep in mind." She took a deep breath. "Walk me up, will you?"

Lando met them at the top of the stairs. "You look fetching as always."

"Why thank you, Lando."

"Do you have your swans?"

"No. Am I supposed to use them tonight?"

"Damn," Beckworth said. "I forgot to tell you." He fished in his pocket and drew out three swans. "In case he asks about them. It's up to you whether you show him one. We also thought it might be a good way to tell us if you need help. Simply drop one when you can. We'll assume you need assistance."

She nodded. "Excellent idea. I have more in the cabin on a bookshelf. Well, there's also probably one or two lying around. Maybe on the sideboard. Oh, and maybe next to the bed. I might have left one or two in Jamie's office."

Beckworth took her hand, a soft smile on his kissable lips. "We know. There are a few in the galley, too."

She gave a shaky laugh. "I admit, I'm a bit nervous."

This time Lando took her arm and placed it through his. "A little walk before dinner will shake away the jitters."

She took a deep breath. "Absolutely. Let's get this party started."

M ost of the stores were closed, but as Lando had said, the walk alone was what she needed. The sea air always calmed her, and though she didn't see any of the team, she sensed them out there.

"Jamie has several of the crew in the pubs and the inn. They'll eat, drink, and keep an eye out, but Michelson will be the only one remaining inside until the two of you leave."

"What about Beckworth, Fitz, and Lane?"

"They'll be out there. Nothing for you to worry about."

"MacDuff probably has his own men out there."

"Beckworth's earlier assignment was to monitor the men leaving the *Grey Ghost* and, if possible, determine which men are the closest to MacDuff. He might say he has his own ship but he's not the captain."

"Interesting. The smuggling business must be good if he can afford to pay a captain."

"It's difficult to know what the man is doing. He doesn't seem to be above chicanery." He slowed as they approached the inn. "Looks like he's waiting for you."

She noticed MacDuff right away. He was taller than the other man, who appeared to be his bodyguard since he stood two steps behind MacDuff. As they drew closer, she also noticed he had selected more expensive clothing for their meeting.

He bowed his head. "Lady Swan, you look more fetching each time we meet."

"You're too kind." She took his proffered hand, ready for the warm kiss he placed on it.

"Will your bodyguard be joining us?" His eyes danced with merriment.

"He'll wait outside with yours."

"Of course." He chuckled as he took her arm and guided her through the door.

She wanted to glance back at Lando for a last sign of encouragement, but she didn't dare. Instead, she lifted her chin and ignored the men, who watched them as they strode to a table in a far corner where a server waited. All the other tables were occupied. MacDuff must have arranged it so they had a table waiting for them. Had he purposely squirreled them away from everyone else?

Before she took a seat, she noticed Michelson leaning against the long wooden bar across the room. He spoke with another man, who looked like a sailor, but she couldn't see his face so wasn't sure if he was someone from the *Daphne*'s crew.

"Do you prefer wine or ale with your meal?" MacDuff asked.

Stella turned her attention to him with an apologetic grin. "I'm sorry. I like to stay aware of those around me, and I prefer wine."

"It's a good practice, especially being a woman. But I doubt you have anything to worry about with your bodyguard."

She sipped the wine and nodded at how good it tasted. He either had expensive taste or was trying to impress. "He's never failed me."

He ordered their meal then leaned his elbows on the table. "This is the second port we've run into each other. Are you following me, Lady Swan?"

She eyed him over the rim of her mug. "I believe I was in port before you. I should probably be asking you that question."

He chuckled. "You're right, of course. If I remember

correctly, you mentioned you were running cargo along the coast."

That didn't take long. "Yes, and we make many stops along the way."

He nodded. "If I'm not mistaken, you sound like you might be from the colonies."

She took another sip of wine then set down the mug, reminding herself too much alcohol wouldn't be a good idea. "We prefer to call it the United States of America."

He smiled, and it was a lovely one. "My apologies. Apparently, your little colony did what Ireland hasn't been able to do."

She had expected him to say Scotland but remembered what Beckworth had told her. While he, Hensley, and the crew of the *Daphne* suspected him of being Scottish, he'd been spending his time playing the part of an Irishman. What a twisted knot of deceit, and it was only going to get messier.

"Well, as they say, try, try, again."

This time his laugh was a deep chuckle. He must have women falling over him in every port. "You have an interesting insight."

"It comes from experience."

He seemed to consider that. "So what made you leave your fledgling country?"

Now, she would learn which of them could spin the better tale. "A tragic accident, actually. My husband was captain of a cargo ship, carrying goods from Boston down the coast and, on occasion, would sail as far as New Orleans."

"He was?"

She took a longer sip of wine and glanced away. When she turned back, she straightened her spine. "He ran afoul of a naval patrol. His ship was sunk, along with him and all the cargo."

MacDuff's surprise didn't look fake. "That's terrible." Then his forehead scrunched in thought. "Was it because of the cargo?"

She shrugged. "There might have been one or two items that could have been considered...let's just say not approved by the new government. Fortunately, I'd decided to stay in port. It was supposed to be a quick run to Jamestown. A few of the hands survived, and from what they told me, my husband thought he could outrun the ship, but a well-placed cannonball was all it took."

"But why leave America?"

"His first and second mate escaped and came to me immediately. I wasn't safe. We had—" She glanced away, bit her lower lip, then turned back to him. "We had stockpiled a stash of coins. More than enough to start a new life, so we found a ship and left for France."

"Was one of them your bodyguard?"

She took her time, appearing to shake off the unpleasant conversation. "No. Adam, the first mate, knew Lando from his time in England. We parted ways when we arrived in Le Havre. He and the second mate had no desire to return to England and spoke French. They'd spent time as fur traders in the Canadian territory, which is where they met my husband." Good grief, she'd never remember this tale. She was supposed to keep the conversation simple. "I don't speak the language, so he found me passage to England and sent me to Southampton with a letter." She laughed. "It took a month before my bodyguard arrived."

"And now?"

"Now, I've taken up the only business I know and one I can do without having to remarry."

"Running cargo?"

She shrugged. "I've learned from the best."

The server arrived with their meal, and while MacDuff

spoke with her, Stella glanced around the room. Michelson was in the same spot. This time he spoke with someone who she'd guess to either be a local or a traveler.

When their server left after refreshing their wine, Stella led the conversation with her own questions.

"You run cargo as well if I remember. Do you normally travel the coast?" She took a bite of fish that had a pleasant, spicy taste but had been overcooked.

He gave her a wink as he ate. "It appears we have business in common. Might I ask what type of shipments you run?"

She finished a bite, washed it down with wine, and gave him an innocent smile. "Oh, you know, things hard to obtain during a war—whiskey, fine lace, hard-to-come-by spices, and the like." She shrugged. "And other things."

She let the "and other things" linger and took a last bite of green beans before pushing the plate away in favor of the mug. Her gaze moved from his quiet inspection to sweep the room. Michelson was still there, this time talking to a sailor she recognized from the *Daphne*.

When her focus returned to him, he was still watching her. "What types of shipments do you run?" She decided to play coy and leaned over. "I'm not having dinner with my competition, am I?"

He took time to survey the room, either because of what he was going to share or simply because she had. Before he spoke, she could tell he was going to play her game. "I prefer to run rum, tobacco, and exotic silks." He gave her a lusty look. "And other things." Then he went back to eating.

She laughed. "That sounds like I might indeed have some competition."

He pointed at her dish. "Is the meal not to your liking?"

She glanced down and frowned. "I hate to admit it." She

glanced around the room again which made him do the same. She grinned. "You won't tell anyone."

He leaned closer. "This conversation is only between us."

"I'm afraid I sometimes get motion sick."

His laugh was robust and honest before he leaned toward her again. "A smuggler who gets seasick?"

"I never said I was a smuggler."

"Fine laces, whiskey, and other things speak to contraband." He finished his plate and his mug of wine. "I'll tell you what. You tell me what you're really carrying, and I'll do the same."

"You first." She added a bit of an edge to her request.

His eyes narrowed. "Now, we're getting somewhere." He considered her, and she held her ground. "I admit I'm on my way to meet another ship." He picked up her hand that had been resting by her mug. "I would give you my word that any lucrative partnership we might arrange would only be between ourselves."

She had an immediate urge to withdraw her hand, but she let it rest in his as he stroked a thumb over the top of it. "I'll be in Tenby in two days. Perhaps you can buy me another dinner."

He considered her statement. "I would have to alter my plans." He released her hand and sat back. "But something tells me it would be worth my time. Shall we take a short stroll?"

He rose, threw some coins on the table, and took her arm.

She noticed Michelson and the sailor from the *Daphne* finish their drinks as she was led out of the inn. Lando nodded to her as she exited and, without a word, fell in step behind her and next to MacDuff's guard as they sauntered along the docks. They walked away from the *Daphne*, which suited Jamie's plans.

MacDuff spoke of his travels and his favorite Irish port. "Have you been to Ireland?"

"No, I'm afraid I have no contacts there, but I hear it's good for the cargo business."

"Perhaps I can help introduce you on one of your next runs."

"Perhaps so."

"Shall I walk you back to your ship?" MacDuff asked.

Before she could answer, Lando responded. "That won't be necessary, sir."

When MacDuff turned to him, Stella was relieved to see Michelson and the sailor from the inn directly behind Lando.

Lando nodded with deference to MacDuff. "You understand, sir."

MacDuff gave the three men a thoughtful look then waved off his bodyguard, who'd taken a step closer. He kissed Stella's hand and gave her a wicked grin. "At least I don't have to worry about your safety."

She reached into her pocket and took his hand, turning it over to run a thumb over his palm. Then she placed a swan in it. "Something to remember me by." She winked. "Until next time."

His laughter followed them as Lando took her arm and strode back the way they'd come. Michelson and the sailor remained behind them as they disappeared into a crowd of sailors.

"Are you alright?" Lando asked.

"Yes." She couldn't stop shaking as he slowly scanned behind them before walking her up the gangplank to the deck of the *Daphne*.

Lando didn't stop until they'd reached the galley where Jamie, Fitz, and Beckworth waited. Beckworth jumped to her side as soon as Lando released her arm, and she leaned into him, welcoming his embrace as he led her to a chair.

"Well?" Jamie asked.

She took a deep breath, shaking off the last of her tremors. "Like shooting thugs in a barrel."

22

"Two days doesn't give us much time." Jamie stared at the chart spread across the navigation table.

"What are you thinking?" Beckworth leaned over the table as he reviewed the ports between where they were and where they needed to be in two days. There wasn't much to work with, and he had no contacts on this side of the coast.

"MacDuff will want to see the cargo, and he'll push Stella to show hers first."

"I don't suppose you're carrying anything that can pass muster?"

Jamie smiled. "Not currently."

"I know someone who might have what we need." Fitz rested his hip against the table and nudged Lando. "Do you think Parsons might have something?"

Lando gave a non-committal shrug. "He's probably our best option, but we'd have to go south before we head back north. It's a gamble, but he's usually got something in that old barn."

"We'd only need one crate," Michelson offered. "Some flint-locks, maybe a few cannonballs."

"A sample of wares." Beckworth nodded. "If we have to show

ours first, we don't want to show them a warehouse, just a single crate of what we have to offer."

"Heading south might confuse the men who've been watching the *Daphne*," Fitz said.

It didn't surprise Beckworth that MacDuff would have been spying as they'd been. "Do you think they've seen Stella aboard?"

"Aye. MacDuff probably has several men watching the ships."

"If we head south, he might think we're headed for hidden cargo." Jamie nodded his head. "If we leave now, we can make it by mid-day tomorrow. If Parsons doesn't have what we need, he might know where we can get something to satisfy MacDuff."

Fitz scratched his beard. "And if we catch the wind right, we should make Tenby in time for Lady Swan's meeting."

"I'm not familiar with Tenby." Beckworth hated to mention his problem to the men. "Stella needs another dress or two. Something that reflects a higher station."

Jamie frowned as he considered their options. "I can't say I'm familiar with the dressmakers in these ports. She might want to take some time while we're under sail to make adjustments to what she has on hand." He glanced at the other men, who all stared at the floor, stymied by the question.

Beckworth barked out a laugh. "I should have known better than to ask you blokes anything about women's apparel. Mark my words, there will come a day when you wish you knew more."

When the meeting ended, everyone but Beckworth went up to prepare the ship for sail. He stopped in the pantry to grab a bottle of wine and two mugs before heading for the cabin.

Stella was asleep, wearing only her undergarments. All of her dresses hung from various spots in the cabin. It didn't take more than a few seconds for him to agree she needed another dress or two.

He sat to remove his boots and had the first one off when she lifted her head.

"Is the meeting over already?" She rolled over and lifted up to her elbow, watching him remove the other boot.

"Yes. Fitz knows a man south of here that might have something that will provide a decent sample for MacDuff."

"South? How far? Will we still make the meet in two days?"

"If we catch a good wind and we don't spend too much time in port, yes." He stood and removed his jacket, then opened the wine. "MacDuff's been watching the *Daphne*. He'll see us head south and assume we're retrieving our contraband. If we're late, he'll wait a day. When one does business with ships, you have to make accommodations for weather and patrols."

She sat up when he handed her a mug. "Thank you."

"Move over."

She scooted over a few inches, leaned against the headboard, and rubbed her stomach. "I don't know what's bothering me most—the motion of the ship or my nerves."

"Was the meeting difficult?"

She hesitated, gave him a side glance, then took a long sip of wine.

"Just say it."

She ran a hand over the bed cover, worrying at a spot. "He's actually quite charming."

His temper instantly flared but he somehow managed to hold it in. "Really."

"I knew you'd be mad."

"I'm not mad."

She laughed. "Of course you are. Or perhaps a bit jealous?"

He drank his wine and looked at the dresses hanging

around the room, anything but at her. "I thought you said it was nerves upsetting your stomach."

"Don't get me wrong. He's dangerous. I can sense it. Not necessarily by his words but by his actions—his nods to his bodyguard, the way he watches a room."

"I would do the same thing."

She nodded as she put her thoughts together. "He has a reputation. One based on facts and his past behaviors." She poked him. "If you remember, I had a problem trusting you in the beginning."

Her lack of trust and her implied statement that AJ didn't trust him had bothered him quite a bit at the time. It had still hurt when she'd admitted that she'd lied. But he couldn't blame her. She'd been dragged from her time by ruffians and was on her own with no one she could rely on. He understood.

She took his hand. "MacDuff was enchanted by my bold nature, just like you. And all men are charming when they're interested. In this time period, he's the type that would woo me just to find his advantage. He knows I have no real rights. That sooner or later I'll need a man if for nothing more than shelter or protection. But for now, I'm a competitor. He'll want this partnership because he assumes he'll be able to not only control me but any contacts I've gained. With male competitors, he's the type that will take an honest enough percentage until he finds a way to screw them." She laughed. "With a woman, he thinks he can just bed me then take my contraband and contacts for his illicit trading. Or, if it's true, the Irish army he's building for Napoleon."

"I don't like this."

"I know." She took his mug and set it next to hers on the bedside table. "Let's not talk anymore. The men are busy. It's time for you to calm my nerves."

He pulled her to him and relished her giggles as he began

stripping off the last of her clothes. Then he made her forget all about MacDuff.

"How long do we have to wait for Parsons?" Beckworth asked.

The *Daphne* had made port in the sleepy seaside village in time for lunch. On the captain's orders, everyone stayed onboard except for the team sent to procure the contraband. Jamie had moored just inside the bay so they could leave as soon as the meeting was over. A weather system was coming, and he was concerned it would impact their arrival in Tenby.

Fitz, Lando, Lane, and Beckworth had rowed the jolly boat to a pier and went directly to the single pub. The only ships at port were small fishing boats, which meant most of the pub's customers were likely local villagers. Fitz ate his stew quickly, then disappeared in search of his contact. The rest of them relaxed and drank ale as they waited.

It was an hour before Fitz returned and waved at the busy server, who dropped a mug of ale in front of him.

"Well?" Lando asked after waiting for Fitz to swallow his first sip.

"He said give him an hour and we'll meet him at an old barn on the far side of his property. It's close and won't take more than a half hour to get there. We might as well drink."

And like the hour before Fitz had returned, no one spoke of MacDuff, Cheval, or the mission. Instead, talk turned to the hunting party.

"Do you think we'll make it back in time for it?" Lando asked.

"It would be a shame to miss your own party." Fitz lit his

pipe, puffing out a pleasant scent with a touch of cherry essence.

"It depends on what happens with MacDuff. I don't think the intent was to set up a full trade." Beckworth hadn't given the hunting weekend more than a passing thought. His focus had been on Stella and the mission. Each step more dangerous than the last.

"The only information we need from the next meeting is where MacDuff usually does his trading and if he'll tell Stella something about his smuggling operation." Lando tapped his fingers on the table, his gaze constantly returning to the door. "Hensley will have to decide what he wants to do with the information."

"What will MacDuff do if we don't make the final meeting place?" Lane asked.

Beckworth shrugged. "He'll either think Stella found the partnership not as lucrative as she'd hoped or simply changed her mind for no specific reason." He grinned. "As women are wont to do."

They laughed but didn't disagree. It wasn't unusual for smugglers to consider an enticing offer too great a risk, or they might have discovered they were being followed by patrols. If MacDuff ever met up with the *Daphne* again, it would be easy enough to say they'd been paid to run cargo for Lady Swan, but it hadn't worked out. Jamie had run the smuggling game since Finn owned the *Daphne* and would know how to handle the situation.

When the time came, they exited the pub to a stronger coastal wind. Beckworth glanced up to a smattering of clouds. It would be best if they got this done and set sail before the storm.

The walk to the property didn't take long. Without Fitz, they would have stumbled around the woods for days. A narrow deer trail was the only direct entrance to the old barn from town. On the far side of the barn, a rut-filled path, just wide enough for a wagon, meandered into the woods.

"Where does that path lead?" Beckworth asked.

Fitz waved off to his right. "It winds around several twists and turns before coming out to another well-disguised path that meets up with the main road. He only uses it when the cargo has to be moved so it looks unused."

The barn door was closed but a horse swished its tail by a nearby tree.

Fitz knocked on the barn door and waited.

An old man, short and stocky, with a wild crop of dust brown hair and a round face, opened the door. He squinted as he peered out and gave the four men a long look. Somewhat satisfied he stepped back. "Come in." He left the door open and disappeared into the dimly lit space.

Lando went first, followed by Beckworth and Lane, while Fitz closed the door. The barn appeared empty. If there had ever been hay stored in it, the forage had disintegrated into the dirt long ago. A single lantern sat toward the back of the barn, and it wasn't until they walked closer that Beckworth made out a door. He stood back. The wall ran the width of the barn. To the casual eye, it appeared to be the backside of the barn.

Parsons picked up the lantern and opened the door, leading them into another room. It was the same width of the barn but only twenty feet deep. Another lantern sat on top of what was one of many crates that took up most of the room. Several stacks of kegs lined the far-right wall. A smuggler's hideaway.

"Fitz said you were interested in a crate of weapons to entice MacDuff." Parsons eyed the group, probably trying to determine if someone other than Fitz was in charge.

Lando nodded. "Flintlocks. A few cannonballs. Maybe a keg of gunpowder."

"And maybe a fine dress or two," Fitz added as he snorted and glanced at Beckworth.

Parsons lifted a brow and gave Beckworth a slight smile. "Like dresses, huh." He studied Beckworth, who blandly stared back. "To each their own. Let's see what I have."

It didn't take long to lift two crates to the ground.

Beckworth whistled when the first one was opened, and he picked up one of the rifles. "These are French."

Parsons nodded. "They're harder to come by but worth the risk for the price I get for them. English ones are easier to get, but I'd rather keep as many of them out of Napoleon's reach as I can."

They settled on a dozen flintlocks, a handful of eighteen-pound cannonballs, and two kegs of powder. Before the old man closed the lid, he picked up the lantern and moved to another stack of crates. He crooked a finger at Beckworth. "I think I have something you might like."

Beckworth's brows rose when Parsons opened a crate filled with linens, lace, and several well-tailored day dresses. "These are French, too."

"Yep. And they cost a pretty penny."

Beckworth removed several, taking a closer look at the size of the dress rather than the color. While he made his selections, the others moved the crate and two kegs to a wagon parked behind the barn. He selected two dresses he thought were close enough in size. Stella was decent with needle and thread that she could make them fit well enough. He smiled and gladly paid Parsons his asking price, already imagining how excited she would be.

A young lad waited with reins in hand as the men climbed into the wagon.

Fitz handed Parsons a bag of coins. He considered the weight and tipped an imaginary hat at Fitz. "Always good to do business with you. Next time you're in port, the drinks are on me." He rapped on the wagon, and Fitz jumped up to the bench seat as the lad clucked at the horses.

The road into town was quiet. The wagon made its way to the end of a narrow trail where the jolly boat waited.

Twenty minutes later, the boat knocked into the side of the *Daphne,* and lines were dropped to raise the cargo. Then a ladder was lowered for the men before the jolly boat was lifted onboard.

Jamie stared into the crate. "French rifles? This is more than we could have hoped for." He grinned. "And you apparently found a dressmaker." He patted Beckworth on the shoulder then turned and yelled the order, "Prepare for sail."

Beckworth found Stella pacing in the cabin.

She turned when she heard him enter, hands on hips. "It's about time. You've been gone for hours."

He chuckled. "Now you know how I feel."

"That's not the same at all. There are at least three or four men with eyes on me all the time. And dinner took two hours at most. First, I'm stuck down here because I can't be seen on deck. As if anyone on the fishing boats would have a clue who I am. Second, you're meeting with some sketchy smuggler that Fitz knows, and who knows who might be watching him because he's a smuggler. You could have been hauled off by—" She tilted her head. "I'm not sure exactly by who, but someone from the law or maybe another smuggler. It's not the same at all."

Not only did she have a list, but she dragged out the last sentence to ensure he understood exactly how perturbed she was.

"Perhaps this will make up for my inconsiderate absence." He laid down the bundle of dresses that had been wrapped in a cloak that he'd also purchased from Parsons.

She didn't waste any time turning the bundle around,

opening the cloak with delicate movements. When she found the dresses inside, her eyes glittered but her focus remained on the cloak which was a deep emerald that complemented her green eyes and luscious, if untamed, auburn hair. She wrapped it around her and ran her cheek across the collar.

"Oh, Teddy. This is marvelous."

He only allowed a small handful of people to call him Teddy. He loved it when she said it, though she didn't use his first name often and rarely in public. It was something she reserved for when it was only the two of them, usually during intimate or special moments—like this. And somehow, that made it all the more endearing.

Then she ripped it off and tossed it on the bed.

He laughed at her theatrics as she picked up the first dress, which was made of silk and lace. It wasn't a dress she'd wear to dinner in London, but for the ports they visited, she'd look like royalty. It was a soft lavender, and though she preferred bolder colors, the men wouldn't be able to take their eyes off her.

"Help me try these on." She turned her back to him and waited for him to untie the laces. He slipped the dress off her shoulders and held her hand as she stepped out of it. He placed the dress on the bed while she stepped into the lavender one.

The bodice fit fine, though it was too revealing. It would be fine if he was taking her to dinner, but not for meeting with MacDuff. It was also a bit tight in the waist.

She looked in the small mirror. "I can take the waist out an inch. I've seen Eleanor do it." She ran a hand across the bodice. "I think Libby packed a couple of linen handkerchiefs that I can tuck in the top." She tapped a finger on her lower lip. "Although, perhaps it's best to keep MacDuff off kilter."

"That dress should do it."

She smirked. "Okay, let's try the other one."

The ship rocked and she fell against him. "We're leaving?"

He set her upright and undid the ties, once again stripping the dress off her. "A storm's coming. Jamie thinks it will be over quickly, but you might want to take one of your pills."

She picked up the second dress. This one was a dusty rose and matched the blooming color in her cheeks. "I'm enjoying having you undress me. I think I'll give Libby the nights off when we return to Waverly."

He felt his manhood stir, and he waited patiently for her to pull the dress on, which she did in twice the amount of time it took her to try on the last one. She was seducing him.

He grinned. Two could play that game.

Once she had her arms through the sleeves, he scraped his knuckles along her back as he slowly tied the strings. Then he lightly brushed her hair away, barely touching her skin.

She shivered, and he dropped his smile as she turned around. Her gaze seared him, and her voice took on a lusty tone when she asked, "How does it look?"

This one fit better and had a higher neckline which pleased him more than he would admit.

"Like it was made for you."

"Take it off."

He couldn't hold back a smile as he turned her around. Since she started it, he took his time, and when the dress fell to the floor, he lifted her into his arms rather than let her step out of it. She wrapped her arms around his neck, light goosebumps erupting over her soft skin. He dumped her on the bed then unbuttoned his jacket.

She didn't stay where he put her. Instead, she yanked off her undergarments then brushed his hands away as she tugged off his jacket, untied his shirt, then rolled it up his chest until he helped her pull it over his head.

Her fingers were already working the buttons of his pants, occasionally slipping down to stroke him. He pushed her back on the bed, then sat down to take off his boots. Her arms wrapped around him, and she pressed her breasts against his back.

It was all he could do to get his pants off.

Then she was pulling him down. "Take me to the moon, Teddy. I don't want to come back down until we're late for dinner."

23

———————

Stella fussed with the rose-colored dress. She loved the lavender one but didn't want to have to deal with the lower neckline. And while her sewing skills would pass muster on letting out the waist, the seas had been rough on their travel north. She'd taken her motion sickness pill last night and that morning, but she didn't want to chance getting sick or continually stabbing herself with a needle during the unpredictable sea.

At breakfast, Jamie said the seas should calm by afternoon, and he was almost right. She'd kept busy in the galley most of the day, which kept her mind off the rocking motion of the ship, though there was one moment the ship took an unexpected dip that sent her and several cooking pots rolling across the floor. If only she'd hit her head. She could use some unconscious time.

Beckworth had slept in with her after a long night of lovemaking but had still risen too early for her liking. He'd brought her a pot of coffee, gave her a toe-tingling kiss, and whispered, "Sleep in. We'll be going over plans once the storm calms."

Then he was gone.

Once the seas had calmed to where she could walk across the galley without stumbling about, she'd made her way topside to stroll the deck and breathe in the fresh salt air. She found Fitz working the lines on the starboard rigging and stopped to lean against the railing. Though the sea still churned, the rain had stopped and the clouds were thinning, otherwise she would've never gotten close to the railing.

There had been a raging storm during the middle of the night the first time she'd been forced to cross the Channel with Beckworth to escape Gemini. They didn't have the coin for a cabin and had shared a tarp-covered spot on deck along with several other travelers. She chuckled. They'd spent more time wet than dry, and during the storm, one of the makeshift tents had collapsed. When Beckworth went to help, she'd heard a woman cry. Worried about Beckworth and acting like a naive idiot, she'd tried to help. She'd only managed several steps from the relative safety of their tent when a rogue wave hit the ship. She fell, sliding toward the railing that was barely waist high as the ship heaved to port. She'd held onto the deck by her finger-nails until the ship righted itself. It was an experience she would never forget.

"I'm surprised to see you on deck."

She glanced over, pulled from her musings, to find Fitz leaning against the railing watching her.

"I thought some fresh air would do me good, and it seemed safe enough to come on deck. I didn't mean to disturb your work."

He nodded. "There's nothing better than the sea air to clean the head and settle the belly. And you're not bothering me. Some days it feels like I could work the rigging with me eyes closed."

"I believe that. How long have you been sailing?"

He gave it some consideration. "Since I was a wee lad of ten. Jamie and I grew up in the same village, not far from where Finn and Maire lived. The two of us sneaked onto the *Daphne* the first time Finn took her for a sail. It was a small cargo run to Dublin. He caught us not an hour from shore and threatened to throw us overboard if we didn't work for passage. I don't think either of us slept a wink during the entire round trip. We even helped move the cargo, though neither of us could carry much of a load."

He chuckled. "One trip was all it took for the both of us. We were lucky it was Finn's ship. Not all captains are as kind as him. When it was time for the next sail, he sent us a message asking if we wanted to join. Neither of us has looked back since."

"Didn't you have family in Ireland?"

He nodded. "Still do. Jamie finds a way to get us back once or twice a year to see them. We both have many brothers and sisters, so our mams don't miss us too much—one less mouth to feed. But we send them money and letters."

He leaned close. "I don't think they like us working for the English, but they don't seem bothered taking the money."

She wasn't sure how to respond, but when she noted the spark of humor in his gaze, she shook her head. "Family. I left mine a long time ago." She looked out to sea, wondering what her mother would make of her life. She'd most likely shake her head, wondering what she'd done to make her child so rebellious. Nothing at all like her brothers.

"Are you ready for this evening?"

She appreciated the change of topic. "As ready as I can be. Weren't you supposed to be in meetings?"

"Aye. I sat in for the first of it, but with Jamie and Lando in the meeting, my time is better spent up here." He glanced up, then stepped aside to loosen a line before tightening and retying it. "Why aren't you at the meeting?"

"I'm nervous enough. I think talking about it would only make me more anxious."

He turned to her, and this time his tone was serious.

"There's only one thing to keep in mind with these blokes. As kind and nice as they might seem, underneath it all, a smuggler thinks about money first and his men second. Anything or—" he pointed a finger at her, "—anyone else isn't worth their time. Even a pretty lady. You're a smart woman, just like AJ. Keep your dagger close, and don't be afraid to use it. I don't mean to scare you, but MacDuff is a ruthless man. Don't let his charm make you forget that."

She sobered instantly. And while his words should have scared her, they snapped her out of whatever fugue state she'd been living in while onboard the ship. She nodded. "That helped more than you know."

He studied her for a moment, then his good-natured grin appeared. "That's a good lass." He rubbed his stomach. "You wouldn't by any chance know if lunch is almost ready?"

She laughed. "Let me go see what Cook is up to. Come down when you're ready. I'll find something you can eat."

She patted his arm before striding down the deck, taking a last look at the clearing sky before descending the stairs. After helping Cook with lunch and cleaning the galley, she fell asleep. When she woke, she'd expected Beckworth to be back. Then she found a swan lying on the pillow next to her. He had been there and had let her sleep.

Did he do that on purpose? He wasn't happy with this latest change in the mission. Did he blame her? He would never admit it. And on the surface, he would believe it. But down deep —buried in his subconscious—was he sorry he'd fallen in love with such a bold woman? The jury was still out on whether she was smart or stupid, sane or just plain crazy.

It was too late to do anything about it now. They were in too deep, and while she could tell Jamie she couldn't go through with it, she wouldn't disappoint Hensley or the rest of the men who would have to come up with another plan.

The cold truth was that she was the only one who could get close enough to MacDuff within the time period allotted. With any luck, she and Beckworth would come out of it unscathed. Then she'd play the good little woman the entire hunting party weekend.

She tugged on the day dress, though, in her opinion, it was too nice for daytime. Beckworth said they were from France. Even now, with the war, Paris was the height of fashion. She couldn't reach the ties and struggled with pulling her hair back while trying to keep the sleeves from slipping down her arms. Frustrated with the entire situation, she stabbed the hairpins in her hair, but try as she might she would never tame her hair like Libby could.

She was in the middle of yanking the pins out of her hair, which made her curls turn into knots when the door opened with barely a knock.

Beckworth strode in, a frown on his face and a storm in his gaze until he saw her and stopped. He tried. She could tell. But the laugh slipped from him until she felt like throwing something at him.

"Stop laughing and help me." She flapped her arms. "I can't do anything with the dress untied."

He held a hand to his side, his laughter still bubbling out. When he was able to catch a breath, he worked hard to cover his grin. "Why didn't you wait for me?" He strode over and turned her around so he could get to the ties.

"I haven't seen you all day. And you didn't even wake me when you came back. How long were you here before leaving again?"

"Only long enough to see you sleeping. Somehow, we've simply passed each other without knowing it."

She grunted. Unlikely, but she wouldn't push. She picked up

the brush and attacked her hair. After two tangled pulls, Beckworth stayed her hand, then pried the brush from her fingers.

"Let me. The last thing MacDuff will be interested in is a bald woman. Nice cheekbones or not."

She let his complement pass, not willing to engage. He was upset, and the last thing they needed was a fight. She had to keep her head in the game, and second-guessing herself worrying about his mood wasn't helping.

When he was done with her hair, she took a quick look in the mirror and nodded. "Thank you. That's better."

She folded the other dress and put it away. Silence between them had never been a problem before, but she felt the tension increase and released a thankful sigh when the knock came.

She let Beckworth answer it.

It was Lando.

"It's time. MacDuff's ship is already here."

Without another word, she picked up her new cloak, wrapped it around her, and followed Lando to the upper deck. Beckworth trailed behind. He'd be out there somewhere—watching. Protecting. But he stopped at the gangplank with Fitz, Michelson, and Lane as Lando led her to the dock and toward an inn.

"Where's the crate?"

"It's already been moved to a warehouse." He pushed their way through a throng of sailors. "We have a handful of sailors watching it until Fitz and the others arrive."

"Do we know where MacDuff is?"

He tapped her arm, and she glanced up.

MacDuff leaned against a post in front of the inn. His bodyguard stood a few steps behind him. He gave Lando a cursory glance then held out an arm for her.

"I thought we'd get a quick meal and discuss our next steps."

"Excellent. I'm famished. It's good to have my feet on solid ground."

He chuckled and led her in. As usual, Lando and the guard stayed outside.

He ordered for them both, and Stella, wanting to down the first mug of ale in one swallow, took a long sip instead. She didn't see any reason to be dainty but didn't want to appear nervous, even if she was shaking inside.

They ate while MacDuff shared funny anecdotes of his travels with storms at sea. Stella described her venture across the Channel to France, modifying the story by saying she'd left her cabin, saw the captain's niece going up the stairs during the storm, and decided to follow her, eventually saving her from falling overboard. It was mostly true.

Once the plates were removed, MacDuff's jovial mood shifted to business.

"Did you bring something to show me?" His gaze had hardened.

She swallowed the lump in her throat and ran a finger around the top of her mug, his gaze dropping to watch.

"I have a crate waiting in a warehouse."

"Don't trust me to take me to your ship?"

"Do you plan on taking me to your ship to show me your cargo?"

His expression softened with a wide grin. He glanced around the room, which was busy but not overly crowded. They were in a corner with three sailors at the next table, more concerned for their food than listening to those around them.

"Can you give me a hint?" He placed his hand next to hers on the table. Close but not touching.

She ran a finger along his hand as she looked him in the eye, leaned in, and lowered her voice. "Just a few rifles, a handful of cannonballs, and some powder." When he didn't show any enthusiasm, she added, "Straight from France."

His eyes widened, and he grabbed her hand. "You're teasing."

"I never tease." She sat back, pulling her hand away as she took another swallow of ale from her second one of the night. A light buzz made her more comfortable. "There's also some fine dresses." She tugged at the bodice. "I thought I'd wear one for you."

He'd followed her hands to her neckline, and she thanked the stars she hadn't worn the lavender gown. He reached out to touch the fabric at her wrist. "It's indeed fine." His gaze sharpened. "How did you get French arms?"

She winked. "I have connections." She thought of Sebastian and the smuggling ring he'd run with Jamie. He'd called it a syndicate. He thought it sounded better than smuggling since he was doing the work of the Brotherhood of Monks. The ill-gotten gains from the smuggling went to purchasing artifacts that had been stolen from the monastery during the Reign of Terror. "It's a syndicate of other like-minded entrepreneurs."

He sat back and emptied his mug then waved for a server, who quickly appeared with two fresh mugs. He took a drink then leaned his elbows on the table. "I also have a network that trades between Ireland, Scotland, and England. On rare occasions, we have an opportunity to trade with someone coming from France. If you could provide a regular shipment of French weapons—" He smiled. "Or fine dresses, I could make you more money than you thought possible."

He gave the room a quick scan. "The Irish are hungry for weapons. There's a building group of individuals who'd like to see French ships at their ports. Perhaps you have some influence in that direction."

Stella racked her brain. Finn had mentioned the time when

Jamie had dropped off Maire and Ethan to search for one of the Mórdha chronicles. Before he sailed to London, he'd made a cargo run to Ireland. The crew had seen MacDuff and tracked him to several ports where he'd riled up the locals in search of friendly ports for France. Jamie and Hensley thought he'd given up the game. Apparently not.

She shrugged in response to MacDuff's query, staring at the ale. When she glanced up, she grinned, feeling the effects of the ale. *Stay calm.* "I have friends along the northwest coast of France. We make a run every couple of months." She tilted her head. "How many are in this network of yours?"

Before he had a chance to answer, the door to the inn blasted open, and a man stalked to their table. Stella sat back in surprise as he stood over them. What the hell?

"Thomas?"

"You thought you could run. The viscount has men every-where looking for you. It was just a matter of time finding the right port."

He grabbed her arm and yanked her up. She'd barely reached her feet when he picked her up and tossed her over his shoulder. What the hell was he doing here? Had Hensley sent him?

"Let me go." She wasn't sure what was happening but decided to play it out. She beat on his shoulders.

His voice was loud and clear as he easily contained her struggles. "You'll not escape the marriage."

Marriage? Good grief, was that the best Beckworth could come up with? This whole ploy reeked of his games. "I'm not marrying that man," she screamed.

"The banns were printed. There's no getting out of them."

"Oomph." The air was momentarily knocked out of her as he repositioned her over his strong shoulders. "I told him I didn't want to marry him."

"You have no say in the matter. And if you keep screaming, I have a rag and rope handy."

"You wouldn't."

He nodded at MacDuff. "Sorry for interrupting your meal."

Stella lifted her head enough to catch the smuggler's gaze. He didn't like what was happening, but he glanced around the room, quickly making a decision not to get involved. Though, there was a storm roiling in his expression. He probably wasn't going to get those French firearms.

Damn it. She'd been so close.

T homas didn't slow as he stormed out of the inn. Lando was still outside, and he blocked the guard as Thomas stormed by with her still beating on his back.

He carried her past several buildings before turning into an alley with Lando right behind him. When he was far enough away from the street, he set her down.

She was spitting mad as she glared at the two men. "You fools. I was seconds from getting the information about his network."

"Change of plans, luv." Beckworth stepped out of the shadows.

She spun around, her anger still burning. With one hand on her hip, she pointed a finger at him. "You know he'll just follow us."

He gave her his cheeky grin. "Good god, let's hope so. Otherwise, listening to all that caterwauling is time I won't get back."

24

———

"Take Stella back to the ship." Beckworth took a step backward then disappeared into the shadows.

Stella turned on the rest of the men. Fitz, Thomas, and Lando glanced up, down, and around the alley, anywhere but at her. "What the hell? MacDuff was going to tell me about his network."

"We didn't have a choice." Fitz stepped forward. Brave man. "Cheval is here, and he's looking for MacDuff."

She hadn't expected that and paced a tight line in front of the men. "So, you had to pull me out." She began to nod, then stopped and looked at Thomas. "Where did you come from? I mean, it's nice to see you, but how?"

"Hensley sent me once he received Jamie's letter with his next two stops. I rode like hell to get here."

"They say timing is everything." She turned back to Fitz. "Where did Beckworth go?"

He glanced at his feet then at Lando before saying, "He needed to get back to Lane. He's watching Cheval on his own."

She wasn't fooled. Beckworth wasn't handling this well. He

hadn't wanted her to be the conduit with MacDuff, and Cheval showing up increased the risk. Once again, he was fighting between his commitment to the mission and his concern for her. But walking off in a snit during a mission wasn't professional and, well, it pissed her off, regardless of how much she understood it.

"Fine." She took Lando's arm. "Take me back to the ship. Or should I be going back with Thomas?"

"Thomas will go back with us," Lando said. "Fitz will continue his surveillance."

She dropped her hand from Lando's arm and walked quietly with her head down between the two men. If anyone spotted her, she would appear defeated. It certainly matched her emotions.

She remained detached as they boarded the ship, crossed the deck, and descended to the galley. When she turned for her cabin, Lando called her back.

"Jamie will want us in his office."

She didn't think her shoulders could drop any lower, but they did. Instead of turning left, she turned right then leaned against the wall, waiting for Lando to take the lead. She dropped onto a stool closest to the door, irritated that she wanted to dart out of it like a bunny chased by a fox, unable to shake the depressed feeling of watching Beckworth walk away without a word.

She understood it. Of course, she did. And she kept saying it over and over in her head, but the mantra did little to restore her energy.

"Stella. Stella, did you hear me?" Jamie asked.

Her head popped up. "Sorry. Did you ask me something?"

He gave her a gentle smile and a nod, tugging at his ear. Not for the first time, she imagined him with an earring. He'd even look good with an eye patch. Not that she wanted him to lose his eye, but if he did, he'd still be hot. "I asked if you were alright, but I think I have my answer. I'll make this quick." He glanced up when Lane entered. "Any news?"

Lane shook his head. "We expected Cheval to meet with MacDuff, but he either hasn't found him or changed his plans."

"It's possible he wasn't expecting MacDuff to be here." Lando pulled out his dagger and whetstone.

The soft, consistent sound of steel on stone was soothing, and Stella's shoulders relaxed. Funny. She hadn't realized when they went from drooping to filled with tension.

"Maybe MacDuff knew Cheval would be here and wanted him to know there was competition." Thomas, sitting next to Jamie's desk, leaned forward. "I know I'm new here, but Hensley let me read your messages. His question was which of them held the power, MacDuff or Cheval? Or were they truly equal partners?"

"If MacDuff had agreed to a meeting with Stella because he knew it was an easy way to prove to Cheval he didn't need him, Hensley has his answer." Jamie turned to Stella. "Did MacDuff ever mention Cheval or any other smuggler?"

She glared at Jamie. It had occurred to her as she vaguely listened to the conversation that she didn't know who had pulled her from dinner. She'd assumed Beckworth, but maybe it was Jamie.

"We were just getting to that when someone dragged me out of there like some Neanderthal." She glanced at Thomas. "Nothing personal."

Thomas just grinned. She didn't know him well, but what little she'd seen of him in his role with taking down Gemini, he'd seemed distant and rarely smiled. Now he was relaxed and grinned easily which gave him a pleasant face.

"What did MacDuff tell you?" Jamie asked.

"He was excited to see the French weapons. He didn't get that opportunity often."

"That sounds like he doesn't have many contacts outside of the isles," Lando said.

She nodded, feeling better now with her thoughts engaged elsewhere. "He said he ran cargo in Ireland, Scotland, and England. He was extremely interested in trading with someone who had access to French supplies. One thing that's important. He wanted to know if I had any contacts that could help bring French ships to Ireland."

Before they could ask her anything else, a knock came before the door opened.

Michelson held a message. "Sorry, Captain. I was on my way back to report MacDuff leaving the inn. He appeared to be heading for his ship. I had just stepped onto the gangplank when a sailor called out. He handed me this note."

He passed it to Jamie and, instead of leaving, leaned against a bookcase that held rolled charts, ledgers, and a variety of books.

Jamie read the top of the folded letter. "It's for Lady Swan." He held up the note.

She was surprised but nodded and waved her hand. "You read it. I'm too tired."

He opened it and read it before glancing at the group. "He's demanding a meeting at a pub on the far end of the docks. His request is for now or he'll send men to see to your safety." He turned to Thomas first. "Looks like he doesn't think of you as much of a threat." Then he looked to Michelson. "Are you sure MacDuff was headed for his ship?"

Michelson considered his original statement before shrugging. "He was headed in that direction, but it's the same path to the pub. I should have followed."

"No matter." Jamie leaned back and tapped the note on his desk.

"It sounds like a trap," Lando said.

"Is it possible he's worried for her?" Thomas asked.

Stella snorted. "More like he's worried about the French firearms."

Jamie pondered his dilemma as the others went back and forth as to whether this was an advantage or a ploy.

"Quiet down." Jamie stood. "I don't think we have a choice. Stella, are you alright with going to the pub? I'll send Lando, Lane, Michelson, and Thomas with you. While you're meeting with MacDuff, I'll send someone to collect the crate. If MacDuff still wants to see the goods, I want to arrange a new location."

Stella, still worried about Beckworth's mood, didn't hesitate. "That's what we're here for, right? To try to get names or something of value?" She glanced at Lando, who nodded. "I'm ready. I just need to know where the crate will be." How would she explain getting away from the viscount's man? "I can tell him my ship's crew saved me from Thomas, so I think he should stay on the ship."

Jamie shook his head. "No. Thomas will go with you. We'll give him a hat and a different shirt. If he stays behind the others and keeps his head down, you'll be fine."

It wasn't her call. She could protest, but Thomas had been Sergeant of Arms for the Earl of Hereford. Ethan trusted him with his life. She couldn't think of a better man to have on her detail. She nodded in agreement.

"Tell him we'll meet him back in Burry Port in order to avoid the viscount's men." He looked to Lando. "Take the best route to the pub. If Cheval is out there, I don't want him to see Stella. If he's with MacDuff, terminate the mission. I'll have a note ready to be sent to MacDuff's ship with our request to meet at Burry Port. If Cheval follows MacDuff there, then we'll end the mission and return to Bristol. We have enough for Hensley."

The men stood but waited for Stella.

She stood and faced Jamie. "Beckworth isn't going to be happy about this, so I expect you to take responsibility for his anger."

He didn't smile, but his gaze was earnest as if he'd expected her request. "We have your back."

B eckworth walked through the dark alleys on his way to MacDuff's ship. He stopped long enough to pound his fist into a crate, then lowered his forehead to it. His emotions were in turmoil—fear, anger, pride. Everything had been working as planned until Cheval showed up.

Had MacDuff known? Had he been playing Stella for some reason? And why in all that's holy had he walked away without giving her some assurance that everything would be alright? He'd wanted to hold her, to feel her body close to his. Somehow, the horrors of the world disappeared when she was in his arms.

But the other men were there, and he was too proud to show his weakness. He would have to have a long talk with Finn when they returned to Baywood. How did the man deal with his fear for AJ when she went off and did something mad?

He rubbed his fist, then wiped the blood on his pants. Stella would demand to know how he'd scraped his knuckles. He breathed deeply. The soft evening air did little to calm his anxiety, but he shook it off and focused on the mission. Stay focused. That was the key, even if he had to remind himself every five minutes.

MacDuff had moored his ship at port this time. Was that important? He'd moored it in the bay at the last port. There were dozens of reasons why that would be, and speculation was pointless. He reached the docks and stopped at the end of a building to peer around the corner.

The *Grey Ghost* was easy to spot. The crew were furling the sails in preparation for departure. He hated that he'd had Stella pulled out before she could gather more information. But it had been too dangerous, and if it had been any of the men, he would have had them pulled out as well.

The last thing they needed was to come between MacDuff and Cheval. It was too early in the mission for that. The two men might be working together, but was it a congenial partnership or one out of necessity? Or did they share other business more risky than smuggling?

He watched for several minutes, and when the crew began releasing the mooring lines, he had what he needed. After looking to his left and right, ensuring he didn't spot anyone following him, he made his way back to the *Daphne*. He was whistling as he boarded the ship. Fitz had been watching Cheval's ship, which was docked on the other end of the pier. Even in the shadows, Beckworth had seen the masts and knew *The Horseman* was still in port.

He was eager to see Stella. His first thoughts were how to apologize. It was time for a long-overdue discussion. Did she understand his concerns? She always had before, but she'd been so mad at him. And his walking away like a coward wouldn't have eased her temper.

The crew was busy, and while the sails remained tied down, he recognized the early signs of readiness to sail. With Cheval in port, he couldn't blame Jamie for not wanting to stay. He ran down the stairs and strode directly to their cabin.

It was empty.

Everyone must still be with Jamie. No one had been in the

galley, so he went to Jamie's office. The door was open, and the only person there was the captain.

"Where's Stella?" he asked after tapping lightly on the doorframe.

Jamie was writing a letter, and Beckworth assumed it was for Thomas to take back to Hensley. Although the *Daphne* would be returning to Bristol soon, Jamie liked to keep the spymaster informed.

After another few scratches, Jamie set the quill aside and closed the inkpot. "She received a personal note from MacDuff asking for another meeting." He must have caught Beckworth's concern because he stood.

"The *Grey Ghost* slipped its mooring lines. They're departing."

Jamie pulled on his jacket then picked up his pistol and sword. "I sent four men with her."

They jogged up the stairs and across the deck to the gangplank. Jamie stopped long enough to give an order.

"Prepare for sail. Send a couple of men to round up anyone still in town."

Once they were on the pier, Beckworth asked, "When was the note delivered?"

"About thirty minutes ago. He asked to meet at a pub on the far end of town towards where the *Grey Ghost* was docked."

They raced that way, and when they reached it, Jamie stopped him from going in. "Let me check."

Beckworth knew it was for nothing. Not one of the men was there, and at least one of them would have remained outside.

Jamie was back in less than a minute. "They're not here."

They hadn't seen anyone on their rush to the pub. Beckworth glanced at the people roaming the docks. Nothing. He went to kick a nearby post when he spotted the paper swan. He picked it up, and Jamie stepped next to him.

"Look for another one," Beckworth said.

Jamie went one way, Beckworth the other.

"Here." Jamie picked up another swan. They continued in that direction, watching the ground until they reached an alley where another swan had been dropped. They turned down it and didn't have to go far before spotting four bodies lying on the dark street.

They were the men sent to guard Stella. Beckworth blew out a breath of relief to find them alive with no apparent injury other than bumps on their heads. They roused the men, who were groggy and slow to come around.

"Where's Stella?" Beckworth yelled at Lando, who was the first one to come to his senses.

"I don't know. There were at least twenty of them waiting at the pub."

"Stella was screaming for them to stop." Thomas raised up on an elbow, rubbed his head, then his stomach. "Promised to go with them if they'd leave us alive."

Lando used a stack of nearby crates to help him stand and wobbled before getting his legs under him. "She saved us. I think they would have killed us, but the leader, whoever it was, stopped his men who were wailing on us, but not before slamming us in the head." He glanced at Beckworth. "I'm sorry. I don't know which way they went."

Beckworth circled the area but didn't find any more swans. Stella most likely had her hands bound or arms held so she couldn't drop any others. He refused to think of any other reason.

"I have a pretty good idea who took her." Beckworth helped Lane up. "We need to get back to the ship."

"Michelson's wound is bad," Jamie said. "He'll need help." He took an arm and began lifting the unconscious man. Beckworth grabbed the other arm, and they dragged Michelson toward the ship.

Halfway there, Lando, his equilibrium restored, took Michelson from Jamie. "Prepare the ship. We're right behind you."

Jamie ran, but they couldn't move any faster than Lane and Thomas, who still struggled but were moving on their own two feet.

When Beckworth reached the ship, he found Fitz waiting for them.

"Cheval has Stella."

"You're sure." His worst nightmare was coming alive, and he was helpless to do anything.

Fitz nodded. "I saw her walk up the gangplank surrounded by over a dozen men. The ship was ready to sail. They left about fifteen minutes ago."

"How long before we can follow?"

"We still have men in port. Jamie sent men to round them up, but it will take another half hour to get the ship underway."

"Do you know which way they went?"

Fitz nodded. "I think they're heading south. I have someone in the nest watching. I gave them your glasses. I hope you don't mind."

Beckworth slapped him on the back. "Good man."

Jamie strode over, his forehead crinkled as he took in Michelson. "Get him below." The stomping of running boots made them turn. Sailors returning. "Get a head count. Thomas, I have a message for Hensley."

"You sure you won't need me?" Thomas was still rubbing his head.

"We need to send him what information we have. And we're not waiting for the men. I'll need you to gather up anyone who gets left behind. Get them to Bristol. We leave as soon as the sails are raised."

He strode off, shouting commands while Fitz remained to determine who was on the ship and who was still on shore.

Beckworth shook Thomas's hand. "We'll try to make the party. Safe travels, mate." He headed for the galley to check on Michelson. Anything to get his mind off Stella.

"Beckworth," Jamie called. "I could use you on the forward deck to help with the lines."

He'd only taken a few steps in the new direction when Jamie called out again.

"Beckworth. Do you mind taking the nest instead? We need to keep an eye on their sails, but I don't want them knowing we're behind them."

Beckworth glanced up at the nest. It made sense. By using his binoculars, they had an advantage in sighting ships over the single glass scopes. He began his climb. It would have been easier to work the lines, forcing his mind to stay focused while listening for orders from Jamie or Fitz. In the nest, he'd be alone with his binoculars and his thoughts.

He knew this mission would go bad. But why would Cheval want Stella? How did he even know about her?

He hadn't heard Lando approach and startled when the big man laid a hand on his shoulder.

"You need to remain focused on the mission. This is no time for mistakes."

He nodded, unable to find the proper words for a response. Then he climbed, allowing each breath of sea air to soothe him and clear his head. When he reached the nest, he tapped the sailor. He thought the lad's name was Stephen.

Stephen jumped and turned, surprised to see Beckworth. "My shift just started."

"Captain's orders. I'll take the glasses. You're needed on the lines."

Stephen handed him the glasses as soon as he climbed in. "The ship is straight ahead. Based on the set of the sails, they appear to be turning to their port side, but they need to get beyond the rocks on the point. They might continue straight for Ireland, but word on the ship is that they'll sail along the coast and disappear into a cove."

"Understood. Thanks, mate." Beckworth waited for the lad to start his descent then brought the glasses up to find his mark. Sure enough. The ship was set to change course.

Hold on, Stella. We're coming for you.

25

———————

Nails. Someone was pounding nails into her head. It seemed familiar.

Stella didn't want to open her eyes. Before her brain could overrule the action, the signal most likely blocked by the sound of the hammer hitting home, she pried one open.

Darkness.

She waited. Nothing changed. The blackness was complete. Not a single ounce of light.

The atrocious stink attacked her senses, and she forgot all about the intense headache. Urine and fecal scents were the first to hit, followed closely by the rot of dead fish. But what made her gag was the sickly sweet scent of a spice she couldn't name that wove through the other acrid smells.

Her first thought was that she was in an alley. Maybe behind the inn or a pub. If that were true, there should be more light.

The rest of her senses rushed in. The sway of a ship battling waves. The creak of wood rebelling against such rough handling.

Giving up on where she was, she tried to remember what happened.

When she considered the question, the throbbing returned with a debilitating tempo.

A door creaked open.

A startling bright light forced her to slam her lids shut. The pain would have brought her to her knees if she hadn't already been sitting.

"Hello, pretty lady." The voice was English and gave her a cold chill.

A rough hand ran over her hair. "You must be thirsty. Drink some water."

Without opening her eyes, she felt the metal lip of the mug and tasted the cool water as it ran into her mouth, and she felt the chill as it spilled onto her chin and down her neck. She'd taken two swallows before the sweet scent sounded an alarm as the bitter taste brought back her gag reflexes.

"If the captain wasn't saving you for himself, we could have some fun. But he doesn't trust you and prefers you sleep."

His body pressed into hers, and she stifled a groan.

The pain in her head receded, and a light euphoria chased away the anxiety as the deep darkness returned.

Several hours had passed since leaving port. Beckworth leaned against the railing as the *Daphne* plowed into the sea in its dogged pursuit of *The Horseman*, nothing but a dot of light in the darkened skies. Soft raindrops struck his face and mixed with salty spray each time the bow struck another wave.

He raged against their inability to overtake the ship. Cheval had gotten ahead of them, but Jamie assured Beckworth they'd catch up, it was just a matter of time.

But how much time did Stella have? Was she already gone?

No. He couldn't afford to think like that. His feelings for Stella had to be pushed aside so he could focus on the mission. She was strong. She survived Gemini. She was of value as long as her cover hadn't been blown.

If Cheval considered her competition and not a spy for the Crown, then he'd be wise to keep her for barter. Or he could sell her to another captain. That idea didn't sit well, but Cheval wouldn't have time to put those plans in motion with the *Daphne* chasing him.

The wind had shifted shortly after leaving the bay, and the ship lost ground before Jamie and the crew had time to readjust the sails. Yet, Jamie, Lando, and Fitz had all agreed they could make up the lost time. But, the yellow dot of light seemed to grow dimmer not closer.

If he only understood why she'd ended up on that ship. He should have forced his hand and made her stay at Waverly. He snorted. She would have probably stolen a horse and chased after him. Barrington would've had to lock her in a room with no windows until it was too late to follow.

He laughed into the night.

What would he have come home to then?

A spitfire.

Would she have forgiven him?

Finn had warned him about this. He hadn't given the man as much credit as he should have in dealing with headstrong women. And he cursed himself for the hundredth time for the pain he'd caused them both when he'd stolen AJ away through the fog. At the time, he hadn't been able to trust them any more than they could have trusted him. Then Finn had given himself up to Dugan, allowing Beckworth to escape and mount a rescue. But it had taken months, and Finn almost died.

It hadn't been his fault, yet he'd held the guilt. And it had been heartbreaking to watch AJ's stubbornness in finding Finn. It had all miraculously worked out.

Would everything work out this time?

He was well aware that he was a nineteenth-century man at heart. Possessive. Overly protective.

But he'd been attracted by Stella's independent nature, her strength, and her intelligence. She'd been the woman he'd fallen hard and fast for. The only woman who'd broken through his shell—that truly understood him. The one woman who could make his life better. Complete.

However Cheval had become aware of her and then considered her a threat no longer mattered.

He'd get her back. She was his life.

He let the rage dissipate, and as a deeper purpose rose, his focus sharpened. It was time to stop wallowing like the insipid lords at the London parties. Lando was right. This was a mission, and the enemy had taken one of their own.

It was time to push the offensive.

The rain increased as he strode along the deck. He studied the sailors as they worked until he found one that was slower than the rest. The man needed sleep.

"Get some rest. I'll take the rest of your shift."

The sailor stared at him and must have noted the conviction on Beckworth's face. Maybe he saw the devil. Either way, he muttered a thank you and, without a word, headed for his hammock. The other man who'd watched the short discussion, nodded at Beckworth before going back to work.

He leaned back to see what he could of the sails then worked the lines to keep the sails trimmed. He didn't pay attention to Jamie or Fitz when they'd strode by. Nor did he question the orders given as the rain and storm increased.

Had Stella taken her herbs before her meeting with MacDuff?

The men around him didn't say a word, and perhaps they couldn't hear past the storm as Beckworth laughed into the night.

He almost felt sorry for Cheval.

One thing was for certain. Stella wouldn't remain idle. She would bring nothing but chaos to that ship.

The next time Stella woke, her chin rested on her chest. She lifted her head, and a soft moan escaped. Pain radiated through her body, and she wasn't sure what hurt more—her stiff neck or the jackhammer in her head.

She moved her limbs, but nothing happened. Her eyes snapped open, and when she grimaced at the light from the lanterns, she shut them again. She attempted to move her arms again but found them tied to a wooden chair. Memories flashed of the first time she'd been kidnapped. It had been in Baywood when AJ and Finn had taken a sail down the coast. She'd made her daily stop at the inn to water plants and fill the bird feeders. That was when she'd found Gaines waiting in the kitchen. He'd mistaken her for AJ, and that had been her first step down the rabbit hole of the fog. A trip that had changed her entire life. On a good note, Beckworth had rescued her, and that had made the whole experience worth it.

Who would rescue her this time?

She couldn't move her legs. They were also tied, but she could move her feet, and she did so to ensure the blood continued to flow. She sensed someone enter the room, which was proven correct by the soft scuff of boots on wood. More than one?

She could pretend she wasn't awake, but what would be the

point? There wasn't going to be an easy way out of this so she might as well get this over.

She slowly lifted her head, scowling at the kink as she slowly rolled her head from side to side. Two men filled her line of sight before a third came into view.

He bent down, his face close enough for her to smell his foul breath and the remnants of alcohol. "Lady Swan. It's a pleasure to finally meet you. My name is Cheval."

Great. Of all the luck.

She didn't see a reason to respond, so she remained silent while she wrestled with her fear.

He lifted her head with a single finger under her chin before using it to caress one of her cheeks. "I can see why MacDuff has become enamored with you. Or was it the promise of French rifles?"

Her eyes widened. She couldn't help it. How the hell did he know about the rifles?

He stepped back and laughed. "Oh, yes, I know all about the little trade you were trying to make with him." He pulled a dagger from his pocket.

She blinked. "That's mine." Her throat was sore, and the words came out raspy.

He took a long look at the dagger. "Yes, I found it in your pocket. Too light for my liking but well crafted. It will make a nice addition to my collection."

He tapped the side of the dagger on her cheek. "I've been working my way into MacDuff's lucrative network for months. I don't need another competitor moving in. If it wasn't for your French rifles, you'd be feeding the fish by now—or perhaps pleasuring my crew."

Her skin crawled. This was really bad. Then the rest of his words worked their way through her foggy brain.

"You don't have a contact for French rifles."

He grinned and his brown teeth explained the rotten smell. "Now I see why MacDuff canceled his meeting with me. You're a smart one—for a woman."

Maybe there was a way out of this. "If you think I'll give up my contact, you're not as smart as you think." This might not be the best approach, but she couldn't appear weak. She needed time. Beckworth had to have found the swans. Had to know where she went. Was he already following them?

Cheval strode to the other side of the room, and one of his men moved with him holding a lantern, which he placed on a tall barrel. Another man was there in what she now recognized as a cargo hold filled with crates and barrels. This man was also tied to a chair, but she didn't recognize him. At least it wasn't someone from the *Daphne*.

The man looked terrified. That didn't lessen the jackhammer that had moved from her head to her chest.

Cheval pulled the man's head back and slowly sliced her dagger across the man's neck. It wasn't deep, but the man flinched as a line of crimson formed. "I'd considered torture to see how long it would take before you gave up a name." He used the blood-stained dagger to point a finger at his men who stood several feet away. "You see, I have a crew of betting men. Risk takers. They like making bets on how long a prisoner will last before giving up information. They even place bets on how long before one dies."

His men chuckled and nodded.

Good grief. He should change the name of his ship to the *Ship of Horrors*.

"The men would have had a good time betting on you, but you provide a unique opportunity. The current bet is how long before I convince you to work for me. It can be quite simple and relatively painless."

He strode back to her and pulled her head back by her hair

as the dagger sliced in front of her face. It didn't touch her, but she understood his point.

"You can become richer than you thought possible working for me. I have my own network. Not nearly as large as MacDuff's." He bent closer. "But everything he has will one day be mine. All you have to do is partner with me. You get your contact to trade with me and you get a nice fat share."

She swallowed hard and considered how Beckworth would play this. He'd tell her to play along. Stay alive as long as she could until help arrived.

She squared her shoulders and ignored the ripples of pain along her spine. "So rather than work a deal with MacDuff, I trade with you." The men always promised she'd get a nice share of the profits. Like she was supposed to believe that. She'd laugh in his face if she wasn't concerned about her dagger still gripped in his fist. So, she appeared to consider it. "I'd have to discuss it with the captain of my ship."

He chuckled and shook his head. "Consider your ship a loss."

What did that mean? Had they done something to the *Daphne*?

"Your men have no idea where you went. This is your new home—by my side." That ugly grin was back. "And in my bed."

"Not likely."

"You see, I had a feeling you'd be stubborn. A woman trying to barter with men is always like that—at first." He walked to a table on the far side of the hold. He pocketed her dagger and picked up a crossbow. It was a smaller version, maybe eighteen inches long. Any other day she'd consider it cute.

"I find examples are the best form of persuasion." Cheval selected a crossbow bolt. She knew the general idea of how they worked but never paid attention to the mechanics. Now, she followed every step he took in loading the bolt.

Cheval pointed it at the man tied in the chair. The shot was quick, and the man grunted as the bolt pierced his right shoulder.

Her eyes snapped wide. Was he going to use that on her? She wanted to struggle against the ropes but that would only show weakness—and her terror. Her gaze flashed to Cheval.

"Oh, don't worry. I don't intend to use this on you. This is a teaching moment." He picked up another bolt and rolled it around in his fingers. "I've found that my most loyal men remain loyal because they know the penalty for crossing me. Yet, the promise of riches from others sometimes makes them forget."

He set the string and bolt in place, and as horrified as she was to what would happen next, she watched each movement he made.

The second bolt hit the man in his upper thigh and this time he screamed. She expected a huge spurt of blood, and while the wound bled, the crimson drops seeping into the wood floor, he'd missed the femoral artery. Did he know if he'd hit the right spot the man could have bled out in minutes?

"I trusted this man. He'd found someone on MacDuff's ship willing to share a bit of news for a few crowns. That's how I found out about you. But MacDuff found out and paid my man more—" he nodded to the man bleeding from two bolts, "—in an attempt to give me false information. It would have worked."

He picked up another bolt, and she glanced at the injured man. His grimace of pain had morphed into terror with his widening gaze, and then he closed his eyes in acceptance as his ragged breaths slowed. He knew he was going to die. The question was how many more bolts he would suffer before that happened. One. Two. Or would Cheval fill him with several then leave him to bleed out on his own?

"Do you know why it didn't work?" His gaze bored into hers

as he rolled the next bolt in his fingers. He was apparently going to hold off until she answered, which only built the horrid tension to an excruciating level.

"No." It was all the words she had strength for.

He smiled. "See how quickly you're learning?" He slid the bolt in but held the crossbow so it pointed to the ceiling. "I don't trust my men."

She snorted. She couldn't help it.

He grinned. "It's the business, I'm afraid. If you haven't had that problem yet it would only have been a matter of time." He scratched his stubbled jaw. "I never send one spy. I always send two. The second is to spy on the first. See? I can't tell you how many times I've caught my men trying to double-cross me. You'd think the rumors of torture and death alone would deter them. But they're greedy men." He shrugged. "That's why they're smugglers."

This time the bolt struck the man's chest. His gaze went wide before his body slumped the few inches his restraints allowed. His eyes never closed as his face slackened. It wasn't the first time she'd watched someone die, and it didn't get any easier.

Cheval dropped the crossbow to his side and marched toward her. It required every last bit of strength not to flinch. He bent to her ear. "Remember this. Not that you'll be leaving this ship anytime soon. But if you think you can talk any of my men into helping you, remember the punishment."

He pulled her head back and studied her.

She tried to reflect both understanding and fearful respect. Whatever he read in her expression seemed to satisfy him.

He turned to his men. "Cut her loose. She won't be causing any problems." He turned back and considered her. "Take her to the hold next to my cabin." He grinned. "Tomorrow you'll be put to work scrubbing the deck. Everyone works on this ship." Before he left, he added one last order.

"Put a blanket or two on the floor of my cabin. Let's see how long she'll sleep on a hard floor after a long day of work. I'll wager two crowns she'll willingly come to my bed in three days."

The men laughed as they began placing their own bets. One strode toward her, removing a knife from his belt to cut her free. She glanced at the other man. Their belts were adorned with a sheathed dagger and gunpowder cartridges. Their pistols were stored in holsters either on their thigh or underneath their jackets.

Weapons within easy reach. She just needed the right moment. A single question made her smile.

What would Beckworth do?

26

———

Beckworth startled when someone shoved his shoulder. He jerked around to find Lando grinning at him. "What?"

"You're sleeping on your feet." He pushed Beckworth out of the way and loosened the lines.

"I'll stay if you stay."

Lando shook his head. "I've just come from a rest. Jamie's making everyone take one before we catch *The Horseman*."

Beckworth wiped his eyes and leaned over the railing. The other ship was still far off but could easily be spotted without a spyglass. "We're catching up."

"Jamie wants to be on top of them when we reach Langland Bay. Do as you're ordered. You're no good to us as you are."

Beckworth glanced at the sailor next to him and noticed it was the sailor he'd relieved earlier.

The sailor grinned at him. "Your turn, mate."

They were right. He'd be no good to Stella or the ship once they caught up to Cheval. He patted Lando's shoulder and stumbled his way across the deck. The cabin was dark when he reached it, but he didn't bother lighting the lantern.

He fell face-first into the bed. Stella's intoxicating scent had hit him the moment he'd walked in, and it only grew stronger. His hand clutched the silk robe she'd left tossed on the bed, and it filled his senses. He pulled it close. The last thought that crossed his mind as he tumbled into a deep sleep was what he'd tell AJ if anything happened to Stella.

***

Stella dragged the bucket along the deck to a spot near the running rigging where a sailor was staring up, his focus clearly on the sails. She glanced around, noting that everyone was busy. From what she'd heard from the sailors as she'd scrubbed her way across the deck, they were nearing a port.

At first, she'd been thrilled to hear the news, hoping there was a way for her to find a way off the ship. She couldn't spend another night onboard. Cheval had kept her locked in the small room next to his cabin all night. She'd been grateful for small favors, but when he'd opened the door that morning, he made it clear she wouldn't be alone tonight.

When she was eating her porridge under the watchful eye of two sailors, one of them mentioned the guns were being prepared for a ship that wasn't only following but was gaining on them.

The *Daphne*. It had to be.

While she might be learning about ships on this mission, there was more she didn't know than what she did. But she was a good listener and had excellent memory retention. Skills that had gotten her out of more scrapes than she cared to admit. Not just in this time period but her own.

She'd listened to Finn share the story about how he and Ethan had chased AJ and Maire across the Channel to save them from Beckworth, who'd been attempting to reach the safety of the monastery controlled by the duke and his men. Beckworth's ship had left port two hours before Finn could get the *Daphne* prepared to follow. Yet, Finn had made it to France first in time to prepare a trap for Beckworth and rescue the women.

Two things had worked in the *Daphne*'s favor. The first was simple physics. Beckworth's ship had been larger but had been weighed down by more cargo. The *Daphne* carried the bare minimum, mostly crew and a group of the Earl of Hereford's guards.

The second reason, and what Stella thought made the real difference, was Finn's ability to sense the winds and when they would shift, keeping his crew ready for new orders. This allowed the *Daphne* to maintain the speed required to overtake the other ship, though they never laid eyes on it during the crossing.

Finn no longer captained the *Daphne*, but Jamie, Fitz, and Lando had been trained by Finn. And Beckworth had once told her Jamie had the same sense for the wind as Finn had. So, she was confident it was the *Daphne* chasing them, though she couldn't see her from where she worked. The threat of guns changed everything. By being on *The Horseman*, Stella had the opportunity to assist, assuming she could figure out how.

She kept an eye on the sailor in front of her while she scrubbed the deck. Her beautiful French dress was ruined. It had been soaked wet from crawling around on her knees scrubbing the deck, and the fabric was ripped in multiple places from the rough wood and nails. As she inched her way closer to him, she scanned the deck. The other men ignored her, their focus on the *Daphne*, their own tasks, and their growing excitement over a battle at sea.

She slowly stood, stretched her back, then pushed the bucket closer to the rigging so it was directly behind the sailor, sloshing more water than was necessary. When the man stepped back to tighten the sheets, he tripped over the bucket, and Stella was on him in an instant.

"Oh my god, I'm so sorry." She bent to help him up but pretended to slip and knocked him down again as he attempted to rise.

"Get off me, woman."

She sprawled over the top of him and used a hand on his upper thigh, close to his privates, to lift herself up. He flinched, and she shifted more weight to the hand pushing on his leg while grabbing two gunpowder cartridges from his belt.

She grinned.

While she'd been on the run with Beckworth, she'd demanded to know how to load a flintlock. She knew how to handle firearms but didn't know the first thing about loading a rifle in this time period. Beckworth had balked at first, but he'd agreed she needed the ability to protect herself in case something happened to him. By the time Gemini was no longer a threat, she'd had a few opportunities to work with a belt of cartridges. Two cartridges didn't hold a lot of gunpowder but should be enough for her plan. Well, the plan she was making up as she went along.

The sailor rolled over to get on his knees, but before he could stand, she scrambled up and fell across his back, forcing him back down.

"Damn it, woman."

Her hand ran up his leg again and scraped across his crotch. She almost gagged when she felt it twitch, but her nimble fingers found what they were seeking before he shoved her aside as he made another attempt to get up.

Stella rolled into a ball, fumbled with her pockets, then complained, "The deck is so slippery."

Once he got to his feet, he glared down at her. "You're

supposed to be over at the forecastle, not near the rigging." The man kicked the bucket away, forcing the remaining water, what little of it there was, to run over her shoes. He didn't notice because he'd already returned his focus to the sails.

Stella pushed herself to her knees and crawled toward the bucket as she surveyed the men. Most hadn't seen the mishap, and the few who had were laughing as they returned to their tasks.

No one had noticed her slip the dagger she'd taken into the pocket of her sodden dress. When she reached the bucket, she stood and raced for the galley to refill it.

On the way, she noticed the lines running to the sails. She glanced around, wondering why these weren't manned but shrugged, pulled out the knife, and quickly tested its sharpness. There was only time for one quick pass, and though the lines weren't cut through they were now frayed. Gravity could do the rest.

She kept her head down as she kept moving. The lower decks were eerily quiet, and she set the bucket near a barrel of water. There was one on the top deck, but she needed an excuse why she was down here. If she'd learned anything from Beckworth during times like this, it was how to create a diversion. It was something he was exceptionally good at.

What was the one thing most feared on a ship? She grinned.

Fire.

The gunpowder cartridges should be enough to get the party started, and the flame to light it up was easy to find. There were lanterns everywhere below deck. What she needed was a good tinder.

She wasn't familiar with this ship, but she closed her eyes and ran through a quick replay of the tour on the *Daphne*. Her first thought went to where the rest of the gunpowder was stored, but it would be with the guns, and there would be men preparing them for battle.

She considered the crew's quarters, but there could be men there as well. Then she remembered spotting the navigation station when she'd been released from the hold.

Charts made of paper. What better tinder than that?

She grabbed a lantern and hurried into a passageway that should have led to the navigation station. It only took a few steps to realize she'd gotten turned around and had to backtrack down a different hallway until she stumbled across the room. She glanced over her shoulder, concerned she hadn't run into anyone. Cheval probably needed all hands on deck, and she almost laughed out loud at finally understanding how the phrase must have started.

She set the lantern on a bookcase and got to work. The question was the best way to start the fire. A chart was already spread out on the table, and she quickly unrolled another one and spread it across the top of the first, ensuring the edges of both covered the wooden table. She piled the rest of the scrolls on top of the charts.

A lone unlit lantern sat on the table. She poured oil over the rolls. It was a start, but she wasn't sure it was enough.

She took the cartridges from her pocket, thankful they weren't wet, though the paper was damp, and she held her breath as she ripped the first one open. The powder was dry. She released a shaky breath and dumped the powder into a pile on one corner of the chart, then repeated the step with the second cartridge on the opposite side.

Then she discovered her problem. She needed a fuse that would give her time to get topside before the blast. The next problem was whether the charts were enough to keep the fire going. They would have to do. She lifted her lantern then looked down at the bookcase it had been sitting on. It was filled with books. She grabbed several and set them on the edge of the table and around the legs, dribbling what was left of the oil over the books.

After giving it a full ten seconds of consideration, her best option would be making the charts the fuse. The fire would spread quickly to the powder but there was no way around it. She ripped a few pages from one of the books and rolled them up, and using it like a torch, lit the end from her lantern. She touched it to the topmost chart, which immediately burst into flame. She dropped the torch near the pile of books, not caring if it went out or not, and ran.

A sailor entered the galley a second after she did. She picked up the bucket and tried to storm past him.

"What are you doing down here, girl?"

"I had to pee. There's no privacy up top."

If he was shocked by her words, she didn't waste time to find out. Since he didn't stop her, she dragged the heavy bucket up the stairs. She grinned when his words floated up to her as she breached the doorway.

"What's that smell?"

She squinted at the brightness. The sun had been playing hide-and-seek as soon as the rain had stopped. She turned in time to see Cheval baring down on her.

"Where have you been?"

"The first bucket got knocked over. I needed fresh water and privacy to relieve myself."

He gripped her arm and stared at her. Had he caught her deception? If he'd seen her take the dagger, he'd have already ripped the dress from her to search for it. She held her ground, even though her heart was ready to burst out of her chest.

"I'm beginning to understand why women shouldn't be aboard a ship. You're nothing but trouble." He glanced around then pointed toward the back of the ship. "Go aft. You should be out of the way for the battle." His grin made her take a step back, which was all she could do since he still held her arm. "Your ship won't save you, little bird. And there's nowhere for you to fly."

He pushed her back and stormed off.

She held her smile as she watched him head toward the bow.

Let's see who has the last laugh, asshole.

27

———

The ringing of a bell woke Beckworth from a dead sleep.

He barely remembered stumbling to the cabin and falling fully clothed onto the bed. His constant need to stay busy while not worrying about Stella, which only worked for five minutes at a time, had completely exhausted him.

When the clanging of the bell continued, he popped up, Stella's robe still clutched in his hand. He held it to his nose. Her scent was a balm, and he sucked in a final deep breath before tossing it on the bed and racing from the cabin.

The top deck was a flurry of activity. He searched for Jamie or Fitz but spotted Lando first. By the time he reached the bow, Jamie and Fitz were there. He didn't need to use a spyglass to see *The Horseman*.

The *Daphne* was bearing down on it.

"What's happening?" Beckworth shouted as he approached.

No one turned around, their eyes fixed on the ship that appeared to be turning to port. When he reached the railing, Lando gave Beckworth his spyglass.

"We think Stella is on deck."

"We thought they were turning to fire on us, but they're too close to the shore," Jamie said.

"Either a sheet came loose or the canvas tore." Fitz used his own spyglass. "It's hard to tell with the men working to fix it."

"Where are we?" Beckworth glanced at the shore that seemed rather close, but he was still disoriented after waking so quickly.

"Langland Bay is right around the point," Lando answered.

"Is it possible they're aiming for a cove?" he asked.

"There's nothing more than a short beach before the point." Jamie turned around and yelled, "Heave to."

"We're stopping?" Beckworth asked. He felt like an idiot with the questions, but he was playing catch up.

"Her gunports are open. Until we know what they're doing, we need to stop. I don't want to get too close if they're attempting a turn to fire." Jamie held out his hand for the spyglass Beckworth was holding.

"The captain must have lost his senses if he's trying to turn to port just before the point." Fitz scratched his beard. "Turning starboard is the only thing that makes sense."

Beckworth remembered his binoculars and pulled them out, focusing them as he slowly scanned the deck of *The Horseman*. He caught sight of the auburn hair immediately. Stella. The air rushed out of him. She was alive. Thank god. But what was she up to?

She turned her head toward the *Daphne*. Then she faced the shore and watched it for a long minute before glancing up at the sails. When her attention turned toward what he assumed was the crew, his gut roiled in turmoil.

She was up to something. He didn't know how or why, but his gut told him the loose top sail hadn't been an accident.

With the glasses still glued on her, Beckworth said, "You'd better prepare a jolly boat."

"Why?" Jamie asked.

"I don't know. But something tells me whatever happens next will be a surprise for both ships."

The words barely left his mouth when all hell broke loose.

Stella dragged the bucket toward the back of the ship, hoping she hadn't jinxed herself with her thoughts on who'd have the last laugh. She grinned when she noticed how close to shore they were. Cheval had unwittingly positioned her exactly where she wanted to be.

She leaned over the railing first gauging the distance to the thin strip of beach and then toward the bow. Though the ship had slowed, the rocky point wasn't far away. If she was going to do something—something really stupid—she needed to do it now.

Once she had her bucket placed, she turned to look at the *Daphne*. It appeared that Jamie had also slowed. Maybe he suspected Cheval would be crazy enough to fire its guns.

"Fire!" someone yelled, and then everyone was yelling.

Her mind snapped back to her current dilemma as her distraction paid off.

Not knowing if any of the shouts had anything to do with her, she began ripping the torn material from her dress. She tore off as much as she could, not worried about modesty, only knowing extra material would weigh her down.

She grabbed the railing and took a last look at the *Daphne*. It was close enough for her to see the men on the bow and thought she'd seen Beckworth, but he'd turned and ran off. Then she noticed a jolly boat being lowered. She didn't have time to contemplate the why, though she had noticed two men with spyglasses. Most likely Jamie and Fitz. She waved her arms before taking another look over the railing.

The water was farther away than she'd expected. She'd once jumped from a ship that had docked. It was from an open gunport, and her landing on the wooden pier had sprained her ankle. She and Sebastian had still gotten away. Would she be as lucky this time?

She glanced over her shoulder to see Cheval running for her. The ship heaved backward at the perfect time and with enough force that he lost his balance and had to grab onto the mast to stop his fall.

Stella hung onto the railing at the unexpected movement. While the ship settled, she climbed onto the railing. Cheval had recovered his step and ran for her.

She swallowed the lump in her throat. Without a second thought, she flung her arms wide and leaped into the air.

Beckworth was still on the bow standing next to Jamie, Lando, and Fitz, as they watched a second sail falter. It wasn't enough to stop the ship or even slow it down.

"Someone must have cut the lines." Lando's voice was one of confusion and perhaps wonder.

"There's smoke coming from the starboard side," Fitz added. "There's a fire onboard."

Beckworth ran to mid-ship where the men were lowering the boat. He hung over the rail, watching its slow descent. When it appeared it would take another five minutes before he could climb down, he pushed away from the railing and moved forward to get a glimpse of *The Horseman*.

Lando ran up to him. "The fire seems to be spreading. They're heaving to." He glanced over the side to check the progress of the boat and nodded. "How did you know that would happen?"

Beckworth shrugged, unsure what was happening or what he thought a jolly boat would do. But he had to do something. This might not work out at all—nothing more than a fool's mission. Jamie might put the ship under sail again, leaving him stranded on a beach. At least he'd be close to a port. He'd have to put his faith in Jamie to save Stella.

Before he answered, he glanced at the other ship, then laughed. It also terrified him as he swung around and headed for the boat.

Lando followed him. "What's so funny?"

"I'm not sure who to be sorry for. Stella, who's preparing to do something both courageous and stupid, or Cheval when he realizes he was a fool to bring her onboard. Whatever's happening on that ship, you can bet Stella had a hand in it." He climbed over the railing to the rope ladder. "Now it's time to save the damsel in distress."

He climbed halfway down before jumping the rest of it. Michelson had taken a position at one of the oars.

Beckworth shook his head. "Sorry, mate. You're needed on the *Daphne*."

Michelson shook his head in return. "Captain's orders. And even if they weren't, you can't row to shore without help."

He could argue but the man was right. It would be a helluva row, and he'd be exhausted when he got there. He took the other oars and pushed off.

"Man overboard."

It sounded like Fitz. He didn't have to look to know who it was, but he glanced back just the same. Now that she was in the water, the only thing they could do was row. And that's what they did. Neither glanced around. They kept their heads down and rowed to the closest point. They could have steered for

Stella, but they needed to stay away from *The Horseman* in case someone fired a shot.

He couldn't help it, and he stole a quick glance. Cheval was lowering his own jolly boat. He paddled faster.

It took longer than he expected against the outgoing tide. Before they reached the shore, he laid down the oars and stood.

"The tide's going out. It will be an easier row back."

Michaelson shook his head. "Jamie meant for me to go with you to shore."

Beckworth took in the unfolding scene. Both ships had come to a stop but *The Horseman* appeared too close to the point. He doubted they hit rocks, but it was still a dangerous position to be in. The fact they'd lowered a boat told him everything he needed to know.

"Go back and get more men. I'll get Stella." Then he jumped out, pushed the boat toward the outgoing wave, and waded through the waist-deep water toward shore. He didn't look back. His focus was solely on the water and any sign of Stella.

She hated ships because she got seasick, but could she swim? He racked his brain to remember if that was one of the items he'd added to her list of phobias or things she wouldn't do. It had become a running joke between them.

When they'd been on Gemini's ship and had discussed their options to escape, there had been a possibility they'd have to jump in the water and swim for the dock. They'd never discussed swimming since then. Surely she wouldn't have jumped if she couldn't make it to shore. Who was he kidding? She might be one of the most intelligent women he knew, but she didn't always think things through before listening to her gut. He had to grin. Sometimes they were too similar for their own good.

He ran up and down the shoreline, searching the waves. Michelson was almost back to the *Daphne*, and men were lined up on deck, no doubt ready to come ashore. He turned to run back the other way, considering swimming out in search of her, when he stopped short.

Cheval stood on the beach. He was soaking wet from head to toe. He must have decided not to wait for the boat. But why had he beaten Stella ashore? That question would have to wait as he noted the man had a dagger and pistol tucked in his belt and a crossbow dangled in his left hand.

The pistol wouldn't be any good without dry powder, but the crossbow was a definite threat.

"Who the hell are you?" Cheval asked as his eyes narrowed. "You look familiar."

"Just a bloke out for a swim." He glanced up at the gray skies, the sun having slipped behind them. "Not the best day for it, but when is it ever in England?"

Cheval took a few steps closer, clearly unsure what to make of Beckworth before he glanced at the *Daphne*.

"It seems you're important enough to have a crew boarding a jolly boat." He chuckled. "Was that little drowned bird someone of importance to you?"

The question drew Beckworth's temper. If she was dead, this man was the cause of it. Before he could think, he launched himself at the man, who'd drawn up the crossbow but didn't have a chance of putting a bolt in it.

The crossbow and bolt flew from Cheval's hands as Beckworth slammed into him. The two tumbled onto the sand and rolled toward the water. He managed a solid hit to the chin and one to the man's gut before Cheval used his larger bulk to roll Beckworth over, pinning him to the ground with the combined weight of his body and soaked clothing.

Beckworth's hands were still free, and he punched the man in the kidney, but, unable to throw a full punch, there wasn't enough force to make a difference. His next blow hit the man's chin again, and though it forced a shout of pain, it didn't dislodge him.

Cheval gripped his throat as a wave washed over them. Beckworth hadn't paid attention to the waves and wasn't prepared, catching some of the water and choking as he expelled it, gasping for air. The pressure on his throat increased, and Beckworth wrapped his legs around his opponent's, but he didn't have enough strength to push or roll the man.

Beckworth, struggling for breath as another wave hit, tugged on the man's wrists.

Darkness blurred the edges of his vision, and it terrified him. Not for himself but for Stella.

Stella was exhausted after barely making it to shore. She wasn't a strong swimmer, more of a dog paddler, and with the tide going out, she was being pulled with it faster than she could swim. Rather than continuing to the shore, she stopped and treaded water as she considered her options.

Cheval had lowered a boat that was heading her way. That wasn't going to happen. Instead, she turned toward the rocks that ran along the southern side of the small inlet. They were denser the closer they got to the point, but as they approached the beach, the rocks were spaced farther apart. With the tide going out, there was sand visible between the stones.

She kept swimming until sand and stone scraped along her belly, then she grabbed a rock and pulled herself onto the sand, rolling over to stare at the darkening skies. Her teeth chattered, and though she wanted to roll into a ball and sleep, the boat of men following her forced her to move. Her shoes, which she'd thankfully kept on, sloshed as she stepped around the rocks, following the sandy path to the beach.

Stella had been too busy watching the winding path to notice the two men on shore until she cleared the last rocks. She watched in horrified silence as Beckworth wrestled Cheval to the ground. Beckworth was on top for a while until Cheval, with a good fifty pounds over Beckworth, rolled him over, keeping him defenseless beneath him.

When a wave washed over them, a spurt of energy shot through her like a firecracker, and she raced for them. She could jump on Cheval, but she doubted that would be enough to free Beckworth. Maybe if she rammed him from the side. She glanced around for driftwood or a rock.

Then her gaze fell on something better.

The crossbow.

She picked it up. It was useless without a bolt unless she hit Cheval over the head with it. Would it be enough? She scanned the sand where the two had been wrestling, about twenty feet from where they tussled in the waves. If she didn't do something soon, Beckworth would either be strangled to death or drowned.

Then she saw it. The bolt wasn't that small, but its natural coloring blended with the sand. She picked it up and held it between her teeth as she used the lever to pull back the string. Her arms shook from the strain, but the string caught behind the hook, or whatever the hell it was called, that held it in position.

She slid the bolt in place and turned toward the men.

The next wave was larger than the last. Cheval must not have expected it, and his fingers loosened, though it didn't last long enough for Beckworth to do anything about it. Two boats had been lowered—one from each ship.

There wouldn't be enough time for Jamie's crew to save him. Another wave hit, and he managed to close his mouth before the cold sea water splashed over him.

When he opened his mouth to suck in air—the pressure on his neck was gone.

Cheval's fingers slackened, and Beckworth tried to see past the saltwater blurring his vision. When his eyes refocused, Cheval stared down at him, his mouth gaping open as if he couldn't remember what he wanted to say. The light in his eyes faded, and when the next wave came and with one last burst of energy, Beckworth pushed the man off him.

Cheval rolled to his side. Unmoving.

He scrambled away and wiped at his eyes, which only proved to get more sand in them rather than clear them.

But what he saw was good enough.

Stella, his damsel in distress, stood in front of him, her chest heaving from exertion. Her hair dripped with seawater and what little clothing she wore clung to every curve. A crossbow dangled from her hand.

Stella had only taken a few seconds to sight her target. When Cheval had used the crossbow, he appeared to hit where he aimed. She went with her self-dense training —aim at the largest target.

She shot the damn smuggler in the back.

Cheval went still. There might have been a small spasm. Then Beckworth pushed him away. She stared down at the crossbow.

That worked better than expected.

Beckworth was sitting up, staring at her. She studied every

inch of her man but didn't see any blood. He'd tried to save her. He was always there for her.

She strode toward him but stopped at Cheval. First things first. She used her foot to push him onto his back and checked his pockets. Her dagger was in the first pocket she checked, and she pulled it out, then stumbled through the wet sand to drop on her knees in front of Beckworth, the weapons slipping from her fingers.

"Let's not do that again."

He pulled her to him. "You're my hero." Then he coughed.

She pulled back, giving him another longer inspection. "Are you alright?"

"Just some seawater."

Tears leaked down her face. Maybe it was water from her drenched hair. She pushed his dripping ponytail off his shoulder, then caressed his face. "I'm so sorry. I didn't go with him on purpose."

He pulled her to him again, hugging her so tightly it was difficult to breathe, but she didn't fight it. "I know."

"I love you."

"I know."

She curved into his body as she turned to look for *The Horseman*. Smoke billowed from the aft portion of the ship. "I hope they get the fire out before it reaches the gunpowder stores."

Beckworth settled onto the sand so he had a better view, keeping her close. The jolly boat lowered from *The Horseman* had turned around and was heading back to the ship. A flash of motion to his right was from the *Daphne*'s boat reaching the shore. Michelson had returned with Lando, Fitz, and two other sailors.

"What made you think of starting a fire?" he asked. "And was it you that cut the sheets to the sails?"

She shrugged. "Michelson taught me a bit about the lines and rigging and all that stuff. I wanted to bring all the sails down but that would have been too difficult, and the crew would have stopped me. I had just taken a dagger from one of the sailors." She shrugged. "I wanted to see how sharp the blade was. The lines weren't cut through, but I hoped gravity would do the rest." She laughed. "I needed another option so I thought —what would Beckworth do? The men were busy preparing to turn the ship to fire the guns. I couldn't let them destroy the *Daphne*. I lifted a couple powder cartridges from that poor sailor before I took his dagger." She held up her hand. "Don't ask. I'm too tired to explain it all but suffice to say, Cheval didn't realize he'd given me a lesson on how to work the crossbow." She glanced up at him and gave him her most innocent look then hesitated as she bit her lower lip. "I really didn't like that man."

He just stared at her for the longest moment. Then he threw his head back and laughed. "You're as mad as I am. What a pair we make, Lady Caldway. Or should I say, Lady Swan?"

"Indeed, Lord Beckworth."

His kiss told her everything she needed to know. They would be okay.

28

———

Stella hadn't wanted to let go of the crossbow, but Beckworth pointed out she wouldn't be able to climb the rope ladder to the *Daphne*. Once he stepped onto the deck, she immediately took it from him. She was still gripping it when Jamie laid his hands on her shoulders.

"Are you alright, lass?" Jamie's wrinkled brow seemed contrary with his handsome grin.

"I'm fine. Thank you for the rescue."

"I'm not sure who rescued who." Beckworth took the blanket Lando handed him and wrapped it around Stella.

She grasped it with one hand, still shivering but at least her teeth had stopped chattering. Jamie and Lando glanced down at the crossbow but didn't say anything when Beckworth pulled the blanket over it.

"We need to get the ship underway." Jamie nodded to Lando, who strode off to where Fitz watched *The Horseman* through a spyglass. "You can get out of your wet clothes and get some rest, then we can talk about what happened."

"If it's alright with you..." Stella fumbled with both edges of the blanket. Her fingers were still numb from the cold, and she couldn't grasp it tightly enough. Beckworth helped get her fist wrapped around it. "I'd like to get this over so I can just pass out afterwards."

Jamie glanced at Beckworth before nodding. "Wait in my office. We'll be down as soon as we can." He winked at her. "I think there's a bottle of good Irish whiskey on my desk."

She snorted. "And if not, I know where there's a case or two."

He laughed as Beckworth led her away. She couldn't blame them for their worry. Beckworth had mothered her from the moment they walked away from Cheval's body until the jolly boat bumped against the ship. At first, it was comforting, then it became annoying—until she realized it wasn't all about her. Beckworth must have been terrified the minute he found the first swan. His worst nightmare. Everything he'd imagined about this mission had come true.

She had chuckled to herself. Maybe he was psychic. She pictured him sitting at a table at the annual mystic fair held about twenty miles north of Baywood. He was dressed in a black robe lined in red satin and a tall black hat staring into a crystal ball as he rubbed his chin while predicting someone's future.

She'd sobered quickly enough when the boat came alongside the *Daphne* where the crew had lined up next to the railing. Their faces had been similar to Jamie's, a combination of worry, grins, and a few cheers. She didn't know what their plans had been to rescue her. Maybe she should have waited like her previous kidnappings, but this hadn't been the same. She'd had the opportunity, and Beckworth had taught her skills—and she had a few of her own.

But that wouldn't have stopped Beckworth from worrying or wondering if she was still alive.

He settled her into a chair in Jamie's office. "Are you sure you don't want to change?" When she shook her head, he poured her a glass of whiskey. "At least let me get you another blanket."

He plucked at the one around her shoulders. "This one is soaking wet. You need something drier." Before she could nod, he was out the door.

She took a sip of whiskey and shuddered as the burn worked its way through her, then finished the shot as Beckworth returned. He stood her up and peeled the old blanket away and wrapped the fresh one around her.

"Why don't I set your crossbow on the table?"

She handed him the empty glass and repositioned the blanket so it covered most of her body, then laid the crossbow across her lap. Her hand trembled until it gripped the cool wood of the crossbow. "I could use another shot."

He poured her a double and ignored the crossbow.

"What will they do about Cheval's body?" Her voice sounded stronger to her ears.

"Jamie will send a message to the magistrate at our next port."

"Wouldn't his crew do that?"

"Doubtful. Too many questions would be asked. If Jamie has a problem, he'll provide Hensley's name and that will be that." He glanced at her lap. "Did you want to tell me about your souvenir?"

She grinned. "You know how I like to bring one home from every vacation." He smiled in return. She'd kept a silk purse— more like a pouch—she'd taken from one of Gemini's several trunks when she'd first been kidnapped. It now hung over a standing mirror in their bedroom in Baywood. It was a pretty purse with a light floral print. One day she'd pack it away with her other treasures from the past.

They sat in silence for fifteen minutes, holding hands, calmed by the gentle sway of the ship. When Jamie joined them, Lando and Fitz followed him in. They each glanced at the crossbow as they walked past her. Fitz poured everyone a glass of whiskey and refilled Stella's glass.

Jamie swallowed his down and took a moment to savor it. "Now that the *Daphne* is underway let's do a quick recap. We can talk more at dinner tonight."

"Is the other ship alright?" Stella asked.

"It's sure to have a fair bit of damage, but nothing that will prevent the crew from getting it to a port," Fitz answered. "What did you use to get it started?"

Jamie held up his hands. "Let's start from the beginning, shall we?"

Stella sipped the whiskey and let the blanket slip off her shoulders. She was finally warm inside and out, and though she kept one hand on it and could feel its weight, she glanced down to confirm the crossbow was still there. Beckworth placed a hand on her arm, and she wasn't positive which of them the action was meant to comfort.

"I imagine Lando told you about the men who seemed to be waiting for us." She glanced around. "I saw Michelson rowing the dinghy. Where's Thomas? Is he alright? And Lane?"

"Thomas is on his way back to Waverly. Lane is fine. Michelson's hit on the head was more grievous, but as you saw, he wants to work. Although, I think he still suffers from a headache."

She nodded. "I have some medicine that might help. Anyway, I remembered the swans and managed to drop one when we were surrounded and obviously outnumbered. I slipped more out when I could."

"Fitz saw them take you aboard *The Horseman*," Jamie said. "Go on."

She told them about waking up someplace dark and then someone giving her water, but she'd realized too late they'd put something in it. It had smelled sweet but tasted bitter.

"Laudanum," Lando said. "Opium. It would have made you sleepy."

"Yes, the man said that was what the captain wanted, and it definitely did the trick." She continued her story and told them about Cheval's paranoia over his crew's loyalty and how he always sent a second spy because he didn't trust the first. For some reason, that seemed important to Jamie and the others. She finished with how she started the fire, her daring jump off the ship, and then finding the crossbow, the only instrument available to stop Beckworth from being strangled.

"Did Cheval ask you anything about England or suspect you had other motives?" Jamie asked.

She considered the question, not sure why he asked it, then she understood. "You want to know if my cover was blown?"

"In so many words, yes."

"No." She straightened in her seat, pulling the crossbow closer. "He was interested in the French rifles. He wanted to be the only source feeding the weapons to MacDuff. It sounded like there might have been a mole on MacDuff's ship. Let's see. Oh, this is important, I think. He said MacDuff's network was larger than his, but he had plans to take whatever MacDuff owned. Wait. You coming to my rescue means you lost where MacDuff went."

"Nay, lass," Fitz said. "We have plenty of information to take back to Hensley. We know MacDuff has a network, Cheval is no longer a problem, and as far as anyone knows, there's a mysterious smuggler of French weapons called Lady Swan." His laugh was one of those diabolic ones and everyone chuckled.

"I suppose."

"That's enough for now," Jamie said. "Get some sleep. If the winds are kind, we should be in Bristol by tomorrow afternoon, and while you'll miss dinner, you should be sleeping in your own bed at Waverly."

eckworth pushed Stella toward their cabin. "I'll follow in a few minutes."

She nodded and pulled the blanket up as she trudged down the passageway. The blanket fell when she opened the door and she kicked it into the room, refusing to let go of the crossbow. It was silly. She knew that. But she wasn't ready to let it go.

She'd killed a man. It hadn't been her first. That had been Gaines, who had been ready to shoot Beckworth at close range. It would have killed him. She'd had no choice. Just like this time.

She jumped when Beckworth used his foot to push the open door she hadn't closed all the way. He had a bucket of water in one hand and a coffee pot in another. She gave him a smile in an attempt to disguise her whirlwind emotions. If he noticed anything strange, he didn't say anything.

He set the bucket down by the wash basin and the coffee pot on the table. He pulled a mug out of one pocket and another one from his other pocket. He poured the coffee and handed one to her.

When he poured water into the basin, she noted the light steam.

"Hot water?"

"Warm enough." He added a few sprinkles of lavender that he must have taken from her herbal stash.

He carried the basin over and set it on the floor next to the chair then waved her over to sit. She hesitated but did as he asked. He rummaged for a hand rag and a towel before he knelt in front of her then sat back on his heels.

"What are you doing?"

"Hush. Just sit back and enjoy the coffee." He lifted her foot and placed it on his thigh. Inch by inch he ran the warm rag over her skin, washing away the dirt and sand. He ran his hand over her calf then along her thigh, caressing and softly massaging her tense muscles. When he finished the first leg, he set her foot down and picked up the next.

She finished her coffee and dropped the mug on the table. The crossbow slipped to the floor, and she leaned her head back as the last of her anxiety drained away. He moved to her left arm, starting with each finger before working his way up, leaving her warm, tingly, and boneless. Once he finished, he kissed the soft skin under her wrist before placing her hand on her belly and repeating the process with her other arm.

He never looked at her as he worked, instead keeping his focus on his task. There wasn't anything to say, and once again, she considered his actions something he needed as well as her. This was something he could control. Something he could predict the outcome with a hundred percent accuracy. It was his way of dealing with his own tumultuous emotions over the last two days. Hell, the entire mission.

When he finished with her arm, he pulled her up and untied the remains of her dress. Now naked, he began with her face, his touch gentle on her cheeks and forehead. His fingers followed the rag as it moved down her neck, across her shoulders, and over her breasts.

He didn't stop to kiss or linger on her most sensitive spots, and when she'd been washed from head to toe, he moved her to the bed until she lay prone, staring at the ceiling. Though the air was cool, and goosebumps erupted over her flushed skin, she was warm and tingly inside. She thought he was done as he dropped the rag in the basin and moved it back to the washstand.

She was wrong.

He gave her a complete body massage, once again starting at

her feet, his strong fingers squeezing and caressing as they moved over her. When he reached her shoulders, he rolled her over. She was nothing but a limp rag as his fingers trailed down her back, his thumbs working every knot out of her muscles.

She wanted to say something. Thank him. Tell him she loved him. But speaking a single word seemed beyond her capability. She was so tired, and her lids fluttered as sleep overtook her.

At some point, she woke in Teddy's arms. He was naked, their bodies touching. She stirred and his hand immediately began stroking her arm.

"Ssh. Go back to sleep." He rolled into her, trapping her from rising.

"Jamie's expecting us for dinner."

"I took care of that. If we get hungry later, I'll pilfer something from the galley. He knows we both need the rest."

She snuggled closer. "You take such good care of me. I love you, Teddy."

He squeezed her to him, holding her in a tight cocoon, as she drifted back to sleep.

29

———

Stella stood at the railing and watched the number of seaside homes that dotted the coastline increase as the *Daphne* made its final approach to the port in Bristol. She'd woken early, starving and jonesing for coffee. It didn't surprise her to find a pot of coffee waiting for her with no Beckworth in sight. His side of the bed was still warm, so he hadn't been gone for long.

She'd sipped the coffee and ignored her growling stomach as she dressed for the day. Jamie said they wouldn't reach Bristol until late afternoon. She picked through her clothes and considered how she'd spend the day. Sitting around the cabin reading held no interest, and she could only spend so much time in the galley.

She slid on her pants and was tying her shirt when Beckworth returned. If her choice of clothes surprised him, he didn't show it.

He pulled her in for a dizzying kiss.

"If I'd known you were going to do that, I would have stayed in bed." She ran a hand over his hair and tugged at his ponytail.

He smiled down at her. The light in his eyes expressed his

love more than words. It also reminded her how she'd scared him to his core.

"I have special plans for when we reach Waverly. A fire, a bottle of fine wine, and nothing but you and me." He kissed the tip of her nose, squeezed her backside, and tugged her out of the room. "Jamie's holding breakfast for us."

During breakfast, the team gave her a recap of the activity on the *Daphne* once their pursuit of *The Horseman* began. It was shared with a jovial air, mostly by Fitz, who Stella was now convinced was the ship's storyteller. The day went by quickly, and as much as she wanted to see Waverly, she would miss the *Daphne* and her crew. Who would have believed it?

Her final task was to assist Cook with a late lunch or early dinner, depending on how one looked at it. The crew had worked hard during the mission with little downtime at the ports. When they reached Bristol, they would have several days to relax in port, but Jamie wanted them fed before they docked. No one had to tell her the crew would be spending the majority of their time pub hopping.

She'd barely cleared the galley of the last of the pots and pans when Beckworth dragged her back to the cabin to change. He'd asked to help with her hair, and she didn't have the heart to say no. She was pleasantly surprised to see his skills were improving as he went with a simple approach of pulling her hair back with a couple of hairpins.

She decided to wear the best day dress she'd brought from Waverly. Everything was packed in their trunk, with the crossbow placed on top. Beckworth had lifted a brow but didn't say anything.

Neither of them spoke of Cheval or his ending, just like they never spoke of Gaines. Maybe someday she'd need a shrink. But what would she tell them? She couldn't mention time travel or she'd end up in a padded cell. If she ever needed to talk about it with someone other than Beckworth, she had AJ. She'd faced her own demons from the past. And if Stella ever felt the need to confess her sins there was Sebastian, and knowing all of that somehow lightened her burden.

She lifted her face to the sky and stared at the burnt colors of what was sure to be a spectacular sunset. The sun had shown itself several hours earlier, and it had lightened her mood. When the *Daphne* turned toward one of the piers, she felt a sense of coming home.

How strange was that?

———

Beckworth tugged at his sleeves, feeling like the viscount once again in his breeches and waistcoat. Once he had the trunk transferred to the deck, he stopped by Jamie's office on his way up to wait with Stella.

The door was open, but he stopped and tapped before entering. "You have a minute?"

Jamie pushed back the ledger he'd been staring at and rubbed his eyes. The man needed a good long rest. "Always for you." He sat back, his face a bit haggard yet he managed a grin. "How's Stella?"

"She's a bit quieter than normal but she'll be better once she gets to Waverly."

"It won't take long once Mary gets a hold of her."

Beckworth chuckled. "Mary is food for the soul."

"That she is." Jamie studied him until he began to fidget. "How are you?"

That was a good question. Stella hadn't asked, but she seemed to intuitively understand his moods and responded accordingly. They would talk eventually. If not at Waverly, then once they returned to Baywood.

"I'm happy to be returning home from a successful mission with the same number of crew as when we left." He stared at a spot on Jamie's desk, his mind more on Stella than himself. "Cheval wasn't the first man Stella killed. Not that it makes it any easier, but I've discovered it's better for her to internalize her emotions. She'll let me know when it's time to talk."

"Taking a life is never a good thing, but sometimes there's no other way."

"Certainly not in this century." He played at the edge of his sleeve. "What will you tell Hensley about the lost opportunity with MacDuff?"

Jamie shrugged. "You're worried that pulling her out of her meeting with MacDuff when we discovered Cheval in town was a mistake." He picked up an orange that had been sitting on his desk and peeled it. "It was a fifty-fifty chance that he would have told Stella anything important. And as it turned out, you were right to be concerned."

"I never suspected Cheval would have known about Lady Swan."

"No one did." Jamie ate two slices of orange as he stared at the ceiling. He dropped the unfinished orange on the corner of his deck and wiped his hands on his pants. "As to your question about Hensley, I suspect you don't share everything about your missions with him. No reason to think I do."

Beckworth stood, and Jamie followed him to the upper deck.

When they stepped outside, Beckworth held out his hand. "It was a good mission, wasn't it?"

Jamie shook it without hesitation. "That woman of yours is rather special."

"And reckless."

"And just as devious as you."

Beckworth laughed. "That she is. Thank you for keeping her safe."

"In the end, that was all on the two of you."

Beckworth looked toward the bay and the setting sun. He sucked in a long scent of strong salt air mixed with the stench of fish. It brought back memories of his youth in London living next to the Thames. He gave Jamie a last look. "Will we see you at the hunting party?"

"Aye. We wouldn't miss it. We'll need a day or two for maintenance and restocking the stores, then we'll be on our way."

Beckworth clapped Jamie on the shoulder and strode toward Stella. When he stepped next to her, she reached for his hand. He gripped it tightly, and without saying a word, they watched the *Daphne* dock. Before they went ashore, she pulled him down for a long kiss. When she released him, she gave him her best broker smile.

"Take me home."

S tella was surprised to see Thomas standing next to a coach when they reached the end of the dock.

"How did you know when we'd be arriving?" Stella asked, smiling and happy to see for herself he was alright after Cheval's men had taken her from the alley.

"I didn't." He opened the coach door. "I arrived yesterday and planned on waiting for as long as it took for you to arrive."

She touched his arm. "It's good to see you well."

"Enjoy your ride to Waverly." He helped her into the coach, then smiled at Beckworth. "You should see that foal of yours. I think Hensley spends more time in the stables than anywhere else." He lowered his voice but Stella, who was peering out the window, managed to hear him say, "Hensley has a lot of questions."

"Thanks, mate. I wouldn't expect anything less." Beckworth

jumped in the coach and sat next to her.

She leaned her head against his shoulder, wondered what questions Hensley would have, then forgot it all when she closed her eyes.

When she sensed the coach slow and make a turn, she sat up, jarring Beckworth.

"Sorry. Are we home?" She scooted across the bench to stare into the darkness. The coach passed tree after tree. She rubbed her eyes, noting the trees appeared the same and were evenly spaced, and knew they were on the drive into the estate.

"Is this what you meant when you asked to go home?" His voice seemed thick with emotion.

She turned to him, words ready to tumble from her mouth, but she stopped. He'd thought she'd meant Baywood. Of course, he would. That was her home—and his too now.

But so was Waverly. He had to know that. She reached across the bench and grabbed his hand.

"Of course, I meant Waverly. Until it's time to go to our other home. Lots of people have two homes."

He laughed. "Yes, they do. I'd always imagined someday having to marry and settle down. Be the proper viscount and all. Then I'd have to buy a home in London for the season."

"And would you take the children with you?"

He shrugged. "I imagine that would be expected. In addition to the governess. All so tedious."

"Would they have blond hair or brown?" She didn't know why she wanted to know. As a viscount, he would be expected to marry.

The coach pulled up in front of the manor, and she lost her train of thought when she leaned over Beckworth to look out the window. The manor was ablaze with light not only from the windows but the torches that lit the outside, as if it had its own spotlights shining upward.

The front door opened, and Barrington barely stepped out before he was pushed aside by Mary, with Eleanor and Dame Elizabeth not far behind.

Before Thomas opened the coach door, Beckworth whispered in her ear. "I was thinking ginger-haired."

Then he was outside waiting to take her hand.

She didn't know how to react to his response, and the merriment in his eyes said she didn't have to. She grinned and stepped down seconds before Mary's arms wrapped her in a hug.

"It's so good to see you home safe and sound. We want to hear all about it. Barrington has arranged for a light repast. You must be famished."

"How did you know when we'd arrive?" Stella breathed in Mary's familiar rose scent. It was good to be home.

"Because Jamie sent a man ahead before he knew Thomas was already in Bristol." Hensley stepped next to the women and shook Beckworth's hand. "Good to have you home. Your guests arrived early this morning, and we weren't sure if we'd have to start the hunt without you."

"After a good meal and a good rest, I wouldn't think of missing the hunt."

"I think he just wants to be on a horse regardless of the hunt," Stella said, and they all laughed at the truth of it.

The women ushered Stella inside while the men marched toward the stables. Beckworth wanted to see the foal. She did too, but it could wait until morning. It was doubtful Mary would let her out of her sight.

Dinner was a light fare, being the second one of the day, and the conversation was boisterous. Stella worried they'd have to discuss the mission and the way it ended. She should have known better. Hensley would never discuss a mission with their guests present. Of their new guests, she knew Dame Elizabeth and Lord and Lady Osborne. No one ever forgot Lady Abigail Osborne—AJ's nemesis. She would have to ask Beckworth for a quick overview of Lord and Lady Melville and Lord Standish.

She also should have remembered Hensley and Mary's ability to carry on a conversation without a pause. Other than a slight discussion on the weather during their sailing adventure, Mary shared every detail of the upcoming events for the weekend.

Stella was excited to see everything Mary and Eleanor had put together, but exhaustion from the journey home was taking its toll, and she made an early excuse so she'd be fresh for the morning activities. No one questioned it, and Mary all but insisted. Beckworth promised to join her soon, which meant Hensley would want to discuss the mission once the men adjourned to the west study.

Before she left the dining room, she took a last glance back and caught Dame Elizabeth's gaze. Elizabeth had been watching her all night, and Stella felt the woman's eyes on her all the way out of the room.

After dinner, Beckworth followed the men to his west study and played host as he poured brandy for the others. He wasn't surprised that Hensley had already informed Lord Osborne, Lord Melville, and Lord Standish of the mission. Everyone who was anyone worried about the war —or, more specifically, about Napoleon.

While Stella had laid her head on his shoulder and slept during their ride to Waverly, he'd been preparing his report. It was Jamie's mission, not his, so he had no plans to go into detail. That could wait until Jamie joined them.

He waited while everyone had a chance to light up their

cigars as Hensley positioned himself behind the desk with an approving nod from Beckworth. While he was happy to be home, he wasn't ready to play viscount. He'd wait for tomorrow, and he saw no reason to shoo Hensley out of his office when he had another in the east wing.

He went through his practiced report, sharing their luck at finding not only MacDuff but Cheval as well. Then he explained that the two smugglers appeared to be joining forces until Cheval got greedy over possible competition. He didn't mention Stella's role in the mission. While Hensley must have been aware of it, if not through Jamie's messages, then certainly from Thomas, he didn't mention it either. The group in attendance only needed the highlights of the mission, not the details.

Once the talk turned away from the mission and to rumors and gossip within the King's Court and war council, Beckworth took his leave, claiming a similar excuse to Stella's.

He left the running of the house to Barrington and climbed the stairs to the second floor, feeling oddly strange to be home after the last week. Perhaps it was because he'd only been home two days before leaving for the mission. Maybe it was coming home to a manor full of guests. Deep down, he wanted the manor empty of everyone but his staff and Stella.

When he entered their room, the only light came from the fire and a single lantern burning by the bed. A bed with an unmoving lump in the middle of it. He smiled as he undressed, tossed another log on the fire, then doused the lantern.

He snuggled next to Stella, who turned into him mumbling something he couldn't understand. He'd planned for a special homecoming night, but it would wait for tomorrow. This was everything he needed. They were home, and she was safe. Life didn't get any better than that.

30

———

Stella stretched and rolled over. That moment between sleep and wakefulness nagged that something was different. There wasn't the gentle swaying she normally woke up to. Her head popped up, one eye stuck close, and she wiped it until the lashes separated and her vision cleared. Beckworth was gone, his side of the bed cold. She glanced around the room and then laughed, falling back to the pillow to stare at the ceiling.

She wasn't on the *Daphne* anymore. They were home at Waverly. She'd been so exhausted, no doubt from the stress of the mission finally behind her, the entire homecoming and dinner had been a blur.

Except for Dame Elizabeth, who'd watched her like a hawk all evening. She'd worry about that later.

She sat up, her head stuffy from sleep but not enough to miss the scent of coffee wafting over from the pot hanging by the fire. She registered it had to be morning, but with the drapes closed, she had no sense of the time.

Maybe Beckworth had gone downstairs to bring back breakfast. She crawled out of bed, fumbled for her robe that Libby must have left on the bed, and pushed the curtains away from the window that overlooked the gardens.

The sun was hazy, and dew glistened off the evergreens. Chances were good the clouds would lift and give them a sunny day. She carried the coffee pot to the table and placed it next to two mugs. One of the mugs had the remains of what was now cold coffee, and she poured coffee into the other one.

She must have slept like the dead to not have heard Beckworth come to bed or leave. So where had he gone? She took a sip of coffee, gave it a minute, then considered her question again.

Duh.

Hunting, of course. Parts of the night before were returning, and she took two more gulps of coffee. Mary had arranged for an early-morning hunt and a late breakfast upon their return. Well, at least she hadn't slept through that, and her stomach, timely as ever, grumbled in agreement.

No sooner had she wondered where Libby might be when a knock on the door preceded her lady's maid. Though she considered Libby more a friend than a maid.

"Good morning." Libby flew into the room, setting a pitcher on the washstand, tossing a log on the fire, and opening the rest of the drapes on her way to the dressing room. "Beckworth wasn't sure when you'd wake, but I thought you'd want to be dressed for breakfast," she yelled from the closet. She came out holding a deep sea-green day dress. "They should be back from their hunt any moment. Most of the women took an early breakfast in their rooms, but they'll be down to nibble when the men arrive."

She stopped and stared at Stella, her head tilting to the side. "You look like you spent a night at the pub, but I know that isn't true." She glanced around the room. "I don't see any dirty glasses, so unless you drank straight from the bottle, you must have been dog-tired." She held up the dress. "Will this do?"

Stella nodded as she took a longer swallow of coffee. She needed to catch up. Maybe a splash of water on her face would clear the rest of the cobwebs. She'd barely poured water in the basin when Libby rushed over.

"Here's some hot water. Let me add a bit."

Once Libby stirred the water in the basin with her finger, she nodded. "That's better. Nice and warm."

"Thank you. I guess the trip tired me out more than I thought."

Libby moved to the trunk that had been brought up the night before. "Is that all it is?" She held up the crossbow. "I don't remember packing this for your trip."

Stella's hands flexed with some weird instinct to grab it from her. She drained the mug and poured more. She was losing it. Was it some guilt over Cheval? She hadn't experienced these rollercoaster emotions after Gaines. So, why now? Sure, it had bothered her until she remembered Beckworth would have been dead rather than him. Maybe it wasn't how it ended. Maybe it was the terror when Cheval had tortured his spy with the crossbow before so ruthlessly killing him. If that was the case, why had she become so attached to the damn thing?

Libby patted the chair. "Come over and let's get your hair done." When Stella sat, Libby selected a few strands and began to brush. "I had to kill a man once."

Stella had been staring at her reflection, but at her words, her gaze flashed to Libby, whose focus remained on her task. Had the whole manor heard about Cheval's demise? She wasn't sure if she should respond, but it didn't matter because Libby kept talking.

"It was two or three years ago. He dragged me into an alley, wanting to do nasty things to me. He didn't think much of a young girl living on the streets. A year before that, I'd been given a job by the crew to follow some shady guy. Don't know why. Never thought to ask back then. What I hadn't expected was that someone else was following the man. He caught me and dragged me into a warehouse. Gave me this scar, he did."

She stopped brushing and pulled up the sleeve of her dress to show a long, ragged scar under her forearm. "Then he pushed me into a crate. I barely fit. My blood was gushing everywhere. Thought I was gonna die in that crate. But Beckworth found me."

"How long were you in there?"

She shrugged as she pulled up another section of hair to brush. "It seemed like forever, but Beckworth said it was about fifteen minutes. He would have killed the man right then, but two others showed up, so he had to wait for them to leave. They were just going to leave me there stuffed like a pigeon in a pastry shell.

"Beckworth carried me to Eleanor. She was a seamstress with an acting troop at the time. I think you know she used to do that."

"Yes. She's a marvelous seamstress."

"She sewed my skin together. Even with the alcohol, I screamed. Two days later, Beckworth came to check on me and gave me a bone-handled dagger of my very own. Wasn't very big but easy enough to fit in my pocket. Said it was up to me whether I wanted to stay in the crew now that I knew how dangerous it was. But either way, he wanted me to have protection, no matter what I decided."

"Why did you stay?"

She glanced at her through the mirror and grinned. "The money."

Stella laughed.

"So, anyway, when this guy dragged me into the alley, I still carried that dagger. I don't know what that man would have done with me or whether he'd leave me alive, but I wasn't going to wait to find out. I stabbed him in the gut and then in the chest, then I ran."

"How do you know he died?"

She laid the brush down and scattered the hairpins out before pushing three aside. "It's the eyes." She pointed to hers. "They get glassy, you know?"

Stella did know. No other words were spoken, but Libby hummed something soft and melodic as she finished her hair.

"Okay, let's get you dressed. I know you've made somewhat of a friendship with Lady Abigail, but there's no reason you can't still outshine her."

Stella stood, feeling better than she had since finding herself on Cheval's ship. Once she was dressed, she pulled Libby in for a hug. The maid kept her arms limp by her side, but when Stella refused to let go, Libby's arms came around her, and she felt the young woman hug back.

Once they pulled apart, Libby pointed a finger at her. "Don't you ever tell Beckworth I did that."

She held up three fingers. "Scout's honor."

Libby narrowed her eyes for a moment, then seemed to accept the strange oath. "Scout's honor. I like that."

She scampered from the room, and Stella released a long breath as she did an internal survey. She believed Libby's story. The young woman was tough, and it wasn't hard to imagine what life was like for her in the East End, having seen it for herself.

Beckworth had been watching out for Libby, just like he did for others. For her.

Stella picked up the crossbow. It was heavier than her pistol and wouldn't fit in her oversized pockets, but it was faster to load. There was no reason to think she'd ever use it again.

She opened the wardrobe closet where she kept her more personal items and searched for a hook, but there wasn't one. Not sure what else to do with it, she moved clothes aside and leaned it against the back wall.

"I'll have Barrington add a peg so you can hang it up if you prefer."

She spun around to find Beckworth watching her. "I didn't hear you come in."

He smiled. "There's nothing that gets a man's heart thumping faster than an elegantly dressed woman with a crossbow."

Her laugh was throaty. "From fear?"

He pulled her to him. "Not in my case." His kiss was hot, passionate, and never seemed to end, but when he released her, she wouldn't have minded a few more minutes of it.

"I spent too much time with the colt. Can you help me change?"

"It's a shame Libby's already dressed me."

He touched the tip of her nose. "We're home now, with obligations to our guests."

She pouted. "I suppose."

He pulled her close again. "But I have a surprise for later." His eyes filled with mischief.

She shoved him away. "Let's get you dressed before Barrington comes looking for you. Where's your valet, anyway?"

"I gave Nigel the day off. His missus has been under the weather."

Worry made her pause. Sickness in this century was nothing to laugh at. "Has a doctor seen her?"

"Yes, she just needs some rest. She'll be fine soon enough." He strolled to the dressing room with her following. "I should have an emerald jacket in here somewhere. I'm told the Osbornes are wearing blue."

She grinned at Beckworth's concern over fashion. Everything was going to work itself out.

***

Stella stopped in the kitchen before going up to the dining room. Mrs. Walker, the housekeeper, and Nellie, the cook, were busy inspecting the meal preparation while three footmen fussed with trays.

"Lady Stella. You didn't need to come down." Mrs. Walker glanced around as if ensuring everything was in order.

"Of course, I did. I wanted to tell you how marvelous everything looks and what a wonderful job you've all been doing in pampering our guests."

She didn't think it was possible for Mrs. Walker to blush.

"It's no trouble at all, Lady Stella."

"Stella! I'm surprised to find you down here."

She turned in sync with Mrs. Walker. "Good morning, Mary." She slid a glance to the housekeeper. "I was just telling everyone what a great job they were doing."

"Oh, yes." Mary wandered from counter to counter, eyeballing every detail, picking at this and that. "Not bad. Do we only have the strawberry tarts? Are there any more mince?"

Nellie hurried over. "They're still in the oven, my lady. They should be out soon."

"Very good." Mary winked at Stella. "They're Fitz's favorite."

"Is Fitz here? I thought it would be at least another day."

She nodded. "From what Hensley said, they arrived just as everyone was returning from the morning hunt. They've been given rooms in the east wing, which they prefer, but promised to join us for breakfast."

She took my arm as she steered me toward the stairs. "It's so good to see you down here checking on the staff. From what I've observed..."

Stella turned and waved at the women, who smiled in return.

"Beckworth runs a very good household. So surprising without a woman's touch. But you mustn't let that deter you from checking before every meal."

Breakfast bled into games of whist and chess in the solarium before an afternoon hunt, which Stella gracefully bowed out of, claiming she hadn't had time to properly meet with the women. Thank god for some of this century's archaic traditions. After lunch, once the riders were off, Dame Elizabeth cornered Stella as she walked out of the solarium and into the hazy sunny day.

The woman didn't wait for any preamble as she pulled her wrap around her. "Walk with me."

Stella grabbed a wrap from inside the door and quickly raced to catch up with her. Elizabeth didn't say a word as they meandered through the winter garden where a few sprigs of green revealed themselves between the brown detritus of summer blooms. It wasn't until they reached the lake that she found a bench for them to sit.

Stella wasn't sure what this was about, but she sucked in a deep breath, preparing for whatever was bothering Elizabeth. No doubt it would explain the woman closely observing her since they'd returned home.

"I hear you ran into some trouble on your mission."

She sighed. Another brave soul wanting to ensure she hadn't jumped aboard the shuttle to crazy town.

"Nothing we couldn't handle."

Elizabeth snorted. "I wouldn't have expected anything else. Have you recovered?"

Stella opened her mouth to give her standard rote response

but stopped. She wouldn't do that with Elizabeth. "It took a while, but I think I'm okay now."

Elizabeth reached over and patted her hand. "Of course, you are. It will be easier the next time."

It took a moment for her words to sink in, but before Stella could ask what she meant, she heard Mary's voice calling out.

She turned around to see Mary bulldozing her way down the garden path, Eleanor on her heels. Mary was huffing and puffing by the time she reached them. Both women were grinning like the proverbial Cheshire Cat, so Stella relaxed.

Mary pulled out a fan and started waving it. "I'm afraid we rushed out so quickly, I think I'd better sit down." Stella moved over and patted the seat next to her.

"What's the rush?" she asked.

Mary leaned over to glance at Elizabeth since Stella sat between them. Then she looked up at Eleanor, who had stepped in front of the bench, not seeming to care there wasn't a spot for her to sit.

"Well..." Mary started, then stopped.

"For heaven's sake," Eleanor said. "We miss Beckworth. And you. We wanted to know if this was the only visit you would be making."

Stella stared at the three women. "I don't know. Beckworth hasn't said anything, and I haven't asked. We've been focused on the hunting party and the mission kind of blindsided us. We've been taking it one day at a time."

"Well, I know my Hensley misses him. And not just for the missions. Beckworth lives so close, only a few hours' travel, that he used to stop by for long talks and games of chess." Mary pulled out a handkerchief and dotted at her eyes.

Good grief. She'd feel sorry for Mary if she didn't think she was being duped. She would have gotten away with it if Stella hadn't seen her quick glance at Eleanor. Stella wouldn't think of calling her on it. Instead, she patted Mary's arm.

"You wouldn't have found a reason to get me alone out here unless the three of you didn't already have something cooked up."

"I've always been impressed with your wits." Elizabeth pulled her wrap tighter. "It saves time." She nodded to Eleanor. "Do you want to ask her, or should I?"

"You could have asked her by now," Eleanor replied. "That would have saved time."

Elizabeth chuffed then looked at Stella. "Barrington mentioned you have an incantation that can be modified to send you back to a specific time and place."

Stella nodded. "Maire discovered it based on the one that was used when I was first kidnapped. She made some adjustments to it with the help of Sebastian."

"Oh, I hope he's doing alright living in the future," Mary interrupted.

Stella patted her arm again. "He's having a wonderful time. He's planning a trip to France with AJ and Maire to see the monastery."

"Oh my," Mary giggled. "For a monk, he's certainly adventurous."

"And that incantation worked when you came back this time." Elizabeth guided them back to the point of the conversation.

"Yes. To the day anyway. The actual hour is up to the fog."

"What about going back?" Eleanor asked. "AJ mentioned something about it when she was last here. The timing is different when you go back."

Stella nodded again. "The time spent in this century is much longer than the time a person is gone in the future. So, we've already been here almost two weeks, and Beckworth wants to make an overnight visit to see Bart and Lincoln. By the time we go home, only a couple of days should have passed.

The three women all glanced at each other. They were smiling. Then Mary and Eleanor turned to Elizabeth, who shook her head, a bit irritated that she was being put on the spot again. Then she gave Stella one of her earnest Dame Ellingsworth smiles—the one that always terrified AJ.

"We'd like to talk to you about the London season."

31

Five days later, Stella and Beckworth stood among the trees just beyond the gardens, holding hands, a duffel over each of their shoulders. Jamie, Fitz, and Lando were there, in addition to Hensley, Mary, and Elizabeth, who would be leaving with Mary and Hensley for London the following morning. Eleanor stood with Barrington and Libby.

Everyone was smiling, if not just a bit sad.

Stella, Beckworth, and Eleanor had returned the day before from what ended up being a two-day trip to visit Bart and Lincoln. She was already missing this group. Her focus shifted to the gardens and the manor beyond.

Waverly had become home to her, even with the short time she'd spent there. She and Beckworth had spent the morning lounging in bed with a pot of coffee while developing a story to share with the group in Baywood. They wouldn't lie about sailing on the *Daphne*, but they would gloss over most of the details.

Beckworth had laughed. His desire to stay longer could be blamed on the new foal. She couldn't argue his reasoning, knowing how passionate Finn was about horses.

"Make sure you give that envelope to Finn." Jamie shook his hand and surprised Stella with a kiss on her cheek.

"You have my word. He'll be happy to hear from you." Beckworth nodded to Hensley, who'd also given him a packet of letters for Finn and Sebastian. "Try to keep them out of trouble. MacDuff isn't one to trifle with."

Beckworth didn't say anything to Barrington or Libby other than to nod and give them a smile as he read the incantation. The four of them had had a long talk after breakfast and shared everything they needed to.

When the fog came, the women waved goodbye—even Libby—and Stella waved back. Her grip was tight in Beckworth's hand when the first tug of the fog came.

She closed her eyes and lowered her head to avoid the brightness of the light. It didn't help. Within seconds her stomach wrenched, and she doubled over, leaning into Beckworth. When the pain receded and the light dimmed, she was spit out of the fog like she'd been shot out of a cannon. Her feet dangled in midair, and she kicked her legs in a vain attempt to find the ground.

Her feet scraped the wood dock, and she thought she'd stuck the landing. It wasn't the dock. It was Beckworth and the two tumbled, duffel bags and all, until they rolled to a stop, the bags dropping on top of them.

She shoved hers aside. "Good god, there has to be a better way to do that."

Beckworth lifted up on his elbows and glanced around. "At least we're in the right spot."

The sun was bright for a winter day but softer than the light in the fog. Stella glanced at the path leading up to the inn. "I don't see anyone."

"Maybe they're not home." He stood and brushed off his pants then pulled Stella up.

"I was so looking forward to concierge service for my bag."

"Come on." He pushed her duffel toward her. "We'll take it slow."

They trudged up the path and were walking across the lawn toward the back deck when Finn's truck barreled down the driveway and into the parking lot in front of the inn. Stella dropped her bag, which landed with a thud on the grass as she made her way onto the deck.

"I either need stronger arm muscles or I need to pack lighter." Stella collapsed at the outdoor table and leaned her head back. Her arms hung by her side, unwilling to move.

Beckworth sat next to her and grabbed her hand. "It's the impact of the fog. Your energy will come back soon. Some food will help."

Stella was running through which foods she'd missed the most while in England when the French doors blew open and AJ burst out.

"You're home!" AJ pulled Stella out of her chair, hugging her tightly.

Stella's throaty laugh couldn't be helped as she clutched AJ to her. When she pulled back, she admonished her friend. "With absolutely no welcoming committee."

Finn was shaking Beckworth's hand and passed him a beer before sitting at the table. "To be honest, we thought it would be another day or two before you returned."

Stella slid Beckworth a glance. "We were gone almost three weeks. I thought that would be a couple of days on this side of the fog."

AJ picked at the edge of the table. "It was. We thought you might stay longer than you planned once you got there."

Beckworth jumped in before Stella. "If it had been a better time of year, we probably would have. But, as you know, England in January isn't the best climate."

Stella didn't glance at Beckworth, but she wanted to. They'd had decent weather, and while it had been on the cooler side it wasn't any different than winter in Oregon.

"So, tell us everything." AJ stood and looked at Finn. "Did you start the coffee?" When he nodded, she ran for the door. "Give me a minute to get Stella some coffee." She was back quickly with a cup for her and Stella.

Stella ran the mug under her nose. "Heavenly." She took a sip and glanced at Beckworth, who dove into their rehearsed tale. She had to give him credit, the man was a master at weaving a tale, focusing on the hunting party and providing an update on all the people they'd visited.

"I'm relieved to know everyone is safe and living their lives without all the theatrics whenever we showed up." AJ tucked her legs under her and savored the coffee.

"Well, everyone missed the two of you." Stella emptied her mug, and feeling better, shuffled into the house, returning with the coffee pot and a hot pad. She refilled cups before sitting down.

"Do you know how the *Daphne* is fairing?" Finn asked.

"She's still a fine ship and the crew sharp as ever under Jamie's hand." Beckworth grinned at Finn, who raised a brow.

"And you know this firsthand?" Finn asked.

"We might have taken a short sailing trip while we were there." Stella straightened and sipped her coffee, staring at AJ over the rim of her mug. She was rather proud she'd been able to spit that out.

AJ almost choked on her coffee. "You went for a sail on the *Daphne*?"

"Just up the coast to Swansea." Beckworth smiled at Stella like a proud father. "We had fair weather, and Stella didn't get sick once."

"Mostly just using the herbs, but I admit I took a motion sickness tablet twice."

"That seems odd." AJ squinted at Stella, her truth radar on high alert.

"Stop that," Stella scolded. "Jamie all but dared me. What choice did I have?" She couldn't believe how flippant that sounded, but it did the trick.

AJ relaxed and settled back in her seat.

"Oh, I almost forgot." Beckworth pulled the envelope and a stack of letters out of his pocket and slid it to Finn. "For you to read later. Letters from your mates and a few for Sebastian."

Finn's expression softened when he ran his fingers over the top of them. "I appreciate this."

"And we arrived to discover a new foal in the barn."

The two men fell into horse discussions as AJ asked Stella more detailed questions about the people.

Soon, the rest of their family and friends began arriving, all bringing food that Stella immediately sampled. They stayed for another hour before Finn and Ethan took their duffels to Stella's car.

"Give us a day to acclimate," Beckworth said. "Then maybe dinner at Joe's?"

"Sounds good." Finn rubbed the back of his neck, his signature grin sneaking through. "It's a shame you didn't have a camera to take a picture of that colt."

"He's going to be a fine stud. I think Hensley will be spending more time at Waverly than his own manor." Both men laughed at the truth of it before Beckworth climbed into the passenger seat. He knew how to drive, but he preferred taking the wheel on long drives. City driving drove him crazy, and as many times as Stella had shown him the shortcuts, he would lean his head back to watch the city—or as Stella knew—the people.

Neither spoke as they drove to their bungalow-style house. It was in her name, purchased with well-earned money from her broker business, but as far as she was concerned it was theirs, just like Beckworth considered Waverly theirs, though they weren't married.

When she pulled into the driveway and parked, Beckworth turned to her.

"I think Finn knows we're lying to them."

***

Stella dropped the duffel on the bed and stared at the floor. She'd wanted to turn on music and dance with Beckworth, excited for their ability to keep their secret. Instead, she collapsed on the bed. Beckworth placed his duffel on a chair and opened it, removing his clothes and laying them on the dresser.

The bedroom originally had a king-sized bed, a stuffed chair with a round side table, two dressers, two nightstands, an electric fireplace, and a walk-in closet. When Beckworth moved in, they found a second chair that complemented the original one, and then a bookcase was added. It was only the first step in making the room efficient for their lazy streaks.

An LCD monitor was added to a wall, and some days they only left the room for food. Beckworth had drawn the line at adding a mini fridge, declaring they wouldn't leave the room for days and they might as well give the food delivery man a key so he could just bring the food to their bed. Stella had laughed, and he'd picked her up and tossed her on the bed. She was fairly certain sex had ensued afterward.

Beckworth placed his boots next to the door so he could take them to the utility room for cleaning. Once his duffel was empty, he placed it next to the boots where it would end up in the guestroom closet. Then he sat next to her on the bed.

"Why do you think Finn knows we're lying?" Stella picked at a loose string on her sweater. "I've been playing back all the conversations. I don't remember saying anything that would've given it away. And AJ would have called me on it the moment she caught the lie. She was suspicious enough about the *Daphne* story."

"We didn't really lie. We simply left out what we did on our sailing trip."

"That's walking a mighty fine line."

"I don't think Finn caught us in any specific deception. I think it's more intuitive. He senses we left something out, he's just not sure what."

"Do you think he suspects we were on a mission?"

Beckworth grabbed her hand. "You're going to unravel that. And, no, I doubt it. I believe it to be more of a feeling. Something he can't put his finger on."

She sighed. "And he'll most likely say something to AJ."

"I'm not so sure."

That surprised her. She turned to him, pulling a leg up on the bed. "Why not?"

"Because he knows how she gets. She'll jump to conclusions —most of them wild speculations. He won't want to stir that pot."

"I suppose." But she worried her bottom lip.

Beckworth laughed. "And I probably shouldn't have said anything to you."

"What about Ethan?"

"I think Ethan and Maire were more nostalgic."

"You think they wanted to go with us?"

"Maybe not before we left, but now? Yes, I think they do."

"We're going to have to be more careful."

"Let's not worry about it for now. But I agree we need to be careful we don't slip. I'm sure our trip will come up more than a few times over the next week or so."

He pulled her hands away from her sweater where she was still slowly tugging at the loose piece of yarn. She was indeed unraveling it. He slid the sweater off her shoulders then unbuttoned her blouse.

"I think we're in need of a better way to celebrate our homecoming." When his fingers brushed over her bra, then slipped behind her back, expertly unsnapping it, her mind refocused on the man in front of her.

Soon they were both rolling across the bed, and someone kicked the duffel off.

Beckworth hugged her to him, but Stella pushed him onto his back then straddled him. She ran her hands up his chest then more slowly on the return trip down. She kissed him, one hand running through his hair and the other trailing down his stomach.

He was more than ready for her, and her first thought was to take it slow. Until he reached between her legs. She pushed his hands away but didn't stay on top for long before he rolled her over. It was like surfing a rogue wave—wild and freeing and intoxicating.

Nothing stayed hidden between them when they made love. It was raw. Even at the tenderest of moments. Jamie had said the two of them were alike, and he'd been right. Their coming together fed a hunger they'd needed all their lives. And it was hot enough and deep enough to fulfill them the rest of their days.

Sometime later—for some reason her ability to sense the general time never worked when the two of them were in bed— her eyes opened.

It took a moment before she glanced over to find Beckworth

staring at the ceiling. They were holding hands like new lovers. They did that a lot, as if they had to touch each other, just to make sure the other person was there. Maybe it was more than that. Some innate knowledge that there was a stronger connection between them than mere touch could provide, yet the feel of skin on skin deepened it.

She released a long sigh and squeezed his hand. "Don't be mad."

When she didn't say any more, he squeezed back. "Just tell me."

A minute passed before she finally spilled it. "I kind of promised Elizabeth, Mary, and Eleanor that we'd try to come back for the London season."

She gave him a side glance to find he'd turned his stare on her. She fidgeted under his intense cornflower-blue gaze. Maybe she should have discussed it with him while they were still at Waverly. But it hadn't been her fault the women had cornered her.

He was still staring at her when he said, "I have something to confess myself."

She squinted at him, not expecting that response.

"I told Barrington to have Lord Templeton's London house prepared for an April visit. Hensley said he'd find a reason for the *Daphne* to be in London."

They stared at each other for the longest moment. Then they broke out in laughter.

Once their jovial mood faded, so did his smile, and his tone became earnest. "Do you know how much I love you?"

Stella stroked his cheek. "I have some idea, but it wouldn't hurt to remind me."

His kiss was heated with a hunger she hadn't seen before, which seemed impossible after the many shared nights of heartfelt passion. Nights where they simply held each other or stripped the sheets with hot sex.

"We are two lucky people, Lady Swan. What adventures wait for us."

"Until then, I only have one thing to ask of you, Teddy."

He didn't wait for her to finish before tugging her to him for more intimate adventures.

THANK YOU FOR READING!

Stella's and Beckworth's adventures will continue!

The question is whether their love story can handle the stress of constant peril that seems to follow them...or perhaps, follows Stella. But then, what can one expect when they take a chance on traveling through the fog.

I haven't started Book 2 of the series yet, but I did take the time to write a scene. It won't be Chapter 1. I'm not sure where it falls within the story yet, but I can pretty much guarantee it will be there, and I think it provides the best tease on where the story might go...or maybe not. I do like my twists and turns!

The Swan Syndicate - Book 2
(Actual title still pending)

tella and Beckworth make a decision that their friends in Baywood, Oregon aren't all that happy about. Is it because they worry about what dangers the adventurous couple might fall victim to, or because they might be a wee bit jealous they're not going too?

When the couple returns to Waverly Manor in time to enjoy the London season with their friends from the past, chances are pretty high that something will inevitably go wrong.

***

Keep reading for a preview from the next edition of *The Swan Syndicate.*

***

Enjoy!

THE SWAN SYNDICATE - BOOK 2

London - 1806

Stella tugged at the bodice of her rose-colored dress, then ran her hands over the skirts before reaching for her opal necklace as she glanced around the ballroom. Her eyes bulged at the sight, having never seen anything so grand.

"You're not nervous, are you?" Beckworth's warm breath caressed her neck as he leaned closer, a wicked smile on his handsome face.

"What are you up to?"

He chuckled. "Nothing. It's rare to find an astonished expression on your beautiful face."

She tapped his shoulder with her lace fan, then glanced at the fancy accessory and laughed. "I can't believe I just did that." She straightened her shoulders. "It appears I'll fit in just fine."

He put her arm through his and guided her down the steps. "I think you'll be perfect, but I understand how overwhelming a ball of this size can be for the first time. The fashion alone could make one marvel all evening."

"I should have known fashion would be the first thing on your mind. So, where do we start? I don't see Elizabeth or Mary."

"I thought I saw Hensley in the crowd when we first walked in, but I don't see him now. Mary is most likely with her circle of friends from the Cotswolds. She's known to circulate more widely at the various parties and balls, but for this particular one, she usually hovers with her local friends from Bristol. Elizabeth, considering her stature as Dame Ellingsworth, will be with Agatha and Lord Osborne. I think I caught sight of the Melvilles, too, but let's steer our own course for now."

Stella wouldn't argue. She'd attended other parties since arriving in London for the season and had disregarded Beckworth's and Mary's excitement for this particular ball, believing them to be too enamored by it all. She'd been dead wrong. AJ never mentioned a party so lavish, but she might not have attended anything this massive.

From what Mary said, the duke's ball was one of the most anticipated of the season, and anyone who was anyone expected an invitation. Elizabeth had seen to theirs, though Stella had a feeling all Beckworth had to do was send a letter, and an invitation would have been on its way. She might be wrong, but she didn't think so. Beckworth had friends in the most unexpected of places.

They greeted a half dozen couples, constantly dragged into conversations about the war, fashion, and sometimes a little gossip. Stella held onto those tidbits for her planned lunch date with Mary and Elizabeth the following day. It wasn't often she had gossip to share. Not that she didn't have a rowdy tale or two that Libby always shared about these events. The stories always ended with Mary quickly fanning herself while Elizabeth howled with laughter.

"Let's see if we can find someone in one of the less crowded rooms." He snagged two glasses of champagne from a passing server and handed one to Stella. "If I see anyone I know along the way, I'll keep the introductions short."

"Gee, I thought you knew everyone."

He nudged her shoulder. "As you often say—funny."

She grinned. "I have no problem meeting people, but you need to tell me if they're important before greeting them. As hard as it is to believe, there's only so much information I can store in my head in one evening. I'd prefer to keep the important stuff in there."

"Fair enough." He chuckled as he glanced around, sliding his arm around her waist. "How about every time I squeeze your waist, it indicates you're about to meet an important person."

She leaned in, her lips gently brushing his ear. "You just want to keep touching me."

"Keep that up, and I'll have to lock us in an empty drawing room."

Her laugh was lusty. "Now you're talking." She nudged him back. "Thank you for erasing the nerves."

He gave her a long look. "Anything for you, luv."

She shook her head, and then her face brightened. "Lord and Lady Melville. How good to see you again."

"You look lovely, my dear." Lord Edgar Melville kissed her hand, then shook Beckworth's. "I'm glad you made it. Hensley found himself a competent opponent at chess. They're currently tied at one game each and are now battling to the end."

"Really," Beckworth responded after kissing Lady Flora Melville's hand. "Perhaps we should go cheer him on."

"I was thinking the same thing."

"Why don't you both go do that," Lady Melville said. "Stella and I have other interests."

Beckworth glanced at Stella, who nodded. She wouldn't have minded watching the chess match, but she promised Beckworth she'd behave like the lady of his manor tonight, and that's what she'd do. "I'll be in good hands with Flora." She took the woman's arm, and as they strolled away, she gave Beckworth one last look over her shoulder. His worried expression made her lift a brow. How much trouble could she get into at a ball?

Once the men had melted into the crowd, Flora steered Stella back toward the crowd of the ballroom.

"Elizabeth is holding court across the room from the musicians." Flora nodded at a couple of women and stopped long enough for quick introductions before moving on again. "She doesn't like shouting over them, but then who does?"

"Wouldn't a drawing room be quieter?" Stella nodded to a younger couple Beckworth had introduced her to earlier. They didn't seem high on his list of friends, but they'd seemed nice enough.

"Yes, but then she wouldn't be seen by enough people. It's not that she needs to be sought out by so many, but one must keep up appearances and their reputation."

Stella never got the impression Elizabeth cared for such things, but she'd yet to spend much time with her in London. She supposed what one said and did at their country estates stayed at their country estates.

"There you are, my dear." Elizabeth moved away from two women, who Stella guessed were a mother and daughter. "Sorry, Eloise, but you have all the information I know about Lord Hutton. I still think you'd be better off with Lord Fillmore, but that's a decision you'll need to make."

Elizabeth took Stella's arm and moved her and Flora toward the front of the ballroom. "I think I've had enough socializing for the moment. That woman can talk until it's time for the carriages. And I don't know why she bothered asking my opinion on who the best match is for her daughter when she's never listened to a thing I've said before."

"Well, she might have to this time," Flora said as they worked their way through the crowd. She stopped long enough to unfold her fan and cover her mouth. She leaned over so only Elizabeth and Stella could hear. "I have it on good authority that Lord Hutton has already made a proposal to Lord Dorsey for his oldest daughter's hand."

"Dorsey, really?" Elizabeth seemed surprised then she shook her head. "He must want that country estate."

"That's what Edgar said." Flora stopped long enough to grab a glass of champagne, and Stella gave the server her empty glass.

She was tempted to grab a new glass, but it would be a long night, and she needed to pace herself.

The threesome made it to the hallway, where it wasn't quite as crowded, and Stella appreciated the cooler air. They were almost to what Stella assumed would be one of the drawing rooms when there was a commotion behind them.

She turned as a group surged toward them. Flora's arm was bumped, forcing champagne to splash from her glass. Stella attempted to step out of the way, but droplets sprayed over her dress. Then she heard Elizabeth gasp.

When Stella turned to her, Elizabeth was holding her neck.

"Someone took my necklace." Her face was pale. "Someone shoved me, and now it's gone." Her voice was becoming shrill.

"Are you sure it didn't fall on the floor?" Stella pushed the women back and searched the floor, which was difficult with the hall becoming more crowded.

Elizabeth was shaking her head. "I felt fingers on the back of my neck." She dramatically shivered. "I must have froze because the next thing I knew, I was jostled, and now my precious necklace is gone. It was a priceless heirloom."

Stella could see how distraught her friend was, but she wasn't sure what to do.

"I saw it."

The women turned to find a middle-aged gentleman with rather long sideburns wiping what looked like champagne from his shirt. It might have been from Flora's glass, but several people had been bumped, so it could have been from anyone. "The man was quick, but his hand gripped a silver and jeweled item before he stuffed it in his pocket. It happened in a flash, but I saw what I saw."

"Which way did he go?" Stella asked as she began searching the crowd.

"Down the hallway toward the back of the manor."

"Stay here," Stella shouted to the women, and she took off down the hall.

She shoved people out of the way, shouting "Sorry, sorry, sorry," as she stopped every so often to stand on tiptoes in an attempt to catch sight of the man in question. She'd been watching Flora and her glass of champagne, trying to dodge out of the way, and hadn't seen the man at all.

The crowd was thinning as she moved farther away from the ballroom. She knew she was on the right track because some of the guests appeared flustered as they glanced down the hall. Was it the thief?

Then she saw him. He wasn't moving very fast, but he kept his head down as he kept an even pace. She quickened her steps as she followed. Would one of the crews be daring enough to steal jewelry from around someone's neck during a ball? Had there been more than one thief? Chester, who ran one of the larger gangs—or crews as Beckworth called them—in the city, would never do anything so risky. Beckworth never mentioned a crew running a job during a ball. The topic never came up, but still. If it was common, wouldn't he have mentioned it?

She ignored the stares of the men and women around her as she hurried along, ready to break out into a run. When he turned for what Stella thought might be the solarium, and the people were becoming scarce, she decided it was time to call for help. Maybe she should have done it sooner, but she was close enough now, he shouldn't be able to get away.

Four men were coming toward them, and the man she chased had slowed as he stuffed his hands in his pockets. He still kept his head down.

"Stop that man!" Stella broke into a run, swearing at her shoes, which started to pinch. "He's a thief!"

The four men looked around, and Stella rolled her eyes as she gained on the man. Before she could reach him, the four men suddenly understood, but the man bent over as he picked up speed and, leading with his shoulder, plowed into them like they were bowling pins.

While the four men weren't able to stop the thief, they slowed him down. Stella almost grabbed his coat, but just as her fingers brushed it, she tripped over one of the men. She landed on all fours and, after two attempts, was able to lift her skirts high enough to get back on her feet as she raced after the thief, no longer caring who was watching or that she wasn't acting like a proper English lady of the manor.

The thief ran through the solarium and out the back patio, almost flying down the steps. Stella was hot on his trail. When he reached the grassy lawn of the classic English garden, he stopped and turned. Stella zeroed in on his face, somewhat shocked by what she saw, though she didn't know the man. But she knew the leer.

She reached into her pocket with one hand while pulling up her dress with the other so she didn't trip down the stairs. The man was waiting for her, but his eyes went wide when he saw her pull out her dagger.

He turned to run, and, with one huge lunge, Stella leaped. It was enough to grab a leg, which threw the man off balance, and they tumbled onto the grass.

He had size and weight on his side, but she swung out with her dagger and heard a quick intake of breath. Then a fist slammed into the side of her head, and it sent her wheeling. She reached out one last time, but once again, his coat slipped through her fingers.

Her head hurt like a mother, and when her breath returned, she tried to stand as she watched the man flee into the night. Three other men raced past her as they chased after the thief.

Then Stella, who was having difficulty getting her feet under her, was suddenly lifted up and spun around. She reached for her head.

"Don't do that."

Someone stripped the dagger from her hand.

"What the bloody hell were you thinking? You could have gotten yourself killed or stabbed."

She heaved, gasping for breath, her head pounding, but managed to glance up into Beckworth's angry and worried face.

Concern overruled his irritation as he shoved the knife into an inside pocket before he held her face in his hands. They were gentle as he took in every inch of her. When his hand moved over the right side of her head, she winced and pulled back.

"Ouch."

"All right. It's all right. Let's get you back inside, or at least to the patio so you can sit and catch your breath."

Then she was pulled tight against him in a bear hug she couldn't possibly escape from. His cheek rested on the top of her head, and she wrapped her arms around his waist, turning her head to lean her left cheek against his chest.

"If I'd lost you to a pickpocket, I'd hunt down every crew member until I found the one who did it. I might do that anyway. I know the necklace that was stolen and how important it was to Elizabeth, but you should never have taken it upon yourself to run recklessly into danger."

"No," she managed to spit out before his grip tightened.

"I love you, Stella, but you scare me every time you do something so foolhardy."

She pulled back from him. "I don't think he belonged to a crew."

Beckworth pushed her to arm's length and read her face. His anger over her actions might be returning, but he knew her well enough to listen to her. He might not believe what she had to say, but he'd give her the chance to speak.

"Go on. What do you mean he's not crew? How could you possibly know that?"

She shook her head, then thought better of it as she held a hand to it.

"I don't know, and I know you're going to find it hard to believe. After being on the *Daphne Marie*, living among sailors, and watching for smugglers in all those pubs and inns while searching for MacDuff—well, I can't put my finger on any one thing. Not at the moment. Something might come to me later. Assuming I didn't have a concussion or a brain aneurysm. Maybe it's just a headache, but I feel like my head might explode."

"Stella. Just for this moment, can you please say it without all the preamble?"

She stared at him. There was little light on the back patio, and it darkened his cornflower-blue eyes to a midnight blue. Thin lines marred his forehead in worry. She sucked in a breath and straightened, though it made her head pound more.

"There was something about him that seemed different yet familiar, and I can't explain it any better right now. But the minute he ran, my first thought was sailor."

THANK YOU FOR READING!

I sincerely hope you enjoyed a glimpse of *The Swan Syndicate - Book 2.*

If you haven't already read the original series, here's your chance to catch up on how it all began!

A Stone in Time
The Mórdha Stone Chronicles - Book 1

AJ Moore stands on a precipice. Her ambitions stalled after an unexpected loss.

A two-hundred-year-old sailing vessel appears through the fog. This could be the story she's been waiting for. The story to salvage her sluggish career.

When she meets Finn Murphy, the enigmatic captain, he's nothing but arrogant, annoying, and tight-lipped. But she's not one to give up easily. He's just not aware that he's met his match.

Finn Murphy has only one thing on his mind. Find an ancient stone necklace and return home. But he wasn't expecting to be hounded by a reporter. The more she comes around, the more he wants her to stay.

But the stakes are too high, the mission too important to be tempted. The longer it takes to find the necklace, the weaker his resolve becomes.

Join AJ on an adventure where honor and friendship can beat the odds—and love transcends time.

"Time travel with unique twists and many layers..."
"This is a captivating story! The atmosphere is richly evocative and well-rendered, and the characters are brought to life beautifully!" InD'tale Magazine.

A Stone in Time is the first book in a time travel romance adventure series, and it comes with cliffhangers...just so you know.

Buy Now

You can read the <u>prequel</u> to **The Mordha Stone Chronicles**
for **FREE**

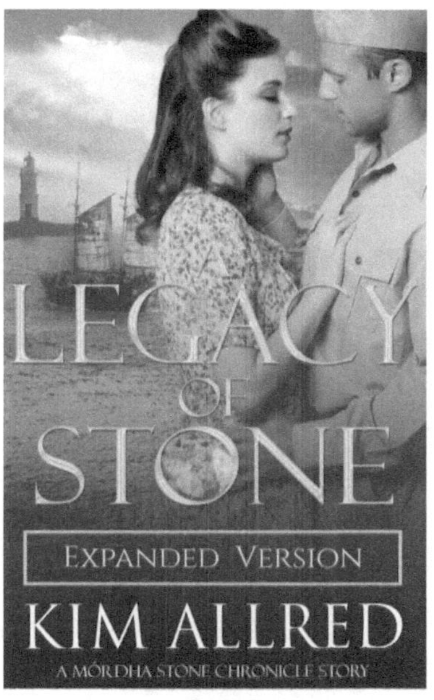

Download Now

If you're interested in other stories written by me, you might enjoy my urban fantasy series, *Of Blood & Dreams*. A touch of mystery...with just a pinch of spice.

Seduction in Blood, Of Blood and Dreams - Book 1

A thief. A vamp. A walk on the wild side.

Cressa Langtry is the best cat burglar on the West Coast. But she owes a large debt to the wrong kind of people. Her only way clear is to steal something for the city's notorious and ancient vampire – Devon Trelane.

Devon Trelane can't forgive the one man who cost him a seat on the Council. Luckily, a thief has fallen into his lap. A woman with the skills he requires to take down his greatest enemy.

There's only one hitch—a simple business arrangement becomes complicated when their dreams collide.

Pick up your **FREE** copy today - available on Amazon and other retailers in ebook, print, and audio.

Download Now

Want to know when my next book will be available?
Sign up for my newsletter!

You can also follow me on Amazon, Goodreads, Bookbub,
Facebook, or Instagram

ABOUT THE AUTHOR

Kim Allred grew up in Southern California but now enjoys the quiet life in an old timber town in the Pacific Northwest where she raises alpacas, llamas, and an undetermined number of free-range chickens. Just like her characters, Kim loves sharing stories while sipping a glass of wine or slurping a strong cup of brew.

Her spirit of adventure has taken her on many journeys, including a ten-day dogsledding trip in northern Alaska and sleeping under the stars on the savannas of eastern Africa.

Kim is currently creating worlds while shooing cats and dogs away from her lap, and the mighty parrot, Willow, from her keyboard. Willow can peel the keys from the board in fifteen seconds flat.

Kim's current works include her time travel romance series, the Mórdha Stone Chronicles and The Swan Syndicate, and the urban fantasy romance series, Of Blood & Dreams.

To stay in contact with Kim visit her website.